# Collision

# Collision

## Joanna Orwin

HarperCollins*Publishers*

National Library of New Zealand Cataloguing-in-Publication Data
Orwin, Joanna.
Collision / Joanna Orwin.
ISBN 978-1-86950-778-7
I. Title.
NZ823.2—dc 22

First published 2009
HarperCollins*Publishers (New Zealand) Limited*
P.O. Box 1, Shortland Street, Auckland, 1140

ISBN 978 1 86950 778 7

Cover design by Matt Stanton
Cover images: top — Getty Images; bottom — Alexander
Turnbull Library; background — Shutterstock.
Typesetting by Springfield West

Printed by Griffin Press, Australia

70gsm Bulky Book Ivory used by HarperCollins*Publishers* is
a natural, recyclable product made from wood grown in sustainable
forests. The manufacturing processes conform to the environmental
regulations in the country of origin, New Zealand.

# Historical background

In mid-October 1771, two French ships sailed from the French island colony of Mauritius (Île-de-France) in the Indian Ocean, heading for the Pacific on an eighteen-month voyage of exploration and trading.

The late eighteenth century — the Age of Enlightenment — was an exhilarating time in France. Scientific voyages to the Pacific and the Indian Oceans in 1760 and 1769 to witness transits of Venus rekindled French interest in searching for the elusive Southern Continent and finding new prospects for trade in the Pacific. But the Seven Years' War (1756–1763) had exhausted Louis XV's coffers, ensured the naval supremacy of England, and put an end to French imperial aspirations in Canada and India. The associated liquidation of the entrepreneurial French India Company (Compagnie des Indes) in 1769 left many able and experienced 'blue' officers of the merchant marine without prospects.

Amongst these officers was a well-established member of the wealthy Breton merchant classes based in St-Malo, Marc-Joseph Marion du Fresne, who had a brilliant record in both the King's Navy and the French India Company. Known to his contemporaries as a skilled sailor and navigator, an energetic and honorable man with a sense of adventure and a willingness to take risks, Marion had settled on the Île-de-France in 1766, where he bought land, held the post of harbour master for Port Louis, commanded several scientific voyages in the Indian Ocean and traded on his own account.

In 1770, the restless and ambitious Marion saw the opportunity he was waiting for when the Tahitian native, Ahu-toru, arrived in Port Louis, seeking repatriation to his homeland after accompanying the French explorer Bougainville to Paris in 1768. Marion promptly proposed a voyage that would combine the return of Ahu-toru to Tahiti with exploration in the southern Pacific Ocean. What was more, he was willing to mortgage his own estates to finance an expedition he hoped would win him glory. In return, the French administrators of the Île-de-France arranged for Marion to have the use of a King's ship to accompany the larger ship he had already purchased. Both ships were fitted out at the King's expense, wages and provisions for both crews were advanced, and a substantial trading cargo was provided — the costs to be reimbursed on Marion's return or his estates forfeited.

Such willingness to risk personal financial ruin was at least partly driven by Marion's feelings of social inadequacy and a continuing deep need for approval — despite his undoubted abilities and acclaimed reputation. Like many privileged members of the French bourgeoisie at this time, Marion had aspirations for ennoblement into the aristocracy and the desirable social acceptance that this embodied. These aspirations and the gamble he was taking meant he accepted some less-than-ideal conditions imposed on his expedition. All these factors coloured Marion's choices and the decisions he made during the voyage, contributing to what eventuated during his stay in the Bay of Islands, New Zealand, in May, June and July 1772.

Although preceded in northern New Zealand by Cook and another ex-French India Company officer, de Surville (both in 1769), Marion and his men were the first Europeans to spend significant time ashore. During their stay, gaps in understanding and tolerance developed between the French and the local Maori people as a result of language barriers, cultural ignorance, local political upheavals, and the undue pressure imposed on local resources by the sudden and prolonged influx of more than two hundred Frenchmen. That this seminal encounter ended in calamity for both sides was probably inevitable, and the result had ongoing consequences for New Zealand's later history. Northern Maori allegiances were affected well into the period of European colonization, in turn shaping the relationships between the two peoples that in 1840 led to the unprecedented formal signing of an agreement between indigenous inhabitants and colonists — the Treaty of Waitangi.

This novel is the story of the events that took place in the Bay of Islands in the winter of 1772 and what precipitated them.

# The French ships and their officers named in the story

*Mascarin*

Ship-rigged, three-masted flute on loan from the King of France, 450 tons, 22 guns; crew 140 men:

*Captain and expedition commander*
Marc-Joseph Marion du Fresne

*2nd-in-command*
Julien Crozet

*2nd Lieutenant*
Lehoux

*Ensign and clerk*
Paul Chevillard de Montaison

*Senior Ensign*
Jean Roux

*Ensign*
André Tallec (fictional)

*Surgeon*
Thirion

*Sub-Lieutenant of the Legion*
de Vaudricourt

*Sergeant-at-arms*
Thomas Ballu

*Ship's cook*
Anthonie

*Domestic slave*
François (fictional)

## Marquis de Castries

Ship-rigged, three-masted flute and consort ship owned by du Fresne, 700 tons, 16 guns; crew 100 men:

*Captain*
   Ambroise-Bernard-Marie le Jar du Clesmeur

*2nd-in-command*
   Josselin Le Corre

*1st Lieutenant*
   Le Dez

## Locations mentioned in the story

| French names | Modern names |
|---|---|
| Île-de-France | Mauritius |
| Malagasy | Madagascar (a native of) |
| Terre d'Espérance | Marion and Prince Edward Islands |
| Prise de Possession | Crozet Islands |
| New Holland | Australia |
| Van Diemen's Land | Tasmania |
| Pic Mascarin | Taranaki/Mt Egmont |
| Anchor Bay | Spirits Bay |
| Rotterdam and Amsterdam Islands | Tongan Group (probably) |
| Square Cape | Cape Brett |
| Port Marion | Bay of Islands |
| Marion Island | Moturua |
| Cape of Currents | Tapeka Point |
| Tacoury's Cove | Manawaora |

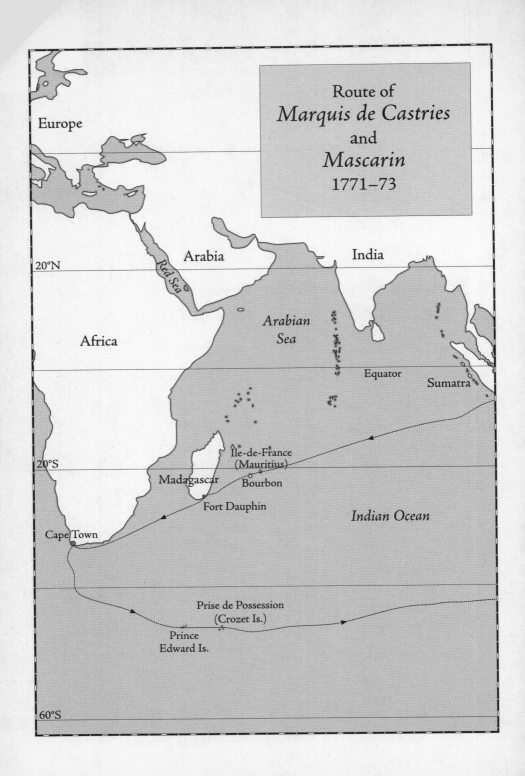

Route of
*Marquis de Castries*
and
*Mascarin*
1771–73

Europe

20°N

Red Sea

Arabia

India

Africa

Arabian
Sea

Equator

Sumatra

Île-de-France
(Mauritius)

20°S

Madagascar

Bourbon

Fort Dauphin

Indian Ocean

Cape Town

Prise de Possession
(Crozet Is.)

Prince
Edward Is.

60°S

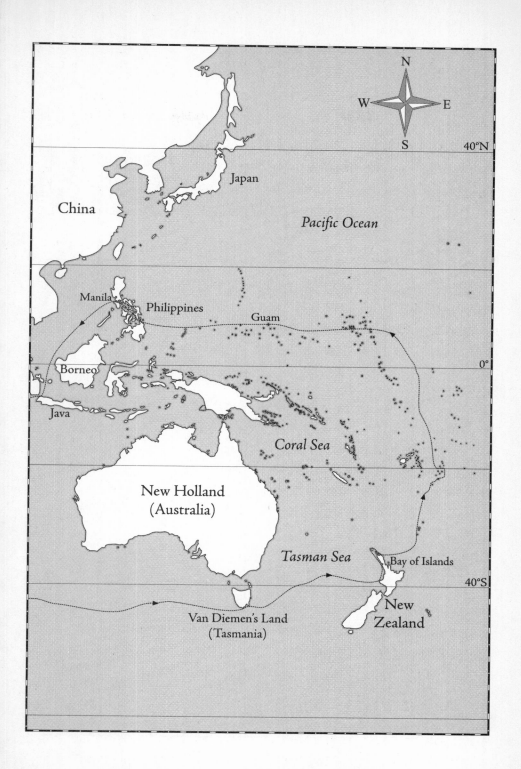

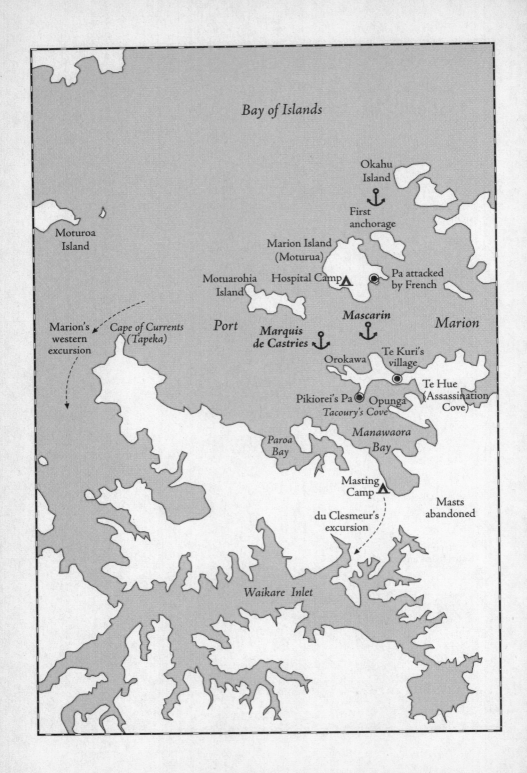

Bay of Islands

Okahu
Island

First
anchorage

Moturoa
Island

Marion Island
(Moturua)

Pa attacked
by French

Motuarohia
Island

Hospital Camp

Mascarin

Marion

Marion's
western
excursion

Cape of Currents
(Tapeka)

Port

Marquis
de Castries

Orokawa

Te Kuri's
village

Te Hue
(Assassination
Cove)

Pikiorei's Pa

Opunga

*Tacoury's Cove*

Paroa
Bay

Manawaora
Bay

Masting
Camp

Masts
abandoned

du Clesmeur's
excursion

Waikare Inlet

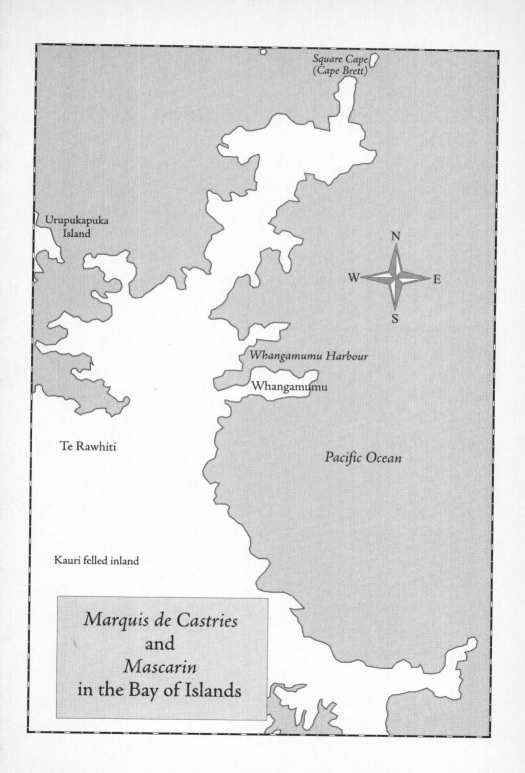

Square Cape
(Cape Brett)

Urupukapuka
Island

N
W   E
S

Whangamumu Harbour

Whangamumu

Te Rawhiti

Pacific Ocean

Kauri felled inland

*Marquis de Castries*
and
*Mascarin*
in the Bay of Islands

# Chapter 1

Not more than a musket shot ahead, the *Marquis de Castries* fell directly across the *Mascarin*'s path. Ensign André Tallec glanced over, his eye caught by the sudden movement. He stared in disbelief at the rapidly approaching ship. The two sailors casting lead lines from the bow of the *Mascarin* chanted their next soundings, but the young ensign barely heard them. Ignoring the slate and chalk in his hand, he called urgently to the officer of the watch: 'Monsieur Crozet!'

One arm thrust through the foremast shrouds for balance, the collar of his greatcoat turned up around his ears for warmth, the *Mascarin*'s second-in-command had his eyeglass trained on the two mist-cloaked islands a few leagues distant. Alerted by the urgency in André's voice, Monsieur Crozet looked towards the consort ship, then barked curses and orders in quick succession. 'Quel diable? Stand by the topsail braces!'

As the petty officers relayed his orders and barefooted sailors ran to their stations, André and Monsieur Crozet continued to peer through the drifting veils of mist and sleet that once again obscured the larger ship to starboard. The *Castries* still bore down on them. She seemed to be making no attempt to alter her course.

'Mort-diable!' Monsieur Crozet exclaimed. 'Does that imbecile not see us? Is he mad?' He raised his voice. 'Brace the topsails to larboard!'

André watched helplessly as the men struggled to get their own hove-to ship underway, even simple tasks hindered by ice-swollen ropes that jammed in the blocks and refused to run freely. The backed yards responded only slowly to the men hauling on the braces, but at last they swung across and the topsails started to draw. Above him on the quarterdeck, Monsieur Marion, their captain and the expedition leader, told the men on the wheel to hold steady as the ship began to move through the water, his voice calm as always amidst the shouting and frantic activity.

A little further along the deck from where he stood, André could hear the senior ensign, his cousin, maître and protector, twenty-five-year-old Jean Roux, muttering, 'Allons, allons! Come on, come on! Sacré Dieu!' Impatience darkened his cousin's already swarthy face.

But their imperturbable captain waited until the *Mascarin* had gathered more way before he ordered the wheel thrust hard over. As the ship at last started to turn, André felt a hand grip his shoulder. He glanced at Monsieur Crozet, but the ship's second-in-command was staring into the mist, seemingly unaware of the youth at his side, his long, angular face taut with tension. Monsieur Marion had judged the manoeuvre well, and their ship was already picking up speed. They could hear shouts from the other ship. On their own deck, men stood momentarily transfixed, gazing towards the mist-blurred menace now less than half a musket shot away. The ensign focused on the narrow wedge of grey water that separated the two ships, willing it to widen as the *Mascarin* turned away from danger.

For a brief moment, he thought they would make it; that the two ships would scrape by each other and avert disaster. But even as the thought formed, the beakhead of the *Castries* loomed out of the mist alongside them. Her long bowsprit swept along their starboard side like a jouster's lance. Men scattered in all directions. Timbers graunched and squealed. Ropes parted and heavy blocks plummeted to the deck as the bowsprit cut through their mizzen rigging, then snapped off the *Mascarin*'s mizzenmast at deck level. The *Castries*' bowsprit itself splintered into a jagged stump. Her foremast started to sway dangerously as its supporting stays parted — one severed by the loss of her bowsprit, the others torn away by the *Mascarin*'s falling mizzenmast.

The collision scarcely slowed the momentum of the larger ship. Flung to the *Mascarin*'s deck by the impact, the two ensigns and the second-in-command instinctively rolled into the larboard scuppers. André covered his head with his arms as the *Castries*' bower anchor crushed part of the *Mascarin*'s starboard gallery, swept away the officers' latrine, then demolished the poop taffrail. Amidst the chaos and the cries of the men, he distinctly heard the indignant cackle of the hens as several chicken coops disappeared over the side.

Almost before he had time to draw breath, the *Castries* shook herself free of the smaller ship and dropped astern. On board the *Mascarin*, men slowly picked themselves up from where they had fallen, checking themselves and their companions for injury. André untangled his long legs from the stockier ones belonging to his cousin Jean and scrambled awkwardly to his feet. He rubbed the knee that had taken the brunt of his fall. Only minutes had passed since his first shout of warning.

Beside him, Jean cursed quietly, a purple bruise spreading on his forehead, then asked, 'Are you hurt?'

André shook his head, not ungrateful that the senior ensign still looked out for him, having taken him under his wing as his fidèle when he joined the Compagnie des Indes six years ago as an eleven-year-old apprentice. Jean clapped him on the shoulder affectionately, then picked his way after Monsieur Crozet, who was already crossing the cluttered deck towards the steps up to the quarterdeck.

A sudden shout drew André's attention back to the *Castries*, now drifting astern. As he turned to look, the other ship's unsupported foremast toppled. The man on lookout was flung from his perch in the foremast top. André watched in horror as he fell in an arc of flailing limbs, his thin scream cut off abruptly as he disappeared amidst the tangled heap of yards, sails and tackle that cascaded onto the deck. The ensign hastily crossed himself and muttered a brief prayer. Surely no one could survive such a fall?

For a long moment, the two ships seemed suspended in time, held motionless on the sullen sea. Then from their quarterdeck, the expedition leader took up his speaking trumpet and hailed the captain of the consort ship. 'Monsieur du Clesmeur, report on board the *Mascarin* as soon as you have secured your ship.'

André was glad not to be in the shoes of the *Castries'* young captain. Even before the collision, the expedition leader had commented unfavourably on various manoeuvres undertaken by the consort ship. The ensign thought it must be all the more galling for Monsieur Marion, as the owner of the *Castries,* to see his precious ship so mishandled. Their own vessel, the much smaller *Mascarin*, belonged to the King, on lease for this eighteen-month expedition that would take them from the Île-de-France off the African coast deep into the unknown Southern Ocean. It made little sense to him that the inexperienced twenty-year-old du Clesmeur could be entrusted with the command of any ship. But André's more worldly cousin reasoned that being lumbered with Monsieur du Clesmeur was the price Monsieur Marion paid for the use of the King's ship, and the young captain's promotion was the result of the patronage and undeniable influence of his uncle, Governor of the Île-de-France and one of the expedition's sponsors. No doubt, Jean added, the captain of the *Castries* considered himself the equal of any of their older and more experienced ex-Compagnie des Indes officers, being of aristocratic birth with a pedigree as long as his pompous name — Ambroise-Bernard-Marie le Jar du Clesmeur. The cynical Jean thought Monsieur Marion would have willingly made any concession necessary to get his expedition underway, the promise of fame and fortune accompanying the discovery of new lands and new outlets for trade in the Southern Ocean being sufficient recompense for any such imposition. The expedition leader must have decided that giving the young aristocrat the charge of his own ship, the *Castries*, was the lesser evil, seeing she was more seaworthy and less temperamental under sail than the King's somewhat dilapidated smaller ship.

Now, as his heart rate slowed to normal, André gazed around him at the wreckage-strewn deck, realizing the young captain's ineptitude had inflicted considerable damage on the King's ship. He looked across at the disabled *Marquis de Castries*, drifting without its most essential spars. Monsieur Marion would not be appreciating the irony of his decision.

A few hours later, when some order had been restored to both ships, the consort's yawl brought her captain and second-in-command across to the *Mascarin*. As the two officers came aboard, Monsieur Crozet beckoned André. 'Vite, vite!' he said. 'Quickly now — go and tidy yourself, Monsieur Tallec. The captain needs you in the great cabin to take notes.' He explained that the captain's clerk, Paul Chevillard, had severely sprained his right wrist when the ships collided and could not hold a pen.

Below deck in the cramped gunroom, André changed into his spare pair of slightly cleaner breeches and the merchant seaman's blue jacket he had already outgrown. He tried in vain to tug the sleeves down over his protruding knobbly wrists. Giving up, he ran his fingers through his unruly russet-red hair then retied the queue at the nape of his neck. The disconsolate Chevillard sat on the bench at the gunroom table, nursing his strapped wrist.

'You lucky young pup, Tallec, I'd give anything to see Monsieur du Clesmeur try and explain this one away.' He paused, then could not resist adding, 'Mind you take particular care with your lettering.'

André held his tongue. Even if he were the best calligrapher in all of France, the captain's clerk would find fault with his work. Of similar age and experience to Jean Roux, Chevillard jealously guarded his role. What was more, as a native of Poitou, he considered himself superior to Bretons — most of the men on board both ships — and was quick to criticize. It did not endear him to his two Breton fellow ensigns.

By the time the young ensign reported for duty, the senior officers of both ships were already seated on either side of the great cabin table. Monsieur Crozet, the *Mascarin's* second-in-command, glanced up as André hovered in the doorway, then nodded towards a small side desk equipped with paper, inkwell and pens. The ensign settled down as unobtrusively as he could, then took in the scene as he sharpened a couple of quills.

Subdued light filtered through the wide stern windows of the great cabin. Its shifting patterns glimmered on the low deck-head above them, slid across the polished table then glinted briefly on the silver-chased hilt of Monsieur Marion's dress sword. The two captains had dressed formally for the occasion, the expedition leader in his favourite blue velvet frockcoat with the matching waistcoat and breeches. The coveted gold cross of the Order of St Louis, awarded in recognition of his many exploits in the Seven Years' War against England, hung on its red ribbon from his top buttonhole. Monsieur du Clesmeur, slighter in build than the expedition leader and fine-boned, was of course wearing the splendid scarlet and gold uniform that gave the nickname of 'red' officers to the aristocrats who formed the Gardes de la Marine, the élite training corps for the King's Navy. The ruffles of his fine linen shirt were on show at collar and cuffs, and he sported large gold buckles on his black shoes, gold lace on the three-cornered black beaver hat now laid carelessly on the table, and enough gold braid elsewhere on his person to rig an entire ship. Unlike Monsieur Marion and the other senior officers, who always wore the stiff wool wig favoured by sailors because its side rolls did not need constant attention, the young aristocrat had taken the time to have his wig of human hair freshly curled, pomaded and powdered.

To André's secret satisfaction, the captain of the *Castries* seemed somewhat ill at ease, despite the elegance of his attire. He barely sipped the excellent Cape Burgundy poured by François, Monsieur Marion's black Malagasy slave, before putting the glass down on the table. Monsieur Le Corre, the consort ship's second-in-command, sat beside his captain, his own glass already drained. His massive thighs were spread wide to ease the binding of his tight breeches, and his faded blue Compagnie frockcoat was unbuttoned over his straining waistcoat. André caught him swapping a slight nod and sardonically raised eyebrow with Monsieur Crozet, his opposite number on the *Mascarin*, as the expedition leader put his own glass down and said briskly, 'Now, gentlemen, I suggest we begin. Monsieur du Clesmeur, I await your explanation for the unfortunate manoeuvre that has brought our ships to such a sorry state.'

The young captain took his time. He stared down his long nose then took a pinch of snuff from his silver snuff box, ignoring the communal box placed in the centre of the table. When he finally spoke, his tone was haughty. 'Surely, sir, the fault lies with the clumsy steering of the *Mascarin*? It's unreasonable to expect my larger ship to have taken evasive action. We were hove-to, foresails aback . . .'

Ma fois, what nonsense, thought André, who had seen the *Castries'* foresails fill as the ship turned towards the *Mascarin*.

Monsieur Le Corre intervened as the expedition leader raised his eyebrows. 'Perhaps, sir, I can supply the explanation? Our captain had gone below at the time.'

Monsieur Crozet snorted, but the second-in-command of the *Castries* continued smoothly, 'One of those williwaws swept off the land adjacent — our vessel was closer inshore than yours. We were caught unawares by the sudden violent gust of wind and fell immediately aboard your ship.'

'So, you're claiming there was no time to correct?' Monsieur Marion sounded dubious.

'In my opinion,' said Monsieur Le Corre, 'even a captain of your vast experience could not have averted the collision.'

André knew the *Castries'* second-in-command was taking a risk with such a bold statement, even though — like the *Mascarin's* Monsieur Crozet — he had known the expedition leader for years. All in their mid- to late forties, the three men had shared ships and experiences in the Compagnie des Indes and then as 'blue' merchant officers recruited into the King's Navy during the recent war against England. The room grew quiet. The ensign could hear the click of Monsieur du Clesmeur's carefully manicured fingernails as he tapped out an unconscious rhythm on the lid of his snuff box.

Monsieur Marion considered for a moment, then nodded slowly. 'Fort bien. Very well.' He looked across at the ensign sitting riveted in the corner. 'Make a note, Monsieur Tallec, if you please. The incident is to be logged as an accident.'

André dutifully complied, thinking that Monsieur Le Corre's explanation would seem inadequate even to the most inexperienced sailor. But as he put his pen down, the expedition leader added, 'Your loyalty towards your captain is commendable, Monsieur Le Corre. Nevertheless, it needs to be said that a captain of my experience — as you put it — would not have taken his ship so close to high land under such circumstances. Unexpected downdrafts off such terrain are commonplace, are they not?'

Before the *Castries'* second-in-command could respond, Monsieur Marion took a pinch of snuff himself from the communal box, blew his nose heartily, then pushed the snuff box towards him. 'Let's move on. I see you have your list there.' He nodded to the attentive François to pour more wine.

As the officers helped themselves to snuff, André watched the captain of the *Castries* out of the corner of his eye. It was slowly dawning on him that the expedition leader had put Monsieur du Clesmeur firmly in his place. At the same time Monsieur Marion had, he now realized, subtly acknowledged the difficult position occupied by the *Castries'* far more experienced 'blue' officer. For a moment, Monsieur du Clesmeur bristled, then visibly resigned himself to accepting the indirect rebuke without comment. The young aristocrat might be arrogant, but he was far from stupid. Even cousin Jean conceded that.

Monsieur Le Corre was already itemizing the damage suffered by the *Castries*, a stubby finger stabbing at each entry as he read out his list. André hastily jotted them down. One man killed on board the *Castries* when the foremast fell — the lookout — and three with fractures, all hit by debris as the mast fell. Although the ship's hull had suffered little damage, she had lost two essential spars. Both her bowsprit and foremast and their associated rigging were now nothing but a tangled heap of flotsam, already cut away from the ship and set adrift.

Monsieur Crozet followed with the report for the *Mascarin*. Although the damage to the smaller ship was mostly confined to her stern superstructure, it was bad enough. 'Our gallery's stove in on the starboard side, sir, and the carpenters say our mizzenmast's splintered beyond salvaging.'

There was silence while the senior officers contemplated their situation. They would need to make urgent repairs before they could risk venturing any further into the turbulent Southern Ocean. At best, both ships would be forced to make do with jury rigs, replacing their lost spars with spare topmasts — smaller and lacking the necessary strength to be effective if the gale-force winds they had already experienced should recur. As the brooding silence wore on, André understood from the glum faces around the table that any loss of sailing efficiency could prove their undoing. He swallowed uneasily. They were already a long way south of frequented waters, and therefore unlikely to encounter other vessels or find anyone to assist them. Even the *Marquis de Castries*, at seven hundred tons, suddenly seemed too small and too fragile a ship for this venture into a vast and unknown ocean.

From the hastily repaired taffrail of the *Mascarin*, André looked longingly at the still-visible coastline of the larger of the two islands. The sea was calmer than it had been for days, and this was the first land they had encountered since leaving the Cape of Good Hope a fortnight ago. They were still close enough for the ensign to see the line of bright surf fringing the shore. Whenever the mist cleared, he could make out several tiers of high snow-capped mountains rising behind green lower slopes. With land in view, his qualms about their vulnerability had soon been replaced by his more usual appetite for adventure.

Jean Roux joined him at the taffrail. 'I was looking forward to being one of the landing party.' His cousin was in a bad mood. 'Monsieur Crozet says going ashore's probably out of the question now.'

André was more optimistic. 'Don't lose hope. If the weather holds—'

'Hope?' Jean grimaced. 'Monsieur Marion must regret naming that island Terre d'Espérance, Land of Hope — Land of Hope Dashed would seem more appropriate.'

André crossed himself. 'Prenez garde, Jean! Take care! Saying such things is asking for more bad luck.'

For the next three days, both ships lay at a safe distance from the islands as the carpenters made what repairs they could. Apart from retaining one topmast to replace their own destroyed mizzenmast, Monsieur Marion sent his other spare spars across to the *Castries*. Heavy rain set in, making the work more difficult as the men handled the cumbersome spars and wet ropes, their fingers numbed with cold. They were enveloped in thick fog once more, but at least the sea was flattened by the persistent rain. The only sounds were the constant groaning of the ships' timbers and the creak of gear aloft as they drifted under bare masts, rolling on a long swell.

Work stopped only to commit the unfortunate lookout to the sea, sewn up in his hammock and weighted with shot to prevent his body lingering on the surface as prey for sharks or predatory seabirds. The two ships lay close together in calm seas, their men mustered on the main decks. On board the smaller *Mascarin*, there was only room for the hundred ship's people to assemble in the waist of the ship, so the forty-strong company of soldiers lined up on the forecastle. André stood on the quarterdeck with the other officers, their tricorn hats tucked under their arms, as across the water Monsieur du Clesmeur conducted the brief Mass for the Dead in front of his own one hundred men.

That evening, the ensigns joined the men gathered on the *Mascarin*'s forecastle while the musicians played their melancholy Breton tunes, the harsh fluting cry of the double-reed bombarde weaving an octave below the skirling drone of a biniou, the familiar sound eerily intensified by the fog. Monsieur Marion had ordered that the men receive an extra serving of wine, but the mood remained sombre. No one had the heart for their usual singing and dancing, and most of the sailors soon became sullen drunk. It was not long before André retreated to his hammock in the ensigns' corner of the gunroom. He buried his head in his blankets, waiting for sleep to dispel the unwelcome thoughts Jean had stirred up once more — that Monsieur Marion's expedition to the Southern Ocean was dogged by misfortune.

By the time the ships were seaworthy, they had drifted far from the islands. Rain and fog continued to beset them, and the weather remained bitter. Before they set sail, André was called again to the great cabin when the expedition leader met with the senior officers of both ships to decide how best to progress.

The captain of the *Castries* wanted to return to the islands and continue their interrupted survey. 'We neglect our duty if we do otherwise, gentlemen. We've not truly ascertained the nature of the larger island. It may well be a promontory extending from the Southern Continent we seek.' His fingers tapped once more on the lid of his silver snuff box.

Monsieur Crozet disagreed. 'Returning would mean tacking close-hauled to windward, Monsieur du Clesmeur. I'm far from convinced your ship's makeshift masts would withstand the strain. That westerly is picking up strength.'

They listened to the whine of the rising wind in the rigging. Already, the sea visible through the stern windows was white-capped and rough, and the ship was beginning to pitch uncomfortably.

The expedition leader shook his head. 'Monsieur Crozet's right, sir — we can't risk the stress to your ship of tacking against such a wind.'

Monsieur du Clesmeur was inclined to argue, somehow managing to imply by his over-polite language that such pragmatism — to be expected of unimaginative 'blue' officers — was in danger of impeding their ultimate goal; that only a 'red' officer of aristocratic birth could possibly understand the far-reaching implications of any decision they made.

Ignoring both the young aristocrat's posturing and the responding bristling of his fellow 'blue' officers, Monsieur Marion made up his mind. 'If we're indeed off the coast of the Southern Continent, no doubt we'll encounter land again by continuing eastwards along this forty-sixth parallel. These currents will carry us further into the Southern Ocean anyway.' His tone becoming steely, he added, 'Return immediately to your ship, Monsieur du Clesmeur, and prepare to set sail.'

André ducked his head to his paper and pen to hide his satisfaction as the captain of the *Castries* and his visibly smirking officers rose to their feet and prepared to leave the great cabin.

Over the next few days, the ships were driven south-eastwards under shortened sail. It soon became clear that the jury-rigged *Castries*, previously the faster of the two ships, could no longer keep up with the *Mascarin*. Progress was slow. When it was not blowing a gale, dense fog enveloped the ships and they had to fire the guns night and day to signal their respective positions — both to remain in contact and to avoid any further collision. Even at noon, André could not see the bow of the *Mascarin* from the quarterdeck, where he met with the other ensigns and Monsieur Crozet in mostly thwarted attempts to take sightings. As he fumbled with his sextant, chilled to the bone, the ensign was secretly relieved the horizon was usually too obscure for accurate sightings. His figures would fall far short of the standard expected by the second-in-command, who was known to be an excellent navigator, as good as Monsieur Marion himself. The difficulties of navigating in such weather added to the frustration of seeing almost daily the banks of seaweed, seabirds and seals that indicated they were not far from land. At night, their sleep was often disturbed by the shrill, unnerving cries of penguins swimming near the ship, sounding more like fractious infants than seabirds.

The only real excitement came late one afternoon when André, on watch in the mainmast top, noticed a wedge of brilliant whiteness on the horizon, gleaming under the lowering sky. In response to his holler, Monsieur Marion joined him in the top with his eyeglass.

'Well spotted, Monsieur Tallec — it's an iceberg, and a large one,' the captain confirmed after examining the distant object. He handed André the eyeglass. 'From its size, I'd conclude it's been ejected from a substantial river.'

'Meaning substantial land — the Southern Continent, sir?' André asked, his excitement growing as he reluctantly returned the eyeglass.

'D'accord,' said Monsieur Marion. 'But don't get too excited. Such a large iceberg could've drifted many hundreds of leagues from its source.'

By seven that evening, the ships were within a league of the iceberg. Everyone crowded the rails as they sailed past. The descending sun suddenly emerged below the layer of grey cloud. The western side of the iceberg blazed a white so dazzling that André's eyes watered whenever he tried to look at it directly. Huge caverns worn at sea level glowed a cold turquoise, which darkened to blue below the surface. Long after they had sailed on, and the iceberg's silhouette had merged into the darkening night, he could hear the hollow boom of the waves as they rolled steadily into these caverns.

Although the weather did not improve and conditions remained foggy, they continued to catch tantalizing glimpses of land. Six days after leaving the collision site, they approached another island, large and mountainous. For the best part of a day and a night, the two ships tried to tack closer in a wind that blew offshore directly against them. Poorly clad in what was meant to be summer in the Southern Hemisphere, the ship's people froze in their loose knee-length cotton trousers and inadequate short jackets. Although most had woollen bonnets and Monsieur Marion had them issued with knitted Guernsey frocks from the slop chest, few owned shoes or stockings. The men's fingers were so numb with cold and their bodies wracked with shivering that their sluggish efforts meant the ships often missed stays and fell back onto the previous tack. Even when they succeeded in bringing the ships onto the opposite tack, they found it difficult to trim the sails to Monsieur Marion's liking. The limitations of their adapted sailing rigs became only too obvious, and the shoreline remained stubbornly distant.

At the end of his deck watches, André stumbled below. By day's close, he was too tired to eat the pannikin of lukewarm soup thickened with dried peas and crumbled ship's biscuit that constituted supper. Even drinking his ration of wine seemed almost too much trouble. He draped his sodden outer clothing from the ropes of his hammock, although he knew it would not dry. The deck-head oozed damp and the floor was puddled wet from the moisture they inevitably tracked into the gunroom. Sleep overwhelmed him almost before he had time to wrap himself tightly in his musty blankets and roll into bed. His four hours below passed too quickly to bring much respite.

Dawn at last brought clear bright skies. Sunlight coloured the great waves that rolled endlessly to the horizon. A deep indigo overall, each white-capped wave glowed translucent green at its crest, deepening through blue to violet in its trough. By mid-morning, they had succeeded in bringing the ships close enough to land for Monsieur Marion to order his second-in-command to row ashore and claim possession of the large island for the King.

André and his cousin Jean accompanied their senior officer in the yawl. They landed in a small cove backed by a steep boulder beach, the sole break in a line of stern black cliffs. As the three officers made their way up the beach, the ensign staggered on rough boulders that did not yield under his feet the way the deck of the ship did, then stumbled amongst the thick strands of dried brown seaweed piled at the high tide line, cursing his clumsiness after so long at sea.

Monsieur Crozet indicated a natural cairn at the end of the beach, maybe fifty feet high, built from large chunks of rock tumbled from the sea-eroded cliffs. 'Up you go, Monsieur Roux,' he said, handing the senior ensign the bottle containing the deed André had clean-copied before they left the ship, claiming the island for France and the King and naming it Prise de Possession. 'Your young muscles should be more agile than mine.'

After Jean had lodged the bottle in a cranny at the top of the pyramid, Monsieur Crozet told both ensigns to remove their tricorns. When the second-in-command finished intoning the words of possession, the two young men spontaneously shouted 'Vive le Roi!' and tossed their hats high into the air. André's chest swelled with pride at participating in the first of perhaps many new discoveries for France. There was no sign other men had ever come ashore on this island. Neither the seabirds sitting on nests scattered in the rushes nor the seals gambolling on the beach showed any fear at their presence. He was able to walk right up to the penguins standing around on large clumsy feet, bright eyes examining him back with equal curiosity.

The expedition leader had given them only an hour or two ashore, barely time to climb the hill behind the beach and glimpse the island's interior. From the hill's summit, André took in the desolate snow-patched valleys below the mountain range they had seen emerging from the sea. If there were streams in the valleys, they were too distant to be of any use for replenishing the ships' water supplies, foul-tasting and getting low after nearly four weeks at sea. No trees or even shrubby plants softened the barren landscape before them. Yellow-green lichen studded the black rocks, and a brown, tussocky grass provided the only other colour.

'This is truly the most inhospitable place,' muttered Jean as they slowly made their way back to the beach, leg muscles already weary after the unaccustomed exercise.

'Toutàfait — absolutely!' André agreed. 'Fit only for the birds.' His earlier excitement ebbed away as he realized that discovery of this island was unlikely to win them much honour, let alone provide a suitable southern Pacific trading base for France.

To make matters worse, Monsieur Marion now reluctantly decided they could not penetrate further south in search of the elusive Southern Continent. The constant need to put the ship's people on watch and watch-about in bad weather was eroding everyone's strength. Their poor sailing ability, particularly of the jury-rigged *Castries*, and the cold prevented the ill-equipped sailors from working the ships effectively. Even in better weather and good visibility when the men could be kept on three watches, giving them eight hours' rest below deck and regular meals for every four worked on deck, injuries aloft were increasing.

The expedition leader explained his decision to the assembled officers of both ships. 'Our people can only grow weaker in these deplorable conditions.'

Monsieur Thirion, the elderly surgeon, agreed. 'I've several cases of severe rheumatics amongst the younger men. Many others have hacking coughs and fevers. Some of these have all the appearance of consumption.' The surgeon was bleeding the more severe cases, but the benefit gained was slight and short-lived. Minor complaints such as saltwater boils were rife.

Although the captain of the *Castries* predictably expressed his aristocratic disapproval at the decision to curtail their probe southwards, implying the expedition leader lacked fortitude, Monsieur Marion would brook no argument. Although his voice remained neutral, he effectively silenced the captain by pointing out that the damage to their ships caused by the collision had tipped the scales against proceeding further south. 'To add to our difficulties, these damnable fogs show no sign of dispersing. It's almost impossible to navigate accurately in such conditions. We're putting our ships and our people at too great a risk.'

André thought it typical of him to put the safety of his men first. The expedition leader's demeanour showed no sign of what must be acute frustration and disappointment at their failure to discover the Southern Continent. But Jean commented later that — with the encouragement of his Malagasy slave, François — he was probably sticking pins into an effigy of Monsieur du Clesmeur in the privacy of his cabin.

Without further delay, they weighed anchor and sailed directly eastwards.

February brought gales and heavy seas. Not only the men but the ships themselves were now showing increased signs of the continual strain of sailing at such latitudes. The *Mascarin*, dilapidated before the added stress to her timbers caused by the collision, developed enough leaks for the pumps to need manning every day, hard physical work that taxed men already weak. Her decks badly needed recaulking, and the tightly packed hammocks where the sailors slept between decks were subject to continuous icy shower baths. The number of men sick and unfit for duty aloft increased by the day. To add to their problems, Monsieur Thirion reported that some malcontents were now constantly drunk.

Conditions on board the *Castries* were even worse, and Monsieur du Clesmeur resorted to frequent floggings for what André and Jean suspected were minor transgressions. Even though the expedition leader had ensured that, as on his own command, the *Castries* had able musicians on board, her people seldom congregated on the forecastle of an evening to sing and dance. Following traditional Compagnie des Indes practice, Monsieur Marion encouraged such entertainment on the *Mascarin* whenever the weather was kind enough. Even the officers were expected to join in the country dances and rounds. He saw the physical activity as good for morale, as well as keeping the men warm and less susceptible to illness. Jean claimed the *Castries* was an unhappy ship under Monsieur du Clesmeur. 'He's not respected,' he said. 'You can't expect unhappy men to dance or sing for a captain they don't respect.'

André had his own private miseries to contend with. His hands had developed chilblains. The fair, sensitive skin that came with his accursed red hair broke open and bled whenever he handled wet gear or could not resist rubbing his fingers to alleviate the itch that drove him to distraction. Eventually taking pity on him, Jean sent him to the ship's surgeon.

Monsieur Thirion's tiny cabin, partitioned off the gunroom on the lower deck, was cluttered with books, papers and stacked boxes. When André knocked and stooped to enter, the elderly surgeon was engrossed in his copy of de Brosses' book on Pacific voyaging. He waved the ensign to a seat on a convenient sea chest, then proceeded to précis what he had just read. 'These islands we're encountering could well be part of the southern land mass the philosophers say must counterbalance our northern continents.' He added, 'Indeed, I'm beginning to think the Southern Continent may be made up of a vast archipelago of such islands — enough of them to provide the necessary land symmetry in both hemispheres.'

Without waiting for André's response, he went on: 'We're bound to find plants and animals on these islands that are new to science and trade.' He reluctantly closed the book, marking his place with a slender ivory paperknife. 'And that of course should allow our esteemed captain to establish the trading connections so dear to his heart.'

'I doubt, sir, whether even Monsieur Marion could trade with penguins,' said André, his voice sour.

Monsieur Thirion looked at him, his eyes sharp under his tufted grey eyebrows. 'Mockery signals ignorance more often than not, young man.'

André apologized. 'I find myself doubting we'll ever leave these desolate waters and reach inhabited lands. I constantly dream of the warmer latitudes of the East Indies.'

'Certainly it's hard to accept it's midsummer here.' The surgeon nodded at the ensign's inflamed hands. 'Those the reason you've come to see me? I can make you up a good salve.' He busied himself with mortar and pestle.

The ships continued to labour on. The Southern Continent they suspected lay only a few degrees further south stayed hidden — whether it were land mass or archipelago. It was not until ten days into February, nearly seven weeks after setting sail from the Cape of Good Hope and four months since leaving the Île-de-France, that Monsieur Crozet and the ensigns were at last able to take advantage of a full moon, a well-defined horizon and a clear evening sky to obtain good lunar sightings. But when Monsieur du Clesmeur and his officers took advantage of the favourable conditions to bring their yawl across from the *Castries* to the *Mascarin* to compare readings, it was soon clear that the consort ship's navigators had achieved quite different results. Even the reckonings made daily using the ships' runs differed. Both captains considered their ready reckoning was more reliable than the infrequent attempts they could make at observing longitude, so the discrepancy was puzzling.

'Lack of expertise has much to answer for,' said Monsieur de Clesmeur, looking down his long nose. 'It's most unfortunate we have neither an astronomer on board nor one of these new and reliable chronometers.' He took a large portion of snuff, his head characteristically thrust back — just like a turkey about to gobble, in Jean's irreverent opinion.

André winced. He knew the expedition leader had hoped to have the experienced astronomer Rochon appointed for the voyage — along with his Berthoud chronometer, but at the last minute the Governor of the Île-de-France refused permission. Monsieur Marion constantly lamented the inevitable limits this imposed on accurate navigation or any mapping of new lands. The ensign realized from Monsieur du Clesmeur's expectant expression that the captain knew this full well.

Visibly choking back his ire, the expedition leader chose not to react. He merely pointed out that, regardless of discrepancies in their calculations, they had certainly reached a suitable longitude to change direction and head north until they reached the forty-third parallel. By sailing eastwards along that, they could expect to find Van Diemen's Land at the southern extremity of New Holland, using Abel Tasman's one-hundred-and-thirty-five-year-old chart. This should prove a welcome refuge where they could rest the ship's people, trade for food and water with the native inhabitants, and cut timber for more permanent repairs to their struggling ships.

# Chapter 2

O n deck for the dawn anchor watch, André Tallec gazed shorewards as the rapidly increasing light transformed the black bulk of the forested slope behind the beach into a pattern of shifting grey and sage-green shadows. Through the eyeglass, he caught glimpses of darker shapes amongst the trees that he thought might be human, but when he blinked and looked again, he saw only tree trunks. Mist lay in wreaths amongst the trees and along the beach. When the sun rose, flocks of large parrots — some black with scarlet crests, some white with yellow crests — burst in noisy flurries from amongst the trees. A strong sea was running, and he could hear the roar of the waves as they surged up the beach. He was scanning the length of grey sand when quite suddenly, there they were, a large group of people, thirty or more, standing where he was sure only a moment before there had been nothing but driftwood and sand.

Tall, lean black men armed with staves or long spears, he was not sure which, were accompanied by women and children. All of them stark naked. Not even the women had their private parts covered. Curious, he stared intently for a moment, then looked away, ashamed of himself. He hastily sketched the sign of the cross and muttered a short prayer of contrition. Monsieur Marion was somehow expecting to establish cordial relations with these primitives. They looked nothing like the only Pacific inhabitant the ensign was familiar with, the affable Tahitian who had died on board of smallpox soon after the ships left the Île-de-France.

Variously known as Ahu-toru, Poutavery — after the explorer and circumnavigator Louis de Bougainville, whom he had accompanied in 1768 from Tahiti to Paris where he had been fêted in the salons — and finally as Mayoa, his own approximation of Monsieur Marion's name, the constantly smiling Tahitian had quickly won their hearts. Stranded for ten months in Port Louis on the Île-de-France, with much baggage containing gifts of seeds and implements for his people from his aristocratic admirers in Paris, the man had been patiently waiting for a ship to undertake the next stage of his return home. Although the return of Ahu-toru to Tahiti was the overt reason for their expedition and its official sponsorship, an enterprising Monsieur Marion had not been slow to see the potential for extending such a voyage into southern waters — a chance to win glory by finding the Southern Continent and other lands to provide France with a trading base in the South Pacific. He then intended reaping a profit by trading in the Spice Islands of the East Indies on their way back across the Pacific to the Île-de-France.

After the unfortunate and untimely death of Ahu-toru, some of the officers had argued for an immediate return to the Île-de-France — Monsieur du Clesmeur being the most vociferous. Jean believed Monsieur Marion would have faced certain ruin by doing so. 'I've heard he's staked everything on this expedition, mortgaged all his estates as well as borrowing vast sums of money. He's a known risk-taker.'

Not that the senior ensign was being critical, he hastened to add. Once peace had been brokered with England in 1763, 'blue' merchant officers inevitably lost their temporary postings in the King's Navy. Even worse, in 1769 their main source of employment and promotion, the Compagnie des Indes, had been dissolved. As a result, they had all been scratching for a living these last few years. The usual note of bitterness crept into Jean's voice. 'It's all very well for aristocrats like Monsieur du Clesmeur, guaranteed life-long retention in the King's Navy and sure of promotion — regardless of ability. It doesn't matter how many honours someone like Monsieur Marion wins in battle, he's still tossed onto the midden with the rest of us. We're dependent on such as him being willing to gamble.'

It seemed to André that the chances of Monsieur Marion's gamble paying off were diminishing rapidly. Ahu-toru's death, the collision and their forced abandonment of the search for the Southern Continent were bad enough. Now, watching the Diemenlanders clustered together at the water's edge, he had few illusions about their chances of profitable trade in this place. From their state of dress and apparent lack of any of the attributes of civilization, these people seemed unlikely to have items of interest to the French other than primitive curiosities. With uneasy thoughts occupying his mind, the ensign continued to watch them as they in turn stared towards the ships. They stood so still he became unnerved. From what he knew about Ahu-toru's people, he had been expecting a crowd of smiling, garlanded beauties, dancing and singing on the beach in welcome, not these grave, unmoving effigies.

Suddenly feeling the need to break the impasse, he waved and called a greeting. When the primitives did not so much as look in his direction or respond, he felt foolish. Busying himself with his duties, few at that hour of the morning, he kept an eye on them in case they should try and attack — although they seemed ill-equipped to do so. He consoled himself with the thought that, at the very least, Monsieur Thirion would find the opportunity to look for new plant and animal species once they went ashore. He could certainly test his theories about the desirable attributes of Natural Man. No one could seem closer to a state of Nature that these Diemenlanders.

On the evenings André was bidden to the captain's table for supper — one of Monsieur Marion's regular weekly invitations to each ensign in turn — the conversation often revolved around the advantages of living close to Nature in the way of Adam and Eve before the Fall. The book-loving surgeon promoted the philosophic argument, popular in the learned circles of French society, that primitive peoples uncorrupted by the desires and ambitions accompanying civilization and learning had the more contented lives. Only a few nights ago, the ensign had been present when the conversation turned in this direction.

Monsieur Thirion declared he had proof from Commerson, the botanist who had been with Bougainville on his recent circumnavigation. 'He told me in person that these laughter-loving Tahitians indeed live without vice.' The surgeon once more expounded the theory he favoured. 'Such people aren't degraded by intellectual reasoning and the lure of luxuries. Instead, knowing nothing else, primitives are content with their simple life and rely on instinct to dictate their gentle ways.'

Certainly, the ensign thought Ahu-toru's genial personality had lent some credence to such ideas, but the *Mascarin*'s second-in-command, as well-read as the surgeon, was inclined to be sceptical. Monsieur Crozet pointed out that Bougainville himself had commented negatively on other aspects of Tahitian society. 'Far from being content with their simple possessions, these so-called gentle primitives soon proved themselves capable of avarice. They stole anything they could lay their hands on.'

'Fi, fi, sir — surely such behaviour merely reflects how quickly contact with civilized men debases such innocent souls?' Monsieur Thirion was adept at turning an argument.

'Innocent souls? How then do you explain their indulgence

in human sacrifice, bloodshed and other such cruelties?' asked Monsieur Crozet. 'Monsieur Bougainville cites many examples of such behaviour.'

The expedition leader became impatient. He added a note of pragmatism. 'From my own experiences of the darker races, I find their state of mind invariably childlike and unsophisticated.'

André thought no one could argue with his wealth of experience. As well as being a slave-owner on his estates on the Île-de-France, Monsieur Marion had often traded along the coasts of Africa, China and India. The expedition leader beckoned for more wine and put an end to the discussion for the time being by saying, 'For our purposes, gentlemen, all we need to know is that, like domestic animals, such primitives respond to kindness. Treat them well and you'll get good results, every time. In my opinion, speculations on their underlying nature are therefore irrelevant.'

Although the surgeon and the second-in-command conceded with good grace, the ensign knew both officers would relish the chance to put their own views to the test. Now, in the cool light of early morning, he sneaked another look at the impassive group of Diemenlanders still standing motionless on the beach. As far as this lot went, if he were a gambling man he would place his money on Monsieur Marion.

Before the end of the watch, both the expedition leader and his second-in-command joined the ensign on the quarterdeck. Monsieur Marion nodded at the group on the beach. 'How long have our friends been with us, Monsieur Tallec?'

'Since first light, sir,' André said. 'They've not moved a muscle in all that time.'

Monsieur Marion looked at the naked men leaning on their long spears, the unarmed women and children. 'They seem harmless enough.' He smiled. 'Indeed, Monsieur Thirion is sure to see in them his Naturals, Men of the Woods — Savages. Call them what you will.'

Immediately after breakfast, the expedition leader hailed the *Castries* through his speaking trumpet. 'Monsieur du Clesmeur — bring your officers and join me on board the *Mascarin*, if you please.'

The officers gathered in the great cabin to receive their instructions. Paul Chevillard had resumed his clerical duties, so André stood at the entrance with the other junior officers. In the tiny officers' pantry beside him, the captain's slave was washing dishes, his ears no doubt pricked for any interesting gossip he could share later with Anthonie, the ship's Malagasy cook.

Monsieur Marion addressed them. 'Take the longboats to opposite ends of this bay, gentlemen. Traverse back within the breaker line if at all possible, keeping an eye out for any freshwater stream suitable for filling the water casks.'

'Are we to be armed, sir?' asked Lieutenant Lehoux, delegated to accompany Monsieur Crozet in the *Mascarin*'s boat. An energetic man and inclined to be belligerent, it was clear he would like nothing better than an invigorating skirmish with a bunch of naked primitives.

'Oui, oui!' said Monsieur Marion. 'By all means take a contingent of soldiers in each boat.' He fixed the eager lieutenant with a stern look. 'Take note, Monsieur Lehoux! A precaution only — I don't want these Diemenlanders alarmed in any way.'

As the crestfallen lieutenant subsided, the expedition leader continued, 'I intend taking my yawl direct to the middle of the cove, where you'll meet me in due course.'

Monsieur Le Corre of the *Castries* looked dubious. 'The middle of the cove? Is that wise, sir? That's where those savages have congregated.'

'Toutàfait — the sooner we establish contact and assure them we mean no harm, the better.' The expedition leader turned to Monsieur du Clesmeur. 'Would you care to accompany me in the yawl, sir?'

The *Castries*' captain looked less than enthused about directly encountering such uncouth beings as the waiting primitives, but answered, 'Fort bien, sir — as you wish.'

The young ensign was detailed to accompany the two captains in the yawl. Somewhat to his relief — and no doubt Monsieur du Clesmeur's — it was to be armed with a detachment of eight soldiers and six swivel-mounted blunderbusses. De Vaudricourt, the Sub-Lieutenant of the Legion detachment on board, was also to accompany them. Quiet to the point of taciturnity, the experienced military commander was punctilious with his duties, and his soldiers were well-drilled, despite the difficult conditions of the voyage. They would be in good hands if trouble developed.

Monsieur Marion then suggested his personal slave should go with them. As Monsieur du Clesmeur raised his eyebrows, he calmly explained. 'François' black skin will give us the advantage of familiarity. These Naturals will recognize him as similar to themselves. That should ease any apprehension.'

François, dressed in his master's cast-off finery and accustomed to a comfortable life in the great cabin, had none of his master's faith in primitives. André was close enough to hear him muttering protests in the officers' pantry.

When the yawl set out for the shore, the slave was on board, still grumbling. Monsieur Marion took no notice, being well-used to François. Jean believed the only reason the captain tolerated such insubordination was the slave's extraordinary ability to make the ship's food edible. Although the best chunks of salt beef in each cask were of course put aside for the captain's table, as well as the fresh meat butchered from the livestock pens once a week, the officers still received the same basic rations as the ship's people. Dried vegetables, salted meat and ship's biscuit with a little butter were eaten on flesh days; rice, dried or fresh fish and cheese replacing the meat on fast days — monotonous fare at best. But François could work magic with a splash of Burgundy and his private supply of spices. All the ensigns looked forward to their weekly supper with the senior officers in the great cabin, Jean allowing that he would tolerate any amount of theorizing from Monsieur Thirion so long as he had his spoon deep into a plateful of François' rich beef and bean cassoulet.

Once the yawl reached the breaker line, the Diemenlanders began calling to them and gesturing with their spears. 'They seem to think we speak their language,' André said as an old man launched into a long speech. 'Quelle folie! That's as crazy as us expecting them to speak French.' He laughed to hide his sudden attack of nerves.

'Think before you speak, Monsieur Tallec!' said Monsieur Marion. 'These simple people know nothing of any other world but their own. Of course they assume we understand their language.' He stood up in the stern sheets, doffed his hat, and called a greeting to the old man, smiling broadly to show friendship.

The boatmen took the yawl in closer, but the undertow was too strong for them to beach the boat. As they rowed along the breaker line, looking for a more suitable landing place, the Diemenlanders followed them on the edge of the water. One even ventured into the waves up to his knees, waving his spear, in what Monsieur Marion said was an invitation to join them.

'An invitation to join the contents of their pot, more like,' a sceptical Sub-Lieutenant de Vaudricourt muttered, thinking the gesture more threatening than friendly, earning another mild rebuke.

'They *have* sent their women and children away,' demurred Monsieur du Clesmeur. 'We should remain vigilant.'

'D'accord, Monsieur du Clesmeur,' said the expedition leader. 'Nevertheless, I see no signs of aggression.'

André looked cautiously at the Diemenlanders. They were now close enough for him to see their woolly heads, deep-set eyes and prominent cheekbones. He noticed the lines of raised scars on their broad yet bony chests. They were small-boned but tall — about the same height as him. They looked decidedly uncivilized. Monsieur Thirion's philosophy of equating primitiveness with natural nobility was fast losing its appeal. He exchanged glances with the lieutenant, but decided it wiser to keep such opinions to himself.

As Monsieur Crozet's longboat was now approaching not far along the shore, Monsieur Marion ordered the yawl to anchor just beyond the breaker line. 'I need two volunteers to strip naked and swim ashore,' he said. 'This would be the best way of showing these Diemenlanders we're men like them.'

André's jaw dropped at such an unorthodox suggestion. Equally disapproving, Monsieur du Clesmeur raised his eyebrows to a supercilious height. When none of the startled officers or sailors rushed to volunteer, Monsieur Marion told the coxswain to point out two men who could swim.

Joking nervously, the two well-built young Bretons chosen took off their clothes and plunged over the side. As they clung to the sides of the boat while they adjusted to the cold water, the expedition leader handed them some trinkets and a mirror as gifts for the primitives. André watched them swim ashore, his heart beating faster than usual. When the two men waded onto the beach unmolested, he heard Monsieur Marion let out his pent-up breath. For all his expressed confidence, he was obviously aware that such a tactic had its risks.

The Frenchmen watched from the boat as the Breton sailors stood on the edge of the sand, water streaming off their white bodies. For a long moment, the Diemenlanders stared at them, then huddled together conversing amongst themselves, some gesticulating with their spears. At last they put their weapons down and started capering about, singing some sort of song. The tension broke. Monsieur Marion called to the sailors and waved them up the beach. As they cautiously moved towards the prancing primitives, the old man who had earlier spoken so vehemently stepped forward and presented one of them with a burning stick. He gestured towards a pile of driftwood his companions had created above the tide line, indicating that the sailor should light it.

'Some sort of welcome ceremony, wouldn't you agree?' said Monsieur Marion, well satisfied. As the primitives continued to dance and sing, it would seem he was right.

'Dieu soit loué!' André heard the *Castries*' captain mutter his thanks to God, and looked up to see him cross himself. Hastily, he followed suit, then turned his attention back to the beach, anxious not to miss a moment of the encounter.

'You see, gentlemen,' Monsieur Marion could not help remarking, 'my strategy has proved successful.'

Monsieur du Clesmeur merely shrugged. It seemed he was not interested in the wooing of such uncivilized creatures. No doubt, André thought, he put them in a category below that of peasants and therefore quite beneath his consideration.

Those on board the yawl watched as the primitives gathered close around the two sailors, examining their white skin and cautiously poking at them. The Bretons presented their gifts. Only the mirror aroused any interest. The Diemenlanders grabbed it from one another, peering at their reflection and exclaiming. After some time, the old man stepped into the water and gestured at Monsieur Marion to take the boats further along the beach to a suitable landing place. With the two sailors gathered up amongst them, the primitives followed on foot. When they landed at the place indicated, Monsieur du Clesmeur insisted the boatmen and soldiers stay with the boats, ready to come to their assistance at a moment's notice. In his eagerness to meet the Diemenlanders, the expedition leader failed to notice that his black ambassador, François, resolutely stayed with the yawl.

André hung back to join his cousin, then followed the senior officers up the beach. They were soon surrounded by a milling crowd. The ensign tried not to flinch as one of the naked men plucked at his jacket sleeve then thrust his face close to his own. Somewhat disconcerted, he realized the man's woolly hair was a dusty ginger — much the same colour as his own when he attempted to tone down its flamboyant red with powder. The primitive's skin was filthy, smeared with dust or ashes and stinking of fish. When he opened his mouth and jabbered something incomprehensible, André just shook his head, unable to think of anything sensible to say in response. The man gave him a powerful punch on the arm, then turned away. The ensign broke out in a sweat despite the chill in the air. This rough encounter bore no relationship to the meeting with friendly Naturals he had anticipated.

The senior officers now approached the old man who seemed to be the leader or chief of the Diemenlanders, making gestures to indicate that they sought fresh food and water. Monsieur Crozet broke a piece off a flat round of ship's biscuit and ate it, then presented the rest to the old man. He sniffed cautiously at it, then threw it down, his lips drawn back in obvious disgust.

Jean suppressed a snort of laughter, then said quietly to André, 'Monsieur Crozet's taking a risk — a gift of ship's biscuit could be seen as an insult! We can hardly stomach it ourselves, and we're hungry enough to eat anything.'

André was too apprehensive to raise a smile, unable to make up his mind whether the expedition leader was being brave or foolhardy in taking them unarmed amongst these primitives. The soldiers left guarding the boats were a long way away, and the surgeon's philosophies seemed less robust by the minute.

Monsieur Marion's sharp ears picked up their whispered comments, but he did not rebuke his junior officers. Obviously relishing the encounter, his tone light-hearted, he said, 'Perhaps Monsieur Crozet's demonstrating just that — how desperate we are for fresh food!'

The expedition leader showed the old man a bottle with some water, then drank some, hoping his action would explain they were seeking water. But the man upended the proffered bottle and poured out its contents. After sniffing cautiously at the bottle, he gave it to one of his companions, who ran off. When the man did not come back, Monsieur Marion shrugged and gave up. They would have to find their own source of fresh water to replenish the ships' dwindling supplies.

Offering the Diemenlanders two of the last ducks and hens from the quarterdeck coops was no more successful as a bid to gain fresh food. The primitives fought over who was to have the hen, snatching the bird from each other and laughing at its increasingly outraged squawks. Eventually, they tore the unfortunate bird to pieces and flung it aside. André shifted uncomfortably. How could Monsieur Marion expect good treatment from people who behaved so barbarously? His unease grew when the Diemenlanders threw the hapless wing-clipped duck into the sea, then amused themselves by driving the bird in front of them, hurling spears until it was killed.

Monsieur du Clesmeur was also perturbed. André heard him mutter an aside to Lieutenant Le Dez from the *Castries*. 'What are these savages telling us — that they're capable of killing us in the same way?'

His lieutenant shrugged, then fastidiously brushed a smear of dust from his sleeve where one of the primitives had clutched at him. 'Who could account for such bizarre behaviour?'

Before long, several of the Diemenlanders approached the boats, apparently wanting to exchange their spears for the soldiers' muskets. It was Monsieur Crozet's turn to become concerned. 'They obviously recognize the muskets as weapons,' the second-in-command of the *Mascarin* said to his captain.

'They may be somewhat uncouth, but they're not fools,' replied Monsieur Marion. 'Our men can take care of themselves.'

Once they realized the soldiers would not relinquish their muskets, the primitives turned their attention to the officers' clothing. Anything coloured excited them, particularly scarlet jackets or capes. Elegant Lieutenant Le Dez had to fend off a man who tried to remove his velvet frockcoat. As he firmly buttoned the coat, he said to Monsieur Marion, 'If we stay much longer, they'll have their way with us. We'll soon all be reduced to their standard of dress!'

Although the other officers laughed, their unease was growing. Despite Monsieur Marion's belief that the increased jostling was nothing but good-natured excitement, Monsieur du Clesmeur now insisted that things were getting out of hand. 'These are not playful children, but rude primitives with no inkling of what constitutes civilized behaviour. It's only a matter of time before some of our people are hurt.'

Distracted by the old man, who offered him another burning firebrand and pushed him towards a small pile of driftwood, Monsieur Marion made no reply. He had just lit the fire with a flourish when the *Castries*' boat approached, coming from the other end of the beach. As the longboat made to land, its contingent of soldiers fixed their bayonets. The atmosphere suddenly changed. A small group of the Diemenlanders who had been keeping watch on the crest of the sand dunes nearby set up a caterwauling. They began throwing stones down at the Frenchmen already on the beach.

Hastily, Monsieur Marion ordered the longboat's commander to retreat. 'We become too many for them to be comfortable. Take your men back offshore.'

Although the longboat was immediately rowed back out beyond the breaker line, it made no difference. The Diemenlanders' excitement had turned to fear. Those on the beach started to shout angrily at the Frenchmen and wave their spears as they retreated to join their fellows on the sand dunes.

'Gentlemen, we should return to our boats,' Monsieur Marion said quietly. 'Fall back gradually. We don't want to alarm them further or be forced to retaliate.'

But as soon as they began to re-embark, the primitives hurled their spears towards them. A barrage of rocks then found targets, and both captains were hit. Rubbing his bruised upper arm, Monsieur Marion reluctantly ordered the soldiers to fire a volley. 'Aim away from them, Monsieur de Vaudricourt. A warning only. I don't want them hurt.'

At the sharp sound of the musket volley, the Diemenlanders ran off into the sand dunes, uttering howls of terror. But once they realized none of them was wounded, they returned to the water's edge. By then all the ship's people were safely back in the boats and out of their reach.

Monsieur Marion had the boatmen row further along the beach to find a place where they could land without interference. To their dismay, the primitives followed along the shore, continuing to shout abuse and wave their spears. When the boatmen turned the boats to try to land again, the primitives gathered at the landing place. 'Another volley,' the expedition leader ordered. 'Warn them off.'

This time the volley fired into the air had no effect. The Diemenlanders held their ground.

'Mordieu, they think our muskets merely mimic thunder or some such noise!' Monsieur du Clesmeur exclaimed. 'We must fire directly amongst them.'

Reluctant to do so, the expedition leader asked the boatmen to hold the boats beyond the breaker line. But now several of the primitives were wading out into the water and hurling their spears into the yawl. One hit François. The slave cowered in the well of the boat, blood oozing from a jagged wound in his leg, squealing like a cornered pig. André saw that the spear had broken off, leaving its tip in the wound. As he tried to assist the wailing slave, the rest of the Diemenlanders began wading towards the boats, their spears raised ready to throw.

'Fire immediately, Monsieur de Vaudricourt!' Monsieur Marion now had no choice. 'Aim directly at them this time.'

The volley of musket balls scattered the primitives, and some of them fell wounded. This had the desired result, as the Diemenlanders fled into the forest, carrying their injured.

When they did not return, Monsieur Marion decided it was now safe to land. As the boats crunched on the sand and the boatmen hauled them ashore, André kept an anxious eye on the line of sparse, grey-leaved trees behind the sand dunes. He was sure he could see people lurking in the flickering shadows. His skin crawled at the thought of one of those spears finding him as its target. But nothing human moved amongst the trees, and the beach remained deserted.

Although Monsieur Marion insisted his shoulder was merely bruised, his second-in-command advised both captains to return to their ships with the wounded slave. 'I'll take an armed landing party and pursue the primitives. We'll make sure they don't intend returning.'

Not wishing to risk further injury, Monsieur du Clesmeur was only too happy to take this advice, but the expedition leader agreed reluctantly, not liking to miss any of the action. He looked unwell, two patches of red flamed on his cheekbones and his face was white. 'Try not to kill any of them, Monsieur Crozet, but disperse them sufficiently to allow us an unimpeded search for water.'

As well as the soldiers from the yawl, Monsieur Crozet selected the fittest officers to accompany him, the three ensigns from the *Mascarin* amongst them. After being equipped with muskets, the landing party picked their way through the sand dunes, following a trail of drying blood. Although André was preoccupied with looking out for stealthily approaching Diemenlanders, he could not help noticing that the sandy ground was everywhere covered with ash and the bases of most trees were scorched black — presumably burnt by the inhabitants for some inexplicable reason. Van Diemen's Land was far from the verdant paradise he had anticipated. Overhead, raucous black crow-like birds cawed and screeched, a hideous noise that served to underline the harshness of the country they were traversing. After an hour of steady walking, they emerged on the edge of a large, swampy plain. By then they had lost sight of the trail of blood. They saw no other sign of the primitives they were pursuing.

'We'll follow around the edges of this swamp before returning to the shore,' Monsieur Crozet decided. 'Keep a sharp eye out for Diemenlanders, gentlemen, but focus on finding water.'

In that task they had no success, the swamp yielding only a few brackish, muddy pools. So several hours later, the disheartened landing party straggled back towards the shore, no longer bothering to watch out for the absent inhabitants. Exhausted and thirsty, André was plodding along in the rear when movement caught his eye. He turned aside to check. Half-protruding from behind a low-growing bush was a pair of sprawled legs that ended in dusty black feet.

Heart beginning to pound, André stood still and watched. The feet twitched slightly. 'Monsieur Crozet!' he called urgently after the landing party, already disappearing through the scrub. He waited for them to return, unable to bring himself to investigate more closely. The feet did not twitch again.

Pushing aside the low branches, the *Mascarin*'s second-in-command exposed the body of one of the primitives. He crouched to examine him. 'He's been hit by at least three of our musket balls.'

André looked down at the naked body. The man seemed quite young, but he was pitifully thin, the skinniness of his long legs emphasized by over-large, bony knee caps. The ensign could see a line of bilious white exposed under the man's half-closed crusted eyelids. His thick lips were fixed in a grimace of pain, and sweat had cut reddish trails in his black skin. Below a series of crescent-shaped parallel scars, his chest and stomach were a mass of congealed blood and entrails. The ensign swallowed a rush of nausea and turned his head away.

Lieutenant Le Dez asked, 'Is there anything we can do for this poor unfortunate?'

The senior officer shook his head and stood up. 'Alas, he's dying, if not already dead.' He cautiously prodded at the inert body with his musket. The man did not react. His head lolled to one side, blood now trickling from his ears and nose.

'Ma fois, these Diemenlanders are nothing but wild beasts,' said Sub-Lieutenant de Vaudricourt. 'His fellows abandoned him to his fate without compunction.'

'I think not,' Monsieur Crozet said quietly. He indicated the circle of broken darts and spears surrounding the body. 'Those would suggest some element of ritual, however rudimentary. We were pursuing them, don't forget.'

'Should we bury him, sir?' André asked. He had overlooked the broken weapons, and felt a pang of shame at his own ready dismissal of these people. 'Show our regret somehow?'

The senior officer shook his head. 'Unwise, however kindly meant, Monsieur Tallec. We don't know their customs. Any such action on our part might bring retaliation.'

'We should at least make note of his particulars,' said Chevillard briskly. 'Monsieur Marion would expect us to take advantage of the opportunity for scientific records. Those red marks on his skin, for example, would indicate he's not as black as he seems.'

André wondered how the clerk could be so callous, disliking him even more than usual.

Monsieur Crozet looked down at the body. 'He's beyond any further harm we can do him.'

After waiting a few more moments to be sure the man was indeed dead, the senior officer took his handkerchief and gently washed a portion of the Diemenlander's skin with the last of their water. His blackness proved to be a layer of encrusted dirt, the skin underneath the filth the reddish brown suggested by the sweat trails on his body. The clerk took one of the broken spears and, using it as a measure, estimated the man was of average height, about five foot and three inches. Much to André's disgust, he then used the spear to prise apart the primitive's jaws. Although his small teeth were white, worms of some sort wriggled inside his mouth.

'Those would seem to indicate poor health,' said Lieutenant Le Dez. 'These people must lead a wretched existence.'

There being nothing more they could do, the landing party left the man as they found him and made their weary way through the sand dunes back to the beach. It was already evening and the air was growing cold. They waited in dispirited silence for the hailed *Mascarin* to send a boat to fetch them. Behind them in the darkening trees, the black crows mocked them with their raucous cawing. There was no sign of the Diemenlanders. No fires were lit ashore that night.

For the next few days, Monsieur Marion sent armed parties ashore at various points along the bay in search of water and timber for repairing their ships. Suffering a recurrence of the fevers that had plagued him since his years of trading along the African coast for the Compagnie des Indes, the expedition leader had been ordered by the surgeon to stay in his cabin and rest. His Malagasy slave, François, his leg ostentatiously bandaged and limping heavily long after the spear wound showed signs of healing, looked after him, his ministrations accompanied by his habitual grumbling. Monsieur du Clesmeur needed no encouragement to stay on board his ship. Once it was clear they could expect no help from the Diemenlanders nor find anything of use to them in this Godforsaken landscape, he used his own minor injury as an excuse to refrain from further exploration. Jean said he was malingering.

The Diemenlanders had vanished. They left little behind them, and seemed to possess little to leave. On one trip ashore, André's party found where some of the primitives had camped. A score of crude shelters made from bark stripped from the surrounding trees were scattered in a hollow behind the sand dunes. The ensign stirred the ashes of a cooking fire. All he could find were a few fish skeletons and a heap of mussel and cockle shells, apparently roasted on the embers. Wherever the party went, they came across great piles of such shells and mounds of ashes where they had been cooked. There was no sign of other food remains. He wondered how even primitives could survive in such harsh conditions, living naked and without adequate shelter. The nights were already growing cold as autumn set in.

After six days, Monsieur Marion lost his enthusiasm for staying on. He decided they were wasting precious time in a country where people could barely find sustenance, its wild inhabitants surviving only by living like animals. This first encounter with peoples of the Pacific had yielded nothing but disappointment and disillusionment. On 10 March, the ships weighed anchor and sailed for New Zealand in the hope that there they would encounter inhabitants of a more hospitable disposition — true Naturals or Men of the Woods — and find all they needed in the way of supplies and the timber needed for the now-urgent repairs to their ships.

# Chapter 3

*25 March–26 April 1772*
*New Zealand coast 39°15'–34°25' S*

L and ahoy!' The lookout's early-morning shout from the *Mascarin*'s masthead had everyone scrambling into the rigging. It was their first sight of land after an uneventful run from Van Diemen's Land, which had taken a fortnight. By midday, André could see the sugar-loafed shaped peak from the deck, although it was still eight to ten leagues away. Monsieur Marion decided to name it Pic Mascarin after the ship. By the end of the day, it became clear that the distinctive snow-capped peak was part of a larger land mass. They had reached the western coast of New Zealand.

Much to everyone's surprise, the *Marquis de Castries* had managed to retain visual contact with the *Mascarin*. Early in the expedition — after losing contact soon after leaving the Île-de-France and only meeting up again at the Cape of Good Hope — the two captains made arrangements to meet off the Three Kings Islands at the northern tip of New Zealand should they become separated. The Dutch voyager Tasman had left clearly defined positions for these islands, waxing enthusiastic about them as a reliable source of fresh water and firewood. Before leaving Van Diemen's Land, some of the officers on board the *Mascarin* laid wagers on how long it would take on their crossing of the Tasman Sea before Monsieur du Clesmeur and the *Castries* disappeared from sight during the hours of darkness.

Jean was one of those who gambled on the larger ship's slowness and the inexperience of her captain. Now seriously out of pocket, he complained to André. 'I have to assume Monsieur Le Corre took charge, mordieu! He must've decided that leaving that popinjay to make mistakes was no longer in his own best interests.'

'Meaning he'd done so before?' André was shocked at the implication. 'You're saying Monsieur Le Corre could've avoided the collision that's caused us so many problems?'

'Well, maybe I'd not go that far,' Jean conceded. 'But you can't tell me that a "blue" officer of his calibre finds it easy having such a young and incompetent captain in charge — with nothing to recommend him but his aristocratic connections and his book-learning in the Gardes de la Marine.'

'Maybe even Monsieur du Clesmeur has no trouble sailing in open ocean with a favourable wind,' said André. 'Once we're negotiating this coastline, things might be different.'

'Too late to help me, tant pis!' said Jean. 'I've had to pay out already.'

André knew Monsieur Marion had ordered the *Castries* to lead the way across the Tasman because the larger ship was overstrained in trying to keep up with his own command. He thought it was probably the expedition leader's prowess that had kept the two ships in contact, and Monsieur du Clesmeur's competence or otherwise was irrelevant. He kept his mouth shut — Jean would not appreciate hearing this.

It seemed he was right in thinking Monsieur Marion wanted to ensure that Monsieur du Clesmeur could not make any more serious mistakes and delay their landing. As they approached closer to the New Zealand coast, the expedition leader began signalling the *Castries* whenever he wanted the other ship to change tack or alter sail. André was kept busy running up the signal flags.

For the next week, the two ships reconnoitred northwards along the New Zealand coast, standing close towards the land whenever their soundings showed deep enough water. They passed beautiful sandy beaches and apparent inlets with entrances blocked by fierce lines of breakers. Every day they saw the smoke of fires. Once, they were close enough to shore for André to see distant human figures, but he could not pick up any detail. He could only hope this time Monsieur Marion was right, that by offering kindnesses they would receive hospitality and help from the local inhabitants. It would be better still if they proved to be the gentle and amiable Pacific people promised by Monsieur Thirion's philosophers. He tried to ignore the doubting part of his brain that reminded him that their first New Zealand landfall was called Murderers' Bay by Tasman after three of his men were attacked and killed there; that the Zealanders might therefore prove even less hospitable than the inhabitants of Van Diemen's Land.

On a calm day when they could make no progress, Monsieur Marion signalled for the officers of the *Castries* to come aboard, bringing their navigational records so the two captains could compare their calculations once more. Both ships had corrected their estimates of longitude during their stay at Van Diemen's Land, where they had been able to get good lunar readings. The expedition leader told his three ensigns to join the senior officers in the great cabin. 'An excellent opportunity for you to learn something more of these modern skills, gentlemen.'

Once the senior officers were seated, the charts, almanacs and sheets of calculations spread out before them, Monsieur Marion beckoned the hovering ensigns to stand close enough to see. André ended up directly opposite Monsieur du Clesmeur, who as usual was fashionably wigged and wearing his formal scarlet and gold uniform. Jean said he never wasted an opportunity to rub it in that he was the only 'red' officer on the expedition — not that it would do him much good. Irked by losing their money on the cross-Tasman wager, the officers on board the *Mascarin* had taken to making jokes at the young aristocrat's expense. None of them had much time for him, although they were careful not to express their opinions in Monsieur Marion's hearing. The ensign assumed this was because they knew the expedition leader would not tolerate such signs of disunity, but Jean had snorted impatiently. 'Make no mistake, cousin. Monsieur Marion's greatest ambition is to buy into the nobility. You'd think he'd realize he's worth more than any feckless aristocrat who's never worked an honest day in his life. But no, he'll even lick the boots of a poltroon like Monsieur du Clesmeur if he thinks it'll win him prestige and acceptance in aristocratic circles back home.'

André wanted to protest. He admired their expedition leader's drive, and thought that, rather than aristocratic acceptance, it was honour and glory, adventure and fame, he was seeking. Besides, surely Monsieur Marion had no need to be sycophantic? He had little to gain from toadying up to Monsieur du Clesmeur, being himself a man of considerable property, with family well-connected in the Church and the prosperous Breton merchant class back in St-Malo. But there was no point getting Jean started on that subject. The senior ensign could rant on endlessly about the iniquities of the aristocracy and their determination to deprive the more worthy and able bourgeoisie of any real political or social power.

From the sardonic glances now being exchanged with their counterparts from the *Castries*, the ensign was uncomfortably aware that if it were put to the test, the officers from the other ship would likely be more loyal to their ex-Compagnie des Indes' comrades on the *Mascarin* than to the inexperienced captain they had to tolerate. But there was no time for further distracting thoughts. Monsieur Marion was calling the meeting to attention.

'Let's start by hearing your readings, sir,' he said, nodding to the *Castries*' captain.

Monsieur du Clesmeur cleared his throat. His tone neutral, he said, 'According to my corrected longitudes, two days ago we were high and dry eight leagues or so inland of Pic Mascarin.'

Startled, André laughed. But no one else joined him. In the silence that followed, he dared to look at Monsieur du Clesmeur. The captain met his eye and nodded so slightly the ensign wondered whether he had imagined this acknowledgement. After a pause, the captain continued with his report, his voice if anything even more neutral. But André noticed that he held himself stiffly, and the hand that took his habitual pinch of snuff trembled slightly. The ensign glanced around the table at the other officers. The older men were all studiously looking down at their own papers. The awkward moment passed, and they began discussing the discrepancies that had arisen, both amongst themselves and with Tasman's chart.

Monsieur Marion soon dismissed the calculations made from lunar sightings. 'I see no value in them, gentlemen,' he said. 'They're too difficult for ordinary sailors to waste time in trying to achieve results. Our ready reckonings prove more accurate, time and time again.'

Contrary to André's expectation, Monsieur du Clesmeur did not raise the contentious matter of chronometers or the need for expert astronomers. For once, he offered no opinion, but merely sat listening, fingers drumming softly on his snuff box.

After the *Castries*' yawl returned to her ship, André found a moment to ask Jean why the officers had all snubbed Monsieur du Clesmeur. 'He was cracking a joke, mordieu. Against himself, what's more. It's the first time he's seemed remotely human!'

His cousin shrugged. 'Tant pis! We all lost money wagering on his ineptitude.'

As they progressed further up the coast, anyone would think the *Castries'* captain was deliberately rubbing salt in that wound. Certainly Jean thought so. He cited the other ship's often bungled manoeuvres. More than once the consort ship came close to falling aboard the *Mascarin* again, only bearing away in the nick of time. André pointed out that their own people were struggling to work their ship. As well as the men suffering from chronic ailments brought on by their weeks in the Southern Ocean, many others were weakened by the scurvy now taking its toll day by day. 'We've missed stays as often as the *Castries*.'

But his scornful cousin insisted the faulty manoeuvres were all down to the young captain seeking revenge. André gave up. He was too weary himself to argue about such a lack of logic — it was hardly likely Monsieur du Clesmeur knew anything of a wager laid on board the *Mascarin*. It did seem, though, that the *Castries'* captain had lost some of his confidence. At night, whenever the ships strayed out of sight of each other's lights, he wasted no time in firing his cannon — and repeated firing them until the *Mascarin* responded with a return shot or by placing braziers to light up her sails. During the day, he stayed so close to the smaller ship that Jean claimed he could see the whites of his eyes. 'Rolling, what's more, like those of a startled horse!'

Monsieur Crozet, who usually guarded his tongue in front of the ensigns, lost patience. He was heard to say, 'Peste soit du sot! A plague on the young idiot! Next thing, he'll be asking for a wet nurse.'

Monsieur Marion made no attempt to hide his own impatience — impatience André thought gave the lie to his cousin's insistence that the expedition leader would make endless allowances for the captain's inexperience because of his aristocratic status. Before long, Monsieur Marion signalled the *Castries* to follow each and every one of his own manoeuvres, going as far as giving her captain the headings he wanted him to follow.

André had his own reasons for wanting to make landfall without further delays. For the last week he had been aware that his gums were sore and tender, and that morning they started to bleed. Reluctantly, he took himself off to Monsieur Thirion's cabin. The surgeon examined him, then nodded. 'You have the first signs of scurvy, Monsieur Tallec. Many of the men are showing graver signs — putrid gums, loose teeth and foul breath, spots on their thighs. At least you've not yet developed those.'

As the ensign dressed, he asked, 'Is there anything I can do, sir?' He was apprehensive. Although like all sailors, he knew of scurvy, this voyage was his first one long enough to be at personal risk of experiencing the dreaded disease.

'Spend as much time on deck as possible,' said the surgeon. 'Many authorities believe shipboard air's one of the major causes of scurvy. The air below deck is foul after so long at sea — not helped by still having animals in the pens. But now we're close to shore, you should gain some benefit from the land air. I'll also put you on the list of those to receive chicken broth rather than salt beef.' He looked at André's expression and laughed. 'Allons, allons, young man — why the long face? You'll most likely survive.'

When André nodded, even though he did not find the surgeon particularly reasssuring, Monsieur Thirion made a note then turned to his medicine chest. 'I have here a mix of anti-scorbutic worts I'm experimenting with.' He made the ensign open his mouth and take a spoonful of a herbal concoction so foul-tasting it must do him good. 'It's most unfortunate we found no suitable greens or spruce at Van Diemen's Land.'

'Spruce, sir?' asked André, curious despite himself.

'For brewing spruce beer,' explained Monsieur Thirion. 'An Indian recipe recently brought back by Frenchmen who served in Canada. Most effective, I'm told.'

The two ships came within sight of the longed-for Three Kings Islands before a severe storm drove them out to sea. When they struggled back a wearisome nine days later, to their disappointment they could not find a suitable landing place. In contrast to Tasman's description of lush vegetation and a torrent of fresh water, they saw only patchy scrub and a few windswept trees. Although they spotted some men and what looked like houses, there was no sign of fresh water.

As the two ships sailed around the largest island looking for ground where they could anchor, Jean stared in disbelief. 'That damned Dutchman's a lying rogue! Sacré Dieu! These islands are nothing more than arid rocks.'

When they found no suitable anchorage, and the weather continued stormy, Monsieur Marion finally decided they had no choice but to abandon their planned landing on the Three Kings and head for the New Zealand mainland. The surgeon was attending new cases of scurvy each day, the worst sufferers now confined below deck and unable to walk, their limbs swollen, their skin blotched and the colour of lead. The stench of their illness added to the general misery they were all experiencing after so long without respite. Although himself still only in the early stages of scurvy, André struggled to roll out of his hammock at the start of a watch, no amount of sleep enough to relieve the lassitude that affected his very bones. His spirits were low. For the first time since he had been a junior apprentice new to the sea, he found he was dreaming of Brittany. Once he woke with tears still wet on his cheeks. Monsieur Thirion assured him such longings for home were part and parcel of the disease. The surgeon dosed him thoroughly once more. 'You'll soon recover once we find a good anchorage and get ashore,' he said firmly.

To add to their woes, the *Mascarin* was leaking worse than ever. They were forced to man the pumps night and day, further sapping the men's failing energy. The chief carpenter reported that her bow timbers were now in poor condition, with most of the planking rotted. 'We also lost the cheeks supporting the bowsprit in that last violent blow. If this weather continues, we risk losing the spar itself.'

It was a few days before their luck at last turned and they were able to approach close to the northern coast of New Zealand. In calm weather, the ships hove-to two leagues or less offshore under small sails while Lieutenant Lehoux took the longboat into a bay where two wooded coves promised much needed firewood and fresh water. He returned at four that afternoon with favourable reports of reasonable ground for anchoring the ships and a stream suitable for watering. Much to Monsieur Marion's delight, the lieutenant also returned with news of a group of huts in the western bay, well-built and containing evidence their inhabitants had skills far exceeding those of the Diemenlanders who had proved such a disappointment.

'No sign of any inhabitants, sir,' he said, regret in his voice. 'They seem to have abandoned these huts. We did bring back some examples of their industry.'

The members of the landing party spread their spoils on the deck for Monsieur Marion and the other officers to inspect. André picked up a small finely carved wooden box and opened it, full of curiosity. Much to his disappointment, instead of the ornaments he expected, it contained only a handful of white feathers.

'What's more,' said the lieutenant, gratified by the attention his trophies were receiving, 'we found seine nets and a superbly carved canoe in the other bay.' He added that he had thought it best to leave them there for collecting after the ships anchored.

Early next morning, under a steel-bright eastern sky and a brisk breeze, Monsieur Marion ordered the ships to sail into the western bay. They followed the longboat into the anchorage Lieutenant Lehoux had buoyed the previous afternoon. A swift current was running, and the expedition leader signalled the *Castries* to lower the strongest of her two bower anchors. Although the ground seemed firm enough, neither ship could swing head to the wind until the tide changed mid-morning and the current reversed in their favour. By then, the wind had picked up and the sea was becoming rough.

Monsieur Marion spent some time scanning the eastern horizon, then consulted with his second-in-command. The anchorage was not particularly safe, the wind blowing towards a headland where a line of rocks and islets stretched well out to sea to block easy escape, but they decided to take the risk that there was time to go ashore before the weather deteriorated any further. 'Our water supplies are desperately low,' the expedition leader pointed out. 'Return as soon as you've secured a watering place, Monsieur Crozet.'

Within a few hours, the wind rose to a gale and the sea was rougher still. It began to rain steadily. There was no sign of the longboat. Concerned about the worsening conditions, Monsieur Marion had the cannon fired, a pre-arranged signal for the second-in-command to return immediately. André was checking the shore for the reappearance of the boat when a sailor came running to report that the *Mascarin* was dragging her anchor. He was then fully occupied, the men hard at work lowering the other bower anchor. Once they were sure it was holding, they slipped the cable of the dragging anchor, attaching it to a strong line and buoy so it could be retrieved later. At that point, the man on lookout shouted that he could see the boat leaving the beach.

The ensign paused to watch the longboat plunge through the surf, bucking like a bad-tempered horse. It was only with the greatest of skill that Monsieur Crozet was able to bring the boat back up to the ship, battling both the high seas and the gale blowing against them. It was a close call. The expedition leader had ordered a buoy suspended off the stern gallery to assist them. Standing in the stern sheets of the longboat, his feet braced as well as he could, Monsieur Crozet made two attempts before he managed to steer close enough. At his shout, the coxswain leant dangerously far over the side with his boathook. Just as the boat looked to be swept past yet again, he succeeded in hooking the buoy. For a moment, it looked as though the force of their momentum would pluck the boathook from his hands, but he held on grimly as the boat rounded up and was brought to an abrupt standstill against the straining buoy. As soon as the boatmen worked the boat forward to the chains, they fastened and scrambled up the violently swaying rope ladder. Without delay, but with some difficulty, the longboat was hoisted aboard and secured on deck.

The risk taken had been to no avail. The landing party brought back only brackish water. The senior officers gathered on the quarterdeck to discuss their situation. 'We took the boat well upstream, sir,' Monsieur Crozet reported, his long face set. 'Unfortunately, the river remained tidal. No fresh water to be had anywhere.'

At that moment, the *Castries* signalled that her anchor was dragging. Her captain flew flags to say he intended putting out to sea and safety. André reported the signals to the expedition leader.

'Diable!' Monsieur Marion lost his temper. 'Peste! Bougre!' He took his hat off and dashed it against the taffrail. 'How dare he presume? *I* make the decisions here.' He told the open-mouthed ensign to fly a signal ordering the *Castries* to stay where she was. 'Tell him to lower his other bower anchor. Mordieu!'

But as André scuttled away to do as he was told, he heard his captain give orders — in a more moderate tone — to prepare the small sails and slip stoppers on the second anchor cable in case they did need to set sail in haste. A little later he saw the *Castries* obediently put out a larboard anchor.

As darkness fell, the gale increased in force. They were in for a rough night. The ship was now being pounded by violent squalls. Each time a squall struck, André found it impossible to stay upright. Throughout his watch, he clung to a stay as sheets of water were flung over the steeply angled deck. The ship's timbers groaned and the wind shrieked overhead in the rigging. He could just make out figures on the *Castries* struggling to pay out a third anchor. She must be dragging again. Their own anchor seemed to be holding, and he prayed aloud that it would continue to do so. Their position was ominously close to the headland and its line of rocks.

Soon after three in the morning, the *Castries* began drifting downwind towards them. Just as Monsieur Marion was about to signal her to set sail, they saw her get underway, with triple-reefed topsails set. The people on the *Mascarin* watched anxiously as the other ship clawed a passage out of the bay, then disappeared into the wild night.

A few hours later, their own situation became perilous. As an imperceptible dawn broke, the wind increased. From where he was clinging once more to the foremast stay, André saw a great wall of water rushing towards them. He tried to shout a warning, but the wind snatched his words away. No one heard. He watched helplessly as the surging wave towered above them. Its crest broke just as it reached the ship and tons of water poured down on them. Its relentless weight pinned the forepart of the ship below the surface for longer than he could hold his breath. Desperate, he gulped in water, sure he was about to drown.

At the last moment, the *Mascarin*'s bows rose up out of the sea.

The ship shook herself free. As the water drained from the waist of the ship, André saw the officers on the quarterdeck stagger to their feet, drenched to the skin, their hats floating in the scuppers and their wigs awry.

There was no time to draw breath — the anchor was dragging. They were already too close for comfort to the line of rocky islets to leeward.

Monsieur Marion decided they had no choice but to try to sail out of the bay. He ordered the men to stand by. 'Clap a spring on that anchor cable, Monsieur Crozet!' he shouted into the senior officer's ear. 'We need to improve our chances of not being driven to leeward quite so fast once we cut the cable.'

As soon as the second-in-command signalled they were ready, the captain had the inner jib hoisted and sheeted in, then ordered the men to cut the anchor cable inboard of the one now attached as a spring. Despite his precautions, when the ship's bow immediately fell off the wind, the strain coming onto the end of the spring attached to their stern was so violent that the cable parted. Although the force of the wind drove the lee gunwale under, they were able to sheet the foresail home. With the control provided by jib and foresail, the ship pointed up into the wind and away from the rocks — assisted by the strong offshore current. André crossed himself and muttered a heartfelt prayer of thanks for a captain who knew what he was doing and a ship that was so responsive.

They were not yet out of danger. The *Mascarin* was still embayed. Monsieur Marion now had the men set as much sail as the ship could carry. They pitched head-on into turbulent seas that threatened to breach their already strained bow timbers, or worse, dismast them. The sails were trimmed so sharp, André thought they would round up into the wind at any moment. Despite the expedition leader's skill, the wind was forcing the ship sideways, closer and closer to the line of rocky islets blocking their escape to open sea. For two hours they laboured, Monsieur Marion constantly encouraging the exhausted men to haul on sheets and braces as he tried to glean maximum headway against the screaming wind.

The ensign could not take his eyes off the black rocks now less than a musket shot away. Jagged and fanged, they reared above the huge seas breaking on the ship's sides. His knuckles white, he stared at the fiercest of the rocks as though he could fend them off by the force of his gaze. Just when he thought they were doomed and shipwreck inevitable, the wind shifted direction. Not more than a point or two, but it was enough. The rocks — now only half a musket shot away — came no closer. Holding his breath and hardly daring to believe the change in their fortune, he watched as, imperceptibly at first then more surely, the ship slowly drew away from danger.

They cleared the point and the sea opened out in front of them.

'Steady as she goes, if you please, gentlemen,' said Monsieur Marion. He turned away from the binnacle where he had been standing beside the man on the wheel. As he strolled to the weather side of the quarterdeck — the customary place for a commander at ease, the ship's people turned spontaneously towards him. 'Vive le Capitaine!' they shouted. 'Vive le Roi!' As André raised his hat in the air and shouted with the men, he felt tears of relief mixing with the saltwater still streaming down his face.

At midday, the gale subsided, the rain eased and the sky cleared. The lookout sighted the faint grey smudge on the horizon that was the sails of the *Castries*. Late in the afternoon, the two ships came back together, and Monsieur Marion signalled for her captain and senior officers to come aboard.

After the men had been mustered on the deck for the expedition leader to conduct a Te Deum in thanks for the survival of both their ships and not a life lost, the officers assembled in the great cabin to share their news. Unlike the badly battered *Mascarin*, the *Castries* had not suffered any damage, although she had been forced to abandon three anchors — possibly with inadequate buoys.

Before the expedition leader could take him to task, Monsieur du Clesmeur went on the offensive. The captain had regained his earlier arrogance. He sat back in his chair, his legs stretched out before him and his head thrust back so he could look down his nose. His voice almost a drawl, he said, 'I was most surprised at your initial decision to anchor in such an exposed bay, sir, then send your boat ashore with the wind already rising.' He took a pinch of snuff, then continued speaking just as the expedition leader opened his mouth to respond. André had seen that the captain was watching Monsieur Marion out of the corner of his eye, so his timing was deliberate. 'I was even more surprised, sir, when you did not accede to my suggestion that we set sail before dark. Our anchors were already beginning to drag.'

Under such provocation, André thought the expedition leader would lose his temper — it did not take much these days. But he merely looked at Monsieur du Clesmeur, allowing the tension to build for a moment before replying. 'It's a matter of weighing risks, sir, not anchors . . . as you may one day learn.' As the officers hid their grins, he went on. 'Your first point. Our need for water is urgent. Monsieur Crozet's skills in small-boat handling are more than sufficient to deal with any likely contingency.'

None of the *Mascarin*'s officers dared comment that Monsieur Crozet's skills had been sorely tested. Nor did anyone note that the second-in-command's language, once he had regained the ship, had left a lot to be desired. They studiously looked anywhere but at the senior officer, who sat there, a blank expression on his long face.

Monsieur Marion raised his eyebrows at the silence, then

continued. 'As for your wish to set sail before dark, I would point out that you failed to take the contrary current into account. It's my considered opinion, sir, that if you *had* set sail then, your ship would've been driven onto the rocks.'

No one could argue he was wrong; the strong current in the bay had indeed been unfavourable. But even André, whose faith in his captain was unquestioning, knew full well that currents, favourable or otherwise, had not been mentioned at the time.

'You had no trouble clearing the bay when you did sail later — after the current reversed.' Monsieur Marion said nothing of the grave peril they had experienced on board the *Mascarin*, nothing of how close they had come themselves to being wrecked on those very same rocks. He merely mentioned the huge wave that had pinned them down, then gave a brief account of how they were forced to abandon their own two anchors. 'Securely buoyed, however — that risk having been anticipated.'

The other captain had been outplayed. Visibly fuming, his high cheekbones flushed red, he sat silent.

Well satisfied and in better humour than for some time, the expedition leader had François serve wine before he sent the *Castries'* officers back to their ship. 'We'll return tomorrow in the hope of retrieving the five anchors we've left behind. Be ready for my signal, Monsieur du Clesmeur.'

But it was the best part of another week before the two ships could return to the cove they had appropriately named Anchor Bay. Further gales and heavy rain drove them offshore far from the coastline. When at last the weather abated, and the ships could lie to safely, Monsieur Marion sent his second-in-command across to the *Castries*. This time he had no wish to speak with Monsieur du Clesmeur. Instead, he consulted with his own officers, then had his clerk pen a letter: the delay now posed them considerable difficulty;

their need for water was urgent; their abandoned five anchors were an irreparable loss — both financial (borne by Monsieur Marion himself) and in terms of their continuing safety in the likelihood of further storms; and their ships badly needed attention. Should they return and retrieve the anchors, then hope to find resources on the unknown eastern coast of New Zealand? Or should they risk that Tasman's account of the now closer islands of Rotterdam and Amsterdam was more accurate than the one he had given for the Three Kings?

In response, Monsieur du Clesmeur opted for abandoning their anchors, considering it too dangerous a risk to return to the exposed bay. The boat had barely returned to the *Mascarin* with his written reply when the expedition leader picked up his speaking trumpet and ordered him to return immediately to Anchor Bay.

André joined Jean at the taffrail as their own ship set sail. 'So what was *that* all about?' the ensign asked his cousin. 'Monsieur Marion took no heed of his opinion.'

'Keeping up appearances,' said Jean. 'He won't risk getting offside completely with our fine-feathered aristocrat. This way, he can't say he wasn't consulted.'

After several days' sailing in good conditions, they reached Anchor Bay late in the afternoon. The *Mascarin* spotted their two buoys before nightfall, but there was no sign of any buoys for the *Castries*. Monsieur Marion had the boats lowered to retrieve the buoyed bower anchors, the men working all night to raise and stow them. The weather still held the next morning, so he sent his own men to help in the search for the three anchors abandoned by the *Castries*. All they found was one frayed buoy rope.

'No wonder Monsieur du Clesmeur didn't want to come back,' said Jean, sniggering. 'He obviously failed to buoy the others! Ma fois, his foolishness knows no bounds.'

# Chapter 4

The old man stood his ground. At first, he did not respond as Jean beckoned him from the stern sheets of the boat, smiling and spreading his arms wide in a gesture of friendship. After some moments of hesitation, the ancient turned his spear downwards and stepped forward. Behind him, the other three Zealanders, who had now pulled their small canoe up the beach, drew together and watched anxiously. Their glance shifted constantly, from the old man to the Frenchmen in the boat, then back again. André could see they were poised on the balls of their bare feet, ready to run. Behind them, a narrow path led to safety in the small palisaded village on the hill. Unlike the Diemenlanders, these men were clothed, or at least had some sort of matting fastened around their waists. The old man was covered in skins from shoulder to below the knee. His dark eyes took in everything aboard the boat. He began making emphatic gestures, all the time speaking in an unknown tongue. He then stood there waiting, his face expectant, before turning aside.

'Mort-diable!' muttered Jean between his teeth, his mouth still stretched wide. 'Keep smiling!' He called and gestured to the old man again.

André realized the ancient was fetching something from the canoe. He came back towards them, carrying a large fish. He held it out towards them, then, once he was within throwing distance, tossed it into their boat.

'Vite, vite!' said Jean. 'Show him the handkerchiefs and the knife.' He beckoned the old man to come closer.

André held up the red handkerchiefs, then the knife, nodding and smiling. He felt as though he should be shouting his wares like the women in the markets at home, not miming friendship. But when the old man nodded back, speaking a string of words and gesturing back, he felt a flush of triumph. He threw the trinkets ashore, taking aim carefully so they fell at the ancient's feet. But he ignored them, standing there solemnly until one of the other Zealanders rushed forward and picked them up, then presented them to him.

'Ma fois — he could teach Monsieur du Clesmeur a thing or two about dignity,' said Jean. 'He's clearly some sort of chief.'

Looking at the ancient, his cloak of skins drawn around him, his upright stance and proud bearing, André agreed. 'Oui, oui, a fine specimen. These people do seem more like the gentle Naturals of the Pacific we were led to expect.'

When the French boat made no attempt to land, but stayed just off the shore, the other Zealanders slowly ventured back down the beach. They clustered around the ancient, examining the trinkets. One of them tried the knife on the edge of a paddle, then called out his approval at its sharpness. The old man left them to it. He stood on the edge of the water, calling constantly to Jean and André. He pointed out to sea, to the hills and the village behind him, then spread his arms wide. He stood there like that for some time, before beckoning them to come ashore.

'Let's go in — he's obviously friendly.' Jean was keen to comply.

'Monsieur Marion gave us strict instructions not to land,' André demurred. 'We don't want to risk them becoming frightened and attacking us.'

'The ancient's totally in charge,' said Jean. 'Those others will do nothing without his approval. I see no problem.'

'Prenez garde, gentlemen,' cautioned the coxswain. 'None of us is armed. We wouldn't be able to come to your assistance if things go wrong.'

At that moment, another canoe landed further along the shore, and its five occupants came towards them. Seeing they were now outnumbered, Jean reluctantly decided discretion should prevail. He shook his head at the old man, who was now indicating they should accompany him to the village on the hill.

After asking numerous questions, all of which they could only answer with a shrug and a smile, the old man gave up, clearly disappointed at their refusal to come ashore. He sent some of the men back to the newly landed canoe. They launched it and paddled towards the French boat, staying their paddles a short distance away to hold up many large fish. Ashore, the old man called again, then waved towards the fish.

'No mistaking what he means this time — he's offering us more fish!' The delighted Jean beckoned the canoe to come closer.

When the French officers began selecting the fish they wanted, the old man turned his back and walked slowly towards the path leading to the village. Once the Zealanders had offloaded their fish and André had handed over some more trinkets, the canoe returned to shore. Within moments, they had all vanished up the path to the village.

Jean gave the order to return to the *Mascarin*, around the headland in the other bay where the ship's people were still searching for the missing anchors. As they sailed out of the cove, André looked back at the tidy little village perched on the hilltop, surrounded by its palisades. They were not far offshore before its reed-thatched roofs merged into the background and he could no longer pick it out. The ships could have sailed past many such villages without him noticing them, even a mere league or two out to sea.

Beside him in the stern sheets, Jean expressed his satisfaction at this first encounter with Zealanders. 'They do seem to be natural Men of the Woods far superior to the Diemenlanders. We shouldn't encounter any problems dealing with them.'

**Extract from the Te Kape manuscript, 1841**

*I well remember that time. Word of te iwi o Mariou — Marion's people — first came to us from our relatives to the north. Messengers brought word of two apparitions appearing out of the sea mist. With stacked clouds, high wooden sides taller than any building known, and the presence of strange, pale-complexioned beings, many thought those ships were floating islands sent down from the heavens. Accordingly, those beings were thought to be tipua — ancestral spirits. Others thought they could instead be shape-changing demons or the malign ghosts of strangers, because it was not the first time such manifestations had been seen in the north. We all knew that a similar floating island had appeared off Oruru [Doubtless Bay] not long before, swallowed up a chief from there, destroyed his entire village — for no justifiable reason that those people could determine — and then disappeared.*

*Accordingly, when part of Mariou's floating islands detached itself and brought some of the tipua close to shore, those people conferred, and, they agreed a tohunga should go down to the beach to examine the nature of those beings, to determine whether the strangers from the sea intended harm or came in peace.*

*Accordingly, those tipua were challenged by that tohunga, who asked the customary questions. Who were they? Where had they come from? Who had sent them? Why had they come? They made no reply, and, that tohunga thought it wise to placate them with offerings of fish. Those strangers from the sea accepted the offerings, then beckoned him closer, with all the appearance of friendliness, and gave him appropriate gifts of sacred red. The exchanges being completed, that tohunga returned to his village, and, those strangers went away.*

[Editor's note: The Te Kape manuscript was found during restoration work at Pompallier House, Bay of Islands, in the early 1990s. It consists of a series of short items in French, seemingly translated from Maori (genealogical material is included), that relate to the visit to New Zealand of Marion du Fresne in 1772. The narrator, Te Kape, is identified by the translator as a man of eighty-odd who had been a youth living in the Bay at the time of that visit. Unfortunately, the original, dictated Maori document has not been found, and the identity of the Marist brother who translated it remains unknown. Because of its undoubted relevance to the story being told here, I have taken the liberty of including extracts from the Te Kape manuscript (further translated into English) wherever they might add illumination to the French account.]

The next day, as the work of trying to find and retrieve the *Castries'* three anchors continued in calm weather, Jean persuaded Monsieur Marion to let him and André go ashore, this time in Anchor Bay itself, to explore Lieutenant Lehoux's abandoned village. He pointed out there was still no sign of inhabitants in this bay. 'This would be a good opportunity to take more extensive notes about the nature of their habitations and lifestyle without interference,' he said, blatantly appealing to the expedition leader's interest in scientific activity.

Monsieur Marion hid a smile. 'You have a persuasive tongue, Monsieur Roux,' he said. 'I'd not realized you were so interested in such studies — I'd have thought the prospect of shooting some game would be more to your liking?'

When Jean had the grace to blush, then try to justify himself, the expedition leader stopped him. 'Fi, fi, sir. Enough. You may make up a party and take my yawl ashore. I see no useful tasks for you on board. We'll signal when we're ready to sail.' He turned to the hovering André. 'I don't want you overdoing things. Check with the surgeon before accompanying Monsieur Roux.'

The surgeon examined André's gums and prodded at his sore joints, but saw no reason for the ensign to stay behind. 'Fresh air and exercise will do you more good than languishing on board, young man.'

The expedition leader sent them off with detailed instructions about what he wanted them to record. 'We must make the most of this new interest of yours, gentlemen. However, you may also take muskets and birdshot — for your protection.'

In high spirits, like boys let out of school, the two ensigns set off on their explorations, accompanied by some of the soldiers. Taking pot shots at the quail-like birds they found in marshy ground behind the beach, they walked inland along the river.

'We should go far enough to reach fresh water,' André suggested. 'At least make some attempt at being serious.'

Jean pretended indignation. 'You question my motives, cousin?'

It soon became apparent that the river remained tidal for at least a league upstream, well beyond any point of use to them for watering. So they left the river and pushed their way up the bank through a border of tall sword-grasses, which André thought might be some type of pandanus. They emerged onto a plain that had obviously once been cultivated. Every ten paces or so, they found small canals linking with the river, though they could not tell whether these were for drainage or irrigation. André recognized some of the plants, including daisies and some sort of gourd, growing wild in what seemed fertile soil. Not far away, on the edge of the plain, they

78

spotted the abandoned village that was their destination.

On the outskirts of the village, the party paused for some moments and looked around, alert for any sign or sound of Zealanders. The day was still and clear. They could see rounded forested hills stretching inland beyond the swampy plain. All they could hear was the faint hum of insects. Jean sighed. 'This is more like it.'

'These people certainly choose agreeable places to live,' André agreed, looking at the compact group of low houses standing on a terrace of higher ground above the plain, with the sheltering hills behind. He was remembering the other small village they had seen the day before on its palisaded hilltop. Neither village bore any comparison to the skimpy bark shelters of the Diemenlanders, randomly scattered on fire-ravaged ground. He could feel the sun warm on his back and stretched, feeling better than he had for some time. Monsieur Thirion was right about land air being a curative.

Jean ordered the soldiers to wait where they could see anyone approach across the plain, then he and André ventured into the village. They were soon absorbed. On either side were low buildings of various sizes, some fully enclosed with small square doorways, others open-sided. They walked slowly through the whole village until they came across several burnt huts on the far side. Jean sniffed the air. 'Ma fois, you can still smell the smoke!'

The timbers of the burnt huts retained the pungent acrid scent that lingers for days. A shiver ran down André's spine. The stillness suddenly seemed ominous. 'It can't be long since they were burnt,' he said, looking around apprehensively.

'Long enough for everybody to disappear,' said Jean, not concerned.

André forced a laugh. 'D'accord! I'm being foolish, thinking I sense the presence of ghosts.'

His cousin put an arm around his shoulders, embracing him

briefly. 'Always the sensitive one, André! Look around you — there's no sign of anybody having been here for days.' He crouched and sifted through the ashes in one of the small stone hearths located just outside each doorway. 'Voilà — stone cold.'

They retraced their steps, stopping to examine anything that aroused their interest. Not far from the burnt huts was a series of low platforms, each thatched with thick layers of the pandanus, or sword-grass, they had seen on the river bank. Underneath were the seine nets mentioned by Lieutenant Lehoux. André helped Jean drag one out and spread it on the ground. It was five to six feet wide and all of eighty to one hundred fathoms long — they paced it out, two hundred of André's long strides. Just as the lieutenant had described, a finely woven pouch formed one of the net's borders, filled with stones to act as sinkers. Attached to the other border were rounds of some very light wood, like balsa, presumably acting as floats.

'Ingenious!' André fingered a float. 'It's as Monsieur Thirion says: no matter what their circumstances, people everywhere find ways to improve their means of living. Make good use of whatever materials are available to them.'

Jean snorted. 'That hardly applied to primitives like those Diemenlanders.' He had little time for the surgeon's philosophies.

André changed the subject, knowing he would not win a debate with his quick-witted cousin. 'Some of these nets look brand-new. They must've spent days making them. Why would they abandon them?'

Jean shrugged. 'Looks like they were forced out of here in a hurry. Some tribal squabble perhaps — that village we saw yesterday was fortified, remember.' He looked at André's anxious face and laughed. 'Allons donc, cousin! Come on — it means they're unlikely to come *back* in any hurry.'

Nevertheless, André insisted they bundle the net back into its shelter. 'Someone could intend coming back in the summer to fish here. What would a Breton fisherman think if he found his nets tampered with?'

They walked on back through the group of undamaged reed-thatched houses. They proved well-made and sophisticated enough to arouse Jean's admiration. He stopped outside one of the larger huts and pried apart the woven lattice of staves forming its outer walls. 'Look at this! The whole thing's lined with moss of some sort. It must be absolutely waterproof. Let's go inside.'

André watched his cousin push open the sliding panel of the low doorway and crawl in. While he hesitated, thinking how easily they could be trapped inside if the inhabitants returned unexpectedly, the impatient Jean poked his head back out. 'What are you waiting for? It's fascinating!'

Knowing Monsieur Marion would expect a full account, the young ensign reluctantly crawled in after him. It was high enough inside to stand up. He got to his feet, then waited for his eyes to adjust to the dim light filtering through two small latticed windows above the doorway. He had to admit Jean was right; there was plenty of interest to look at. The interior walls were lined with woven mats made from some sort of finer sword-grass. At intervals along these walls, wide planks carved with incised patterns supported the ends of the rafters. The only furniture was a crudely made cot along one wall, filled with dry straw — evidently some sort of sleeping space. The interior was kept dry by an external drain dug along the walls; it smelt no worse than their own gunroom, and certainly not as bad as the below-deck space where the men slung their hammocks.

Jean was gazing up at the main ridge pole that ran between stout posts at each end of the house, with another larger carved post supporting it midway. 'De par tous les diables!' he exclaimed. 'Who would have thought savages capable of such fine work? These joints are all morticed, and the whole framework is strengthened with rope bindings.' He leant heavily on one of the end posts, trying to shake it. 'Solid as a rock.'

André's eye was drawn to a grotesque figure carved at the base of the central support post. He moved closer to examine it. 'Come and look at this, Jean!'

A distorted image of a human face with a long, projecting tongue and large eyes made of inset, glistening shell leered at them from the top of a sinuous body carved with overlapping scales, like those of a lizard. Painted a dark red, the whole figure was almost as tall as André. Although he thought it repulsive, he had to admire the skill with which it was carved. 'Some sort of household god, do you think?'

'Maybe,' said Jean, fingering the carving. 'They're fishermen, so maybe it's a merman or sea god. Handsome work, isn't it! Smell this wood — it's fragrant like sassafras. I'd like to take this back to the ship for Monsieur Marion.'

'But that post holds up the entire hut,' André objected.

'Ma fois, what does that matter?' asked Jean. 'It's been abandoned.'

Before they left to return to the ship, he enlisted some of the soldiers to help him wrench the post out of the house. They had found similar carved posts in other huts, but none so fine as the first one, and the senior ensign was determined to souvenir it. Leaving the ridge pole cracked and the roof sagging, they triumphantly lugged the post with them.

It was mid-afternoon when they returned to the beach, just as the *Mascarin* fired her cannon to signal that they were ready to sail. The yawl from the *Castries* was drawn up alongside theirs, the two boatmen left in charge sharing a companionable box of snuff. Apparently Monsieur du Clesmeur and Lieutenant Le Dez had also come ashore to explore and seek out game. Jean laughed. 'This place must be more to his lordship's liking as it's clearly more civilized than Van Diemen's Land.'

There was no sign of them, and the senior ensign insisted they should not wait. 'Monsieur Marion told us to return immediately we heard the signal. I'm not about to let our friend's tardiness put us at risk of punishment.'

No sooner had they reached the ship, than Monsieur Marion ordered the yawl hoisted aboard — the longboat already being secured on deck, the anchor partly raised and the sails loosened. He obviously had no intention of waiting for the *Castries'* captain. Monsieur Crozet told them not to bother the expedition leader with their report until they had cleared the bay. 'Our captain's not well-pleased,' he explained. 'We've wasted precious time searching for the lost anchors. He's had to send our last spare heavy bower anchor over to the *Castries*.'

André looked across the quarterdeck to where Monsieur Marion was pacing impatiently, his hands behind his back, as they got underway in a steadily increasing wind. They were standing well out of the bay under full sail before he saw the distant small figures of the *Castries'* officers scurrying to launch their boat from the beach. As soon as the boat was afloat and they were pulling for their ship, the ensign saw the *Castries'* sails were being loosened. The consort ship set off after the *Mascarin* almost before her boat had been hoisted aboard.

'Monsieur Le Corre, undoubtedly,' said Jean, grinning, 'making a point.'

Forced offshore once more by unfavourable winds, they tacked within tantalizing sight of wooded land for another five long days. At last the wind changed and they were able to sail around Square Cape, a large headland that ended in a distinctive pierced islet. In calm weather, Monsieur Marion sent off the well-armed longboats to search inlets on both sides of this cape, looking for a sheltered harbour. While the ships short-tacked under small sails, waiting for their boats to return, the *Mascarin*'s lookout spotted several canoes setting out from the shore near the cape, heading straight towards them.

The eight Zealanders in the leading canoe stayed their paddles some distance away. Although the ship's people lined the rails, calling and beckoning them closer, they steadfastly stayed where they were. The other canoes remained even further away from the ship, clearly waiting to see what happened. Monsieur Marion ordered the ship hove-to and the French flag run up, but the canoes still maintained their stations.

'They seem most timorous,' the expedition leader commented, puzzled. 'What reason do they have to be so frightened?'

'Perhaps they've encountered ships such as ours before,' said Monsieur Crozet. 'The lead canoe has paused just beyond the range of a musket shot.'

'Surely mere coincidence, sir,' said Monsieur Marion, frowning. 'As far as we know, no other ship has visited here.'

Monsieur Crozet shrugged. 'They don't look the type to be timid for no good reason.'

André, watching the men in the closest canoe, had to agree. The paddlers were all tall, robust men in their prime, their naked chests broad and well-muscled. Even at this distance he could see they had regular features, with aquiline noses and fine dark eyes. The canoe slowly circled the ship, maintaining its distance. Only after some of the officers held out trinkets did the canoe approach any nearer, but the paddlers still would not come alongside. An elderly man wrapped in a skin cloak stood in the prow of this canoe. He seemed to be examining both the ship and its occupants with intense concentration. He showed no interest in the items being waved at him.

Becoming impatient with such unnecessary caution, Monsieur Marion turned to André. 'Vite, vite — go and dangle some trinkets on a cord from the stern gallery, Monsieur Tallec! Surely something must entice these people. We need to gain their confidence so we can land and replenish our ships without difficulty.'

'Maybe something of more use to them might serve better, sir,' the second-in-command suggested. 'Fish-hooks, perhaps?'

Jean muttered an aside to André: 'I wonder what sort of bait we need to catch us a savage?'

The young ensign went off to place a few tempting items in a small basket, then lowered it from the stern gallery to dangle just above water level. It did seem like fishing and he was tempted to laugh. But when the canoe glided under the stern and the elderly man still standing in the prow gestured to one of the paddlers to retrieve the basket, he remembered the other ancient who had so impressed him. This old man's face was black with the markings of tattoo. His dignified gaze met André's briefly, instantly quelling the ensign's thoughts of levity. After examining the items, the men in the canoe refilled the basket with small, glistening fish and some shellfish. The old man looked up at the now subdued ensign and nodded, gesturing for him to pull up the basket.

The tactic worked. To Monsieur Marion's satisfaction, not long afterwards the canoe come alongside the lowered ladder, and the old man swung himself onto it with an agility that belied his age. But even before he started climbing aboard, the paddlers took their canoe well away from the ship's side. Clearly they were taking no chances. The expedition leader made haste to reassure the ancient, who now stood trembling on the deck. He embraced him and kissed him on both cheeks, then hung glass beads around his neck. The other officers gathered around, smiling and nodding. After a while, Monsieur Marion judged he had gained the Zealander's confidence sufficiently to take him into the great cabin, where he ordered his slave to lay out bread and wine.

'Eat, eat, sir!' the expedition leader urged after he sat the ancient down at the table — ignoring the scandalized François' mutterings of dismay. While the rest of the officers watched with interest, he took a piece of bread himself and broke off a mouthful. He pushed the platter towards the old man, encouraging him to follow suit, then had François pour them both a glass of wine. He lifted his glass towards the old man saying, 'A votre santé, monsieur!'

'Pardieu — anyone would think Monsieur Marion was entertaining aristocracy,' Jean whispered to André, hiding a smile as the old man cautiously tasted the bread, then bit off an approving mouthful while the expedition leader nodded vigorously and took another bite himself. 'Uncalled for, surely? He's just a savage.'

André shrugged. Unlike his cousin, who distrusted anyone with a dark skin, he had to admire Monsieur Marion's courage in dealing so intimately with unknown peoples — even if his own cautious nature perceived a considerable risk. This time, the expedition leader's insistence on approaching primitives with goodwill and kindness seemed appropriate. Anyone could see that this old man had stature amongst his own people — was indeed an aristocrat — and should be treated accordingly.

As if to contradict him, at that very moment the old man took a mouthful of wine, then turned his head aside and spat it out vigorously. Putting down his glass, he kept spitting, trying to get rid of all traces of the wine. François leapt backwards, ostentatiously brushing his clothing. The officers broke into laughter, unable to hide their amusement at the old man's curious distress. But

Monsieur Marion glared at them and told his slave to bring the old man a carafe of water. As the ancient rinsed his mouth carefully, still spitting, then drained the entire carafe, the expedition leader made signs apologizing for both the wine and the poor quality of the water.

The old man, restored to some equanimity, soon seemed to understand the captain's attempts to explain that the ships were seeking supplies of fresh water. He tapped the empty carafe, gestured towards the shore, then began making graceful undulating movements with his hands that conjured up flowing waterfalls and rivers deep enough to swim in — all without the French officers understanding a single word of what he was saying. André could not help contrasting this ancient's quick intelligence with the dumb incomprehension shown by the old Diemenlander similarly faced with a water bottle. If the other Zealanders were equally receptive, surely they would find here what they so sorely needed?

Well satisfied with the progress being made, Monsieur Marion had François bring him one of his own spare linen shirts and pair of breeches. With the slave's disapproving help, he took off the old man's cloak of skins and pulled the shirt over his head, then removed the woven matting fastened around his hips. With some difficulty, they managed to get him into the breeches and their front opening fastened. The captain slung a blue mantle around the old man's shoulders. 'Voilà!' he said, stepping back and indicating his own clothing and those of his senior officers. 'Now you look just like one of us.'

The ancient man said not a word. André thought he looked somewhat bemused. But when Monsieur Marion had some iron axes, adzes and chisels brought in for his inspection, the Zealander at last showed more than cautious interest. He ran his fingers over the cutting edges of each tool, before demonstrating that he knew exactly how they were used. When the captain indicated he could keep them, he smiled for the first time. He asked many questions, none of which the officers could understand, then gestured to the canoe now lying off the ship's stern, making it clear he wanted to recall his paddlers.

A few hours later, the paddlers were all wearing sailors' shirts and trousers — dressing them a procedure that greatly amused the ship's officers and one the Zealanders tolerated, although the ensign suspected they were more embarrassed than anything else. With the Frenchmen calling farewells, they paddled off, each laden with trinkets, the gift of a pig trussed and squealing in the bilge of their canoe. Before they had gone far, they stopped to strip off their unfamiliar clothes — not without difficulty with sleeves and buttons, which caused more mirth aboard the two ships.

Monsieur Crozet watched the Zealanders stop to talk to the occupants of the other canoes. As all the canoes then began coming towards them, some dozen or more, he turned to the captain. 'I think Lieutenant de Vaudricourt should arm his soldiers and post them on the poop, sir. If all those savages come aboard we could easily be overwhelmed.'

'Fort bien, Monsieur Crozet,' said the expedition leader. 'As you wish, though an unnecessary precaution in my opinion.' Remembering the adverse reaction of the Diemenlanders when the soldiers had fixed their bayonets, he added, 'Tell them to be discreet — they're to keep their weapons well hidden.'

No sooner had the soldiers complied, than the fleet of canoes reached the ship. Without any of the fear or caution shown by their first visitors, several hundred Zealanders immediately swarmed aboard after handing up many baskets of fish and some containing a sweet potato of some sort. Although André was relieved to find they had no weapons with them, he was glad of the soldiers standing alert on the poop. The Naturals rushed about the ship, exclaiming at everything they saw and showing great curiosity. It was not long before this curiosity extended to establishing the nature of the sailors themselves. André and Jean submitted to being poked and prodded, their white skin causing much surprise. The young ensign's russet hair and grey-green eyes seemed to attract particular attention.

One youth, about his own age André thought, was more insistent than most. Tall and gangly like himself, this young Zealander kept coming back to him, making gestures of friendship then pulling aside the ensign's jacket and shirt to reveal the white skin beneath. In turn, he would place André's hand on his own brown skin, then laugh. His laugh was infectious, his face open and attractive, not distorted by the tattoo that disfigured so many of the older men. Despite his initial alarm, the ensign found himself responding to such friendliness. Eventually he patted his chest and said, 'Tallec.' He pointed at the youth and raised his eyebrows.

The youth looked puzzled, but when the ensign repeated his name and the gesture, his face suddenly lit up. He nodded and patted his own chest. 'Te Kape.'

'Ta-capaye,' André tried to get his tongue around the words.

'Ae, Te Kape!' The youth seemed delighted. He hesitated, then said, 'Tareka?'

André nodded, 'Oui, oui! Something like that! Tallec.'

They beamed at each other. André turned to share his new friend with Jean, but his cousin had been distracted. He was trying to persuade the one Zealander who had stayed on his canoe to come aboard. An imposing older man wrapped in a handsome fur cloak, he showed every sign of remaining aloof. His canoe was much larger than the others, with tall carved posts at prow and stern. He had four young women with him, who crouched on the floor of the canoe, not paying any attention to the two ensigns looking down at them.

'Always seeking a challenge, Jean!' André was amused. 'From his manner I'd think he's an important chief. Those women must be in attendance.'

'Toutàfait!' said Jean. 'He's interested in my red mantle, though he's pretending not to be.' He took his short cape off and held it out to the man, then pointed at his fur cloak. The chief gestured for him to throw the cape into the canoe.

'He takes me for a fool!' Jean shook his head vigorously, beckoning the chief to come aboard.

After some hesitation, the lure of the red cape proved too much for the chief, and he swung himself up the rope ladder onto the deck, followed by the young women. André became aware that the youth with whom he had exchanged names was muttering something behind him. Te Kape nodded towards the older man, who was now standing imperiously on the deck, waiting for two of the women to take off his cloak. 'Te Kuri.'

André heard what sounded like a name. 'Tacoury?'

'Ae, Te Kuri.' The youth waved at the other Naturals on board, many of whom had stopped to watch the chief being disrobed, his gesture indicating that he was their chief. Then he pointed into the head of the inlet, to the eastern hills behind, and swept his hands in a wide gesture that encompassed much of what they could see.

'Ma fois, Jean,' said André to his cousin. 'You seem to have won over one of the bigwigs of this place.'

They watched as the women offered Jean's cape to the chief. Te Kuri now paid no attention to the ensigns. He glanced at the cape with a show of indifference, then handed it back to the women. While one of them put the cape into the canoe, another brought Jean the fur cloak. The two ensigns inspected it closely. Made of finely woven cloth in which narrow strips of dark and white fur were so cleverly interwoven that it seemed like the single pelt of a very large animal, the heavy cloak was surprisingly supple. Delighted, Jean looked at the chief and nodded to show his appreciation.

Much to his chagrin, Te Kuri merely bowed his head briefly then strode off along the deck to where Monsieur Marion was holding court, surrounded by many Zealanders. After hesitating for a moment, the young women trailed after him.

'Tant pis — he's interested in bigger fish than you, cousin,' said André, laughing. 'Even his women have lost interest in you.'

Jean shrugged. 'Tant mieux — as if I'd be tempted by such ugly specimens.'

They both looked after the women. None of them had the appeal of the men, being squat in build with heavy thighs and large breasts barely hidden by their short capes of woven sword-grass. Their greased hair hung at shoulder length, pomaded with red, and their skin was also liberally smeared with red pigment. Jean shrugged again. 'Let's hope they kept some better-lookers ashore for us.'

Some of the Naturals were already leaving, paddling their canoes swiftly away from the ship towards the *Castries*, hove-to half a league away. Before long, only Te Kuri and another old chief were left on board, with their paddlers — Te Kape amongst them. Monsieur Marion invited both chiefs into the great cabin to share a dinner of fresh pork and newly baked bread rolls.

In the evening, with the wind rising, it became necessary to set sail and stand offshore. Although the captain tried to persuade the Zealanders to go ashore, Te Kuri indicated that they wanted to stay on board; tomorrow they would guide the ship into sheltered waters. The two chiefs sent their reluctant companions off in their canoes. With considerable aplomb, they settled down to sleep on the palliasses laid out for them in the great cabin, showing not the least apprehension at their unfamiliar situation.

Monsieur Marion was delighted. 'The friendliness and confidence of these good people in coming to us unarmed surely means our travail has ended at last. All we have to do is offer hospitality and gifts to ensure we'll reap our reward.'

**Extract from the Te Kape manuscript, 1841**

*The news then came that those strangers from the sea had not been placated by the northern tohunga. The messengers told us that soon afterwards, the people returned from inland where they had been attending their recently dead chief. While they were gone, those strangers plundered their village, ignoring the tapu status of the burnt shelters that indicated someone had died there. The strangers then took away the central ancestral pou of that chief's house. Accordingly, the people of that place sent warning far and wide that those strangers must indeed be malignant supernatural beings, for men like ourselves could not have trespassed so against tapu and survived.*

*Accordingly, when the two ships appeared off our coast, our people here in Tokerau approached them with caution. We also had earlier experienced such manifestations. A few summers before, a similar ship had entered the harbour to lie near Motu-arohia. When some of its occupants came ashore and were challenged in the usual way, they responded by discharging the long tubes they carried. Those tubes emitted sharp cracks like timber splintering, accompanied by bursts of flame and smoke. Much to the fear and astonishment of the challengers, they were instantly afflicted by many small wounds and a sharp stinging as though they had stumbled into a nest of bees, yet they were a full stone's throw distance from those tipua. Then the side of the ship turned towards them, and its many mouths erupted in thunder and lightning, and, a whistling wind conjured up by those strangers threw boulders over the challengers' heads with giant force. Our people therefore knew to stay beyond a stone's throw distance from the strangers.*

*Accordingly, before we approached the new strangers from the sea, the way was cleared by our most senior tohunga, who made offerings to them and placed us under the protection of our atua with many karakia. Even so, those tipua paid no heed to the sacred nature of that tohunga. Instead, he was handled by them and dressed in their garments, yet they suffered no consequences from such violations of tapu. Accordingly, we ventured on board only with caution. Those strangers from the sea were not like us in appearance, having white skin and eyes the colours of the sea and sky, yet they seemed friendly towards us.*

*Great was our joy when in response to our placatory gifts of fish, the tipua presented us with small pieces of iron, which had become valued treasures to our people since the visit of that earlier ship. Even though iron was not as sharp as obsidian, it did not shatter, being as tough as pounamu. Accordingly, as no harm seemed to fall upon us, it was not long before all our people went on board to receive pieces of iron in exchange for whatever we brought with us.*

# Chapter 5

These savages have experienced musket fire before, sir,' said
Lieutenant Lehoux on his return to the ship late that night. A
large number of canoes had come out to surround the *Mascarin*'s
longboat as they approached a deep bay to the southeast of Square
Cape. Fearing an attack, he ordered the soldiers to fire a volley over
the heads of the occupants. 'As soon as we took aim, they all lay
down in the bottom of their canoes,' he explained. 'They sat up only
after we'd fired and the shots had passed overhead. Only then did
they flee.'

'It's as I thought, sir,' said Monsieur Crozet. 'The chief we have
aboard, Tacoury, showed much interest in the muskets carried by the
soldiers on the poop — even though they were not displaying them.
He ferreted them out, what's more.'

'Ta-pou,' said André, suddenly, snapping his fingers. 'What you
say makes sense, sir. He even named them — I've just realized.
Ta-pou.'

Monsieur Marion saw all this as a good sign. 'If these Naturals
have indeed encountered Europeans along their coast before, yet still
approach us with such familiarity and friendship, even coming on
board unarmed, this must give us great confidence, gentlemen.'

Jean thought the expedition leader was perhaps overly optimistic.
He expressed his reservations to his young cousin as they stood

at the taffrail early the next morning, while the ships tacked well offshore against a light but contrary breeze. 'Monsieur Marion forgets the earlier fear shown by these very same people. Even now, that chief — Tacoury — look at him. He becomes uneasy each time we stand off the land.'

André watched the chief cast anxious glances around him, making gestures back towards the land. 'He seemed relaxed enough last night. François said both chiefs slept like babies. He probably doesn't understand that the wind's unfavourable for an entry into the bay, assuming we can manoeuvre our ships as easily as a canoe.'

Jean nodded. 'You're probably right. Maybe he thinks we're going to sail off with him — not that he need worry. We're more anxious than he is to enter this bay and establish a safe anchorage.'

Although the bay southeast of the Cape explored by the *Mascarin*'s longboat offered all that the ships needed, it was exposed to the prevailing winds. That and the greater friendliness shown by the inhabitants of the well-populated western side of the Cape were enough for Monsieur Marion to decide to take the ships into the more sheltered western inlet explored by the *Castries'* longboat. This boat had not returned until after midnight, locating the ships by the braziers set at stern and bow to guide it. The famished explorers scarcely had time to eat a much-delayed supper before the expedition leader sent orders to Monsieur du Clesmeur, requesting his longboat to set sail again before first light. Both longboats set off, a willing Zealander accompanying them as pilot. They were to take soundings beyond the line of islands that formed a seemingly impenetrable barrier across this western inlet, then lead the ships in.

In the afternoon, too impatient to wait for the boats to return, Monsieur Marion ordered the ships to approach the inlet as soon as the breeze shifted in their favour. Under reduced sail with two men sounding constantly from their position in the bow, the *Mascarin* headed towards a channel at the eastern end of the line of islands. A good league behind them, a reluctant Monsieur du Clesmeur followed in the *Castries* — to Jean's approval, her captain's attempt to persuade his superior to delay until the longboats completed their survey had been summarily dismissed.

Before Monsieur Marion was rash enough to commit the ships to the uncharted channel, they saw the two boats returning. They were flying the agreed signals for a safe harbour, clean water, wood and friendly people. On board they had several casks filled with sweet-tasting water from one of the many streams they had been shown by their obliging pilot.

As darkness fell, the *Mascarin* anchored at the entrance to the eastern channel between two islands where every headland seemed occupied by a fortified village. Unable to catch up before darkness made navigation dangerous, the *Castries* anchored in open sea a league further north. The ship's people were in high spirits. It was 4 May, a month since they had left Van Diemen's Land, a month of increasing deprivation and sickness, their water rationed for most of that time to three-quarters of a scum-tainted pint per man per day. For the past week, the *Mascarin's* cook had served a hot meal only every second day, their supplies of firewood close to running out. But now it seemed their fortunes were indeed changing for the better.

All the next day, in light airs and a calm sea, canoes from the nearby islands and the more distant mainland surrounded the ships — at one stage André counted more than a hundred. First aboard the *Mascarin* at dawn, bringing more baskets of fish, Te Kuri's people greeted their chief with cries of gladness, clearly wanting him to return immediately to the mainland with them. The chief waved them away, not showing any signs of the anxiety over the ship's manoeuvres of the day before.

He stood at ease with Monsieur Marion on the quarterdeck, bending his head towards the expedition leader as though he understood every word being spoken. He was once again wrapped in a full-length cloak, brought aboard for him by his companions.

'He's as vain of the trappings of rank as Monsieur du Clesmeur,' said Jean, piqued that the chief had shown no further interest in him after their exchange of gifts. 'Pardieu, will you look at him, giving himself airs. Another popinjay! Who'd have thought we'd find such pretensions to grandeur amongst savages?'

André watched Te Kuri out of the corner of his eye. The chief certainly had a proud bearing, but the young ensign saw no pretension. He thought him impressive, a full head taller than the expedition leader and well-built, a man in the prime of life. Like the other chief who had stayed on board for the night, he wore his thick, dark hair bound up in a tuft on top of his head, fastened with a wooden comb and adorned with a fan of white feathers — like those André had found in the small carved container souvenired from the abandoned village to the north. Despite the full tattoo distorting the chief's features, André found him handsome. His intelligent, sharp eyes darted everywhere, absorbing what he saw. Yet — unlike most of the Zealanders swarming over the ship, who expressed great curiosity and childlike delight in everything — there was nothing of the child about this man. Perhaps it was the deference shown him by the others, who took care not to get in his way, that singled him out.

Before the ensign could speculate further, he heard a great cry of joy behind him. He turned to find his young friend of the day before scrambling aboard from a canoe laden with baskets of dark-skinned, knobbly sweet potatoes.

'Tareka!' the young man shouted, grasping him by the shoulders and embracing him, his nose pressed so firmly to André's that the ensign thought he would suffocate from want of air. When he was at last able to extricate himself, he realized he could not reciprocate the greeting. Embarrassed, he had to ask the youth's name once more. The smiling Zealander seemed unfazed. He repeated his name until André could say 'Ta-Capaye' without hesitation, then accompanied him to supervise the unloading of baskets from the canoe.

Most of the Naturals who came aboard were young men and women, all of them daubed with red pigment from head to foot and glistening with reeking fish oil. The entire deck was soon covered with baskets of fish and various kinds of potatoes. It was not long before all the Frenchmen, sailors and officers, were conducting a brisk trade. The Zealanders seemed only too happy to be offered an old nail or two in return, or some trinkets.

André traded some nails with Te Kape for a basket of sweet potatoes, then gave him a red handkerchief. He was delighted when the Zealander in return gave him a handsome necklace threaded with dark, round seeds or kernels. He took the youth to the forecastle where the enterprising carpenter was setting up his grinding wheel. Te Kape soon understood the carpenter's mimed actions and handed over his nails for sharpening into small chisels and cutting tools. It was not long before the other Naturals on board were crowding around the carpenter to similarly get their traded nails shaped and sharpened — the carpenter gleaning extra fish or examples of handiwork for his trouble. The ensign thought the good-natured scene had much in common with a village market day. Unlike the difficulties of communication experienced with the Diemenlanders, neither side was having any trouble expressing what they wanted. Laughter and shouts of glee accompanying gestures and torrents of speech on both sides seemed well enough understood. Monsieur Marion and his senior officers watched indulgently from the quarterdeck, the chief Te Kuri still at their side.

Much to Monsieur Thirion's approval, some of the Naturals

wanted to trade baskets of fresh greens, some sort of pungent celery, for which the surgeon handed over several small, glass mirrors. He reported his purchase to the quarterdeck. 'These intelligent people seem to know we're in dire need of anti-scorbutic greens for our scurvy sufferers.'

'Yet more confirmation they must have had dealings with European ships before.' Monsieur Marion bowed to his second-in-command. 'I should know better than to doubt your always considered opinions, sir.'

'No matter,' Monsieur Crozet waved his hand, dismissing the acknowledgement. 'It pays to be cautious when dealing with savages.'

At dinner time, the cook brought on deck several great cauldrons of boiled fresh fish and sweet potatoes, made even tastier with the celery. Washed down with all the fresh water they desired, as well as their ration of wine, it was the best meal the ship's people had eaten for weeks. They ate their fill then handed their platters to the nearest Zealanders, who squatted on the deck to devour the leavings with every sign of relish. What the Naturals favoured most was ship's biscuit, which they seemed to recognize, giving it the name 'taro'. Regardless of how small a fragment they were given or how riddled it was with weevils, they ate the biscuit with enthusiasm, especially if it were buttered. Jean said the entire supply would disappear down their gullets if they were not careful. 'These savages have the appetites of gluttons.'

Monsieur Crozet evidently agreed with him, because the order soon went out that only the officers were to offer biscuit, and then sparingly, only to chiefs. 'We still have months at sea ahead of us.'

Communicating with the Zealanders became even easier when both Messieurs Crozet and du Clesmeur independently realized their language seemed to have something in common with that spoken by

Ahu-toru, the Tahitian who had died on board before they reached the Cape of Good Hope. As it happened, Monsieur Thirion had a copy of explorer Bougainville's Tahitian vocabulary amongst his collection of books and papers. The surgeon hunted it out, and the officers perused the list of words while they enjoyed a glass or two of Burgundy in the great cabin after the midday meal. Like the men, they had dined on a simple thick soup of fish, sweet potatoes and celery accompanied by newly baked bread — François said he saw no need to embellish such good fresh fare.

They tested the word list on Te Kuri, who had dined in the great cabin again with both captains and all the *Mascarin*'s officers. Much to their satisfaction, he understood most of the words they tried. When the list passed to André, he read the words with interest, looking forward to trying them out later on Te Kape. But he soon realized that apart from useful words like wood, water and food, most of the list focused on words for different parts of the body — and he saw little scope for conversation based on these.

After his initial enthusiasm, Monsieur Thirion came to the same conclusion. 'Tant pis, it's a great pity that poor unfortunate Tahitian is not still with us,' he said, sighing heavily. 'Imagine how much his help would've improved our ability to communicate with these good people.'

They were all silent for a moment, once more regretting the death of the affable Tahitian. Then Monsieur Marion shrugged. 'Tant mieux — it's not as though we wish to attempt philosophical discussions with these Zealanders, gentlemen. What we have on this list covers our immediate needs.'

As they left the great cabin, Jean said to André that their captain had the right idea. 'These savages do seem highly intelligent. Unlike those wretched Diemenlanders, they certainly understand whatever we want them to.'

Back on deck, where the domestic slaves had cleared the empty platters and returned the cauldrons to the galley, Monsieur Marion had the musicians strike up their instruments and play a few of the more cheerful Breton tunes for the crowd of Naturals still on board. Some of the younger sailors got to their feet at their captain's request and danced a round or two.

Much to Jean's amusement, André's new friend Te Kape clearly disliked both the sharp wail of the bagpipes and the underlying notes of the flute. He sat there with his hands clapped firmly over his ears. No sooner had the musicians finished, than he moved around the deck, urging some of his companions onto their feet — young women as well as men — then lined them up to face the quarterdeck where the senior officers and Te Kuri were watching proceedings. 'He's making quite sure our musicians don't subject them to any further torture.'

Although up until then the Zealanders had shown nothing but their gentle side, they now set about a vigorous performance full of ferocious gesture and hideous grimace. They showed the whites of their eyes and stuck out their tongues, at the same time making bestial grunts. Only the rhythmic stamp of their broad, bare feet on the deck and the apparent co-ordination of their arm movements gave any clue that this was indeed some sort of dance. When they had finished and sat down again, to somewhat disconcerted applause from the watching Frenchmen, André heard Monsieur Crozet comment to the expedition leader, 'Prenez garde, sir — these people may have just shown us their true nature.'

The expedition leader shrugged. 'Our ways are not theirs, obviously. You have to admire the vigour of such a performance.'

Even more disconcerting was the increasing vigour of the embraces with which the Naturals now greeted the French sailors. André himself was more than once subjected not only to the forceful pressing of noses favoured by Te Kape, but also, whenever he was caught unawares, to a curious prolonged sucking of his skin — face or hands. Swapping notes with Jean later, when the expedition leader had at last ordered all the Zealanders off the ship for the night, he found his cousin had also experienced such uncomfortable displays. Neither of them knew quite what to make of such ferocity. 'However gentle and affectionate these savages appear,' said a sobered Jean, his words echoing those of the second-in-command earlier, 'they're primitives at heart. We'd do well to remember that.'

### Extract from the Te Kape manuscript, 1841

*At that time, I was a youth recently become of age to wield the weapons of war, a foster son to the principal fighting chief, Te Kuri. He was the first to visit the new strangers from the sea, and, he received red garments from them. At first we were wary, for they carried the guns we had named pu for the sound they made, and the sides of their ship gaped with the mouths that emit thunder and throw boulders, the weapons we later came to know as cannon. Nevertheless, we urged those tipua to bring their ships into our waters so we could exchange gifts with them in the hope of receiving more iron. Instead they went back out to sea, taking some of our people with them, Te Kuri amongst those taken. We knew of the chief Ranginui of Oruru taken captive by tipua, who then sailed away with him far out to sea so he was thereafter lost to his people, even though that chief offered great friendship to those tipua and looked after their sick when they were stranded ashore. Accordingly, when the ships returned with our people, we took great care to supply those tipua with all they asked for so we should not anger them, for such capricious behaviour led us to believe they could prove to be vengeful beings despite their apparently benign appearance and smiling ways.*

*As the days passed, the tipua showed us nothing but friendliness,* and, although Tokerau remained on alert, some of our concerns were set aside. Indeed, we gradually became more accustomed to their pale skins and strange eyes and to their babbling tongues that sounded like the chirrup and trill of small birds. They had with them many wondrous things whose purpose remained a mystery to us. They allowed us to explore all those things, and, they showed us how to sharpen pieces of iron into useful small tools, then willingly gave those to us in response to our gifts of fish. They shared their meals with us as is customary, and accordingly we grew to relish some of their strange foods. Amongst them were rounds that had the appearance of pumice stone but proved to be a sustaining starch somewhat like our taro, its taste much improved by the yellow grease they applied to it. Also acceptable to us was a sand that dissolved to sweetness on the tongue, and we sometimes drank warmed liquids well sweetened in that way. But those tipua were mostly given to drinking a sour red liquid that was bitter on the tongue, which we soon learned to avoid.

Despite the strangeness of their foods, they cooked the fish, potatoes and kumara we gave them and did not eat them raw. Accordingly, that eating of cooked food in the way of humans and our investigations of their physical nature led us to think they could perhaps be men like us and not supernatural beings. Friendship of a sort then developed amongst us.

Even so, their habits were not ours, and their atua were different from ours. We knew this because they continued to ignore the rituals and protocols that protected the spiritual wellbeing of our people, but did not suffer any consequences. Accordingly, our chiefs conferred, and, they agreed it would be best to continue to gift those strangers from the sea with all they desired so they would soon sail away and leave us to live our normal lives.

Because of the time of year, the hospitality we could offer those strangers was generous, but our chiefs knew feeding so many extra mouths *would soon deplete our winter supplies and sorely stretch their ability to provide for our people, thus testing their mana. We had just returned to the coast after the kumara harvest to capture the autumn shoals of surface-feeding maomao that run in the waters of Te Puaha o Tokerau. According to the saying of our ancestors, once the maomao have finished their run, they do not return, so we could not delay our final effort to supplement food supplies for the approaching winter. Nevertheless, we brought to the ships each day our baskets of fish, potatoes and freshly dug kumara.*

Canoes filled with Zealanders came out to the ships to trade whenever conditions were calm enough. After that first day when both ships had been overrun by Naturals, Monsieur Marion took his second-in-command's advice. Only the chiefs were now allowed on board. Although the others were initially disappointed, they soon settled to a routine of handing up their baskets of fresh food to the sailors lining the rails of the ships, mostly in exchange for nails or small pieces of old iron. Once it was made clear that they would not be allowed on board, the women no longer bothered coming out to the ships. Monsieur Crozet promised the men that the embargo would be in place only until they had established good relationships with the local chiefs. 'We need to ensure we don't trespass in our dealings with their women.'

Jean thought the women were ugly enough to quell the ardour of even the most indiscriminating amongst the men. 'I doubt Monsieur Crozet will have any mutiny on his hands.'

With the *Mascarin*'s longboat and its crew fully occupied in fetching firewood and casks of fresh water from a nearby island, the expedition leader suggested that Monsieur du Clesmeur join him and his officers in taking the *Castries*' boat to explore the islands and the harbour beyond. 'I'm sure you'll agree, sir, that our next priorities are to find wood suitable for repairing the ships and a more sheltered anchorage. We're too exposed here should the wind change.'

Monsieur Marion was showing no sign of the earlier impatience that had coloured his dealings with the captain of the *Castries*. Much to Jean's disgust, he was conciliatory towards him, even standing back to let him take the best seat in the stern of the longboat. 'Ma fois, anyone would think he was the subordinate officer,' he muttered to André as the two ensigns waited to board the boat with the other officers selected for the excursion.

André shrugged. 'What's he got to lose by being polite? Anyway, it's Monsieur du Clesmeur's boat.'

Jean was dismissive. 'Technically, it's Monsieur Marion's boat. Now things are going better for us, he's suddenly remembered that young sot's an aristocrat. And his uncle's our sponsor. So he's toadying up to him once more.'

There was no point arguing with Jean, but André thought Monsieur Marion's behaviour befitted that of a good leader. Surely it made sense to keep the *Castries*' captain on side?

Accompanied by the carpenters, the sergeant-at-arms and some of the soldiers, the officers took the longboat through the eastern channel, heading towards the mainland several leagues distant. The entire coast was lined with villages, most of them situated on headlands and fortified by ditches and palisades. Everywhere they looked, they saw slopes cleared for gardens, although most of these seemed to be lying fallow.

Monsieur Marion concluded they had arrived not long after the annual harvest. 'Our good fortune, gentlemen — these people will have plenty of produce to trade with us.'

Wherever they landed, the Naturals gathered on the beaches to greet them and make them welcome, often performing one of their curious dances. One in particular involved waving branches of green leaves accompanied by a long, wailing dirge. Jean said it sounded more like a wake than a welcome. 'If this is their practice when they're happy, I'd hate to be around when they're sad.'

Best of all, they found a cove backed by overhanging trees with many tough, curved exposed roots that would provide excellent pre-shaped timber for repairing the *Mascarin's* damaged forepart. To André's surprise, Monsieur du Clesmeur volunteered to stay there and supervise the carpenters.

Monsieur Marion hesitated. 'If you insist, sir. I'd hoped for your company in exploring further along the shore.'

'More toadying!' Jean muttered as the captain bowed in acknowledgement. 'Why doesn't he point out that the carpenters know their business well enough without his help?'

'My thought was that one of us should remain here in case an important chief arrives expecting courtesies,' Monsieur du Clesmeur explained, taking out his snuff box.

As the expedition leader nodded in agreement, Jean continued his murmured asides to his cousin. 'No doubt he sees himself granting gracious audiences!'

André shrugged. He was growing tired of sticking up for the *Castries'* captain. 'More likely he's no intention of exposing those elegant shoes to saltwater.'

Leaving the captain to direct the men in cutting planks and cheeks to brace the bowsprit amidst a great crowd of interested Naturals, the other officers strolled further along the beach to enjoy the beauty of this secluded spot. Soon drawing ahead of Monsieur Marion and the main party, André and Jean clambered across rocks towards a headland. Accompanied by Thomas Ballu, the grizzled sergeant-at-arms, they hoped to find some game birds in the bay beyond. As they rounded the point, they heard some sort of commotion. Curiosity overcame caution, and they hastened their steps.

Drawn up on a flat grassed terrace behind the beach were two groups of heavily armed Zealanders, evidently about to join battle. Before the three Frenchmen could retreat, they were spotted. Two men — chiefs from the white feathers they wore in their hair — immediately left their place and walked purposefully towards them. Both carried lethal-looking stone clubs and toothed spears. Other men watched, their own weapons poised.

'No point running for it, gentlemen,' said Ballu. 'That lot would soon have us, with those rocks back there to slow us down.'

'What do you suggest?' Jean deferred to the experienced old soldier.

'Bluff it out — act nonchalant.' Ballu faced the oncoming chiefs, his musket slung casually over his shoulder. He spoke out of the corner of his mouth. 'Not our fight, is it? Wait and see what they want.'

Just when André thought they were within range of those spears, the two chiefs put their weapons down and came on empty-handed, calling out to them. The ensign then recognized both of them. With a deep breath, he said, 'They were on board yesterday — they know us!'

'Seem friendly enough,' agreed Jean. ''But keep that musket close at hand, Monsieur Ballu.'

'Stay relaxed, gentlemen,' said Ballu. He took the musket off his shoulder and grounded it, then continued to wait for the two chiefs.

André did not dare take his eyes off the two Zealanders. They might now be unarmed, but their warriors were watching not far away, wary and on the alert. Beyond them, the other armed group now indulged in some sort of dance, much like the ferocious performance they had witnessed on board the *Mascarin*. Even at this distance, the sound of their screams and deep-throated grunts was enough to make his heart race.

The chiefs reached them. They first approached Ballu and pressed noses with him, then it was the ensigns' turn. The Zealanders' now-familiar smell of sweat and fish oil was even stronger than usual. The two chiefs wasted no time. They gestured at the musket, then took Ballu by the arm, tugging at him.

'They want you to go with them,' said Jean. Relief made him laugh. 'And we thought we were about to be killed — they simply want you as a mascot!'

The sergeant-at-arms allowed the chiefs to lead him along the beach towards their waiting warriors. The ensigns watched as the two chiefs took their places at the head of their party, Ballu with his musket placed between them. On a signal, the opposing groups of warriors moved off in ranks, marching towards each other. When they were a short distance apart, perhaps fifty paces, they halted. André watched, amazed, as one fiercely tattooed warrior came to the front of the other group and began twirling his long spear. His rapid movements, fluid and practised, were accompanied by grimaces and bitten-off grunts. None of the others moved. Both sides waited in silence. Then the whirling warrior suddenly faltered. He lowered his spear and stared.

André exclaimed, 'He's only just spotted Monsieur Ballu!'

At that moment, the two chiefs thrust Ballu right forward. The sergeant-at-arms raised his musket and immediately fired a shot over the head of the warrior facing him.

The sharp percussion startled both sides, but the other group was the first to react. Their challenger following, they turned and fled in complete disarray. With a howl of glee, the victorious warriors set off after them, only abandoning the pursuit after their defeated enemy had disappeared around the distant headland. They then returned to their waiting chiefs. Gathering up Ballu, the whole group returned to where the ensigns were watching, then escorted the Frenchmen back to the longboat, laughing and singing all the way.

'What's it feel like to be the conquering hero?' Jean asked Ballu, grinning, when the Zealanders at last stopped patting the sergeant-at-arms and smothering him with their peculiar embraces.

'Hard to know how serious that skirmish would've been, sir,' said Ballu. 'Looked like a lot of posturing to me. Anyway, I knew those spears were no match for my musket. It seemed wise to go along with what they wanted.' The phlegmatic sergeant-at-arms shrugged. 'Myself, I could do without all this fuss.'

When they told the two captains what had happened, Monsieur Marion congratulated the sergeant-at-arms. 'You've done us a great favour, Monsieur Ballu. These Naturals will look on us as allies from now on.'

'But we'd better steer clear of the ones who ran away,' Jean muttered to André. '*They* mightn't be so enthusiastic!'

'Certainly, their fear of muskets is to our advantage,' said Monsieur du Clesmeur. 'We only have to raise our weapons to bring these savages to order.'

When they turned inquiring faces towards him, the captain hastened to deflect attention from the sergeant-at-arms with an account of his own. He told them at great length what had happened after he was left in charge of the carpenters. Almost as soon as the rest of the landing party had scattered in different directions, the crowd of Zealanders gathered on the beach started to make threatening noises. 'The men had scarcely begun work when some of the Naturals began jostling them. Some even tried to take away their axes and saws.'

Alarmed by the increasing agitation amongst the Naturals — and uncomfortably reminded of their experience in Van Diemen's Land,

Monsieur du Clesmeur said he took firm action. 'I drew a line in the sand around our workers, then took one of the chiefs by the arm and led him beyond it. He seemed to understand my gestures immediately, and withdrew his people behind the line.'

Once the soldiers took positions along this line, their muskets in clear view, all the Zealanders moved back, although the captain said some of them kept murmuring discontent. He preened himself, unable to hide his satisfaction. 'Nevertheless, we were able to complete our work without any further interference.'

'Nicely done, sir,' said Monsieur Marion. 'A firm but friendly hand is all that's needed. Take heed, gentlemen — Monsieur du Clesmeur's approach should be used as a model for all our behaviour towards these people.'

Although Monsieur du Clesmeur pretended modesty, he was obviously gratified by the praise. Jean was unimpressed. 'Ever more toadying from our leader,' he commented later to André. 'Mort-diable — the man had a detachment of soldiers with him. He wasn't in any danger. Not like our friend Ballu. Now *that* was truly brave.'

André thought his cousin a trifle harsh. 'Monsieur du Clesmeur hasn't had much experience. It's hardly fair to compare him with an old campaigner like our sergeant-at-arms. *I* think he kept his composure remarkably well.'

'I don't understand why you keep defending him,' said Jean. 'Either one of us would've done exactly the same. Wait and see — we might yet get the chance to show our own mettle.'

**Extract from the Te Kape manuscript, 1841**

*At that time, many related peoples lived in and around Tokerau with rights to its rich resources, their kinship ties like intermingling grains of sand that pour as one stream from the hand, ties that stretched from the* rich garden-lands of Taiamai inland, west to Hokianga and east to Te Rawhiti, where the whales blow. Ngati Wai and Ngare Raumati held the eastern seaboard. My people were of Ngare Raumati descent, and Te Kuri, our principal fighting chief, had a stronghold on Orokawa in the eastern harbour as well as a large settlement at Whangamumu on the outer coast. Te Kuri himself had links with Te Hikutu, a Hokianga people who had won rights to land in the western harbour. Ngati Pou held the outer islands of the harbour at that time, and lived inland as far as Taiamai and west to Hokianga. We lived in peace with Ngati Pou even though they were not the closest kin to us. Te Roroa, Ngati Hineira, Ngati Manu, Te Kapotai, Ngati Rangi — those are some of the related peoples, eastern and western, I remember in Tokerau at that time, and many were their chiefs. [Ed: genealogical lists of often indecipherable names omitted here] Ngati Rangi mostly lived inland at Waimate and Taiamai but had fishing grounds here in Tokerau, and some of their people were living at Paroa and on Motu-arohia. Descendants of Ngati Awa were also still living here in Tokerau at that time.

The relationships between all those peoples ebbed and flowed like the tides and the intermingling waters of the harbour. Te Pikopiko i Whiti — where the winding inlets flow out into the inner harbour. That is the place where Hine-nui-te-Po receives our dead. Te Puaha o Tokerau — where those inner waters disperse into the outer harbour and merge with the deep sea waters, beyond the point now known as Tapeka. Where those inner and outer waters merge, that boundary shifts according to the inflowing or outflowing tides. At the time we are talking of, eastern and western chiefs were rival authorities in Tokerau, their influence ebbing and flowing like those tides. So that is those names.

Of those chiefs, Te Kuri held a position of strength because of his close ties with both the Hokianga people from the far western coast and Ngare Raumati here on the eastern coast. Accordingly, he was ill-pleased when some of te iwi o Mariou took up arms in support of a rival

Ngati Pou group. Mariou's people also cut timber without first asking permission. I remember Te Kuri saying their presence could quickly become an irritant, a plague of namu namu, whose barely felt stings then set the skin aflame long after the insects themselves have disappeared.

It was only when the ships came into the harbour and anchored off Orokawa where Te Kuri and his close ally Pikiorei had their strongholds, thus bringing those strangers from the sea under his mana as guests, that he was persuaded to tolerate their lack of manners — that, and the iron they were so willing to gift us.

'Come aboard with your senior officers, Monsieur du Clesmeur, if you please,' said Monsieur Marion. 'Pay careful attention to our progress through the channel so you may better bring in your own vessel.'

The young captain seemed happy to comply. 'That would indeed be helpful, sir.' Then, as though he felt the need to emphasize his independence, he added somewhat pompously, 'It'll give me the opportunity to focus on further bearings to supplement the plan I've drawn up for this harbour.'

André noticed the *Castries'* second-in-command, Monsieur Le Corre, stiffen slightly at this pronouncement, then shrug his shoulders. Jean nudged his cousin. 'De par tous les diables, our young aristocrat takes the prize — I know for a fact Monsieur Le Corre does all the chart work on the *Castries*.'

'The captain *has* been out most days taking bearings and soundings,' André objected.

'Anyone can do that,' said Jean. 'The actual cartography's a different matter. He's claiming credit not due to him.'

With the senior officers of both ships crowded on the *Mascarin's* quarterdeck, they set sail as soon as it was light. The wind had changed direction and was now favourable for entering the large harbour that lay behind the line of islands. The morning was fine, the temperatures almost warm after the months of cold and wet they had endured. Moving slowly under small sails in a light breeze, the ship sailed across the bay towards the wider western channel they had carefully sounded over the previous week. A brilliant aquamarine sea reflected the multitude of rocky islets, their colours ranging from ochre to black. Between the rounded humps of larger islands clad in various shades of green, vistas of incomparable beauty constantly opened up before them, revealing yet more islands and sheltered coves. Beyond these, they caught glimpses of the large harbour they had already named Port Marion, where calm, silvered water glimmered against a distant background of high, blue mountains.

Everywhere they looked, the industrious Zealanders who lived in this paradise had shaped the landscape to suit their purposes. André watched as they sailed past the many fortified villages perched on headlands, each one with its strategically placed fosses and smaller ditches, rising in terraces up to the high palisades that surrounded the huts grouped on the summits. In their exploratory excursions around Port Marion, he had already noticed that few of the villages lacked fortifications. As well, apart from those small settlements sited near extensive areas of cultivation, most villages were built on the tops of steep hills where they would be difficult to attack. Such precautions seemed to contradict the apparent friendliness they encountered everywhere they landed.

He shared his thoughts with his cousin as they sailed slowly into the entrance of the channel, barely half a league wide, with the sailors casting the lead lines constantly chanting their soundings. The senior ensign said they should take heed. 'These people might be gentle and affectionate towards us, but don't forget that well-armed and disciplined war party we encountered. Such men seemed capable of considerable bloodshed.'

'D'accord,' said André. 'But the chiefs who come on board are on good enough terms with each other — and they come unarmed.'

'That's as maybe,' said Jean. 'We can't really tell what's going on further afield. We don't know where that other lot of armed savages came from, for instance. There might be more waiting in the wings, ready to attack the ones we've befriended at any time.'

André recalled the abandoned village they had visited on the northern coast. Although he thought Jean was perhaps right, he echoed what the sergeant-at-arms had said earlier. 'Such squabbles are surely nothing to do with us? Monsieur Marion takes care to ensure we remain on good terms with the Zealanders.'

They stopped talking to concentrate on keeping a sharp eye out for submerged reefs and rocks as the ship glided on through the passage, steep cliffs and bush-clad slopes rising on both sides. By mid-morning, although the harbour was now opening up ahead, a shoal extending from a nearby island meant the water became too shallow to proceed safely under sail. As soon as they had furled the sails, the men prepared two boats to tow the ship, suspending the light anchors used for kedging from their stern davits. Canoes full of Naturals crowded around them, impeding the work, until Monsieur Marion was forced to have the soldiers fire a short volley over their heads to get them to withdraw out of the way.

'Just the time when having the Tahitian on board to explain would have been most helpful,' commented Monsieur Thirion from his vantage point at the taffrail.

'Needs must,' said Monsieur Crozet, shrugging. 'These savages are perceptive enough to realize the nature of our warning.'

It seemed the second-in-command was right, for the Zealanders merely took their canoes to a safe distance, then stayed their paddles to watch.

André supervised the boatmen on the yawl as they alternated with the longboat, where Jean was in charge, laying out the two cables in turn. Each time one anchor was let go, the other boat rowed ahead, ready to let go the second anchor as soon as the men on board the ship heaving away at the capstan had winched the vessel forward until she was directly over the first. Both ensigns prided themselves on their ability to carry out such an operation efficiently — aided by a certain element of competition between the two boats. The Naturals quickly understood their purpose and positioned their canoes to lead the way into the harbour ahead of the boats. It became something of a festive procession, what with the bagpipe and flute music struck up on the ship to set the rhythm for the men on the capstan, their raucous singing of the chorus, the beating of the drums on the boats to set the timing for the men on the oars, and finally, the answering chant from the paddlers on the canoes.

After several hours of hard work, they had kedged the ship to their chosen mooring in the deep waters of Port Marion, a spot with a good sandy bottom at thirteen fathoms, well sheltered by land on all sides. They began laying out fixed moorings, a musket shot northeast of a narrow peninsula that jutted towards them from the mainland and about the same distance southwest of a large island. Monsieur Marion intended setting up a hospital camp on the western side of this island, where two small adjoining coves provided good landing beaches and excellent streams of water.

Monsieur du Clesmeur had returned to his own ship early in the afternoon, as soon as the *Mascarin* started kedging. They had already laid out their fixed moorings before the *Castries* came into sight, cautiously sounding her way along the route taken by the smaller ship. Even though there were still several hours of daylight, the larger ship anchored near the island where the water shoaled, more than a league away from the mooring spot. Her captain made no attempt to prepare to kedge.

Showing the first signs of impatience for some days, Monsieur Marion had André signal him to ask why. Apparently, he had left his two kedge anchors behind at the eastern mooring. He intended returning for them at first light and then would be able to begin kedging.

Monsieur Crozet allowed himself to chuckle. 'Our young friend seems to have ongoing problems with anchors, does he not? He must've cast off in too much haste.'

The expedition leader swore an oath under his breath. 'Send the longboat to assist him to kedge in the morning — as soon as he returns to his ship with his damned anchors.'

Jean turned away to hide his own grin. He whispered to André, 'Looks like Monsieur du Clesmeur has his wet nurse. Our captain's no longer leaving him to do *anything* on his own.'

André hissed back, 'Hardly surprising — he'd not want to trust his bigger ship to someone so inexperienced in these confined waters.'

The Zealanders had continued to circle the *Mascarin* while the ship's boats laid out the moorings, and Monsieur Marion now beckoned them to come on board. 'We need to make sure the volley we fired hasn't jeopardized our friendship.'

Monsieur Crozet thought it unlikely. 'These savages seem so eager to get their hands on any old nails, they'll forgive us anything.'

'We must continue to do everything we can to encourage such eagerness to trade, sir,' said the expedition leader.

He had Anthonie, the cook, bring out platters of buttered pieces of broken and weevil-ridden ship's biscuit specially for the Naturals while the ship's people ate their own well-earned supper. He then told André to fetch small trinkets to give to the Naturals when they prepared to leave the ship just before night fell. 'We should be sparing with nails and pieces of iron from now on, gentlemen. That way we'll ensure their trade value remains high.'

'Good thinking, sir,' said Monsieur Crozet. 'Apart from keeping the savages friendly, we want all the fish and vegetables they'll bring us.'

André would not have thought of rationing the articles the Zealanders desired most. He was full of admiration for such astuteness.

But Jean laughed. 'True to form, pardieu!'

Something in his voice made André ask him what he meant.

'Oh, our captain had the reputation of being the sharpest trader in the Compagnie des Indes. He's always been very good at making a profit, and not just for the Compagnie — he was known for taking the right to private trading to extremes.'

'What's wrong with that?' André frowned.

'Why, one voyage they say he had almost as much tonnage of his own private goods on board as those for the Compagnie! What's more, he diverted the ship to an unscheduled port to discharge them.' Jean laughed again. 'Diable! What a rogue — he'd some explaining to do that time, apparently.'

Not liking the senior ensign's lack of respect, André leapt to his captain's defence. 'Surely his trading expertise is to our advantage, cousin?'

Jean grinned at him. 'Toutàfait! There's no point paying out more than we need to provision our ships.'

# Chapter 6

On deck at first light, André leant on the dew-wet rail and absorbed their surroundings. He took in a deep breath of the crisp autumnal air, savouring the mixture of smells coming off the land — damp earth, rotting leaves and pungent wood smoke, sharpened by the rich iodine scent of the seaweed piled along the beaches. He was at last feeling well again, his scurvy quite defeated by fresh air, exercise and a diet of fresh fish and potatoes. Monsieur Thirion had already brewed spruce beer from the aromatic grey-green tips of some myrtle-like shrub that grew prolifically on all the islands, adding malt to enhance its flavour and efficacy. The surgeon also insisted that scurvy sufferers take a good daily dose of the wild-grown celery gathered fresh from the nearby shore. His efforts were paying dividends. Only the worst afflicted, men who could no longer walk, were not yet recovering their strength.

Monsieur Marion and the *Mascarin*'s senior officers had chosen their mooring well. The Zealanders had several villages on the nearby large island — although there were no major settlements in the immediate vicinity of the coves where they planned to land their sick. Only a few people seemed to live there, apparently for the purposes of cultivating the gardens on the slopes rising behind the beach. The young ensign could see smoke drifting above a copse of trees where a few small reed huts crouched on a levelled terrace. He thought

most of the island's inhabitants must live in the big fo
visible from the ship, strategically sited on a narrow pe
where he was standing, he could pick out the palisade...
cliffs that surrounded this village on its seaward sides. From what
he could see, the narrow ridge linking the peninsula to the island
would make any ascent from the landward side impossibly steep. He
could not make out any path from this angle. As he watched, some
Naturals launched their canoes from the bay below the village and
began paddling towards the ship.

By the time Monsieur du Clesmeur had brought the *Castries* to
join them, they were once more surrounded by canoes wanting to
trade. Keeping Monsieur Marion's directive in mind, the ship's people
offered only small numbers of old nails, broken knives or pieces of
the most weevil-ridden biscuit in return for baskets of fish and well-
worked examples of the local axes and weapons.

This time, the Zealanders brought their women with them. The
chiefs handed them all up onto the deck, and then made it clear by
gestures that the Frenchmen were welcome to pay their attentions to
the unmarried ones — recognizable by their unbound hair, worn at
shoulder length. They indicated that their wives were out of bounds,
pointing to the few women present who wore their hair on top of
their heads, fixed by a woven fillet.

Monsieur Crozet asked, 'What are your instructions for our
people, sir? Under such provocation, they'll succumb sooner rather
than later.'

The expedition leader nodded. 'D'accord. We can't expect too
much of them. But make sure they understand the distinction between
these females, and order them to be discreet. These Zealanders have
a certain dignity that should be respected.'

One of the chiefs, who had been on board several times, led a
young woman towards the quarterdeck where the senior officers of

oth ships were gathered. He was followed by several of his people carrying large baskets of various foods, which they deposited near the officers. The chief greeted Monsieur Marion warmly, then indicated the young woman accompanying him. The intention was unmistakable. The embarrassed expedition leader mumbled something, then allowed her to stand beside him. The chief nodded vigorously, then made a long speech before he turned and left the quarterdeck to supervise trading the baskets of fish he had also brought with him.

'Fi, fi, sir!' Monsieur du Clesmeur murmured when the expedition leader studiously ignored the young woman hovering at his side. 'These savages obviously well understand that such ploys are the most effective way of bringing together two such different peoples. Are you not going to rise to the occasion?'

André choked back his laugh when none of the other officers so much as smiled.

'Enough, sir!' Monsieur Marion was in no mood for jokes. He glared at the *Castries'* captain, then unceremoniously pushed the young woman aside. 'I expect all of you to retain some semblance of restraint, gentlemen.'

Ignored by all the senior officers, the young woman stood about disconsolately until the ensigns took pity on her and led her into the gunroom, where they plied her with biscuit and glass beads. Her appearance was pleasant enough, her features well-formed and her skin clear of blemishes. Her short mantle and skirt were better fashioned than most, and she was wearing a finely worked jade ornament on a cord around her neck. Paul Chevillard thought she might be the chief's own daughter. She seemed shy, hanging her head so her thick unbound hair hid her face. She made no attempt to answer their questions, even though she accepted the biscuit and beads eagerly enough. Like all the women, she was plastered from head to foot with red pigment, but she did not stink of fish oil. Jean again voiced his opinion that the ship's people would not have any problem keeping their lust under control. 'It's peculiar that these savages are for the most part so robust and handsome, yet their women are so small and ill-made.'

'Monsieur Thirion has a theory about that,' André ventured. 'He says primitive peoples often expect their women to do all the hard physical work and feed them only scraps, so they don't thrive.'

'Mort-diable!' Jean shrugged. 'So much for our surgeon's insistence that such people live amiable lives. From what you're saying, they treat their women no better than our aristocrats treat their peasants — all work and no play.'

When the Zealanders left the ship at the end of the day, they seemed disappointed that, unlike the sailors, none of the officers had accepted the attentions of their women. Scowling, they pushed them aboard the canoes and paddled off, shouting back at the ship in tones that were unmistakably derogatory.

'Apparently we've caused offence, sir,' observed Monsieur Crozet. 'We might have to compensate for our lack of manhood — give them more iron and trinkets for their goods.'

Monsieur Marion was unmoved. 'All we have to do is continue to show them respect. They'll soon accept their women are beneath the attention of our officers.'

'He speaks for himself,' Jean muttered, his hopes that the chiefs were keeping the best-lookers ashore boosted by the more comely appearance of the young woman they had entertained in the gunroom.

Monsieur Marion heard him and glared. 'I insist all officers maintain their distance, Monsieur Roux. It's a matter of discipline.'

**Extract from the Te Kape manuscript, 1841**

*As day followed day, we continued to bring baskets of fish, potted birds, potatoes and kumara to the ships. Mariou's people received all those gifts eagerly, but responded only with small pieces of iron and other items we soon realized were of little value to them. This they did even when gifts of great value were offered to them, well-worked weapons and finely woven mats. As time passed, it became clear those tipua might have no intention of reciprocating with equivalent gifts, perhaps thinking we remained ignorant of what they valued. Our chiefs conferred, and, they agreed that perhaps even our most precious taonga were not deemed sufficient by a people of such wealth as te iwi o Mariou. Accordingly, the chiefs decided to send the most beautiful and prestigious of our young unmarried women out to the ships to attend Mariou and his senior men, a gesture of hospitality reserved for the most important of guests. Of those young women, the most beautiful and prestigious was a chief's daughter presented to Mariou — the woman Miki, whose name has been handed down amongst our people in songs from that time.*

*Accordingly, when that prestigious woman was spurned by Mariou, the insult to her tapu status was grievous. At the same time, our other valued women were rejected by Mariou's subordinate chiefs, who instead sent them below with men who were clearly of no account. Great was the chagrin of our chiefs at such breaches of hospitality and good manners. To relieve their feelings, many ribald jokes were made about the boorishness of Mariou's subordinate chiefs, and our laughter was loud, but Te Kuri vowed that retaliation would be sought to compensate for the unacceptable behaviour of those strangers from the sea, whom he had claimed as his particular guests.*

They were soon too busy for the embargo to bother Jean. Sent ashore onto the newly named Marion Island to set up the hospital camp, the two ensigns selected a suitable site on a triangular terrace behind the beach where nearby steep hills provided shelter. They set some men to cut poles from the myrtle-like trees that grew on the rocky headland. While others cleared lank grass from the site, André and Jean explored the small curve of beach and ventured around the rocks separating it from the adjacent cove. Extensive bands of oysters grew on these rocks, and they vowed to return as soon as their tasks were completed.

Once the spare main sails were stretched securely over a framework of poles to form a large tent, they sent men to cut armfuls of the coarse bracken fern that grew prolifically on the slopes behind the beach. Jean had got the idea from the abandoned huts they had visited on the northern coast. 'Fasten some of those poles along the ground to make compartments on either side of the tent,' he ordered. Filled with the dry fern, they would make adequate beds for the sick sailors.

'Ingenious, cousin,' said the admiring André as they stood back to survey the finished camp. 'Monsieur Thirion should be well satisfied.'

'Oui, oui,' said Jean. Energized by the physical activity ashore, he was eager to get on. 'There's plenty of room here to set up the forge for the blacksmith and the cooper on the other side of this stream, but I think the adjacent cove's best suited as our watering place, don't you? The stream's deeper for one thing.'

'But that's where those savages have their huts,' André pointed out. 'They might object.'

'Why would that be a problem?' asked Jean. 'There're not that many of them and we'll keep our distance from their huts. But if you like, we'll set up a small guard-post on the far side of the stream. Monsieur Marion would want a contingent of soldiers ashore here anyway. The savages won't bother us when they see our men have muskets.'

They had just finished pitching the tent for the guard-post in the adjacent cove when the youth Te Kape came ashore with a chief, an older robust man whom he introduced as Maru, making it known that this chief came from the island's fortified village. The two Zealanders repeatedly pointed in the direction of this village, which was over the hill and out of sight of the hospital camp.

'They want us to visit them,' said André.

'Why not?' Jean soon made up his mind. 'We need to establish good relationships with that village, seeing it's on the island. Your friend's obviously happy to act as ambassador for us.'

At that moment, Te Kape spotted the longboat coming ashore with its first load of sick men for the newly erected hospital. He gaped, then broke into an alarmed babble of words. Before the ensigns could stop them, the two Naturals fled down the beach and swam out to their canoe, already being paddled rapidly away by its crew. As the bemused ensigns watched, the Zealanders and their canoe disappeared around the point without a backward glance.

'Peste! What was all that about?' asked the exasperated Jean. 'I was looking forward to visiting that village.'

André nodded towards the scurvy sufferers being carried ashore. 'I think they were put off,' he said slowly, looking at the men's awkwardly bent, stiffened limbs and ashen-grey faces distorted by protruding spotted gums.

'You may be right,' Jean agreed. 'They're certainly not a pretty sight.'

André shrugged away his own disappointment. 'Nothing we can do about it now.'

'Allons donc,' said Jean robustly. 'Nothing to stop us going after the savages by land.' He pointed out a track leading up over the saddle that separated their cove from the neighbouring bay where the village was situated. 'Let's see if that takes us where we want to go.'

Accompanied by a couple of soldiers armed with muskets, the two ensigns set out. Although the track was well-formed, it was extremely narrow. As they climbed over the saddle, dense wind-shorn myrtle scrub pressed in on them at head height, and they were forced to walk in single file. Even then, the moss-clad track itself was a deep trough sunk into the clay, barely wide enough for them to put one foot after the other. André found it hard to keep his balance. It was still and quiet but for the hum of insects. The track twisted and dipped so he was unable to see what lay ahead. Beginning to feel claustrophobic, he was relieved when they emerged into the open at the head of the neighbouring bay. From here, the rocky promontory occupied by the fortified village looked even steeper and more difficult to access than it had from the ship.

'Now what?' André muttered as they hesitated at the foot of the path that led up to the village. 'We can hardly charge on up there uninvited.'

'We *were* invited,' Jean pointed out. 'Anyway, we've been seen.'

Above them, they could make out the heads of people peering over the palisades. Before long, Te Kape came down to join them, followed at a distance by several other youths. At first he seemed shy and not sure whether to greet them. André smiled at him, then said his name repeatedly until the young Zealander's infectious grin re-emerged and he forgot his earlier fright. He clasped first André then Jean tightly and pressed noses with them. The others followed suit, the greetings taking some time. At last, Te Kape stepped back and beckoned the small party to follow him up to the village.

As narrow as the path through the scrub, the steep track soon had alarming drops on both sides. André placed his feet carefully, aware that a slip or stumble could result in serious injury or death. Whenever they came to places where the inhabitants had artificially steepened the terrain, Te Kape had to help him scramble up. Even

Jean, more nimble than his cousin with his ungainly long legs, had to accept help from one of the Naturals. By the time they reached the village on the summit, both ensigns were out of breath, their calf muscles aching from the unaccustomed land-based exercise. They collapsed beside a ditch separating them from a stout, eight-foot-high palisade.

'Pardieu,' Jean muttered. 'Even without these ramparts, the climb itself would wear out all but the fittest enemy.'

André was looking along the palisade. 'I don't think we've even reached the village yet — there's no entrance that I can see.'

He was right. When they were sufficiently recovered, Te Kape led them along the edge of the ditch and behind what proved to be a separate rectangular fort, protected by palisades and ditches on all sides. Between this outworks and the village itself was a deep fosse or ditch, at least ten feet wide. On the far side of this, they had to crouch to enter a small gate in the village's outer palisade, then edge their way along a narrow cliff path that skirted the base of the inner palisade towards a second, equally low, gate. André could feel sweat trickling down his back, and his legs were trembling with the effort of maintaining his balance. Above them, from a high platform raised well above this inner palisade, several men kept up a running commentary on their laborious progress. Even though their voices sounded good-natured, André felt exposed and vulnerable and was glad when they emerged onto open ground inside the palisade.

Two rows of thatched huts faced them, each accompanied by an open-sided shelter where André could see piles of blackened stones, fire pits and a stash of calabashes. Half-hidden in shadow near one of the huts, a small prick-eared dog raised a crinkled eyebrow at him, then subsided back into sleep. The ensign then spotted other dogs with fur in shades of brown or black and white. He nudged Jean and pointed them out. 'That fur cloak you got from Tacoury — it's fashioned from dog skins!'

'Perhaps they breed them for that very purpose,' his cousin commented. 'We've not seen any sign of larger animals.'

Te Kape led them along a raised beaten-earth parade ground that extended the whole length of the village, its width varying according to the contours of the narrow ridge it straddled. Just ahead of them, several chiefs were sitting outside a larger building that occupied the centre of this parade ground. These chiefs watched them approach, then the one they recognized as Maru stood to greet them. After all the chiefs had embraced the Frenchmen, he indicated they were welcome to explore the village.

Accompanied by Te Kape and the chiefs, André and Jean first ventured inside the large building, past a weapons rack holding countless wooden spears. Inside the building, which seemed to be the senior chief's house, they looked around curiously once their eyes adjusted to the gloom. Neatly arranged in stacks around the central house posts, they could see numerous weapons sorted by type: more wooden spears, some with carved points, some with bone inserts; long lances made of hardened wood; clubs or bludgeons; an array of axes or tomahawks made of stone; and various other implements, all of them fashioned from wood, bone or stone. Seeing their interest, the chiefs took examples of each weapon from its stack and demonstrated their use. They then conducted the ensigns to two other buildings that clearly served as storehouses, one for fishing equipment and one containing stacks of baskets and bundles of various foods and large calabashes filled with water.

André was somewhat unnerved. 'These savages seem prepared for a siege.'

'D'accord — you have to admire their industry,' said Jean. 'They're certainly well set up. Even Monsieur Thirion couldn't fault such orderly arrangements. What about those communal latrines? Did you notice how well placed they are, jutting out over the sea?'

André was thinking along other lines. 'Maybe it's not such a good thing having our sick men ashore on this island,' he said slowly. 'We could be leaving ourselves open to attack.'

'Nothing here's a match for our weapons,' Jean was quick to scoff. 'A few fusiliers could take out at least a hundred savages armed with spears. Anyway, if they're planning to attack us, they'd hardly show us their defences so eagerly.'

'You're right, of course,' said André, relaxing. 'They've been nothing but friendly.' He turned to Te Kape, who was standing at his elbow, listening with a smile on his face, but clearly not understanding what they said. 'Which house is yours?' He gestured at the rows of huts and tapped the youth on the chest.

Te Kape took André by the arm and led him to the high platform at the entrance to the village. When they had both climbed up the notched post, the youth turned the ensign around until he was looking towards the mainland.

'You live over there?' André nodded. 'Of course — Tacoury's your chief, isn't he, not Malou? I'd forgotten you come from the mainland.'

**Extract from the Te Kape manuscript, 1841**

*Te iwi o Mariou proceeded to unload all their belongings from the ships and deposit them ashore on Moturua, where they built themselves houses and took over the dwellings and gardens of the people who tended the plantings there. They then landed many beings of such ghastly appearance that we first took them to be kehua, whose sickly presence sullied the land and made it unfit for people to use. All this they did without asking permission of Ngati Pou who were living on that island at that time. Accordingly, in the face of such desecration of the land, those people invited two subordinate chiefs from the ships to visit their stronghold on that island with the intention of demonstrating their strength and preparedness.*

After such a friendly reception at the village, the ensigns were surprised to find on their return to the camp that the Naturals who lived there were packing up their belongings. The ensigns tried to indicate that the Frenchmen would stay on their side of the stream, with no intention of intruding. But the Zealanders took no notice. They brushed the hovering officers aside and carried all their things down to a small canoe drawn up on the beach. As soon as they had loaded everything, they paddled away.

'But we took such good care not to provoke or interfere with them in any way.' André was disconcerted. 'Monsieur Marion will be angry — our instructions were clear.'

At the hospital camp in the neighbouring cove, Monsieur Thirion was equally nonplussed. 'We gave them many presents as soon as we came ashore,' he explained. 'They seemed happy enough until we erected a tent for the officers in their cove, beside the guard-post.'

André looked at the cluster of tents and the pile of equipment building up on both beaches as the ship's people laboured to lighten the *Mascarin* so they could start work on repairing her leaking forepart. The blacksmith was setting up his forge under one of the trees, and the cooper had already brought many bundles of staves ashore ready to reassemble the water casks. What with the sixty scurvy sufferers now housed in the large hospital tent, he could see why the inhabitants might have felt uneasy. 'Perhaps they were intimidated by all this activity. It must seem as if we're taking over, settling in like this.'

Jean decided there was no reason to dwell on the misunderstanding. 'No matter, we mean them no harm, after all. Monsieur Marion can hardly blame us — what these savages choose to do is hardly our concern.'

When over the next few days, the Zealanders returned only to dig up the roots they had planted in their gardens and remove some building timber, the French officers realized this was perhaps to their advantage. It was easier not having to worry about the sensitivities of Naturals living so close by. Monsieur Crozet suggested they should use the abandoned huts to store the rigging, sails and rudders they had removed from the ships for maintenance and repair. 'We might as well make use of such God-given facilities.'

A blast of wind hit the *Mascarin*'s longboat as they neared the westernmost cape of the harbour and became exposed to the open sea. The boat heeled sharply. As it plunged head-on into the steep waves, spray dashed against André's face. Huddled beside Jean in the bow, he was soon drenched. In the stern sheets, Monsieur Marion unhurriedly trimmed the sails and adjusted their direction until the motion was more comfortable and they were no longer shipping so much water. 'Are you happy to carry on, gentlemen?' he shouted, his voice whipped away by the wind.

'Pourquoi pas?' replied Jean, his eyes gleaming in his wet face. 'What's a little wind, sir? Besides, we're keen to see what's around the corner.'

The expedition leader laughed. 'Hang on then.' It was not unusual for him to take the helm on such excursions to explore their environs, and he clearly relished this chance to test his own skills. Jean said this habit kept him in touch with the reality of life at sea, and the men admired him for occasionally setting aside the aloof role of captain. But their fellow ensign, the starchy Chevillard, predictably disapproved of such behaviour, believing it undermined Monsieur Marion's authority. He had made excuses not to join them, muttering something about urgent inventories and accounts.

As they weathered the cape with its skirt of treacherous rocks and swirling currents, the expedition leader eased the sheets and turned the longboat towards the far western shore. With their lee gunwale almost awash, they surged onwards, the two ensigns whooping with exhilaration. Even Monsieur Marion had a grin on his face as he coaxed maximum speed from the heavy longboat. The unhappy soldiers delegated to accompany them clutched the gunwale and gritted their teeth, green with seasickness. André heard Thomas Ballu, the old sergeant-at-arms, mutter alternate curses and prayers under his breath.

Far behind them, the ensign saw the *Castries'* yawl pitching in the head-on seas off the cape they had named the Cape of Currents. Even as he watched, he saw the yawl go about and run for shelter. 'Monsieur du Clesmeur's turned back, sir,' he reported. True to form, he thought, the captain would be maintaining both his dignity and his customary caution.

'His boat's not as well suited as ours for these conditions.' Monsieur Marion was diplomatic. 'He's wise not to risk being overturned.'

'Wisdom hardly comes into it,' Jean shouted directly into André's ear, confident he could not be overheard over the boom of straining canvas and the thrum of taut stays. 'That cowardly milksop's wet behind the ears.'

As they crossed the mouth of the bay, endless ranks of still higher waves drove at them, and the wind increased to gale force. Encapsulated by the sound and fury of wind and water, even their robust longboat started to feel like a fragile cockleshell. The soldiers were forced to help the boatmen bail frantically as they shipped wave after wave. André was beginning to think the milksop's caution had indeed been wise. In his opinion, it was only Monsieur Marion's excellent seamanship that was keeping them out of serious difficulties. But neither his captain nor his equally risk-loving cousin was showing any sign of concern. André stifled his growing qualms, having no wish to be classed a coward like the captain of the *Castries*.

'We'll soon reach shelter on the far side of the bay,' the expedition leader shouted reassuringly, as they shipped yet more water.

At last they gained some protection from a cape to the north of them. In less turbulent waters, they turned to run along the western coast of another huge harbour — if anything, even bigger than Port Marion. They negotiated a narrow passage behind an island, first passing close to a bank of curious rounded rocks banded in brown and black that lay like puddings in the sea. Beyond this island, they could see several other large inlets, but the seas were too rough for them to explore further in that direction.

When the sailing became easier, despite the need to negotiate frequent reefs and snags, the expedition leader handed the tiller over to Jean. He took up his eyeglass to scan the shoreline and the land beyond. 'Keep your eyes peeled, Monsieur Tallec — somewhere in this magnificent countryside we're bound to find timber large enough to re-mast the *Castries*.'

Although they cruised along the western coast for the rest of the morning, carefully examining any promising patch of woodland for tall trees, they found nothing suitable. Most of the land had been cleared of trees. Everywhere they looked, the slopes behind the coastline were either cultivated or lying fallow under a green swathe of bracken fern. Forest clad only a few gullies and the distant inland hills. As in Port Marion, fortified villages occupied many of the headlands and hilltops. At midday, cold from their wetting and hungry after a pre-dawn start, they decided to go ashore in a sheltered bay where two small undefended villages nestled on terraces behind the beach.

Almost before they had time to collect driftwood and light a good fire, Zealanders arrived from one of these villages, bringing them fresh fish. After the usual prolonged greetings and the exchange of gifts, the Naturals lingered nearby to watch the Frenchmen. Amidst excited exclamations from their visitors, André and Jean stripped to their drawers so they could drape their wet clothes on sticks to dry near the fire. The soldiers and the boatmen were too self-conscious to do likewise, and Monsieur Marion, in this at least, preferred to retain his dignity.

Leaving their companions to huddle around the fire, the two ensigns made their way along the beach to a rocky platform where they found many large oysters. When they started knocking the shellfish off the rocks, one of the Zealanders, who had followed them at a safe distance, came forward to offer them the use of a woven sack. André, feeling adventurous, tried out some of the words he was learning from Te Kape, now a frequent visitor on board the ship and at the shore camp on Marion Island.

'Pi-pi?' he said, holding out a handful of the oysters. 'Carreca?'

The Natural beamed at him. He opened one of the oysters and slurped up the contents, smacking his lips, then gestured at André to do the same.

'Fort bien, cousin,' said Jean, impressed. 'He definitely understood — what did you say?'

'Nothing difficult,' said André modestly. 'I think it means "good oysters" or something like that.'

Encouraged, the Naturals now crowded around them, helping to pry oysters off the rocks until the sack was full. They then accompanied the ensigns back to the fire, constantly asking questions. André could make nothing of what they were saying, his momentary elation at being understood soon deflated.

Jean consoled him. 'At least you tried, and they seem fast friends with us as a result.'

Before the Frenchmen had finished an excellent meal of fish and oysters, shared with their visitors, Jean spotted a large canoe being paddled towards them, just outside the breaker line. It was a remarkable sight, propelled at great speed through the water by close to a hundred men, all wielding their paddles in unison as they responded with deep grunts to the sonorous call of the fugleman pacing up and down in the centre of the canoe. Streamers flew from a tall, carved stern post, and the bow was adorned with a grotesquely carved figure with the long, sinuous protruding tongue the Naturals seemed to favour in their carvings. Standing in the bow, staring straight ahead, was a chief clad in one of the most magnificent dogskin cloaks André had yet seen.

Somewhat nervous, the Frenchmen clambered to their feet as the paddlers turned the canoe and brought it ashore on the crest of a breaking wave as neatly as any of their own boatmen. The Naturals left them to rush down to greet the occupants of the canoe, shouting cries of welcome. As the chief and his men came ashore, surrounded by a clamouring crowd, the Frenchmen instinctively drew together, the soldiers with their muskets ready by their sides.

'I'm glad we had time to get dressed,' Jean muttered. 'I'd not like to be caught naked by this lot.'

Monsieur Marion overheard. 'Have you not yet learned that we receive nothing but friendliness from these people?' He told the soldiers to put their muskets away. 'Follow me. I'm confident this chief will treat us well.'

The chief, as handsome as his canoe, was indeed friendly. He did not seem surprised to see them, and André realized he must have known of their presence in Port Marion, over four leagues away. He watched as the chief came forward to greet Monsieur Marion, treating him as an equal. Before long, they were able to go and examine the large canoe closely, the chief obviously proud of it and willing to try to answer their questions.

'Look at this hull — it's entirely fashioned from one massive tree trunk!' Monsieur Marion was excited.

They paced out the length of the canoe. It was all of sixty-seven feet long and over six feet wide, the largest they had seen. Superbly made, even the planking around its sides that raised the freeboard was finely carved and decorated with bunches of feathers.

'Ask him where such trees can be found,' Jean urged André.

The young ensign tried, with sign language and many gestures, not having the words to use. The chief seemed to understand and sent them off to explore a stand of trees not far inland. Although they found some fine timber, they came across nothing of a size to match the canoe or suitable for fashioning spars. Disappointed, and with evening drawing near, they returned to their longboat and bade the Zealanders farewell.

It was a long haul against a still-strong wind and wild sea. Darkness had long fallen before the weary explorers saw the welcome red glow from the braziers set to light them back to the ships.

Later, the ensigns joined the senior officers in the great cabin where Monsieur Marion had invited them for supper. Sipping a welcome glass of Burgundy, Jean said disconsolately, 'That was a waste of time, sir. We're no closer to finding a source of timber for the masts.'

Monsieur Marion did not agree. 'You're too quick to lose heart, Monsieur Roux. That canoe proves we'll find suitable trees somewhere in the area.'

'The chief definitely understood what we wanted, sir,' André offered. 'Word will get around.'

'We'll continue to search,' said Monsieur Marion. He added with a glint in his eye. 'Surely you don't object to such excursions, Monsieur Roux? I had the distinct impression you were enjoying yourself. But if not, I can always assign you to shore duties.'

'Mille pardons, sir,' Jean said hastily. 'It was indeed a fine opportunity to explore such beautiful country further. I'm merely impatient to restore our ships to good order.'

'Your zeal does you proud, sir,' observed Monsieur Crozet, who had been stuck on board all day supervising repairs to the ship, laid over on her side to give better access to her hull. 'Tomorrow you can assist me.'

The second-in-command blandly ignored Jean's anguished expression. He had more pressing matters on his mind. He turned to Monsieur Marion. 'We're having a bit of trouble with the savages. Twice today I caught them sneaking aboard and pilfering anything that wasn't fastened down. Monsieur Le Corre's having similar problems at the shore camp. I took the liberty of sending more soldiers to guard both the hospital tent and those huts where we're storing our equipment.'

After the expedition leader had ascertained that only small trifles were being taken by the Zealanders, he said, 'We must be careful not to over-react, gentlemen. All primitive peoples are great thieves, and to them we have much to envy. What's more, these Naturals don't have the same attitude to possessions as us, sharing everything communally.'

The second-in-command nodded patiently. 'Indeed, sir. I take your point, but nevertheless I urge vigilance.'

'D'accord.' Monsieur Marion gave way graciously, but with strict instructions that no one was to retaliate. 'Ensure anything of value is well-guarded night and day, both on the ships and ashore. Boost the shore guard to fifteen soldiers, Monsieur Crozet, and allocate two officers to supervise there from now on. Prevention's better than punishment in my experience. I want no actions taken that risk our friendship with these people.'

Next day, much to Jean's annoyance, the ensigns were indeed put to work overseeing the ongoing work of repairing the *Mascarin's* foreparts, with the ship again being laid over on her side. Later in the day, André was put in charge of the longboat to go and cut firewood along the shore of Marion Island and another island to the west, while Jean took the yawl to load casks of water from the stream. These mundane tasks occupied them for several days, until Monsieur Marion took pity and invited them to join him again, this time exploring the eastern bays of the harbour. The chief Te Kuri, now a frequent visitor to both the ships and the shore camp, had led him to believe they would find some good trees there, not far from his village.

Te Kuri's village sprawled along the top of the large peninsula near where the ships were anchored, above a narrow isthmus linked to the mainland. It was the biggest village they had seen. As the longboat approached the cove below, André could see hundreds of its inhabitants lined up on the hill. Waving branches of greenery, they swayed back and forth, chanting some sort of chorus in response to wailing by the women. Several men came down to the beach to greet them, and insisted on carrying the officers ashore so they kept their feet dry. André's bearer was an enormous man, heavily tattooed and ferocious-looking, but he was handled as gently as a baby, put down on the beach and carefully patted. Jean, already ashore, was watching. 'This is the life, cousin!' he called. 'I don't mind being treated like royalty.'

Monsieur Marion in particular was made a great fuss of, it being obvious the Zealanders now recognized him as the chief of the two ships. Escorted by their bearers, the Frenchmen climbed the hill to the village. The people lined up outside the entrance, women and children amongst them, were still singing and wailing, waving their greenery in a performance André thought must be quite exhausting. Te Kuri was waiting with his family and subordinate chiefs. As soon as the Frenchmen approached, a young warrior emerged from the ranks to grunt and prance in front of them in what they now knew to be a ritual challenge offered to important visitors like Monsieur Marion. When the challenger retreated, the chiefs came forward to greet them. The welcome chorus continued its din throughout the time it took for each of these chiefs to embrace the Frenchmen and press noses with them. Te Kuri made sure they understood that the young boy with him was his favoured son, a personable lad of about fourteen. At last the ceremonies were over. They were led into the village by an enthusiastic crowd, who constantly plucked at their clothing and examined their white skins.

André was relieved when they were finally allowed to sit down on the parade ground outside the chief's house to wait for food to be brought to them. The important men of the village sat with them while the women served small, freshly woven, sword-grass platters heaped with cooked fish wrapped in leaves, some sweet potato and quantities of dried fern root, which they now knew was the Zealanders' staple food. Te Kape and Te Kuri's son sat close beside the two ensigns and encouraged them to try everything. They tasted the fern root cautiously, spitting out the coarse fibres the way their companions showed them. André found the starchy paste somewhat bitter and drying in his mouth, but judging from the relish with which their hosts tackled it, he thought it must be an acquired taste. All around them, family groups were also preparing their morning meal, everyone taking turns to roast fern roots on their small fires, then beat them vigorously between two stones before chewing the result. The meal took a long time.

Jean shifted uncomfortably, his legs becoming cramped from sitting so long on the ground. 'No wonder they eat so much of our ship's biscuit,' he said. 'They're accustomed to eating huge quantities.'

'But none of them seem to get fat,' said André. 'This stuff must be healthy.'

'It's certainly monotonous.' Jean grimaced as he struck a particularly bitter mouthful of fern root he was forced to spit out surreptitiously. The keen-eyed Te Kape saw him and laughed good-naturedly.

The interminable meal at last over, Te Kuri led them on a conducted tour of his village, allowing them to enter any building and hut they pleased. They were followed by a crowd of Zealanders, amongst whom Jean at last spotted a young woman who met his exacting standards of beauty. He nudged André. 'Now she's more like it, cousin,' he hissed. 'Look at her, she's quite comely.'

The young woman was certainly less buxom than most of her companions, and her legs were well-shaped, if still somewhat grossly muscled as was typical of the Naturals. Her glossy black hair hung in waves on either side of her face, and her dark eyes were large and lustrous. Although her lips were painted or tattooed the usual black, both ensigns were now used to this and no longer found it unattractive. She quickly became aware of Jean's interest. Ducking her head so that her hair hid her face, she seemed at first as shy as the young woman the ensigns had entertained on board the *Mascarin*. But André soon realized she was darting bright-eyed glances at his cousin and taking every opportunity to place herself in his view.

The layout of the village and its contents were similar to those of the heavily fortified village they had visited on Marion Island. Situated on a steep hill, it had palisades on one side only. Presumably Te Kuri felt secure enough. It had become obvious to the French officers that his status was the subject of envy in the area. Already some of the other chiefs who visited the ships had asked for their help in attacking him, and the Frenchmen had observed several small skirmishes much like the one in which Ballu had taken part. In Te Kuri's presence, however, these same chiefs showed nothing but good fellowship — if not actual deference. Monsieur Thirion was intrigued by such evidence of political deviousness, but Monsieur Crozet considered the skirmishes were merely muscle-flexing, a bit of posturing. He pointed out that Te Kuri had more than enough warriors to ward off any serious challenge to his authority.

Once the Frenchmen had explored everything, Te Kuri indicated they should embark on the longboat once more so his men could take them to the promised forests of suitable trees. Jean's young woman stood forlornly at the water's edge until he blew her kisses and placed his hand over his heart. Then she laughed and turned away. Te Kape, in close attendance on the two ensigns, did not miss this interchange. He laughed also, then made it clear he was willing to arrange a meeting as soon as it suited Jean.

'Excellent,' said Jean, clapping him on the shoulder.

'And what of Monsieur Marion's embargo?' asked André, grinning.

'What of it?' the senior ensign replied. 'Surely I'd be insulting these savages' notion of hospitality if I spurned her? Besides, I've every intention of being discreet — Monsieur Marion need not know about it.' He gave his cousin a mock glare. 'You, of course, will say nothing.'

'But of course,' said André, pretending indignation. 'None of my business what you get up to when you're off duty.'

Although the ravines they visited that day were indeed forested, they contained no trees tall enough for spars, much to Monsieur Marion's chagrin. Back at the landing place, he pointed out the largest of the accompanying canoes, which was almost as fine as the one they had seen in the western harbour. Getting André to pace its length, he then indicated by many gestures that they needed trees of similar size. Te Kape, quick on the uptake once more, promised to take them to the very place they had obtained the tree for this canoe. He took them onto a hill from where they could see the entire harbour spread out below them, then pointed inland, south to forest growing on a high range of mountains that ran behind the port. 'Apopo,' he said, waving in that direction.

André knew what that meant. 'He'll take us there tomorrow, sir.'

**Extract from the Te Kape manuscript, 1841**

*Te Kuri was ill-pleased by Mariou's people setting up their houses on Moturua instead of near his own stronghold, since this action weakened his position as their host. Accordingly, when Ngati Pou chose to overlook the transgressions of the strangers from the sea, and, instead offered them lavish hospitality on that island, he saw this as a direct challenge to his mana, one that he could not afford to ignore.*

*Accordingly, when other chiefs from the wider district also began approaching te iwi o Mariou and receiving gifts from them, Te Kuri put aside his growing irritation at the uncouth behaviour of the strangers. He renewed his efforts to claim them for himself by offering them the freedom of his own stronghold on Orokawa, and, at the same time he frequently joined Mariou on board his ship and accompanied that principal chief of the strangers wherever he wished to go.*

*When it became clear that the gift Mariou desired most was tall trees to carry the stacked sails on his ships, Te Kuri sent me to lead Mariou's people to the very place where we mark and set aside for many generations the most chiefly kauri trees for our descendants to make into war canoes. He was confident te iwi o Mariou would properly acknowledge such unprecedented generosity, thus upholding his mana and the associated wellbeing of our people.*

# Chapter 7

Reduced to awed silence, André and Jean stood with Monsieur Marion and Te Kape amongst the biggest trees they had ever seen. Some sort of cedar, their massive trunks, many feet in girth, scarcely tapered until they reached a circle of branches high above. André forgot his aching legs, muscles strained from trudging at least two leagues up and down never-ending hills from the bay where they had left the yawl. He forgot his wet breeches, stiff with mud from the fetid swamp they had traversed, sometimes wading up to their waists in ice-cold, black water. He forgot the itching discomfort of bites from the swarms of tiny gnats that besieged them. These trees had an almost regal presence, their trunks uncluttered by moss or clinging ferns. Nothing but some sort of fine-leaved sword-grass grew around their bases. In the dim, filtered forest light, they thrust up through the surrounding smaller trees like the columns of a Greek temple. Tentatively, he reached out and touched the trunk closest to him, fingering the hammered bronze scallops of its smooth bark.

'These trunks must have a clean length of eighty feet at least, sir!' Jean broke the silence. 'Tailor-made for spars!'

'Indeed, Monsieur Roux.' The expedition leader nodded. 'Some of these look tall enough to mast a seventy-four-gun ship. In all my travels, I've never seen such superb trees so well suited to our purposes.'

'There's one problem, sir,' André ventured. 'It's going to be the devil's own job getting them out of here — let alone cutting them down.' He was reliving the more than four hours of hard physical effort it had taken to reach the forest.

They were standing on the crest of a narrow ridge. The most suitable trees were rooted further down the steep slopes that plunged away on either side of them. Those closer to them on the ridge top were ideal for canoe hulls, certainly, but they were too large in girth for spars.

Jean peered over the edge of a precipice. 'Pardieu, cousin!' he exclaimed. 'Trust you to bring us down to earth.' He turned to Monsieur Marion. 'Perhaps we should continue looking, sir — maybe find specimens that grow nearer the shore? André's right. Getting trees out of here would be a Herculean task.'

Monsieur Marion shrugged. 'This young Zealander has probably done his utmost to bring us to the most accessible and suitable trees. We can but hope we do find what we need closer to the sea.'

Buoyed up by their find, they made their way back to the coast. Although they explored every promising patch of woodland that still grew along the many streams meandering across the broad valley behind the bay, it became clear Te Kape had indeed done his best. The Zealanders had felled any suitable trees long since. They had no choice but to tackle the trees on the ridge in the forest far inland. Jean estimated it would take several weeks of hard labour. 'We'll have to form a road of sorts across those hills, then fill that swamp with fascines to provide dry footing before we can even begin to extract any spars.'

Monsieur Marion reminded them that the Zealanders had succeeded in getting out even larger trees for their canoes from the same inland forest. 'You lack fortitude, gentlemen. Surely where Naturals can succeed, we'll have no difficulty — or none that our superior technology won't overcome.' He added, 'It's not as though we're pressed for time. With the Zealanders so willing to supply us with food, I see no reason to leave until our people are fully recovered and the ships in good shape. We're well set up here. Even if it takes a month to extract these spars, it should not cause us any problem.'

Their captain could turn any disadvantage into an apparent positive. No one could doubt the real reason they had already stayed so long was the damage caused by their collision in the Southern Ocean. Now the need to expend even more effort to re-mast the *Castries* meant they would have to prolong their stay in these southern waters well into the depths of winter, further compromising the success of their expedition. A lesser man would take the opportunity to point out the ongoing consequences of Monsieur du Clesmeur's ineptitude. Although André knew his cousin would attribute Monsieur Marion's forebearance to his endless accommodation of the young aristocrat's sensibilities, the ensign admired his captain's restraint.

But it soon proved there were limits to even the expedition leader's tolerance. As soon as they returned to the ships, he ordered Monsieur du Clesmeur to take charge of establishing another shore camp to supply the men who would cut the spars needed to re-mast the *Castries*. 'No doubt you'll want to supervise this vital work in person, sir,' he said firmly. He did not have to spell out the reason.

Although Monsieur du Clesmeur seemed unenthusiastic at the thought of being based on shore, at some distance from the ships and the accustomed comfort of his great cabin, he had no choice but to agree. 'I'd appreciate the help of as many men as possible, sir.'

Monsieur Marion nodded. 'We'll spare as many as we can — from both ships.'

Jean nudged André. 'Our captain's a shrewd one!' he whispered.

'In one stroke, he's forced that idle sot to take some responsibility, leaving himself free to socialize with chiefs and explore.'

The young ensign could only agree. His admiration for Monsieur Marion grew even stronger.

His cousin then took great pleasure in telling Monsieur du Clesmeur about the difficulties of the terrain they had traversed. Regaling him with details of the thick, black mud and the slippery, narrow native trail they had followed up and down steep hills, across scrub country through head-high fern and into dense forest, he soon had the captain looking even less enthusiastic. Enjoying his sport, Jean would have continued, but Monsieur Marion fixed him with a steely glare. 'Seeing you remember the route so well, sir, you'll be the ideal person to guide Monsieur du Clesmeur to the trees we found. You can then help construct the shore camp in the southern bay.'

André choked back laughter as his cousin swallowed his objections, only too aware he had been outplayed at his own game. Jean never learned. Now he also would be stuck ashore, more than four leagues away from the ships — and out of contact with the young woman from Te Kuri's village to whom he had taken such a fancy. Now he thought about it, André would not be surprised if Monsieur Marion had indeed noticed his senior ensign's lustful glances and was seizing the opportunity to remove him from temptation.

Ignoring this side play, Monsieur Crozet was preoccupied with objections of his own. Now he said, a worried frown on his face, 'I'm concerned this means we'll be spreading our men far and wide. Is it wise, sir, to set up a shore station so far out of sight of the ships, a good hour's sailing away?'

'Your point, Monsieur Crozet?' It was the expedition leader's turn to frown.

'You perhaps forget the extent to which we're at the mercy of these savages, sir,' said Monsieur Crozet. He was careful to keep his voice neutral. 'If we're spread so thinly, they may be tempted to attack us. You yourself point out how much they covet the iron we have, and they continue to pilfer anything we leave lying around. What's more, their chiefs seem remarkably interested in the layout of both our ships and the shore camp on Marion Island.'

André watched as the expedition leader made an obvious attempt to control his temper. Only Monsieur Crozet, the captain's long-term trusted companion, would have the temerity to question his judgement in such a way.

His neck flushed red, Monsieur Marion said, 'I put such behaviour down to their natural curiosity and intelligence, sir. Do *we* not explore their villages and fortifications with equal curiosity? We make them welcome, and I see no sign these chiefs would in return abuse our hospitality.'

Monsieur Crozet spread his hands. 'Tant mieux. Nevertheless, I urge that we remain alert, sir. It's clear their customary occupation is warfare. They're battle-ready, and we can have no idea what goes on in the savage mind.'

'We understand each other well enough,' said Monsieur Marion.

André was not sure whether he meant his senior officer or the Zealanders, and he suspected Monsieur Crozet did not know either.

The expedition leader then added, 'But if it would put your mind at rest, by all means maintain armed soldiers at both camps.'

The second-in-command had to accept that this was the only concession he would get. 'I've already sent blunderbusses ashore to the hospital camp, sir. Monsieur du Clesmeur should arm his shore guard-post likewise.'

'Just make sure a few soldiers remain on board the ships to accompany the boats and any excursions.' Gesturing to François to

147

pour more wine, Monsieur Marion made it clear he had heard enough about a concern he felt had little substance.

### Extract from the Te Kape manuscript, 1841

*We expected just payment for the kauri trees thus gifted to be delayed until they had been dragged out of the forest by Mariou's people. But the persistent failure of those strangers to reciprocate the many gifts of food and treasures or the value of the firewood they took began to irk others than Te Kuri. Accordingly, when those strangers continued to point out things of value they fancied in expectation of receiving them, our people took it upon themselves to seize tempting small items left lying around by Mariou's people as plunder to compensate for their lack of adequate repayment. For such was our way of maintaining social control and ensuring balanced exchanges between different peoples.*

*Those strangers failed to respond to such plunder by acknowledging their debt and making amends so the mana of our chiefs would be restored. Accordingly, certain chiefs — amongst them those Ngati Pou chiefs living on Moturua — openly began assessing the strength of te iwi o Mariou as a way of showing their growing contempt for an ignorant people who did not honour their obligations.*

Delayed by yet more bad weather, it was some days before Monsieur du Clesmeur — accompanied by the reluctant Jean — was able to return to the southern bay. André, rostered on duty at the hospital camp on Marion Island with Lieutenant Lehoux, watched the two longboats set off. On board were the fifty men assigned to build huts on the shore as a base for the masting operations. They would then construct a road two leagues into the interior so the trees felled by the carpenters could be dragged back to the shore. It would be some time before he saw his cousin again, but he had no reason to feel lonely. Te Kape now joined him most days, only too willing to help with his tasks.

Every morning, a wooding party went to cut firewood in the forest-clad gully behind the hospital tent, for the use of both the camp and the two ships. Up until now, they had cut anything of suitable size, but much had proved sullen in the burning or over-smoky. André asked Te Kape, close behind him as always, to show them the best trees for the purpose. It took some inspired miming and lots of laughter before the youth understood what was wanted. He then lay hold of one of the sailors' axes, persuading him to let go with smiles and nods.

'Prenez garde — the young devil's running off with that axe!' Lieutenant Lehoux exclaimed, his hand going to his pistol as Te Kape wandered off into the nearest copse. 'Pardieu — you can't trust these savages for one minute.'

André protested. 'He's merely trying to help.'

But the ever-suspicious lieutenant did not relax until he saw what the young Zealander was about. Te Kape examined each tree of suitable size in the copse, then notched some with the axe. He called the lieutenant to join him, gave him the axe with a grin that showed he was well aware of the officer's misgivings, then indicated the marked trees.

'Diable!' Lieutenant Lehoux muttered, discomfited at being shown up by a Natural. He hesitated, then tried to hand the axe back to Te Kape. 'Here — keep it.' When the young Zealander held back, he turned to André. 'What did you say his name was?'

'Ta-Capaye, sir,' said André.

'You then, Ta-Ca— whatever.' The lieutenant had no patience with the local language. He thrust the axe at him with both hands. 'For you.'

Te Kape's face lit up. He mimed exaggerated delight, then gravely taking the axe, he stepped forward and insisted on pressing noses with the lieutenant until the French officer pushed him away. 'Pardieu — it's only an axe. No need to go on so!'

Over his head, Te Kape met André's eye and waggled his eyebrows. It was all the ensign could do to keep a straight face. Monsieur Marion was right, he thought, goodwill and gesture were more than enough to ensure a satisfactory level of understanding with the Zealanders, despite the lack of shared language. As time went on, he liked this youth more and more. They were fast becoming friends.

As if to emphasize his point, Te Kape worked tirelessly with the wooding party, cutting as much firewood with his new axe as three of the sailors could in the same time. And all along, his face never lost its beam of good humour. Even the lieutenant grudgingly admitted he was an asset.

Later, when the off-duty André had Monsieur Marion's permission to accompany Te Kape in his canoe back to Te Kuri's village on the mainland, the young Zealander showed endless patience in trying to answer the ensign's mimed questions and explain his people's curious customs. Even though André was not always sure what Te Kape was talking about, he appreciated his efforts. But one of the things Te Kape could not explain by gesture was his relationship to Te Kuri, that austere figure who seemed to be the leading chief in the whole of Port Marion. André had already realized he could not be one of the chief's sons — he had just the one, the quiet boy who stuck close to his father's side, even sleeping on board the *Mascarin* when Te Kuri chose to do so. But he thought Te Kape must be a relative of some sort as he ate at the chief's fireside, and the ensign was expected to do likewise when he visited the village, even when he was not with the expedition leader. The closest André could get was to assume the chief was

Te Kape's protector and mentor in the same way Jean was his own protector and maître.

Even though Te Kuri always made him and any of the other French officers welcome in his village, extending impeccable hospitality, André still found the chief somewhat unnerving. Unlike most of the Zealanders they came across, Te Kuri seldom smiled, and never laughed. He did not indulge in any of the childlike, expressive or volatile behaviour characteristic of most of the Naturals, one moment rolling around laughing heartily, the next arguing fiercely with one of their companions. There was nothing of the simple sort about Te Kuri. If anything, despite him being the Natural, it was André who felt gauche and inadequate in his presence.

So on this visit, when Te Kape took him to where the chief was sitting with all his senior men on the parade ground outside his house, the ensign was even more uncomfortable than usual. From the Naturals' demeanour, it seemed to be a formal occasion. But when he hesitated, thinking it highly inappropriate to join them, the young Zealander urged him forward until he was standing alone in front of the chief.

André pulled back his shoulders and tried to appear at ease, but in reality his legs were trembling and his heart pumped faster than usual. He was only too aware that he was alone. None of his companions had come ashore with him. Flattered at being invited on his own, he had thought smugly it was a sign of his special friendship with Te Kape. Now he was wondering whether he had been foolish. His only protection was his ensign's dirk, carried as always in its scabbard at his side. He tried to keep his hand from straying to its hilt. More and more of the villagers were now gathering behind the senior people, come to see what was happening. He was surrounded by Naturals. Long moments passed, and he stood his ground, his chin lifted proudly. If he were about to die, he would do so with dignity.

Te Kuri watched him, his tattooed face expressionless as usual. After a time that seemed endless to the ensign, the chief nodded as though satisfied, then gestured to his senior wife, who was sitting just behind him. This woman, as reserved as the chief, had made little attempt to communicate with any of the French officers when they visited the village, nor had she come on board either of the ships. Now she stepped forward and showed André what she was holding in her hand. It was a simple whale tooth, smooth and polished, with the merest suggestion of eyes, nose and mouth etched into one end and a cord threaded through a hole in the other. She lifted this cord over André's head, taking care to avoid touching his hair, then ensured the ivory object lay level against his chest. She smiled slightly at him, then returned to the chief's side. The old man who had first come aboard the *Mascarin* rose to his feet and started some sort of sonorous chant that went on for some time. Then, some of the women joined the chief's wife to sing a lilting, haunting tune accompanied by swaying movements and foot shuffling.

André could hear Te Kape murmuring behind him, but he had no idea what he was saying. Although he was grateful for the chance to recover his equanimity given him by the chanting and singing, he was not sure what he was meant to do now or how to respond. Nothing like this had happened to any of the French officers before, not even to Monsieur Marion. The gift was obviously significant, but he did not dare lift the pendant to examine it more closely. Cursing that he had not thought to bring ashore with him any of the items particularly favoured by the Zealanders, he stepped forward when the women finished, intending to give Te Kuri his dirk. At the last moment, he remembered how the chief did not himself handle any of the exchange gifts he received on board the ship. So he stooped and placed the silver-hilted dagger at the chief's feet. A murmur of approval ran through the assembled people. It seemed he had done the right thing. He put his hand on his heart, then said thank you, nodding and smiling.

Te Kuri inclined his head. After a pause, he stood up and took off the short, feathered cape he was wearing. The Naturals all drew in their breath with a loud hiss. Before the startled ensign could react, the chief was placing the cape around André's shoulders. He stooped to press his nose firmly against André's, then turned and addressed his people, gesturing with a wide sweep of his hand at the village, the surrounding hills and the sea. For a moment there was silence, then the Zealanders burst into wild applause and leapt to their feet, dancing and singing.

Amidst the tumult, Te Kape seized André and embraced him, his eyes sparkling with delight. The ensign embraced him back, elated and relieved. He had clearly been given some sort of honour. Only moments ago he had been sure he was about to be killed.

**Extract from the Te Kape manuscript, 1841**

*It might have been expected that Te Kuri would shun people who so threatened his mana, which undermined the balance of our relationships with the ancestors essential for our wellbeing. Instead, while still assessing their strengths and weaknesses and reserving final judgment about their human status, he renewed his efforts in offering Mariou and his subordinate chiefs hospitality at his stronghold on Orokawa. At the same time, he stayed many nights on board the ship, even allowing his only son to spend time with those strangers.*

*Then, he placed under his chiefly protection the one amongst those strangers whose real nature our tohunga were still assessing. This was the youth with an uncanny likeness to the supernatural beings that inhabit the tops of kauri trees and sometimes snatch away our women, he of the flame-red hair, sea-green eyes and skin the colour of sea spume heaped*

*on the shore. On the advice of our tohunga, it was arranged by Te Kuri
that this youth would willingly — and unwittingly — wear an amulet
that would protect our people against any supernatural powers he might
possess. Not realizing the hostile significance of Te Kuri's action, that
youth's instinctive response was to gift the chief his own shining weapon,
a gift of far greater value than any offered by the other strangers from
the sea. It was this innocent generosity that then prompted Te Kuri to
place his cloak around the youth's shoulders, thus putting him under
his chiefly protection — at the same time that he had protected us
against him.*

*My own friendship with a being of such ambiguous nature was at
first merely in response to a dare from my companions, but it grew to
a genuine attraction to his open friendliness and enthusiastic curiosity
about everything he came across, for above all else he was a likeable
youth without guile.*

No matter how well he was received by the Zealanders, André was
soon reminded of his real status. The day after he returned to his
duties at the hospital camp, he was in trouble with his superiors.
As the morning was mild and fine for once, some of the senior
officers' domestic slaves were sent ashore with him to launder the
linen from the great cabin. André found François, the captain's
personal slave, amusing, but he did not usually have any dealings
with the others. Unlike François and the captain's three female
slaves, who slept in the lobby of the great cabin within beck and call
of the senior officers, the one male slave sent ashore was relegated
to the darkest and dankest corner of the lower deck. He was meant
to be responsible for scrubbing out the officers' latrines and doing
any other rough or dirty work needed for their comfort, but he did
the minimum that would avoid a flogging. A sullen and taciturn

man, he was usually found slumped in the corner of Anthonie's galley, where the fat cook tolerated him only because he was afraid of him. Today, Monsieur Marion had allowed him to accompany the women ashore, thinking the fresh air would do his uncertain temper some good.

Although André knew the man would do little if any work, he set him to tending a fire on the beach near the stream outlet to heat water for the laundry. Once he was sure the slaves were getting on with their task, he left them to go with Te Kape and Monsieur Thirion, who was hoping the young Zealander would lead him to new native herbs he could add to his growing stock of useful worts.

On their return a few hours later, there was no sign of the expected industry at the stream outlet. The slaves had disappeared, the smoking ashes of their fire scarcely warm and the linen abandoned where it had been put to soak in the stream. 'Malheureux! Infame!' the dismayed ensign swore vigorously. 'That rogue, that misbegotten scoundrel — I should never have left him unsupervised.'

'Calm yourself, young man,' said Monsieur Thirion. 'They're probably off having a siesta in the bushes — they can't have gone far without a boat.'

But at that very moment, a Natural from the village, who had been delivering baskets of fish to the hospital tent, came back down to the beach. He stopped and looked puzzled, then started capering up and down, yelling. He rushed up to André and the surgeon, then dragged them bodily along the beach. Pointing at grooves in the sand, he sketched the shape of a canoe with his hands, his aggrieved cries making it clear his means of transport had been taken. It took all their patience, Te Kape's help and an inordinate number of decent-sized nails before he would accept there was nothing they could do. The slaves had absconded. There was no sign of them or the canoe.

When André faced up to Monsieur Crozet back on board the *Mascarin*, the second-in-command was not pleased. 'Diable! I told Monsieur Marion he was taking a risk letting that malcontent ashore.'

'Indeed,' agreed Lieutenant Lehoux. 'If the rogue finds favour with any of the savages, he's more than capable of stirring up trouble for us.'

On hearing the bad news, Monsieur Marion was more put out by the loss of his female slaves than by any fears of trouble. 'I don't think the people here will pay much heed to a lowly male slave.'

❧ ❧

They did not learn what had happened until the following day when Chevillard returned with the longboat from a nearby island, where he had spent the afternoon supervising the collection of boulders suitable for ballast. As soon as the longboat fastened to the chains, the captain's clerk handed up a bedraggled and hungry female slave.

Weeping profusely, she told them their male companion had bullied the three women into taking the small canoe and setting out to escape to the mainland. But as soon as they got beyond the sheltered lee of Marion Island, the waves threatened to swamp the overloaded craft. 'That man,' she wailed, wringing her hands. 'That man, he up with the oar, he split my friend's head, killed her dead, then he tipped her into the sea.'

Terrified she would suffer the same fate, the woman had leapt overboard. Only luck and a favourable current had seen her fetch up on the shore of the island. She spent a miserable, cold day ashore before Chevillard and the men from the longboat came across her. She had no idea whether the other slaves had reached land safely, but she knew they intended making for Te Kuri's village, him being the chief they had seen sleep on board many times.

'That's not good news, sir,' said Monsieur Crozet, frowning. 'I don't trust Tacoury. If the slave gets that far, he could well encourage the chief to attack us.'

'Such fears are surely unfounded,' Monsieur Marion objected. 'You suspect Tacoury simply on the basis that he's a man of obvious intelligence. Merely because he sees himself as our equal and behaves accordingly is no good reason for you to distrust him.'

'I can affirm your good opinion of him, sir.' André showed them his pendant and told them about the ceremony in which it had been presented, the way Te Kuri had draped his own cape around his shoulders. 'Not that I can show you the cape,' he confessed. 'It was taken back from me before I left the village.'

Monsieur Crozet examined the whale tooth and sniffed. 'Clearly not something of value,' he said disparagingly. 'Now, if it'd been one of those splendid frog-like jade ornaments some of the savages wear, Monsieur Tallec, I might be convinced — they're obviously treasured. Or if you still had that cape.'

The expedition leader was at first inclined to be cross. 'You gave your dirk for *this*? Pardieu, Monsieur Tallec — your actions have inflated what the Zealanders will expect us to pay from now on.'

André wanted to explain that trade had not come into it, that Te Kuri had given him something special, an unsolicited gift. In his heart he was confident something significant had taken place, but it was hard to find the right words.

Besides, in his usual way, Monsieur Marion had already relented. 'You're making too much of it, young man,' he said, not unkindly. 'Tacoury simply likes how well you're getting on with that young Zealander who hangs around you like a faithful pup — he seems to be some sort of protégé.'

Before André could explain further, Lieutenant Lehoux said to the expedition leader, 'Ma fois, sir, maybe that in itself is reason enough for caution. That young savage could well be a spy of sorts, with his constant presence wherever we happen to be.'

Monsieur Marion dismissed this as paranoia. 'Monsieur Tallec's hardly the only officer to make a friend amongst the Zealanders — both you gentlemen seem to favour certain of them with your gifts and welcome their attentions.'

Neither would he countenance Monsieur Crozet's claim that it was Te Kuri he was wary of, saying any particular friendships formed between the officers and the Naturals could only foster the good relationships already established. As for Te Kuri, the expedition leader had nothing but admiration for him. 'I would trust him with my life, sir.'

When Te Kuri not only captured the two missing slaves but also returned them to the *Mascarin*, it seemed the expedition leader was vindicated in his stance. Monsieur Crozet was reduced to silence on the matter. He vented some of his frustration by having the male slave flogged at the windlass as a deterrent to the others. Although most of the Naturals seemed peculiarly upset by the punishment, some of them even weeping and wringing their hands, the chief himself watched impassively, only leaving the ship when the flogging was over.

Even more telling in Te Kuri's favour to Monsieur Marion's mind was another incident a few days later. The ship was once again surrounded by dozens of canoes. People from various villages around Port Marion swarmed all over the deck with their baskets of fish, game birds and potatoes, eager to trade. Many of them now targeted particular sailors whom they found obliging. Some of their women disappeared below, a customary practice ever since Monsieur Marion had decided congress between them and the ship's people could only contribute to harmony with the Zealanders. Amidst the cheerful racket, Te Kuri stood on the quarterdeck with the expedition leader. He barely acknowledged André's presence, but the ensign considered that was probably a matter of protocol, seeing the chief had come to visit the captain. He was sure the chief's quick eyes spotted that he was still wearing the whale tooth.

Trade was proceeding nicely when the ever-vigilant sergeant-at-arms, old Thomas Ballu, noticed one of the Naturals climbing out the gunroom porthole back into his canoe. The man was clutching a cutlass he had stolen from the rack of weapons housed in the gunroom. 'Au voleur! Au voleur!' he shouted, pointing. 'Thief!'

Before any of the Frenchmen could react, Te Kuri turned and said something quietly to his companions. The thief was soon bundled back on board and brought in front of Monsieur Marion by the chief's men, who solemnly returned the cutlass to Monsieur Crozet.

'What should we do, sir?' the second-in-command asked. 'We can hardly let such a blatant act of stealing something so valuable go unpunished.'

When Monsieur Marion hesitated, considering what might be appropriate, Te Kuri pointed to the windlass where the runaway slave had been chained and flogged in his presence.

'Tacoury wants you to flog him, sir!' exclaimed Monsieur Crozet.

With the chief nodding approval, the expedition leader had the miscreant chained to the windlass. But no sooner was this done than all except Te Kuri's companions abandoned their trade. Leaving their baskets of food where they were, the Zealanders flung themselves from the deck into the sea. As the bemused Frenchmen watched, they swam to their canoes where they were pulled on board. They immediately paddled well clear of the ship.

Monsieur Marion decided to rescind his order to have the thief flogged. 'Just seizing him seems to have got the message across, gentlemen.'

André heard Monsieur Crozet growl to Ballu that their captain was too soft on the savages, that the man deserved proper punishment. The two were agreeing quietly when Lieutenant Lehoux noticed Te Kuri was also leaving the ship. Although done without haste, he had not announced his departure. His canoe carefully skirted those hovering beyond the ship and made for the mainland.

'Perhaps you're right not to proceed with the flogging, sir,' Monsieur Crozet said slowly, rubbing his angular jaw as he thought the matter through. 'I'm now wondering whether that wily chief has somehow manipulated us.'

Monsieur Marion became impatient. 'I begin to think Tacoury stands no chance with you, no matter what he does. He's simply content to leave the rest to us.'

As soon as Te Kuri's canoe had disappeared from sight, several of the other canoes returned to the ship's side. The Naturals began pleading to have the captive released. Their forlorn upturned faces, beseeching eyes and plaintive cries soon had the expedition leader willing to relent. 'Unchain the man!' he ordered.

As the Zealanders paddled off after embracing their freed companion with floods of tears, the resigned Monsieur Crozet looked around at the several dozen baskets of fish and potatoes lying abandoned on the deck. He muttered, 'Diable! At least we've made on the deal — perhaps lack of payment is sufficient dues.'

'Indeed, sir,' said Monsieur Marion. 'I see no merit in using more force than needed to make it clear we're not to be trifled with. Besides, I've noticed beatings do not seem a means of punishment amongst these people. Tacoury was yet again merely demonstrating his goodwill toward us in offering the man up to be punished according to *our* custom.'

But Jean was watching the retreating canoes. 'Non, pardieu,' he said quietly. 'I fear Monsieur Crozet may've been right about his motive, sir.'

They turned to look. The canoe containing their freed captive had merely retreated beyond musket range. His companions were now facing the ship, their paddles brandished high over their heads. The man they had chained stood in the prow. When he saw the French officers were watching, he thumped his chest repeatedly, each time shouting just the one phrase. Each time, the paddlers echoed him, the sound travelling clearly across the water. No one, not even Monsieur Marion, could mistake that sound for anything but defiance.

**Extract from the Te Kape manuscript, 1841**

*Many were the ways in which authority over those strangers was gained by Te Kuri. At the same time, his rivals were turned against them by him taking advantage of the strangers' inexplicable habits. Accordingly, when a runaway black man and his woman were captured and returned to the ships, and Te Kuri saw that the man was bound in chains and severely beaten as punishment, he encouraged Mariou to similarly punish one of his rival chiefs caught plundering a valuable weapon from the strangers. For the reason that being treated as a captive slave violated his personal tapu, that man feared he was in danger of losing the essential protection of his ancestral atua, exposing him to all manner of evils. Although he was released by Mariou, that chief vowed to seek revenge against those strangers for causing him, and through him his people, such spiritual harm.*

*Te Kuri was satisfied that in such ways rival chiefs might be dissuaded from associating with te iwi o Mariou. The favours of those strangers could thus be retained for himself, and, at the same time his ascendancy over those rival chiefs would be asserted.*

'We are pleasantly enough situated, sir, do you not agree?' Monsieur du Clesmeur showed off the efforts of his men at the masting camp with evident pride.

André looked around the small terrace with its four newly erected reed-thatched huts set in a neat square, one for the officers, another for the men, a smaller guard-post and a store. Sheltered from the sea breeze by a small hill crowned with trees, the camp was set well back from the beach. To the south stretched the broad, swampy plain they would have to traverse each day to reach the inland forest.

Joining his cousin, Jean Roux said, 'Anyone would think we're here to stay, not merely camping for a few weeks! That soft aristocrat insisted tents were inadequate and had us build these mansions. Luckily, the savages abandoned some huts they had nearby as soon as we offloaded everything here. We were able to dismantle those for beams and so forth. Even so, we wasted two whole days that would've been better spent constructing the road to the forest.'

'Winter's setting in,' André pointed out. 'Maybe the captain's thinking of his men's wellbeing, not himself.'

'He did choose a good site,' Jean admitted. 'Savages are already bringing us fish each day from a village in the next cove. And most days we manage to pot a few quail and plenty of ducks within minutes of the camp. Lieutenant Le Dez has proved himself an excellent shot. If I didn't regard him as a most conscientious officer, I'd suspect him of using his hunting skills as an excuse to avoid duties here at the camp.'

'No doubt you found sufficient reason to join him,' said André, grinning.

Jean protested his innocence. 'I've been marking out the line for the road into the interior, I'd have you know. If I succeed in bringing down game as we return each evening, that's merely sensible.'

'Oui, oui, I believe you.' André dodged his cousin's friendly punch.

After inspecting the huts, Monsieur Marion insisted on being shown progress on the road across the plain. 'We may as well take this opportunity to go right on and select the trees,' he added. 'The carpenters have given me the exact measurements.'

Monsieur du Clesmeur objected. 'The footing's exceedingly muddy, sir. I see no merit in troubling yourself with such an arduous journey.'

'You forget I'm already familiar with the route,' said Monsieur Marion, his voice cold. 'A little mud's no obstacle.'

'It's already late in the day,' the captain argued. 'We'll be hard pushed to return before dark'

Jean nudged André. 'He's unwilling to let Monsieur Marion see just how little we've accomplished!' he whispered. 'The road's barely started — we've got less than a quarter league beyond the camp.'

'Fi, fi, sir,' said Monsieur Marion. 'Stay behind if you wish. It seems I've more taste for adventure than you.' He turned to Lieutenant Le Dez. 'Will you accompany me, or do you prefer to remain here with your captain?'

Monsieur du Clesmeur hastened to change his mind. 'But of course we both intend accompanying you, sir! I was merely concerned for your health and comfort.'

The expedition leader relented. His voice warmer, he said. 'I have full clearance from our estimable surgeon and have never felt better. You need not concern yourself on my behalf.'

Without further ado, the officers set out along the path through the swampy plain beyond the camp. As Jean had indicated, it was not long before they left the short length of cleared roadway where he and his party had laid bundles of cut myrtle as fascines to provide dry footing. The narrow path then became even muddier than André remembered, no doubt because of the continual rain experienced the previous week. Soon they were floundering thigh-deep through patches of mud, grabbing onto any bush or handy clump of rush to haul themselves onwards. As the day had grown unseasonably warm and muggy, clouds of pesky gnats swarmed around them. They seemed particularly attracted to the beefy, sweating second-in-command from the *Castries*. Cursing vigorously, Monsieur Le Corre was forced to bat them away constantly to avoid being severely bitten.

Much to Jean's barely concealed satisfaction, the hapless captain from the *Castries* managed to plunge up to his waist on one particularly treacherous section. He whispered to André, 'If he'd bothered coming with us on reconnaissance, he would've known to avoid that bit!'

'No doubt you saw no reason to warn him?' André whispered back. But then, none of the others had bothered warning him either. Monsieur Crozet unceremoniously heaved him back onto drier ground by the slack of his frockcoat, then walked on, leaving the captain to wipe the stinking black mud off his soaked breeches as best he could. The ensign hovered, feeling sorry for him. It seemed that even ashore no one other than Monsieur Marion himself was prepared to make any allowances for the young aristocrat — and his tolerance had its limits. Without saying a word, he cut some switches of myrtle with the cutlass issued to replace the dirk given to Te Kuri and handed them to him.

After casting him a startled glance, the captain took the switches, muttering thanks. 'No need to wait for me, Monsieur Tallec. Even I can scarcely lose the way, seeing the trail's now as trampled as any left by a herd of elephants.'

André laughed. 'How true, sir!' Not for the first time, he wondered why no one else seemed to notice the man's self-deprecating sense of humour.

When some hours later they reached the steep ridge where the splendid cedars grew, Monsieur Marion immediately sent them off to search for two that would serve best as spars for the *Castries*. Discouraged by the steepness of the surrounding terrain, Monsieur du Clesmeur insisted they spend considerable time looking for more suitable sites. He seemed unwilling to accept that the earlier party had done just that. Monsieur Marion did not argue. By the time they had found and marked a cedar suitable for a bowsprit forty-five foot long and another taller tree further inland for the sixty-five-foot foremast — both on the original ridge — it was close to dusk and they were all weary. They plodded down the hill in silence; no doubt, André thought, all cursing the young captain under their breath for the senseless delay.

Near the edge of the forest, Monsieur Marion suddenly stopped them on the banks of a stream. 'I suggest we stay here for the night, gentlemen,' he said, looking around him. 'The ground under that large tree seems level and dry enough, with plenty of fuel for a fire.'

'Surely that's not a good idea, sir!' Monsieur Crozet objected. The others all nodded in support.

'Pourquoi pas?' Monsieur Marion asked impatiently. 'I see no reason to continue across those three mountains still to come, not to mention the swamp. Do you wish to negotiate that in the dark?'

'We'd be across the swamp before dark, if we don't delay any longer,' said Monsieur Le Corre. He slapped at his face. 'I for one have no wish to spend a night in the midst of these gnats.'

'We have no provisions,' said Monsieur Crozet. 'A night in the open might prove more unpleasant than traversing the last of the path in darkness.'

'We're virtually unarmed,' added Monsieur du Clesmeur. 'Only one musket between us and very little powder. We risk attack.'

Monsieur Marion was now in no mood to be conciliatory. 'The night's mild, this spot's idyllic, and we've seen no sign of Zealanders all day. Where's your spirit of adventure? I intend staying put.' He sat down on a convenient log and took out his snuff box.

It was clear no amount of argument would change his mind. No one dared voice the unease they felt at this prospect of spending a night in the open, in an unfamiliar forest where who knew what wild animals might emerge with the onset of darkness. André thought he would not be the only one amongst them wondering whether this apparently uninhabited forest harboured the same sort of evil spirits and beings that featured so prominently in tales told by the old wives at home in Brittany. He crossed himself surreptitiously, then as an added precaution made the sign against the evil eye.

Monsieur du Clesmeur sighed. 'At least let us send back to camp for food and some guards.'

The expedition leader shrugged. 'As you wish, sir.' His tone implied he thought the young captain a fusspot. But André noticed his face was white, his cheeks flushed the hectic red that signalled he was in for a bout of fever, despite his earlier insistence he was now in full health. Monsieur Marion made no allowances for his age or his condition, he thought, feeling concerned. Close to fifty, and most of those hard years spent at sea, the expedition leader was an old man who should be taking things easy, not running around in such rough country. None of the others seemed to have noticed his exhaustion. They had no choice but to spend the night here. 'Some of us'll go back, sir,' he said quietly. 'We could all do with a decent supper.'

Accompanied by the now badly bitten Le Corre, who would stay at the shore camp, the two ensigns made their way back for supplies. By the time they returned with a few blankets, food and three armed soldiers, night had fallen. They lit their passage the way Te Kape had shown André, with torches made from the bundled dry leaves of a curious tufted tree that grew on the edge of swamps. The ensign found it hard not to start at every shifting shadow and determinedly kept his gaze within the area lit by the flaring torches. The journey back seemed to take forever, none of the terrain they were traversing familiar in the dark. The three soldiers kept up a constant cursing as they stumbled behind the ensigns, their rough words a surprising comfort.

At last, they spotted the glow of a fire ahead of them through the forest. When they reached the spot on the stream bank, they found the small party settled in well enough. With a rough shelter made from fallen branches for the two captains, the rest of them had selected suitable spots under the spreading tree. While they sat around the fire, their mud-soaked clothes drying stiff in its heat, the officers ate the welcome supper of cold quail and bread brought from the shore camp. Monsieur Marion then retired to the shelter, rolling himself up in a blanket. Monsieur du Clesmeur reluctantly followed him.

The two ensigns spread armfuls of dry fern out in the open on the stream bank, and lay studying the sky that stretched above them, thickly studded with brilliant stars. The night was calm and surprisingly mild. Soon, only the screeches and whistles of night birds and the occasional cough from the soldiers on guard broke the quiet.

# Chapter 8

The chief carpenter scratched his head. 'Mort-diable — if you'll pardon the expression, sir. It's a fine stem and well-suited to our purpose, no argument. But you couldn't have chosen a more difficult position for felling a tree.'

Their axes forgotten in their hands, the small group of men stood looking at the tall cedar marked for the bowsprit. They were almost level with its crown of dense whorls of thick, pointed leaves and could barely make out the tree's base, rooted far below them down the steep side of the gully. 'We'll be forced to balance on the side of that precipice, sir,' the carpenter said. 'And that's just to fell the tree. After that, we'll have to winch the thing up out of there.'

'But it *is* possible?' Jean looked at him anxiously. 'It was the most accessible tree we could find, I assure you.'

The petty officer scratched his head again. 'Oui, oui, it's *possible*,' he said, although his voice and body language signalled exasperation at the unrealistic demands of his officers. 'Before we even start, we'll have to rig block and tackle to stop the tree from plunging further down the slope once it's cut.'

Jean had the sense not to say any more. He and André listened in respectful silence while the carpenter and his offsiders discussed what might be needed. It was not long before the petty officer's dourness was replaced by interest in the challenge of the task ahead.

He asked the ensigns to return to the ships. 'We'll need strong ropes, heavy blocks, timber and bolts for constructing shear-legs . . . and see if the captain'll let us have one of those three-hundred-pound kedge anchors.'

André opened his mouth to ask what the anchor was for, but hastily shut it again. The petty officer noticed and nodded at him. 'We need a counterweight for the shear-legs, sir,' he explained. 'And it'll prove useful as a brake once we're lowering the spars down all those mountains in our way.'

Monsieur du Clesmeur had returned to his ship as soon as the shore camp was completed. It seemed his distaste for straw huts, gnats and black mud outweighed any acceptance of his responsibility for overseeing the work on the spars for his ship. Now he restricted himself to the occasional excursion ashore to hunt for quail with the elegant Lieutenant Le Dez — the only officer who willingly tolerated his company. Jean made no attempt to hide his exasperation. 'The pair of them ponce about as though they're enjoying a weekend's hunting on some aristocratic estate back in Brittany. The man's a fool, pardieu. Can't he see such fastidiousness does nothing to endear him to his officers or his men? He seems to be implying that shore work's fit only for those beneath him.'

André could only agree. 'They could have the tact to contribute some of their bag for the shore camp's pot instead of taking it all back for the *Castries*.'

'Out of sight, out of mind.' His cousin shrugged. 'If he's not around, at least he can't keep finding fault.'

While the carpenters were setting up to fell the tree for the bowsprit, the two ensigns continued supervising the widening of the narrow track over the three mountains between them and the coastal plain. Two-thirds of the fit men from both ships — more than a hundred-and-twenty in total — were now deployed for the masting party, most at this stage working on the road. With close to sixty men still ill with scurvy or respiratory ailments of various sorts and bed-ridden at the hospital camp, only a handful were left to continue the equally essential work on Marion Island. Apart from the carpenters still working on the repairs to the *Mascarin*, a party was kept busy filling the water casks as the cooper re-assembled them from staves taken ashore to the island, and another was collecting firewood. The blacksmith at the forge, still occupied with heating and fitting hoops for the water casks, was also now starting on the iron bands that would strengthen the new spars. Without the welcome daily supplies of fish and potatoes brought to both camps by Zealanders from the neighbouring villages, the Frenchmen would be hard put to find time to feed themselves.

At Monsieur Crozet's request, Monsieur Marion split the contingent of forty soldiers amongst the two shore camps and the ships — even he conceded this was a necessary precaution against the Naturals stealing valuable goods or essential tools whenever they saw an opportunity. He still insisted that no retaliation be taken in the face of the constant pilfering of lesser items. 'We can afford to lose the odd handkerchief or offcut of hoop iron, gentlemen. What we cannot afford is being put into the position of having to apprehend and punish more serious offences.'

He did not have to remind them of the cutlass episode, which had shown how punishing any of the Zealanders could risk the good relationships they had established with the local people on whom they were so reliant.

Once word reached the shore camp that the cedar selected for the bowsprit had been chopped through, André and Jean returned to the forest to watch how the men overcame the difficult task of hauling the tree trunk out of the ravine. It had taken the carpenter and his most skilled axemen most of a day to fell the tree, working suspended by harnesses above the drop below. It was to take another whole day to winch the severed trunk up the precipice. Although the carpenter had taken the precaution of clearing the undergrowth from its path, the thickly branched head of the tree constantly snagged as the men on the capstan erected on the ridge slowly wound up the stout cable attached to the trunk. As if clearing the obstructions was not difficult enough on the steep slope, they had to keep stopping to reposition the side ropes that held the tree steady on its path. Sailors agile in the rigging of a ship found themselves less adept at maintaining their footing on the treacherous slopes of a New Zealand forest. To make matters worse, the weather was damp and humid. The gnats soon found them, and they were forced to work amidst clouds of the persistent pests. By the time the tree trunk had been winched successfully to the ridge top, several of the men had joined the unfortunate Le Corre at the hospital camp, so severely bitten that their flesh had swollen and festered until they were unable to work.

While some of the men cut the head off the cedar and began trimming the resulting length of satisfyingly straight timber into the octagonal shape needed for the bowsprit, the carpenter took the rest of them further along the ridge to fell the taller tree selected for the foremast. The work was hard and heavy, and not helped by the need to traipse a good two leagues twice each day to and from the shore camp through the swamp and over the mountains. Each evening, the masting party erected a small tent over their equipment and left the allotted five soldiers on guard. The sailors considered the guard had the easier task — at least they were not forced to wade each morning through waist-deep icy water at one place in the swamp, the more shallow sections of which now often froze overnight.

Once both spars were cut and trimmed, the masting party tackled the even harder task of hauling them out of the forest, across the mountains then through the swamp to the shore. Although the carpenter had considered adapting gun carriages from the ships as trucks to support the logs, the season was so wet that it was soon clear that wheels would be an impediment. Despite their best efforts and the constant cutting and placing of fascines of myrtle over the worst spots, the already slippery track soon became knee-deep in mud throughout its length. Even with rollers under the logs, cleverly rigged blocks and tackle and the help of the capstan, progress was slow. On the wettest days they had to stop work altogether. The carpenter estimated it would be another three weeks before they reached the shore.

Most days some of the Zealanders came to watch the log-hauling, often providing a loud commentary. That was less appreciated than the odd occasion they applied themselves to the ropes, their strength sufficient to make an immediately noticeable difference. Even so, André found it difficult to understand how the Naturals had retrieved the much larger tree used to make the canoe they had been told came from this very same spot. He had seen no sign of sophisticated hauling equipment in any of the villages they visited. When he asked Te Kape, the young savage confirmed that they used only ropes and rollers — and manpower.

After being told of the difference the Zealanders made to the log-hauling, Monsieur Marion tried to persuade several of the chiefs, including Te Kuri, to supply the masting party with labour. They all steadfastly refused. Not even the promise of the more valuable trade goods as payment would change their minds. Finding out why was beyond even André's best efforts with the Tahitian vocabulary and Te Kape's skill with gesture and body language.

When he gave up trying, the disappointed Jean shrugged. 'If you ask me, the few savages who *do* help have ulterior motives.'

'Allons, Jean — what makes you think that?' André thought his cousin's judgment harsh, considering the good-natured assistance given by the Zealanders in many of their other tasks.

'Just watch,' said Jean. 'They're putting on a big show for their companions. *I* think they're demonstrating their superior strength, emphasizing how easy they find what to our men is considerable effort.'

André watched for a while. It was hard to argue with Jean's interpretation, although unlike him he saw nothing sinister in it. Then he realized something else was going on, at least some of the time. A group of young men had just taken their places amongst the Frenchmen. As he watched, he realized each of them was subtly mimicking the unaware sailor in front. He found it hard not to smile at their clever antics. 'Ma fois, Jean — they're putting on a show all right, but it's for their own amusement, that's all.'

Whatever their motives, the Zealanders seldom joined in the hauling for long, preferring to watch from the sidelines. It was also hard not to suspect that their commentary was far from complimentary. Before long, the two ensigns found excuses to be elsewhere, both suddenly uncomfortable at their suspicion that the ship's people had become the butt of local humour.

**Extract from the Te Kape manuscript, 1841**

*As winter approached closer, te iwi o Mariou showed no sign of returning to their ships and leaving our waters. Instead, those strangers moved ashore at Manawa-ora and set up yet another of their villages, expelling those who lived there and taking over their houses as they had done before. We thought they intended staying forever.*

*As we grew more familiar with those strangers from the sea, we realized they observed none of the restrictions or obligations — practical or spiritual — that reinforce and nurture our essential relationship with the land itself and with all other forms of life, of which we are an inseparable part. Although those strangers themselves suffered no consequences, confirming that indeed they were not like us, we feared their continuing trespasses would threaten our own physical and spiritual wellbeing.*

*Accordingly, our concern was great when the two kauri gifted from the forest of Tane were felled by te iwi o Mariou without ceremony or offerings of any sort. Accordingly, those strangers were avoided by many of our people when they began hauling those mistreated kauri to the sea, as they feared grave repercussions from such lack of respect. Those few who dared join them in that work protected themselves from harm by mocking those strangers as a way of placating the forest atua thus offended.*

Once the ship's people were settled into their new routines and working willingly enough despite the heaviness of the work, the cold and wet and the occasional heckling from local onlookers, all the officers had time on their hands. Only two were needed to supervise the work at each of the shore camps — officers from the two ships usually alternating at each location. The ship fitting-out required only the presence of the petty officers. Like the other officers, the ensigns now found they had whole days off to fill as they saw fit.

Some of the time, they accompanied Monsieur Marion on his explorations of the villages and various bays around Port Marion. He seemed fully recovered from his tiredness, the onset of a bout of fever stemmed by the surgeon bleeding and purging him, then dosing him with vile herbal mixtures. After ensuring his daily instructions were being carried out, the expedition leader liked nothing better than to take one of the Zealanders as a guide and spend each afternoon walking on the narrow tracks that formed a network throughout the hills and plains behind the port.

Content to leave any further survey work around the harbour to Monsieur du Clesmeur and his much-vaunted Gardes de la Marine training in such matters as detailed charting, the expedition leader was indefatigable in his own efforts to record everything he saw in the way of human endeavours, trees and plants, animals and birds of all kinds, potentially useful mineral deposits and soil types. 'Although these people seem quite knowledgeable in their treatment of their garden patches, with drainage and the use of sand to ameliorate the soil, for example, they grow nothing but roots and gourds,' he commented. 'I'm quite convinced many of these soils would be well-suited to cereal crops.'

Monsieur Marion's main motive was the discovery of useful products for trade purposes, both human-made and natural. He was also greatly interested in having the opportunity to apply modern scientific method. Monsieur Thirion told André that a few years earlier their expedition leader had succumbed to scurvy before he could complete his well-organized strategic and commercial exploratory voyage to the Seychelles archipelago in the Indian Ocean. Apparently his planning was still seen as a model of scientific exactitude. Monsieur Marion had been most frustrated at having to hand over his command to a proxy in the final stages and himself remain convalescent at the Île-de-France. 'Indeed, the experience made him all the more determined that nothing would prevent him carrying out our present enterprise.'

Always anxious to view his captain in a good light, André reported this comment to his cousin. 'Surely this, rather than mere commercial interest, explains why Monsieur Marion was so fixed on continuing our voyage after the Tahitian died of smallpox?'

Jean conceded the point, but added, 'I'm not sure why you see it in his favour that he was so keen to seek glory of *any* sort that he tried to hide the fact we had smallpox on board.'

André had succeeded in forgetting their captain's disgraceful attempt to conceal the two officers who had also fallen sick, hiding them in the ship's hold during the inspection by the Dutch authorities at the Cape of Good Hope — besides, both Chevillard and Sub-Lieutenant de Vaudricourt had survived the illness. He tried to recover his position by saying, 'The authorities were willing to overlook that, once the ship was placed in quarantine. Surely their help in provisioning us indicates they accepted the significance of Monsieur Marion's expedition?'

Jean shrugged. 'Maybe, but they might just have wanted to get rid of us as soon as possible!' He grinned. 'Mind you, I'd be the first to admit disappointment if we *had* turned back — and the last to criticize our captain's zeal.'

The young ensign had to be content with that. There was no doubt the expedition leader's zeal was keeping them busy. At least he was spared the tedious task of writing down Monsieur Marion's meticulous observations — that fell to Chevillard in his role as clerk, but he was often set to work digging holes to assess the quality of the soil. Jean soon grew bored with these endless observations of dirt, sundry trees and nondescript bushes, finding excuses to deviate off into areas that supported a useful variety of game birds. But André relished the excursions, his own curiosity about the usefulness of whatever they came across as enthusiastic as his captain's. Each time, they returned to the ship or shore camp laden with samples of soil, rock and plant material to examine and catalogue with Monsieur Thirion, whenever the surgeon took respite from his duties at the hospital camp.

Te Kape soon proved one of the most favoured guides for these expeditions, his sharp eye picking up tiny details the officers failed to notice. At times, the expedition leader had to exert rank over Monsieur Thirion, who was equally keen to employ the young Zealander's services.

'D'accord, sir, I bow to your prior claim,' the surgeon conceded reluctantly. 'I regret that my old legs prohibit me from accompanying you. If you would be so kind as to ensure the youth remembers to gather up any fungi or herbs of medicinal value, I'll be well content.'

There were still plenty of occasions when the ensigns were left to their own devices. At such times, both André and Jean preferred to go ashore and visit Te Kuri's village, where they always met up with Te Kape. The expedition leader commented tartly, 'Odd how that youth's unavailability for my inland excursions seems to coincide with your leave, Monsieur Tallec.'

André apologized, but Monsieur Marion waved him away. 'I can always go fishing.' Collecting oysters on the rocky headlands or casting the small seine net they carried on board was another favourite pastime of his, one encouraged by the surgeon, who considered it less taxing on his captain's health.

Soon after anchoring off Marion Island, the expedition leader had relaxed his prohibition on the ship's people spending time ashore in the various villages in the nearby bays. Many of the sailors had already struck up relationships with local women on board, and they now spent all their free time with them. Because of the precautions taken to ensure they knew how to distinguish which women were available, none of these liaisons caused any trouble with the Naturals, who seemed more than happy to make the necessary arrangements. 'That's because our people are careful to respect their women and conduct their affairs with circumspection,' said Monsieur Marion with considerable satisfaction.

The expedition leader was also more than happy that his policy of encouraging the friendships between his officers and the chiefs was paying handsome dividends. Relationships with the local chiefs were now so amicable that they often spent nights on board his ship, dining with the officers and taking over their sleeping cabins as of right. Even Monsieur Crozet, initially so suspicious of the chiefs' motives, frequently entertained one of their sons on board, excusing himself by saying the lad reminded him of his own son. The Zealanders knew all the officers by name, although their pronunciation of those alien to their tongue meant not all of their versions were as obvious as Mariou, Ta-recca and Ru.

Only Monsieur du Clesmeur kept himself aloof from more contact with the Zealanders than duty required. André had noticed that after the ships were first overrun by the Naturals, the captain mounted an armed guard to prevent even the chiefs from coming on board the *Castries*. His action seemed at odds with the expedition leader's instructions to extend friendship to the chiefs whenever possible, and the ensign could only assume it was the result of his overweening snobbery. Jean thought it hardly surprising that, as an aristocrat who most likely saw his own peasants as barely human, he considered mere Naturals beneath his notice. 'Mort-diable — he has little enough time for his fellow *officers*.'

When Monsieur Marion himself was not fully occupied with his excursions, he relished the way in which he was fêted by the Zealanders — men, women and children alike. Whenever he went ashore he was besieged by a throng of singing and laughing people. He returned their caresses and showered them with cheap trinkets. Although Jean cynically observed that their captain seemed to have acquired a retinue as fawning as that of the French King, the senior ensign himself benefited from Monsieur Marion's determination to encourage good relationships with the Zealanders.

Anxious not to offend the chiefs who brought him fine turbots each morning and accommodated his every whim — when he could make them understand what these were — Monsieur Marion now also turned a blind eye to the liaisons being formed by his junior officers with the chiefs' encouragement. With Te Kape as willing matchmaker, Jean's relationship with the coquettish young woman he fancied at Te Kuri's village soon blossomed. He spent many pleasurable nights with her in the village. 'She's quite the minx!' he boasted. 'But I have her twisted around my little finger. She'll do anything I wish of her.'

Even their fellow ensign, Paul Chevillard, proved not as cold-blooded as André had thought. He succumbed to the allure of a girl from a village closer to their anchorage than Te Kuri's. Situated on a narrow headland that jutted west from the main peninsula, it was the home of Pikiorei, a chief who often accompanied Te Kuri on board the ship. The clerk waxed poetical about the shapely breasts and ravishing glances of this girl until Jean told him bluntly that action carried more weight than words.

André himself avoided any such relationships. He felt awkward and clumsy in the presence of young women. His feet got in the way, and if not his feet, it was his tongue he tripped over. When it came to the Zealanders, he found the reek of fish oil soon quelled any stirrings of ardour and outweighed the undoubted advantage of not having to summon up snippets of social wit. Besides, Monsieur Thirion drew him aside and warned him that many of the women he had seen in the villages bore the unmistakable marks of the great pox — another indication they were perhaps not the first European ship in these waters. 'Prenez garde, young man,' he said. 'Several of the ship's people reported to me with symptoms of the pox within a few days of our captain allowing the women on board.'

Much to the ensign's secret relief, none of the women showed interest in him. They remained shy, avoiding any contact with him if they could. When they could not, they ducked their heads so their hair covered their faces. Jean teased him about his lack of sex appeal. 'It's that hair of yours, cousin — it's not to their liking. Maybe you should powder it.'

André knew it was indeed his red hair. He often heard the women refer to him by a different name than that used by Te Kape. He had first heard it during the ceremony at which he was given the whale-tooth pendant. Initially he assumed it was his faulty ear or their faltering pronunciation, but as he grew more familiar with the sounds of the Zealanders' language, he realized it was a different name entirely. Something like 'Too-raye-hoo', not 'Ta-recca.' None of the Naturals addressed him directly by this name, but he heard them use it — particularly any group of gossiping women — when it was clear they were discussing him. It occurred to him that maybe the whale-tooth pendant had tabooed him in some way. Eventually he asked Te Kape what the name meant.

'Turehu?' Te Kape repeated. He indicated André's russet hair, his grey-green eyes and his particularly white skin. Then with much gesturing towards the distant forest, he seemed to be saying the term applied to some sort of being of the forest — a supernatural being with similarly red hair and pale skin. When he thought the ensign understood, he then pointed to some women nearby and mounded his hands over his stomach. Wagging his finger at André, then in the direction of the forest, he shook his head vigorously.

'Non, pardieu!' André exclaimed. 'Are you telling me this forest person is responsible for pregnancy?' Self-consciously, he mounded his hands over the front of his breeches in the way Te Kape had and raised his eyebrows.

Te Kape fell about laughing. 'Wi-wi!' he said, using one of the French expressions he had picked up. He thrust his stomach out, placed his hands in the small of his back, then waddled a few steps, rolling his eyes in a face the picture of guilt. He then acted the part of an outraged husband.

'Fort bien!' said André wryly. 'Now you're telling me these pregnancies are the result of misalliance?'

Although Te Kape did not understand the words, the ensign's tone was clear enough. 'Wi-wi!' he said again, grinning.

At that moment, André realized the women nearby had been watching every gesture and were now giggling behind their hands. Although he flushed scarlet with embarrassment, he managed to sweep a bow in their direction, which had them running off, laughing openly. He comforted himself with the thought that at least he had not raised the matter of taboo with Te Kape. He would have made even bigger a fool of himself.

He had no intention of explaining any of this to his cousin.

Like Jean, most of the off-duty officers also enjoyed spending time on hunting expeditions, taking with them a local guide and a few soldiers as protection — although as time went on such precautions seemed increasingly redundant. The days drifted by as they indulged in relaxed and amiable hours with their new companions. Although the weather was now often wet and cold, life in Port Marion had much to commend it. Even the somewhat timid Monsieur du Clesmeur grew confident enough to venture on a longer excursion into the interior with some of his officers from the *Castries*, looking for good hunting opportunities as well as exploring new territory.

Having left the masting shore camp before daybreak, the captain and his party had not returned when darkness fell. Just as those at the camp were becoming concerned for their safety, the soldiers who had accompanied them straggled into the firelight, led by several

Naturals. At some stage in the afternoon, they had become separated from the officers. 'We were surrounded by a large crowd of savages, gentlemen,' their embarrassed leader explained, nervously fingering the hilt of his cutlass. 'As you know, the trails are narrow, and we were forced to follow along different routes through the fern.'

Monsieur Crozet was not impressed. 'You made no attempt to rejoin them?'

The soldier shuffled his feet. 'We had no choice but to rely on our guides, sir. They kept urging us on, and as you see, they did bring us here without any difficulty.'

'Imbeciles — we can only trust Monsieur du Clesmeur's guides are equally reliable,' said Monsieur Crozet dourly, dismissing the soldiers to the guard-post.

As the Zealanders who had brought them back were still hovering, the second-in-command bid them join the men for supper. 'You've no doubt earned it,' he said.

The Zealanders had left before the long-overdue officers returned, also in the company of local guides, tired to the bone and liberally covered in mud, but otherwise none the worse for wear. After making sure their guides were fed and given gifts, André and Jean joined the hunting party in the officers' hut to hear the details of their adventure.

That morning, after several hours of steady walking, the hunters had been surprised to find themselves on a ridge overlooking another large inlet fringed with mangroves where they had expected to see yet more mountain ranges stretching further inland. Monsieur du Clesmeur seized the opportunity to add this southwestern extension of the harbour to his charts. He had no trouble persuading his companions to continue down to this inlet as they could see tempting flocks of ducks on the stretches of mudflat that skirted it. 'We expected to find excellent hunting.'

Much to their dismay, the mud proved too soft for them to get close enough to shoot any of the ducks they could see. As it was, the unfortunate Monsieur Le Corre ventured too far out. Without warning, he sank up to his armpits. 'If we'd not acted immediately, he would've disappeared entirely,' said Monsieur du Clesmeur. 'It took all our strength to pull him to safety.'

Jean nudged André. 'I can well believe that,' he whispered. 'I'm surprised they accomplished it without the block and tackle we're using to drag the logs.'

André glanced at the weighty second-in-command of the *Castries*, who was quaffing a large glass of brandy. He whispered back, 'I bet their success was due to the strength of their guides — without them they wouldn't have stood a chance of pulling him out.'

Monsieur du Clesmeur was continuing his account. 'We carried on around the seashore towards a large fortified village we could see on a distant peninsula. This village proved larger even than that of Tacoury's.'

'But of course,' muttered Jean. 'No doubt its chief was superior too.'

Much to André's reluctant amusement, the captain echoed his words. 'The chief of this place, a most superior type of man, came to greet us in the usual manner. He then invited us to inspect his village, but would not allow us to enter any of the buildings.' He explained that, made uncomfortable by this, they decided not to linger. 'We indicated we wished to cross to the other side of the inlet, and this chief showed himself willing to have his men take us across in several canoes.'

Monsieur Le Corre nodded. 'We were clearly in a different canton,' he said. 'We didn't recognize any of the people, and their refusal to let us explore their huts seemed likely the result of their lack of familiarity with us.'

'Nevertheless, they were in no way surprised to see us,' Monsieur du Clesmeur added. 'We had no doubt they knew of us.'

After presenting the chief with most of their remaining supplies as payment, they were taken across the inlet without mishap. At one stage, one of the canoes fell well behind. 'The rogues wanted to turn back,' said Monsieur Le Corre. 'But once I pointed my musket at the fugleman, they agreed to continue.'

'Probably objecting to the weight of their passenger,' Jean said out of the corner of his mouth to André.

Monsieur du Clesmeur overheard and frowned at him before continuing their story. Accompanied by the paddlers from the canoes, with more Zealanders joining them on the way, they had followed on around the coastline in the rough direction they thought would return them across the head of the inlet and back to the masting camp. It was at this stage that they became separated from the soldiers, which was of course of considerable concern. 'We'd also grossly underestimated the time it would take us,' he said. 'To make matters worse, at four in the afternoon, with the light fast fading, we came across the largest river we'd yet seen.'

As they were only halfway back to the camp, the captain thought it best to stop in the open rather than become benighted in forest at the mercy of Naturals. 'We also hoped that by doing so our soldiers would catch us up.'

But their guides persuaded them to continue, carrying them across the river one by one so they did not get their clothes wet. 'It took two of the biggest of them to carry me,' said Monsieur Le Corre, grinning at Jean. The good-natured second-in-command had clearly heard the ensign's comments at his expense.

'Much to our relief and surprise, the savages delivered us safe and sound back to the camp as you see, gentlemen.' Monsieur du Clesmeur finished his account. 'It took another five hours of steady walking, but they showed no signs of discontent, having nothing but concern for our wellbeing. At times they even carried us on their backs, seeing we were growing exceedingly weary.'

All things considered, Monsieur du Clesmeur's party were elated rather than downcast by their adventure. But the captain did add, 'We must confess to being a dismal failure as a hunting party. All we have to show for our long day are four muddy ducks and two wood pigeons — and the latter had to be pointed out to us by the savages.'

'Indeed,' said Monsieur Le Corre. 'We need not have bothered carrying our muskets all that way.'

'Your soldiers fared no better,' said Monsieur Crozet, his tone tart. 'We must hope our savage friends bring us supplies of fish or game tomorrow or we'll have to resort to salt beef.'

Late that night, they were woken by a disturbance outside the huts. The guard banged on their door, shouting that he thought a canoe was coming in to land on the beach below. 'Peste soit du sot!' Monsieur Crozet exclaimed as he struggled into his breeches and threw his greatcoat on over his nightshirt. 'A plague on the fool — is he trying to make up for his companions' dismal performance, proving he's on the alert? At this hour, it's probably a flock of the ducks they failed to shoot yesterday.'

Before any of the officers had time to leave the hut, Sub-Lieutenant de Vaudricourt appeared at the entrance. 'Pardon, mille pardons, gentlemen, for my intrusion at such a late hour,' he muttered.

Before anyone could respond or the military commander explain his unexpected presence, he staggered off-balance as someone thrust him further into the hut, together with his servant, who was hovering in the shadows behind him. Standing in the doorway, carrying a flaring torch that threatened to set fire to the hut, was a large beaming Natural.

'Ma fois!' muttered Jean. 'Will you look at the state of Lieutenant de Vaudricourt!'

In the light of the torch, André took in the sub-lieutenant's disarray. He had lost both his hat and his wig, his hair mussed and full of twigs. His stockings were torn and his breeches covered in mud. His face was scratched and bloody. His servant was equally dishevelled.

'Que diable?' Monsieur Le Corre lumbered towards his sword. 'We must hasten and find the fiends who attacked you.'

'Non, non, sir — it was nothing like that!' The sub-lieutenant put out his hand to stop him. 'I was foolish enough to get lost.' He went on: 'Late last evening I had the good fortune to stumble across this man's village. Even though we hadn't met these particular people before, they've shown me nothing but kindness, gentlemen. Insisted on feeding us, then brought us here by canoe after we'd rested.'

Apparently, he had been on an excursion with Monsieur Marion to the east of Te Kuri's village. Although they were some five or six leagues from the masting camp, and in country unknown to them, he had felt confident he could find the camp by following the local trails, despite having no guide.

Monsieur Crozet sighed heavily. 'Foolishness indeed, sir. What possessed you, venturing off alone in such a way? Once again, it seems we are in debt to these savages.' He turned to André. 'Take this man to the store hut with you and make sure he's well rewarded.'

Next morning, when Monsieur Marion learned of these various experiences, he promptly decided there was no longer any point in the soldiers accompanying the officers' excursions, whether by boat or on foot. He dressed down the discomfited Sub-Lieutenant de Vaudricourt. 'From now on, sir, you and your men will restrict yourselves to guard duties against pilfering at the shore camps. It's more than clear we're perfectly safe amongst these people, no matter where we stray.'

The exasperated Monsieur Crozet had to agree with this decision. 'Moreover, sir, despite it being of considerable chagrin to me, these . . . savages . . . have proved themselves far more reliable than our own soldiers in every way, whether it be as hunters, protectors or companions.'

'D'accord,' said Monsieur Marion, making no attempt to hide his satisfaction. 'My point exactly, sir.'

**Extract from the Te Kape manuscript, 1841**

*Mindful of those strangers' inexplicable powers and capricious behaviour, our chiefs and tohunga insisted we continue to offer them friendship and hospitality, so they would not turn against us. We continued to eat together and to sleep on board the principal chief's ship, and they continued to sleep in our houses ashore. Many of the ordinary people, including our women and children, persisted in the friendship that grew out of curiosity and pleasure in the attentions they received from those strangers. Mariou himself continued to shower everyone he met with small objects of little value, trinkets enjoyed by children. Our chiefs and tohunga sent us to accompany those strangers on all their incursions ashore in the hope of averting any further harm they might unknowingly inflict.*

*Despite such efforts, the mana of the chiefs and accordingly the wellbeing of all our people became undermined by those strangers' actions. They continued not to reciprocate with equivalent gifts our provision of food supplies and items of value. Our vital winter supplies were fast becoming depleted, for the strangers' appetite showed no sign of diminishing, and, they made few attempts to find food for themselves, having little skill in hunting despite their mysterious guns. Moreover, they continued to send their people to cut firewood wherever they pleased, with no thought to ask permission or to respect any restrictions. Accordingly, great was our dismay when those people heedlessly took wood from a sacred pohutukawa tree that was under such tapu that we ourselves took care not to approach anywhere near.*

*Equally troubling was the continued failure of Mariou's people to acknowledge those who held the real authority in Tokerau. Their indiscriminant and impulsive favouring of various subordinate groups, who gained status as a result, was beginning to stir up strife. Stronger currents began to flow in the harbour, and the tides were now shifting. It was a time of growing turmoil amongst the peoples of Tokerau.*

# Chapter 9

'Savages approaching, gentlemen!' One of the soldiers on guard at the masting camp came running to the officers' hut to report. 'A chief we've not seen before, with a large party of armed men.'

'Any women or children with them?' Jean drained his morning coffee without haste.

'Oui, oui, sir.' The soldier seemed puzzled by the question. 'Shouldn't we be taking up arms ourselves in preparation?' He fidgeted impatiently, waiting for orders. 'They're not more than ten minutes away!'

'Take up arms? Non, pardieu!' Jean got to his feet and stretched. 'Even you should be aware that a war party does not bring children with it.' He waved the man away.

André said, 'We should go outside, wait in front of our hut to meet them — a chief would expect that.'

Jean agreed, although not without a smile at his cousin's desire to fit in with Zealander protocol.

Telling the guard to keep a discreet distance, the two ensigns waited as a chief in full regalia approached the camp. With his tattooed face, the white feathers of chiefdom in his ochre-powdered and oiled hair, and a splendid full-length white dogskin cloak around his shoulders, the imposing chief was accompanied by a tall, attractive woman, equally adorned. Close behind this pair were

189

several other well-dressed men and women, and a host of children of various ages. As the soldier had reported, the chief's group was followed by a large party of armed men, amongst them many heavily laden women. A few young girls trailed behind the main party, but it was not clear whether they belonged to it or were curious onlookers.

'This front lot must be the chief's family,' said André. 'I wonder where they're from? The baggage they're bringing surely means they've come some distance.'

'Au contraire — it might mean they intend staying!' Jean pointed out.

The chief and his family approached the two ensigns without hesitation. Their followers halted on the outskirts of the camp, dropping their bundles and squatting on the ground.

'Wherever they're from, it seems they were expecting to find us here,' said Jean. 'Our fame must be spreading far and wide.'

'Hardly surprising since we've been in Port Marion a full month,' André pointed out. He took a step towards the approaching Zealanders, then called out the greeting used by the Naturals. 'Aré maye, aré maye!'

The women accompanying the chief began calling back, words not so familiar to the ensign but ones he recognized as a response to his own greeting. So he called again.

'Quite the savage you're becoming, cousin,' Jean said, half-teasing, half-admiring, as the chief now came forward to press noses with them and embrace them vigorously, followed in turn by all his family.

Ignoring his cousin, André tried the phrase he thought asked where visitors had come from. He must have got it right, because the chief pointed inland and indicated they had been travelling for several days. He made it clear they had indeed come to see the Frenchmen and their ships, then were carrying on to spend some time at Te Kuri's village. The chief went on to ask all sorts of questions far beyond André's rudimentary grasp of the language. Before long, with his inquiries receiving only puzzled shrugs and well-meaning smiles, the chief rose to his feet and started exploring the camp. He investigated each hut with evident curiosity and showed great interest in all he saw.

'Better give him some gifts before he makes off with whatever he wants,' said Jean. 'He obviously covets our tools.' He told the soldiers to distribute a few trinkets amongst the chief's women, and brought out some offcuts of hoop iron and a handful of nails for the chief himself, with which the man seemed well satisfied.

Although heavy rain had set in, the party of Zealanders donned the shaggy, full-length waterproof cloaks they used in wet weather and went on their way, seemingly unperturbed by travelling in such conditions.

⚜ ⚜

**Extract from the Te Kape manuscript, 1841**

*Chiefs began to gather from far and wide to discuss whether action should be taken against the inflammatory presence of those strangers — namu namu whose delayed sting was now being felt, just as predicted by Te Kuri. All those with interests in Tokerau gathered at Te Kuri's stronghold to discuss those matters, putting aside their rivalry.*

*You question how such co-operation could be possible? Consider then this whakatauki or proverb from ancient times that reinforces the close kinship between the peoples of the east coast (Taumarere) and those of the west coast (Hokianga):*

*Ka mimiti te puna i Taumarere, ka toto te puna i Hokianga.*
*When the spring at Taumarere is used up, that at Hokianga is full.*

*The ancestor Rahiri gave Taumarere to his elder son Uenuku, and Hokianga to his younger son Kaharau, their close relationship as half-brothers being like that of the different tides of the two coasts. That proverb directed those brothers and their descendants to support each other in times of need. That co-operative alliance has held through many generations to the present day. That is the meaning of that proverb. Because of those ancient and continuing kinship ties, Te Kuri was able to call on the chiefs from Hokianga, the chiefs from Te Rawhiti and the chiefs from Taiamai. Despite their continuing rivalry, those chiefs began gathering in Tokerau in response to his call.*

The downpour continued without pause for another day. The carpenter took advantage of the enforced respite from log-hauling to design and build two robust trolleys with runners like those of a sledge in place of wheels, which he thought might make the work easier. 'These trolleys should enable us to move both logs together, gentlemen,' he explained. 'That alone would halve the work required.'

Impatient to try the devices, the masting party did not wait for the rain to stop before returning to where they had left the logs in a sea of mud. Much to their delight, the carpenter's ingenuity proved successful, particularly when it came to lowering the logs down the first mountain slope. Roped securely to each other and to the trolleys, the logs could now be moved as one unit. Although just as many men were needed, from then on the work of hauling the masts towards the shore camp proceeded much faster. The carpenter predicted it would not be long before they were in sight of the sea.

As the *Castries'* officers were due to take over duties at the masting camp that evening, Jean suggested that he and his cousin spend the afternoon hunting along the shoreline. They were not far from the camp when André called a halt. 'Prenez garde — more armed men! And no women or children with them this time.'

They crouched behind a screen of bracken fern to watch as a canoe containing about forty Zealanders was dragged up on the beach just beyond them. They stayed hidden as these men advanced purposefully on a small hamlet of eight or ten houses tucked into the head of the cove. When the occupants of the houses emerged to face the armed party, they seemed cowed. Certainly they offered no resistance as the armed men rounded them up roughly and herded them away from their homes.

'Que diable?' Jean muttered. 'What's going on?'

'Those people are the ones who've been bringing us fish and game,' said André, recognizing several of the inhabitants. 'These rogues are evicting them!' He half rose to his feet, hand going to his musket.

'Don't be a fool!' hissed Jean, pulling him back down. 'What do you think the two of us could possibly do? They're in no mood for negotiation.'

André subsided. His cousin was right. There was nothing they could do but watch in silence as the invaders drove the villagers away, allowing them to take little with them. Once they had left, the armed men sent some of their companions back to the canoe to collect their own belongings. They then moved into the houses, clearly intending to stay.

When all was quiet once more, Jean said, 'Let's get out of here before they spot us.'

Giving the hamlet a wide berth, the ensigns rejoined the coast beyond the cove then continued to walk along the shore. But they had lost their enthusiasm for hunting, and it was not long before they decided to turn back. When they were still about a league away from the camp, they came across a superbly carved war canoe, pulled up high on the beach under some of the gnarled and twisted coastal trees. No one was around, and from the litter of leaves and twigs that had accumulated in the canoe, they at first thought it had been abandoned.

André paced out its length. 'It's all of seventy feet, and carved from one tree trunk. Look at this workmanship — it must've taken months, if not years, to make with stone axes and adzes. I can't believe anyone would abandon a canoe of this sort.'

'D'accord,' said Jean. 'Look, they've stashed the paddles behind that tree. It must belong to some local chief after all.'

Keeping a sharp eye out for the armed intruders observed earlier, they made their way back to the masting camp. Each preoccupied with uneasy thoughts, they did not talk much. Their route took them past the grass huts abandoned by their inhabitants when the masting party had taken up residence nearby. As they drew near, they realized the people they had seen evicted were moving in, even though the huts were now in ruins, their main timbers taken for use at the camp. These people stood and watched the two ensigns walk past, not even calling a greeting.

'I don't like this,' said André. 'Trouble of some sort's brewing.'

'We'd better alert the officers from the *Castries*,' Jean agreed. 'They'd be wise to mount a more vigilant guard tonight.'

But when they told Lieutenant Le Dez and his companions of their concerns, the officers from the *Castries* seemed not at all perturbed by the presence of armed Naturals in the vicinity. Immaculately garbed as always, the urbane lieutenant was preoccupied with preparations for his next hunting excursion. André waited patiently for his attention.

When the senior officer at last replied, he was dismissive. 'Fi, fi, gentlemen, we've been aware ever since we arrived in Port Marion that these people are in a constant state of warfare. Why, only this morning yet another chief tried to persuade Monsieur du Clesmeur to assist them in a raid on Tacoury. If they're building up to another skirmish, it's no concern of ours.'

Monsieur Le Corre was more interested in their mention of the canoe they had found. 'That could well serve us as a tender,' he mused. 'We're often stranded here once the longboat returns to the ship, as Monsieur du Clesmeur usually wants the use of the yawl. With a canoe, we'd be able to move about more.'

Jean urged caution. 'We don't think it's been abandoned, gentlemen. If you just take such a valuable item, you'd be giving the savages every excuse to steal equivalent items from us.'

André was regretting they had ever mentioned the canoe, but as the most junior ensign of the two ships he was in no position to tell his senior officers what to do. Then, thinking the first lieutenant from the *Castries* — an intelligent and perceptive man despite his apparent indolence — might be more receptive to their reservations and exert some influence on his ship's second-in-command, he said to him quietly, 'Could I suggest you at least try to find its owners, Monsieur Le Dez?'

Overhearing, Jean backed him up. 'Trading for it would be the best option — it must belong to someone around here.'

But the very next morning, when the two ensigns arrived back with the longboat bringing daily supplies from the *Mascarin* for the masting camp, they found the canoe pulled up on the beach. On being questioned, the officers at the camp were adamant the canoe had been abandoned. They saw no problems with commandeering it for their own use.

Monsieur Le Corre laughed off Jean's objections. 'Why so much fuss? The savages themselves seem unconcerned. Some of them even watched us launch the thing without protest.'

André thought that might have been simply because they were

not the owners, but there was no point protesting further. The deed was done and they would have to bear any consequences.

**Extract from the Te Kape manuscript, 1841**

*Some people incoming from the west sought recompense against a small hamlet near where te iwi o Mariou had set up their houses in Manawa-ora. Whatever the cause, some offence satisfied by taking over the hamlet, it gave those incomers an advantageous position in Te Rawhiti, close to Mariou's people and their tempting possessions.*

*That in itself would have been no more than an annoyance to Te Kuri, but a war canoe belonging to more powerful relatives of those evicted was then seized by Mariou's people at Manawa-ora. For that reason, they were seen to be aligning themselves with those incoming from the west, a direct challenge to Te Kuri's authority here in Tokerau. Accordingly, several rival chiefs were encouraged to ask Mariou's people on the ships to assist them in mounting an attack on Te Kuri, an alliance that would further weaken his influence. Although those chiefs were refused, that action was understood as evidence of Mariou's interference in the politics of Tokerau. Accordingly, Te Kuri would be obliged to put on a show of strength both to revenge the insult to his mana and to correct the imbalance caused by such interference.*

The next day dawned fine, and being off duty, André and Jean joined Monsieur Marion on a fishing expedition. Although their companions on this occasion came from the large fortified village on Marion Island, the expedition leader had set his heart on going to Tacoury's Cove — the name the Frenchmen had given the whole of the bay bounded by the long peninsula running from the mainland towards their anchorage. André had the distinct impression that neither the two chiefs they knew from the island — Maru and Te Kotahi — had much love for Te Kuri, despite their apparent amity in the mainland chief's presence. Both had at times been amongst the chiefs who had tried to gain French support to attack Te Kuri. So he was not surprised when their island companions seemed unenthusiastic about fishing in the mainland chief's territory.

But Monsieur Marion, by now well-used to the rivalry amongst local chiefs, was not to be diverted. 'I've often fished in those waters with Tacoury's blessing. Besides, I've not found oysters of such excellence elsewhere, and today I fancy some.'

Numerous coves were scattered along the western sheltered side of the peninsula, each with enticing beaches and rocky headlands, with bushes and trees descending to the water's edge. But at this time of the morning they were all in shade, so Monsieur Marion ordered his boatmen to row ashore west of the cove below Te Kuri's village to a beach where the winter sun was already warming the sand.

As soon as it became clear where they intended to land, the Naturals on board the yawl set up a clamour, making it clear they did not wish to go there. Two of them even tried to take control of the tiller and steer the boat away from the chosen beach. They only subsided when the exasperated Monsieur Marion waved his pistol at them.

'Quelle folie!' he exclaimed when they reluctantly followed the officers ashore, but refused to join them in preparing the seine net.

'You don't think we should be taking some heed, sir?' André ventured. 'They clearly don't want us to fish here.'

'I've no idea what their objection could be, Monsieur Tallec.' The expedition leader looked around him. 'I'm quite sure I've fished from this very beach before.' He watched as the Zealanders seated themselves some distance away, then drew their mats up around their faces so only the tops of their heads showed. 'Such children, to sulk in this manner! I've no intention of allowing them to spoil our excursion, gentlemen. We'll proceed as usual.'

So the officers took off their jackets and helped the boatmen lay out the seine net. Once it was hauled in, they occupied themselves collecting large oysters from the nearby rocks. Within a few hours, they were basking in an unseasonably warm sun, still in their shirtsleeves, slurping succulent oysters straight from the shell while the substantial haul of fish from the net baked on the embers of their fire.

His annoyance with the Zealanders set aside, the contented Monsieur Marion sent André to persuade them to join their repast. But when the ensign made his way along the beach to where they had been seated, the Naturals had disappeared. When he reported their absence to his captain, Monsieur Marion shrugged. 'No matter — we can safely assume they'll find their own way back to Marion Island.'

Their meal finished, Jean, as restless as ever, persuaded André to leave the others in their party enjoying a snooze while they went off to hunt a flock of particularly plump ducks within easy reach on a nearby mudflat. It was late in the afternoon when the party of relaxed, sun-sated and well-fed officers reluctantly returned to the *Mascarin*, where they presented the grateful François with sufficient ingredients for several delicious suppers for the great cabin's table. By then, even André had all but forgotten the inexplicable behaviour of the Naturals who had accompanied them.

The following morning, busy preparing for their next tour of duty at the masting camp, the two ensigns failed to notice that the ship was visited by few of the Zealanders from the island's fortified village. Although André did observe that most of the officers' particular friends were not on board, he put their absence down to the fine weather — Te Kape had not turned up either. Besides, there was a lot going on. Two chiefs from mainland villages arrived at the ship's side early, wanting Monsieur Marion to accompany them ashore. He went off in his yawl with his lieutenants and his usual small contingent of soldiers — for Monsieur Crozet had insisted he as the expedition leader needed to keep up appearances. 'You may not feel the need for protection, sir,' he argued, 'but you don't see any of these chiefs without some sort of escort.'

The second-in-command, due with the ensigns at the masting camp, wanted first to check on the garden he was planting on Marion Island. As a result, he was impatient with the young chief's son from the island whom he had befriended. This lad came aboard as usual and kept hovering around despite the senior officer's obvious preoccupation. He seemed keen to present the second-in-command with several items in which Monsieur Crozet had earlier expressed an interest. But the senior officer had come to realize that these items — several valuable jade ornaments, some finely carved wooden spears, and a whalebone club — were probably family heirlooms and beyond the boy's authority to obtain for him. So he was dismayed to find these were the very things he had brought on board. He called André over to help interpret. 'I've not time to try and explain my scruples to him, Monsieur Tallec. See what you can do, if you please.'

Although André was sure the boy understood, he nevertheless seemed determined to present the items to Monsieur Crozet. When André tried to send him away, the boy promptly burst into tears. The ensign relented and took him back to the second-in-command. 'I'm afraid he's unmoving in his intentions, sir. I think you've no choice but to deal with him.'

'Mort-diable!' The senior officer sighed, but turned his attention away from his box of precious seedlings. 'Fetch me an iron hoe and a couple of decent chisels, Monsieur Tallec — and a red handkerchief or two. I can't possibly accept such items without proper recompense.' He stooped to take the weeping boy's hands in his. 'Allons, allons, mon pauvre! What's the cause of such sadness? Where's your usual smile?'

Despite his best efforts, the boy could not be cajoled back to good humour. When André returned with the trade items, Monsieur Crozet handed them to the young Natural. He refused to take them. Losing patience, the second-in-command turned to the ensign. 'Ma fois, surely he can see I'm being more than generous?'

'I don't think it's a question of that, sir,' said André, frowning. 'He seems highly distressed about something.'

Monsieur Crozet then tried to return the gifts, but the boy put his hands behind his back, shaking his head. He also refused to join the officers for breakfast, something he had previously enjoyed, his appetite for newly baked bread huge for someone so slight in build. Neither the senior officer nor André could think of anything else to try. More than somewhat bewildered, they watched the boy, still snivelling, leave the ship and paddle off in his small canoe.

'No matter how long we spend with them, Monsieur Tallec, I don't think we'll ever understand the savage mentality.' Monsieur Crozet watched the rapidly dwindling canoe for a moment longer, then shrugged and turned his attention back to his seedlings.

Before they left for the masting camp, André went ashore with him to help plant out the tiny plants. The second-in-command surveyed his previous efforts with considerable satisfaction. Early in their sojourn in the harbour, he had taken over the gardens in the watering cove abandoned by the Zealanders. Now, only a month later, the new green shoots of rice, wheat and maize were already thrusting up from the freshly dug soil, despite it being winter. Rows of cabbages, garlic and onions were thriving, and even the potatoes were beginning to shoot. He now bordered this area of plantings with a row of various fruit trees, marking with red-painted discarded planks from the ships the spots where he planted the kernels.

'I've made it clear to Malou and our savage friends from the fortified village over the hill that these crops are for their benefit,' Monsieur Crozet said, as he and André finished planting out the latest lot of seedlings — turnips and more cabbages. 'They've promised to look after them.'

'We can only hope they understand enough to harvest any seed, sir,' said André.

'They obviously have gardening skills of their own,' said Monsieur Crozet. 'I'm confident they understand the ways of perpetuating such crops. For that reason, I've taken many opportunities to scatter seed and fruit-tree kernels in appropriate places on all my excursions ashore.'

By the time they left for the masting camp, both satisfied gardeners had forgotten the perplexing behaviour of Monsieur Crozet's young friend.

**Extract from the Te Kape manuscript, 1841**

*It came to pass that revenge was sought by the chief's daughter Miki who had been spurned by Mariou. In revenge for that violation of her tapu, she expressed a desire for fish. In that way, an ancient saying from Hawaiki was invoked; when a chiefly woman desires a food, that food is the heart of a man. Accordingly, when Mariou and some of his subordinate chiefs rowed ashore to net fish on a tapu beach below Te Kuri's stronghold, near Manawa-ora, their actions determined the means by which her craving would be satisfied.*

*Some people of Ngati Pou scolded those strangers and told them not to fish in that place, for the reason of it being tapu to Te Kuri's people because men from the settlement at Whangamumu had recently*

*drowned and washed up ashore there. Taking no heed of their warning,*
*Mariou and his subordinate chiefs persisted in casting their net in that*
*place. Those strangers then cooked fish caught there in their net, and,*
*they further transgressed by eating those fish in that place where they*
*had been caught.*

*Because they had failed to prevent all these desecrations of tapu,*
*those Ngati Pou people knew retribution would come both upon Mariou*
*in accordance with that woman's desire and upon themselves from Te*
*Kuri, whose people had suffered these latest grave offences. Accordingly,*
*those Ngati Pou people were greatly saddened, and, they went away*
*from those strangers and stopped visiting their ships.*

*Not recognizing the finality of their transgressions, Mariou's*
*people retaliated by going ashore on Moturua to the garden lands they*
*had seized. There, they set up rahui posts marked with red along the*
*boundaries of those gardens as a warning for those people living on that*
*island to keep staying away.*

The last few days having been fine, the track across the mountains had
dried out somewhat. With the help of the trolleys, the masting party
succeeded in hauling the logs a good distance. In the evening, André
and Jean returned to the shore camp after helping erect the tent used
as a guard-post. The officers always left a small contingent of soldiers
and sailors with the masts overnight to ensure the Zealanders did not
steal any of the equipment. They were comfortable enough, with a
fire to warm them and the same ingredients for supper as the people
at the main camp.

Shortly after ten that evening, just as the officers were about
to retire for the night, two of the men left inland with the masts
stumbled into the camp. Once they regained their breath, they
had a disturbing tale to tell. 'We were still eating supper when we

heard movement near the tent and went to investigate,' one of them explained. 'We spotted a couple of savages running off with armfuls of our clothes and gear. One of our soldiers fired his musket at them, but they kept running. Several of us set off in hot pursuit.'

His companion took up the story. 'We got close enough to fire a second shot. It was enough to make them drop some of what they'd stolen — a whole bag of biscuit and some rope.'

As the thieves had by then disappeared into the forest, and it was too dark to go after them, they returned to their camp. To their dismay, they found other Naturals had taken advantage of the ruckus. 'The varmints got clean away with an axe, a musket and some greatcoats!'

'We worked out later that those cunning scoundrels had pulled out some tent pegs at the rear of the tent then sneaked in under the loosened canvas, right behind our backs,' added the first man, still flushed with exertion and indignation.

'And that wasn't the end of it, gentlemen,' said his companion. 'No sooner had we secured the tent and set a careful guard, than we heard them at it again — near the masts this time.'

Of all things, the Zealanders made off with the anchor being used to brake the trolleys, but they were in time to prevent them taking anything else. 'The varmints retreated into the forest once more, then set up their unholy caterwauling. We felt most unsafe, and have come to request reinforcements.'

Monsieur Crozet sent André and a dozen armed men back with them. Everything had quietened down by the time they reached the inland camp, but the people there were relieved to see them. 'They've been threatening to set fire to the masts, sir,' one of the soldiers explained. 'We'll need to set a full guard there as well as here for the tent.'

André spent an uneasy night, lying awake and alert despite the men on guard. Every rustle made him start, thinking the Naturals were back. His thoughts kept returning to the incidents of the previous few days. Now, with this unprecedented thievery at the masting camp, he was beginning to think the presence of armed Zealanders in the bay was indeed ominous. But the night dragged on without further incident. Eventually he dozed, one hand clutching his whale-tooth pendant in the obscure hope it might provide him some protection. At dawn, he sent some armed men to search the surrounds for the anchor, thinking the thieves would surely have abandoned something weighing three hundred pounds. There was no sign of it, and no sign of any Naturals. Discounting his fears as the inevitable distortions of a wakeful night, and embarrassed to have woken still clutching the pendant, he left the extra men on guard and returned to the shore camp to report to Monsieur Crozet.

'Mort-diable!' the second-in-command exclaimed. 'These savages have become over-familiar with us. Our policy of ignoring their petty thieving is now making them bold. We need to make it clear we won't tolerate such behaviour.'

The second lieutenant from the *Mascarin*, who had just arrived with the morning's supplies, volunteered to lead a search party to the neighbouring village. 'I've no doubt we'll find our possessions there. They have to be involved — they're always snooping around our camps, using the excuse they're bringing us food.'

'Those people have been moved out, sir,' said André. He saw no point in protesting the slur on Zealanders who had been nothing but generous towards them. He told him about the eviction he and Jean had observed.

'All the more reason to suspect the *present* occupants then.' The second lieutenant was quite happy to adjust his argument. 'We should endeavour to capture one of these miscreants. A show of force is needed here, gentlemen.'

Amidst the growing hubbub of indignation amongst those present, Monsieur Crozet decided the time had come to disregard the expedition leader's instructions about not mistreating any of the Naturals. He sent the second lieutenant off with a party, each of them armed to the teeth and eager to seek redress.

André watched them go with some trepidation. 'Monsieur Marion's not going to like this,' he said quietly to Jean.

'D'accord,' Jean replied. 'But at the same time, I agree with Monsieur Crozet that we can't afford to do nothing.'

The second lieutenant returned victorious later that morning. Finding the village abandoned and no sign of their belongings, he had vented his frustration by setting one of the huts alight. 'The fire soon spread,' he said with considerable satisfaction. 'The blaze made a fine spectacle. Those savages will think twice before taking off with our property again.'

While returning to the camp, they had come across a small group of unsuspecting Zealanders — not people they recognized. They promptly seized two of them. 'Mission accomplished, gentlemen,' said the second lieutenant proudly, pushing his captives forward. One of them was a chief, resplendent in dogskin cloak with feathers in his hair, the other a young man of no account.

'That chief, sir — I recognize him!' A man from the inland camp who had come down with André that morning to report their failure to retrieve the stolen goods now spoke up. He pointed at the chief. 'That's him — that's the scoundrel who made off with the anchor!'

'Quelle folie!' André tried to rebut this assertion. He appealed to Monsieur Crozet. 'This man's merely seeking glory for himself, sir — it was far too dark to identify anyone.'

But the second-in-command refused to listen. Brushing the ensign aside, he ordered the chief to be bound to a stake in front of the huts where he would be in full view of any Naturals who came near. Although the chief protested vigorously that he had nothing to do with any thefts, Monsieur Crozet was in no mood to change his mind. He was determined to make an example of one of these Naturals — and in his opinion, the more prestigious the captive, the better the point would be made.

He then turned to André and said, 'You, Monsieur Tallec, seeing you're so concerned, can make up an armed escort and take this other savage back up to the masting camp. I've noticed you've gained useful knowledge of their language. It's now up to you to make it clear to him that we'll release them both only once our possessions are returned. In the meantime, I'll send word to Monsieur Marion, telling him what's happened here.'

There was nothing the dismayed ensign could do but comply.

### Extract from the Te Kape manuscript, 1841

*As was customary, Ngati Pou sought to recompense Te Kuri for those desecrations of tapu at Manawa-ora. Accordingly, in the darkness of night those people with stealth and boldness took valuable items away from the strangers left to guard the kauri trees — cloaks they took, axes and guns, and a sack of the pumice-like food. Then, while those strangers were rushing about shouting, they took away the heavy iron anchor holding the kauri trees. All those things would be given to Te Kuri and his people in compensation.*

*To the dismay of Ngati Pou, Mariou's people at Manawa-ora ignored that such plunder was just punishment for the offences against tapu committed by those from the ships. Instead, they sent their men to seize the western chief who had settled near their houses, a principal chief of the name Rauhi, [Ed: genealogy of this chief omitted here] and with him a young man. Those two they bound with ropes, intending to keep them prisoner until the plundered items were returned. Those incomers had nothing to do with what had taken place, nor were they relatives of the raiders against whom retaliation might be justified.*

*Not satisfied with those actions, neither acknowledging their denigration of the highly tapu person of that chief nor that they had brought the plunder upon themselves, Mariou's people at Manawa-ora then set fire to those nearby houses and destroyed them.*

*On learning of those further provocations, it was understood by Te Kuri and the chiefs already gathered from Hokianga, from Taiamai, and from Te Rawhiti that they no longer had any choice but to take direct action against te iwi o Mariou.*

# Chapter 10

*9–11 June 1772*
*Port Marion 35°15' S*

Later that morning, André reluctantly returned to the shore camp with his captive. He suspected the Zealander had indeed been involved in the thefts in some way — he certainly seemed aware that the anchor was missing. But the ensign was not at all convinced he had succeeded in explaining the consequences. They could only wait and see whether the gear was returned.

A still-belligerent Monsieur Crozet ordered that the young man remain bound. 'Put him in the guardhouse and keep an eye on him.'

The second-in-command considered his tactics were having the desired effect. On the hilltops all around the shore camp, groups of armed Zealanders were gathering. Every now and then they shouted defiance and waved their spears, but they kept their distance. 'They can see we mean business,' he said. 'It's high time they learnt that we're not to be trifled with.'

Not long afterwards, Jean arrived back from the *Mascarin* with a replacement anchor for the masting operation, more soldiers, and instructions from Monsieur Marion that the captives were to be released immediately. The second-in-command was not inclined to obey. 'Tomorrow morning will be soon enough,' he said firmly.

In no position to argue with his superior officer, Jean merely said, 'Monsieur Marion suggests we keep a closer watch on the savages, sir. He considers that if our guards had been more alert, such thefts wouldn't have been possible.'

Monsieur Crozet snorted. 'Monsieur Marion's not here to see what we're up against. In my opinion, he's too ready to blame our own people in his determination to be lenient towards these savages, no matter what they do.'

Later, Jean told André in private that the expedition leader had been furious about the captives. 'I've never seen him so angry,' he said. 'He railed and swore and called Monsieur Crozet all sorts of names, not caring who heard. He kept repeating that his instructions couldn't have been clearer. He said everyone in command knew they applied to them — regardless of whether they were at the shore camp, on Marion Island or on board the ships.'

'D'accord — no one could argue about that,' André said. 'Ever since we considered having that man flogged on the *Mascarin* and the other savages reacted so badly, he's stuck to his principle that if we do them no harm, they won't harm us.'

'I suspect Monsieur Crozet wouldn't consider that he *is* doing them any harm,' said Jean. 'He's only bound these two, after all. It's not as though he's had them hurt in any way.'

When he found the opportunity, André went to squat beside the bound chief, hoping to reassure him that he would not be harmed, that he would be released once the stolen goods were returned. At first, the man would not look at him. Every muscle tensed, his face contorted with rage, he kept denying any knowledge of the thefts. As the ensign leaned towards him, trying to pick up any words he understood, the whale-tooth pendant swung free from his shirt. He was about to stuff it back inside the neck opening when he realized the chief had noticed it. His eyes flashing, the man nodded his head vigorously, then broke into another spate of words. Amongst them, André distinctly heard the names Te Kuri and Pikiorei. Puzzled that the chief had apparently recognized the pendant, he repeated the names slowly. The chief nodded again, then turned his head away, refusing to say anything more.

The ensign went to find Monsieur Crozet to let him know that the chief seemed to be saying Te Kuri and his ally were responsible for the thefts. He expected this news would result in their captives being released immediately.

The second-in-command listened impatiently, then shrugged. 'It wouldn't surprise me in the least if Tacoury and his henchman Piquioré were responsible,' he said. 'I've never trusted that man. But hasn't it occurred to you, Monsieur Tallec, that our captive may indeed be laying blame elsewhere so we'll release him? I said tomorrow, and tomorrow it will be.'

**Extract from the Te Kape manuscript, 1841**

*That western chief, Rauhi, taken as hostage for the things plundered, was left bound like a slave in full view of any passers-by. Although that chief insisted he had not been involved in the plunder, blaming Te Kuri and Pikiorei, Mariou's subordinate chiefs took no notice. Although that western chief was a skilled practitioner of maketu and uttered powerful incantations against those men, they were not afraid. Accordingly, not only was that chief's mana diminished by such humiliation, but he feared his atua had indeed withdrawn protection from him as a result of the violation of his ancestral tapu. His only recourse was to take immediate revenge.*

*Tension grew as caution was urged by the principal chiefs. Te iwi o Mariou were a powerful people, and any action taken would need to be well-planned. Those chiefs withdrew to discuss what should be done. At the same time, our people stayed away from that place to avoid being contaminated by the evil let loose there.*

*The energy of war rose like smoke from a fire, and, fierce quarrels broke out amongst young, impetuous warriors wishing to attack the strangers without delay. But only the inexperienced net the first of the eel-run; those who wait catch the largest eels, which run last, so the chiefs held back. Those principal chiefs were persuaded by Te Kuri that Mariou's people at Manawa-ora would be on the alert, expecting retaliation for their evil actions. Accordingly, it would be better to negotiate a truce so those strangers would instead think their actions had been accepted as justified revenge and be lulled into complacency.*

*At the same time, it was decided by those principal chiefs that te iwi o Mariou should be subjected to displays of the might of the war parties gathering in Tokerau, thereby instilling some humility in them.*

Despite André's attempt to persuade him otherwise, Jean was determined to go hunting that afternoon. 'Everything's quietened down,' he pointed out. 'Surely it's best we carry on as usual? If we over-react and confine ourselves to the surrounds of the camp, the savages will think they have the upper hand.'

Monsieur Crozet agreed, saying only that he should not venture beyond the territory already familiar to him. 'Unfortunately, I can't release any of the soldiers to accompany you, Monsieur Roux. We need to maintain vigilance at both our camps in case the savages try any more of their tricks.'

As André had other duties, he could not keep his cousin company. Jean decided to go alone, laughing off the young ensign's protests. When evening came and Jean had not returned, André berated himself for not taking a firmer stance. Filled with foreboding, he waited anxiously as darkness fell and there was still no sign of Jean.

Despite his qualms, the senior ensign eventually arrived back in the camp, embarrassed at the anxiety he had caused and weary from walking a long distance. Jean confessed that, intent on tracking some quail, he had lost his way in the forest. 'It was overcast, so I couldn't use the sun to guide me,' he said. 'After a few hours, purely by chance, I ended up on a mountain in sight of the sea. It was only the distance of two musket shots away. I knew that once I got down to the shore, I'd be able to find my way back.'

But while he was clambering down a steep gorge, he heard the unmistakable sound of hand-to-hand combat. Like all the officers, he was used to the sight of warriors practising their fighting skills in games that involved considerable exertion and dexterity. 'These two were armed with those carved spears. They were twirling and thrusting them as they parried each other's blows, showing all the grace and agility of any expert in fencing.' He explained that he withdrew into the fern where he could watch in comfort without disturbing their concentration. Then, after some moments, they suddenly threw aside their spears and drew their war clubs from their belts. 'Before I had time to realize what was happening, they fell upon each other in earnest.'

Without pausing for thought, the ensign ran towards them, shouting. But he was too late. At that very moment, one of the men had his head split open by his opponent. He was killed instantly. 'It was only then the victor became aware of my presence,' said Jean. 'He was so surprised, he immediately ran off.'

Left to examine the victim, Jean was impressed to find the blow had been so severe the man's skull was clove almost in two, the brains scattered at some distance. 'He'd been killed as effectively as though he'd been struck with a cutlass.' He added, his voice full of admiration: 'It's clear, gentlemen, that these savages fight such duels with great courage.'

Realizing he would soon run out of daylight, the senior ensign hastened on his way. Once he reached the sea, he walked along the shore, not at all sure whether he was heading in the right direction. Much to his relief, he had not gone far when he came across a group of Zealanders he recognized. 'I tried to question them about the duel I'd witnessed, but I couldn't make them understand,' he said ruefully. 'So I asked them to put me on the right path back.'

Indicating that he was a long way from the shore camp, half a dozen of the men showed themselves willing to guide him. Just before dark, they stopped in a small village where they were given fish to eat, then carried on. Noticing that he was beginning to stumble with weariness, the Zealanders took it in turn to carry him on their backs. For some reason they would not come with him right into the camp, but stopped where they were certain he could find his own way. 'I tried to persuade them to continue with me so I could fetch gifts for them,' Jean said, still perplexed. 'I'd nothing suitable on me to reward them for their kindness, but they were adamant in their refusal to go any further.'

After he gave them a handkerchief — all he had — the Naturals left him and vanished into the darkness. 'It's the first time I've found them so unwilling to enter our camps.'

'Perhaps they were wary of being taken prisoner.' André risked Monsieur Crozet's wrath.

But the second-in command was well-satisfied with this outcome. 'Monsieur Roux's experience proves I'm right to act in the way I have, gentlemen. We've won back some respect. The word's got around that we won't tolerate them interfering with our possessions. At the same time — despite Monsieur Marion's assertions otherwise — it's clear no harm's being done by holding captives, or those savages wouldn't still be willing to help our officers in such a manner.'

At dawn next morning, Monsieur Crozet had gifts brought for the bound chief, then ordered him released. But the chief ignored the gifts. He ran off immediately the ropes were untied, first slipping off his cloak so he could run unimpeded. Once he was out of reach, he turned and shouted threats at them. As soon as he joined the Zealanders gathered on the nearby hill, they all took off. Even though Monsieur Crozet had the cloak left neatly folded on the edge of the camp, no one returned for it.

Much to his chagrin, the younger man bound in the hut had managed to escape during the night. The soldiers on guard duty insisted they had not heard a thing. 'The savages are as wily as foxes, sir,' they said. 'He somehow got free of his ropes, then pushed his way out through the rear brush wall.'

'Mort-diable, such slackness merely confirms Monsieur Marion's poor opinion of your efforts,' Monsieur Crozet retorted grumpily. But there was nothing he could do.

While they waited in vain for the local villagers to arrive as usual with fish to trade, the first lieutenant from the *Castries* came ashore to take over command. Lieutenant Le Dez decided to take the masting party inland to work on the hauling as usual. No sooner had they begun to cross the swamp than a large crowd of armed Zealanders began gathering on the surrounding hilltops. Then André spotted others silently filtering through a saddle onto the swampy plain behind them. They were soon surrounded by armed and menacing warriors. There were hundreds of them, maybe close to a thousand — the most he had ever seen in one place.

Lieutenant Le Dez said quietly, 'We're about to be attacked, gentlemen. Take up defensive stations.'

Nervously, the masting party formed a square, with the soldiers on the outside, their muskets at the ready. They waited as the warriors moved steadily but cautiously closer, stopping just beyond musket range. There they stayed, motionless, the various groups lined up in the orderly ranks André had observed early in their stay in the port, when they had witnessed a skirmish between rival groups. Several chiefs stood in the front ranks, as seemed customary. They were in no apparent hurry to take any further action. All they did was ostentatiously count the men in the masting party — even though the Frenchmen were clearly outnumbered.

'An impasse, gentlemen,' said the imperturbable Lieutenant Le Dez, examining his pistol. 'This may take some time — we can assume our work's been interrupted for the day.'

As an hour or more dragged by and the Zealanders made no further move, the initially tense masting party grew restless. André could feel the cold from the sodden, swampy ground creeping up his legs. Worse, the gnats had found them. Everyone was shifting from foot to foot, trying to restore feeling in their toes, at the same time surreptitiously slapping at the annoying insects. The ensign could see the warriors were not similarly bothered. They continued to stand unmoving, watching the Frenchmen. Not once had they even leapt into action with one of their hideous challenge performances. The situation was descending into farce. He said quietly to his cousin, 'Nothing's happening — nor seems likely to.'

'Mort-diable — all they have to do is wait for gnats and cold to do the job for them,' said Jean, swiping an insect from the side of his nose.

Before much longer, the stand-off got the better of the senior ensign. He offered to approach the Zealanders. 'I recognize some of them, sir. And two of my guides from yesterday are amongst them. If I go alone and apparently unarmed, I might be able to find out what they want — we can't just stand here forever.'

Lieutenant Le Dez was unconvinced. 'We all recognize some of them. I'm not sure the risk is justified.'

As his cousin was insistent, André suggested, 'He could cut a leafy branch and take it with him as a sign of peace, sir. I've seen them use branches in that way.'

The lieutenant gave in reluctantly. 'But be clear that you do this on your own initiative, Monsieur Roux, not on my orders.'

So, with his cutlass concealed beneath his greatcoat and waving a leafy branch, Jean walked steadily towards the group of warriors nearest them. André watched in some trepidation. What if they sent a challenger out to meet him, expecting him to fight? Now that it was too late, he was wondering whether he should have sent his pendant with his cousin. The captive chief's reaction to it had indicated that it had some sort of status amongst the local people. But even as he was thinking this, four chiefs came out from the ranks to meet the senior ensign. They each embraced him. André heaved a sigh of relief. So far, so good.

Jean then stepped back slightly. He presented first his branch then his naked cutlass, pointing at each in turn. After returning to their men for some lengthy discussion, two of the chiefs eventually came back and took the branch from Jean, waving the cutlass aside. They then embraced the ensign again, and walked with him towards the waiting masting party. Leaving their weapons on the ground, the rest of the Zealanders followed them, still at a distance.

'It seems you young men were right.' Lieutenant Le Dez nodded a gracious acknowledgement to André. 'Put your weapons down, gentlemen, and stand by for the usual greeting ordeal.'

Only the two chiefs subjected them to the pressing of noses and sucking of flesh, constantly saying a phrase André thought meant peace. As the rest of the watching Zealanders then dispersed, the officers took the chiefs and their companions back to the shore camp where they presented them with gifts. Jean was at last able to reward his guides, and the chiefs agreed to bring fish to the camp the following day.

'Sir, perhaps we should give them the cloak left behind by the chief we captured?' André suggested. 'It's valuable, and it would serve us well to have it returned to its owner.'

With Lieutenant Le Dez's agreement, he went to fetch the cloak. After many questions about the fate of its owner, the chiefs sent two young men off with it — but not until the oldest of them had conducted a curious ceremony over the cloak that involved much muttering and the sprinkling of excrement.

Lieutenant Le Dez considered this was all very satisfactory.

'But we still don't know what the confrontation was all about, sir,' Jean pointed out. 'André, see if you can find out.'

After a lot of miming and maximum use of the few phrases at his command, the young ensign came back to the waiting Lieutenant Le Dez. Keeping his face blank to hide his secret glee, he said, 'It seems they want their canoe back, sir.'

The first lieutenant flushed. After a moment of silence, he said, 'Fort bien, Monsieur Tallec. I'll leave you to arrange that.' Nodding abruptly at the chiefs, he stalked off to the privacy of the officers' hut.

Monsieur Le Corre, not in the slightest bit fazed, muttered, 'Quelle folie! A lot of fuss about nothing, if you ask me.'

Leaving the officers from the *Castries* in charge of the shore camp, André and Jean returned to their ship. On the way back across the bay, they spotted Monsieur Marion's yawl in Tacoury's Cove and decided to divert the longboat there. Unlike Messieurs Le Dez and Le Corre, the two ensigns were most uneasy about the escalating presence of armed warriors in the area. 'Monsieur Marion needs to be told what's been happening,' Jean decided.

They found the expedition leader on the bank of a nearby river, surrounded as usual by children from Te Kuri's village. He was watching a group of them taking it in turns on a rope fixed to a stout pole like a maypole. As they ran around the pole, the rope wrapped itself higher and higher, taking them with it until they let go near the top to sail out over the river and plunge into a deep waterhole, apparently not bothered by the coldness of the water. Admiring their skill, Monsieur Marion continued watching while the two ensigns recounted the events at the masting camp and its vicinity during the past few days.

'Fi, fi, gentlemen,' he said when they finished. 'It's to be expected that those people reacted badly to the tying-up of one of their chiefs: these things you're telling me are nothing more than I predicted would happen as a result of such a foolhardy action.' He paused to admire a particularly daring boy spin high up the pole before he added, 'You two, on the other hand, seem to have conducted yourselves well — indeed, perhaps averted further bitterness amongst those particular Zealanders.'

'You don't consider, sir, that we should be worried about the growing number of armed savages?' André ignored the compliment and the activity on the river bank.

'I see no reason to be concerned, Monsieur Tallec,' the expedition leader replied. 'No reason at all. This morning, a chief came to the ship to return the axe and the musket stolen from the hauling site. He was extremely apologetic. I reassured him with several gifts, and we parted on the most amicable of terms. This afternoon, as you can see, I'm enjoying my usual entertainment with these delightful children.' He smiled as a small girl came to squat at his feet and patted her on the head. He then sent the two ensigns back to the ship.

That evening, Monsieur Marion assigned André and Jean to the guard-post at the hospital camp as the officer in charge there had become ill. 'Our excellent relationships with the people on the island should allay any further concerns on your part, gentlemen.'

As the two ensigns packed their gear to go ashore, Jean grumbled, 'Pardieu, cousin, he's treating us exactly like he treats those children.' He was not pleased to have their concerns so easily dismissed.

'Perhaps Monsieur Marion's right,' André tried to argue. 'Perhaps we're not in a position to see the wider picture, not travelling around the district the way he does.'

Jean shrugged impatiently. 'You can't seriously believe that! He's constantly being fêted by chiefs and fawned on by children. Our captain doesn't see what's actually going on beyond that, in the same way the King in his luxurious court isn't aware of the plight of impoverished peasants.'

André thought his cousin was mistaken. Surely someone as astute as Monsieur Marion, someone so skilled at managing the disparate mix of people crowded together in the confines of the ships for months at a time, would not have his judgement clouded so easily by the attentions of unsophisticated Naturals? But he kept his mouth shut, not wanting to set Jean off on one of his political diatribes.

Ashore at the hospital camp, Monsieur Thirion was pleased to see them. 'I've missed your company, young man,' he said to André. 'Or, if I'm honest, I've missed the services of that friend of yours, Ta-capaye. With you away at the masting camp, he's not been once to visit me.'

André realized it was several days since he himself had seen Te Kape. His friend had not joined him at all on this last tour of duty at the masting camp. Somewhat troubled, he left the surgeon to his patients and went off to join his cousin at the guard-post in the neighbouring cove.

Jean was also preoccupied. 'Would you believe our people have become so complacent that no one has even bothered to set up this guard-post properly?' He took André and showed him where the six blunderbusses brought ashore lay just above the tide line, still unmounted and half-covered in sand. 'Criminal foolishness,' he said. 'There're only four soldiers stationed here. With you and me, and Monsieur Thirion — who's really too old to be of any use — that means just seven able-bodied men to guard the sick in the hospital tent *and* the forge, with all that tempting iron lying about.'

'And half the ship's rigging, the rudders and other equipment's still stored in those abandoned huts.' André stared at his cousin, his misgivings growing. 'You have a point, cousin. We wouldn't stand a chance if the savages really wanted to plunder us.'

'D'accord,' said Jean. 'It's about time you came to your senses! So let's get this so-called guard-post set up properly.'

The soldiers took umbrage at their criticism, protesting that they had taken sufficient precautions. 'Assurément, this last week, a few of the savages from the village have been snooping around at night in the hope of stealing anything lying around,' one of them admitted. 'But they soon scarper when they see us alert and armed, gentlemen.'

That was enough for Jean. Without wasting any more time, he sent the sullen soldiers to drag the blunderbusses up to the guard-post. André supervised while they cleaned the bronze guns and put them in working order. In the meantime, Jean had their three-legged wooden stands assembled and placed in a square around the tent, leaving two to guard the entrance to the hospital tent. Only when the blunderbusses were each loaded with two handfuls of musket balls and the guard-post was in ship-shape order would he let the soldiers eat a delayed supper.

Leaving an armed soldier on sentry duty at the hospital tent and another outside the guard-post tent, Jean and André at last retired for the night. But at eleven o'clock, the sentry came to report that five or six Zealanders were prowling around outside. As soon as the ensigns hastened out, these people ran off up the hill. When they did not return, the ensigns left the sentry on the alert and went back to bed, dog-tired. It had been a long day. Much to their relief, they were not disturbed again that night.

Next morning, Monsieur Marion arrived in his yawl on one of his regular visits to the hospital camp to assure the sixty or so men still lying sick that they were not forgotten. After finishing his consultation with the surgeon, he came over to see how the two ensigns had fared during the night.

'I see you've set up the blunderbusses, gentlemen,' he said, raising his eyebrows. 'What's happened that's so out of the ordinary for you to reinforce security?' His tone indulgent, he obviously thought they were still over-reacting to the events at the masting camp.

Gritting his teeth, Jean explained. Monsieur Marion listened patiently, then shrugged. 'In my opinion, Monsieur Roux, the Zealanders are merely trying to steal what they so dearly covet. Such behaviour's understandable, surely? In comparison to them, we have untold riches. I've said before that stealing would become a problem once these people lost their fear of us.'

So much for Jean's theory about our captain being unaware of social inequality, thought André ruefully, as Monsieur Marion continued. He was saying firmly, 'All you need to do is remain vigilant at night to prevent them doing so.'

Behind them, one of the soldiers was smirking. Jean glared at him. Seeing the expression on his senior ensign's face, Monsieur Marion hastened to add, 'Nevertheless, gentlemen, maybe you're right to be taking extra precautions. We've much valuable equipment stored here that we cannot afford to lose.' He then told them that he had heard from the masting camp that morning. 'Just as you experienced here, some Zealanders again appeared during the night, obviously intent on stealing what they could.' He had sent some soldiers to reinforce the guard around the masts.

'Does this not in any way undermine your trust in these people, sir?' André asked. 'Don't you consider it at all possible they may be plotting against us — exactly because of their growing desire to seize our equipment?'

'As long as we do them no harm, I'm quite confident they in turn will not harm us,' the expedition leader replied. He looked at Jean, who was finding it hard to hide his scepticism, then said quietly, 'Perhaps you forget my many dealings with such primitive peoples, both with the Malagasy slaves at my estates on the Île-de-France and with black traders along the African and Indian coasts. I've seen nothing in our six weeks here to change my long-held opinion that treating the darker races with consistent, gentle kindness wins the best results.'

Seeing he was in a discursive mood and therefore perhaps unlikely to lose his temper, André risked expressing further doubts. 'I quite take your point, sir. But these Zealanders seem of higher intelligence and more sophisticated in their customs and industries than the type of savage you speak of.'

Jean added, 'We've already seen instances of their daring and courage, sir. It's clear they're now in a state of readiness for war. All we're suggesting is that we're seeing signs that they're more than capable of using those tendencies against us.'

Monsieur Marion sighed. 'Gentlemen, be assured my understanding of these people is not tinted by the rather naïve philosophies expounded by Monsieur Rousseau's followers in the salons of Paris and so eloquently argued after supper by our good surgeon. I'm not blind to their venal nature, their tendency towards aggression, or their avarice when it comes to the wealth we represent. But I have good grounds for believing my approach applies as successfully to them as it does to the more brutish races.' He then explained that a few days previously two chiefs had come on board to take him ashore. 'You were present when we left, I think?'

When they nodded assent, he went on to tell them that these chiefs took him and his party onto a high hill overlooking Te Kuri's village. Several more chiefs and a great crowd of people were waiting there for him. The chiefs accompanying him sat him and his officers down on several luxurious mats and cloaks spread out on the ground. After the usual solemn greetings, they draped a cloak around his shoulders and placed a crown of feathers on his head. With considerable ceremony, accompanied by songs in which he clearly heard his name mentioned many times, they then took him by the hand and led him from one side of the hilltop to the other, gesturing at the expanse of country that spread beyond. 'I was made to understand in this way that they recognized me as their King, gentlemen. I was treated with the greatest of respect, and all the chiefs made their obeisance to me.'

Monsieur Marion's voice became so affected in recalling his gratification at this reception, he had to pause. He dabbed at his eyes with his handkerchief, then continued his account. The chiefs had come up to him one by one to present him with many gifts, including parcels of his favourite fish and a stone handsomely carved with the figure of some sort of deity. Once this grand occasion had drawn to its conclusion, the chiefs and the whole crowd had conducted him back to the shore. There, they followed his boat out to the *Mascarin* in a flotilla of canoes. 'I gave them many presents and they departed, still singing. So you see, gentlemen, you cannot expect me to have a poor opinion of people who show me so much friendship.' He then repeated what he had said earlier. 'Since I do them nothing but good, surely they'll not do me any harm?'

The two ensigns could find nothing to say. Soon afterwards, the expedition leader left them, confirming his orders that regardless of any provocation they were to continue to treat the Naturals with gentleness.

Once he had gone, Jean shrugged. 'Mort-diable — there'll be no convincing Monsieur Marion that any savage might have dire intentions,' he said gloomily. 'Not now they've made him *King*, no less. He must've thought all his dreams had come true!'

**Extract from the Te Kape manuscript, 1841**

*It came to pass that some of the chiefs were unhappy with Te Kuri's procrastination. Seizing a chance to provoke him, they made pretence of changing their allegiance to Mariou himself. Accordingly, in full view of Te Kuri's stronghold, they gathered their people, and, they entertained the leader of those strangers with great ceremony, giving him the white feathers of chiefdom to indicate their respect. Regardless of their motives, Te Kuri had no choice but to react, for their action put Mariou himself in a position of political strength from which he could threaten Te Kuri's influence in Tokerau. That this was Mariou's purpose could no longer be doubted, for why else would the strangers from the sea carry out so many acts of physical and spiritual aggression against people who had done them no harm?*

*And so it was decided. The inflammatory presence of te iwi o Mariou in Tokerau could no longer be tolerated. Accordingly, those chiefs allied to Te Kuri divided their warriors into three war parties, one at Manawa-ora, one on Moturua, and one at Orokawa where the ships were anchored. After ascertaining the strength of each of Mariou's strongholds, those war parties waited for an opportunity to carry out a three-pronged surprise attack that would satisfy the now urgent need for revenge.*

# Chapter 11

No sooner had Monsieur Marion left than the chief Te Kotahi arrived at the hospital camp from Maru's fortified village on the island. This particular chief had not visited their camp before. He brought the customary gifts of fish for the officers at the guard-post, and sent his companions with baskets of food on to the other cove to trade with the surgeon and the blacksmith. His quick eyes soon spotted the blunderbusses set up on their stands around the tent. Gesturing at them, he asked André what they were.

'Ta-pou,' the ensign replied, using the word the Zealanders gave to the muskets.

When Te Kotahi shook his head in disbelief, Jean went into the tent and returned with a handful of balls. 'Let's make things a bit clearer,' he said. 'It wouldn't be a bad thing if this chief understands exactly what these guns are capable of.'

He loaded one of the blunderbusses, showing the chief each ball as he did so, then swivelled the gun on its stand, aiming its long barrel out to sea, up the hill, and then directly at the chief himself. 'Bam! Bam!' he shouted, enjoying himself.

The startled Te Kotahi backed away, the whites of his eyes wide with alarm.

'I think you've made your point,' said André dryly.

The chief drew his mat across his body and took up a defensive pose. He waved the muzzle of the gun away, making it obvious he not only understood but also thought this type of weapon highly dangerous.

Jean nodded vigorously. 'And don't you forget it!' Satisfied with the result of his demonstration, he left the blunderbuss loaded, but tilted its barrel down at the ground out of harm's way.

Despite the fright he had been given, Te Kotahi lingered around the camp for several hours. Keeping a safe distance from the blunderbusses, he nevertheless examined everything else with great interest. He peered into the tent, taking notice of the four cots set up inside, then indicated that he wanted to go to the other cove.

'Go with him, André,' said Jean. 'Keep a close eye on what he does. Prenez garde — I'm suspicious of such intense curiosity. He's up to something.'

'Fort bien,' said André. 'He does seem to be taking stock, but let's retain some perspective: we've explored his village with equal curiosity, including examining their magazine of arms. It *is* the first time he's visited us.'

'Oui, oui,' Jean spread his hands. 'I'm probably over-reacting. But it would do no harm to be alert.'

At the hospital tent, the chief asked to go inside, where he wrinkled his nose in distaste at the fetid smell of the sick men, but stayed long enough both to count them and satisfy himself that they were incapable of rising from their beds. André, watching him, now thought his cousin might have the truth of it. None of the other Zealanders had ever shown any inclination to go near the hospital tent. They had continued to show fear at the sight of the leaden complexions and distorted limbs of the men still suffering from scurvy. Monsieur Thirion was of the opinion that they thought some demon or other was responsible for this affliction, as he had observed they always left a small parcel of fish at some distance from the tent and muttered incantations over it before approaching him with the baskets of food they wished to trade. At the beginning, the Naturals would not even take gift items in exchange, and it had taken him some time to convince them that he expected to pay some token for what they brought him.

So when Te Kotahi then made his way across the stream to where the blacksmith and the cooper were working at their trades with their offsiders, André followed hard on his heels. Although the chief jumped involuntarily at each blow of the hammers, flinched at the clangour of beaten iron and was obviously uncomfortable in the intense heat emitted by the forge, he again examined everything closely. Before he left, he once more counted all the men present and seemed impressed by their brawn and strength as they wielded the heavy tools of their trade.

André escorted him and his companions, who had waited patiently for their chief on the outskirts of the camp, to the start of the track back to their village, then went to report to Jean at the guard-post. 'Needless to say, I didn't tell him everyone he was counting so carefully at the forge returns to the ship at the end of each day.'

The senior ensign clapped him on the shoulder. 'Dieu soit loué, cousin! I'm glad you at last have your wits about you. He's gone away thinking we have more than double the actual number of able-bodied men stationed here.'

That afternoon, the two ensigns went hunting in the direction of the village. 'I've a mind to see whether anything unusual's going on there,' explained Jean. 'We can drop in, casually, as we pass by.'

'Do our own counting, you mean?' André was in favour.

Somewhat to their surprise, they were made welcome when they arrived at the entrance to the village. The Zealanders greeted them as enthusiastically as usual, with a couple of the young men coming down the steep path to help them over the worst sections. Jean had fully expected they might be turned away. Instead, Maru and Te Kotahi accepted the brace of quail they offered and sat down with them as though they had not a care in the world. In the face of such friendliness, even Jean was forced to revise his suspicions. 'Maybe Monsieur Marion's right after all,' he muttered to André as gifts were brought for them. 'Maybe we're too quick to think the worst.'

But before they left, Te Kotahi questioned them closely about the muskets they were both carrying. He pointed at their bag of quail and nodded, then patted his own chest and shook his head with a look of disdain on his face.

'Ma fois, the rogue's telling us quite plainly that he doesn't think our muskets are up to much!' All Jean's prejudices came crowding back. 'He doesn't think they're capable of killing a man.'

'Hardly surprising, since they've only seen us using birdshot to hunt game,' André pointed out. 'Monsieur Marion's scruples have ensured we've not at any stage fired directly at any savage.'

'Don't you see?' Jean was impatient. 'If these people think we're so poorly armed, they'll believe they can attack us with impunity.'

Before André could reason with him, point out that Te Kotahi had seen the blunderbusses and already knew their camp was well defended, the chief began gesturing at one of the many village dogs wandering past.

'You want another demonstration?' Without further ado, Jean lifted his still-loaded musket and fired at the dog, killing it. Blowing on the lock to disperse the smoke as usual, he then grounded the butt of the musket and waited expectantly.

Te Kotahi, looking most surprised, stooped to examine the dead dog closely. He then came over to the ensigns and asked to see the musket. Jean held it out to him without saying a word. The chief took it cautiously and examined it equally closely. He then wedged the butt against his shoulder, mimicking the way he had seen the Frenchmen wield the weapon. As they watched, he aimed the muzzle carefully towards another dog — then blew vigorously on the lock. The puzzled chief watched the dog amble on its uninterrupted way. He re-examined the musket before giving it back to Jean. In response to his further questions, the senior ensign merely shrugged.

Much to André's amusement, Te Kotahi gave a Gallic shrug of his own. Then losing interest in them and their mystifying weapon, the chief turned and left them to make their own way back down the treacherous path leading from the village.

Jean was well pleased with the outcome of their sortie. 'He should now think twice before assuming we're an easy target.'

In the evening, Monsieur Marion sent for André to return to the ship, wanting his company on his next day's excursion. The ensign was reluctant to leave his cousin one man short, but Jean sent him off without any qualms, considering his precautions more than adequate to deal with savages who were so ignorant of firearms. 'I can't see they'll be in any rush to come back anyway, not after today's demonstrations.'

First assigned to help Paul Chevillard with the day's ballasting efforts, a reluctant André was rousted out of his hammock several hours before daylight. Still bleary-eyed, he joined his fellow ensign in the longboat, grumbling at the early hour. The over-zealous clerk retorted that it was all very well for him, with an excursion ashore later planned with their captain. 'I'm not only required to load two lots of ballast today, but I'm also expected over at the *Castries* mid-afternoon to go over accounts with my counterpart for Monsieur du Clesmeur.'

Chevillard seemed to think he was due sympathy for his heavy workload, but André thought the ridiculously early start was merely a jealous attempt to curry favour with Monsieur Marion. Stifling his yawns, he dozed while the half-dozen equally irritated boatmen rowed them in pitch-darkness in what they hoped was the direction of Tacoury's Cove, where they would spend the morning loading suitable round boulders.

Only the lapping of water on the shore warned them that they were approaching land. It was still a good two hours before there would be enough light to see what they were doing. The boatmen stayed their oars and looked for instructions towards Chevillard, a barely visible blacker shape in the stern sheets. André, wrapped in his greatcoat trying futilely to keep warm, muttered curses under his breath. He could think of better things to be doing — like still being asleep in his hammock in the warm fug of the gunroom.

As their way slowed and the boat rocked gently on the small waves, a huge shout rang out high above them, startling them all out of their lethargy. It was followed in quick succession by more shouts, then the mournful blare of conch shells that sounded much like foghorns. Almost instantly, a fire blazed up, to be followed in quick succession by similar fires all along the coast. The shouting continued, to be echoed by answering shouts from further away, more and more faint as the distance increased. With the heights above them now silhouetted in the light of the fire, André recognized where they were: just below the steep headland of Pikiorei's fortified village. He could not resist saying, 'I think our presence has been noted, Monsieur Chevillard.'

Not able to come up with a suitable retort, his fellow ensign ignored him. 'Lower the grapnel, coxswain, if you please. We'll wait here until it's light.'

'The savages must've set sentries the whole way along the coast, sir,' the coxswain commented as he let out the anchor rope. 'Expecting trouble of some sort.'

'D'accord,' said Chevillard patiently. 'We'll wait until they can see we're unarmed and realize they need not fear any trouble from us.'

André moved into the stern sheets and said quietly in Chevillard's ear, 'We've not even a musket amongst us, Paul. Don't you think we might be wise to return to the ship?'

Chevillard shook his head. 'This isn't the first ballast-run I've done, you know. I've had no trouble from these savages before, and I don't anticipate any now.'

'The coxswain's right, though,' André tried to change his fellow ensign's mind. 'Something's brewing. We'll be sitting ducks if they choose to attack us.'

Chevillard shrugged this away, his tone supercilious. 'I heard all about the little problem you had at the masting camp. That amounted to nothing in the end. I see no reason to abandon our task just because your nerves are frayed.'

André gave up, regretting his earlier quip at the clerk's expense. There was no point trying to reason with him. Chevillard constantly rubbed it in that he was senior and more experienced; he would not be about to take his junior's advice now. So, with the sounds of continued activity above them, although the shouts of the sentries had died away, they sat, increasingly cramped with cold, and waited for daylight.

At last the first streaks of yellow appeared in the sky, and they could distinguish where water ended and land began. Slowly, the headlands and hills surrounding the bay took shape, their summits emerging above the drifts of early-morning mist. Chevillard ordered the boat crew to row them ashore to the boulder beach he had targeted for ballast collection.

No sooner had they landed than they were surrounded by a

hundred or more armed Zealanders. Gesturing fiercely with spears and clubs, the Naturals tried to force them back into the boat. When Chevillard took no notice, ordering the men to start collecting ballast, the Naturals immediately knocked the boulders out of their hands. The exasperated clerk then showed them the Frenchmen were unarmed, holding open his coat so they could see he was not carrying even a pistol or dirk, then pointing into the boat to indicate there were no weapons stashed there either.

But when the Zealanders continued pushing the sailors about and trying to prevent them from collecting boulders, André said, 'Maybe they think we're going to use *them* as weapons?'

Chevillard snorted, 'They've not seen us resort to pebbles before.' He waved his arms about and tried to explain that they were merely taking the boulders out to the ships. At the same time, he told the sailors to keep loading the boat.

André did not know whether to admire the clerk's courage or condemn his persistence as foolhardiness, but slowly the atmosphere changed. Several of the Zealanders — chiefs by their tattooed faces — put their weapons down and started asking the whereabouts of Monsieur Marion. Both he and Chevillard pointed out to sea, towards the anchorage, where the *Mascarin* and the *Castries* could now be seen through the eddying mist. At last the Naturals gave up their harassment. One by one, they withdrew to the beach and watched sullenly as the sailors continued to load the boat. When Chevillard had the men push the heavily-laden boat out into deeper water before they all re-embarked, the Zealanders made no move to stop them leaving.

Back on board, at André's insistence, they reported what had happened to the expedition leader. Monsieur Marion listened, barely concealing his impatience. He told them he had indeed heard the shouted alarm and seen the signal fires from the stern gallery.

He had later noticed the crowd of Zealanders going down to the shore. 'But what is it in these activities that you perceive as such a problem?' he asked. 'Have you not returned unmolested, your task accomplished?'

When neither ensign could find words to counter this disparagement, he said more kindly, 'Probably your going ashore so early made them afraid of your intentions. Obviously, once they realized what you wanted, they were content to leave you alone.'

It was hard to argue with this interpretation. André decided there was no point in pursuing the idea that the Zealanders' level of alertness in the small hours must have some significance, knowing Chevillard would certainly not support him now that their captain had openly criticized his decision to land before dawn.

Later, when Monsieur du Clesmeur arrived from the masting camp with accounts of further attempts at thievery and received the same lecture about property ownership and doing no harm that he and Jean had heard the day before, André was glad he had not bothered. Nothing anybody said would change Monsieur Marion's stance. Jean was right — the expedition leader would remain blind to anything that raised doubts about people who had sufficient appreciation of his qualities to make him their King.

Resigned, he went ashore with Chevillard again soon after midday for the second load of ballast. Monsieur Marion refused them permission to take armed soldiers, saying it would only alarm the Naturals further. 'Carry on in the same way as before, gentlemen. You've no justification for your concerns.'

Even the clerk seemed dubious about the wisdom of this, and André felt some fellow-feeling between them as they were rowed ashore. Once again, the same crowd of Naturals tried first to prevent them from loading the boat with boulders, then to persist in asking for Monsieur Marion.

This time, André voiced his concerns to Chevillard. 'I don't much like this,' he said. 'They've not arrived armed wanting him to come ashore until now. Their intentions may well be sinister.'

'D'accord,' said Chevillard, frowning. 'Several of them were intent on attacking *me*, I'm sure of it. It was only because their chiefs made them desist that they didn't proceed. It was then they started asking for Monsieur Marion again.'

Sobered, they went back to the ship with their load of ballast. Somehow they would have to try to persuade the expedition leader that their concerns were warranted.

As the two captains were still dining together in the great cabin, the returning ensigns had no opportunity to present a united front. When the captains emerged onto the deck, their heads bent together in animated discussion of some matter, they did not at first even notice the hovering ensigns. Monsieur du Clesmeur then left in some hurry, impatiently urging Chevillard to board his yawl as he had no time to waste. 'Before we return to my command, I must first inspect the rudder I sent ashore a few days ago,' he said. 'I trust you have all the papers you need for your balancing of accounts with my clerk, Monsieur Chevillard?'

Momentarily distracted from his worries, André watched in some amusement as Chevillard bristled at the implication it was he not the *Castries'* clerk who was required to account for himself and his receipts, instead of the other way around. He thought they made a good pair, the expedition clerk and the captain, both full of impotent self-importance. He must remember to ask Jean how Monsieur du Clesmeur's so-called inspection of the rudder had gone. The blacksmith no doubt would similarly resent a superfluous inspection that implied he did not know his job.

Roused from his musings by the chant of a fugleman and the rhythmic splash of paddles, he watched the approach of a large canoe. It was soon close enough for him to recognize Te Kuri's canoe, the chief standing as usual in its prow, the hold laden with baskets of fish. André felt tension drain from his shoulders. The chief would hardly be coming out to the ship to trade if he were busy plotting mayhem — at the very least they still had allies amongst the Zealanders. To his delight, he could already pick out the familiar figure of Te Kape amongst the paddlers. Whatever was going on in the bay, his friend had not deserted him after all. He hastened to greet him when the chief and his retinue came aboard.

Although Te Kape embraced him and pressed noses with him, he seemed distracted, even subdued, his usual broad smile fleeting. Before André could find out what was bothering him, Monsieur Marion was calling for his yawl to be brought around to the gangway and the seine net put on board. It seemed Te Kuri had come to invite him and his officers to go fishing on the expedition leader's favourite stretch of coastline, the sheltered coves and beaches below his village. Fussing, Monsieur Marion was now looking around for the officers he wanted to accompany him. He beckoned André over.

Before the ensign could join his captain, he felt a tug on his jacket, holding him back. It was Te Kape, shaking his head and making signs that he should stay on board the ship. But when he asked what was wrong, the youth mutely shook his head once more. Pulled in two directions, with Monsieur Marion now shouting for him impatiently, André shrugged and spread his arms wide, smiling encouragement at Te Kape. 'Allons donc, mon ami,' he said. 'I'll see you once we get ashore — we can talk then.'

Te Kape hesitated, then turned away to join his own commander, now back in his canoe. He had no sooner done so than one of the young Naturals from the island flung himself at the feet of Monsieur

Marion and clutched his legs, crying piteously and saying something over and over. At the same time, keeping well down below the gunwale, he was taking good care not to be seen by his fellows.

'De par tous les diables!' the expedition leader exclaimed. 'See if you can work out what this fellow wants, Monsieur Tallec.' Ignoring the Natural tugging at his shins, he turned to his boatmen busy putting a rack of muskets into the boat and ordered them to take them back out. 'And you soldiers, too: out — the yawl's far too crowded and you'll be in the way.'

The officers accompanying him on the fishing trip exchanged glances. 'Is that wise, sir?' Sub-Lieutenant de Vaudricourt spoke up.

'Mort-diable!' Monsieur Marion lost his temper. 'We're hardly about to go to war. Take your pistols, gentlemen, if you insist. I'm only taking my bird gun in case we see some game.' He impatiently thrust at the youth still clutching him around the legs. 'Have you established what this is all about, Monsieur Tallec?'

André got slowly to his feet, struggling to absorb what he had just been told. He took a deep breath. 'He says Tacoury plans to kill you, sir.'

The officers stood still, shocked into silence.

Monsieur Marion glared at him, then abruptly freed himself from the Zealander at his feet. He beckoned the officers to follow him back onto the quarterdeck. When they had gathered around him, he said, 'Monsieur Tallec now hears as well as sees evidence of conspiracy everywhere he goes. His command of the language might be better than most, but this time he's clearly got the syntax muddled. Look at that poor wretch — surely it's obvious it's his *own* life he fears for?'

Thomas Ballu scratched his head. 'If you say so, sir, but we might be wise to pay heed.'

'You may take your musket, sergeant,' said Monsieur Marion.

'Gentlemen, I will not hear another word. This chief Tacoury has shown me nothing but kindness. I will not insult him by succumbing to unfounded and mistaken suspicions. Please join me immediately in the boat.' As he swept off the quarterdeck, bright spots of anger flushing his cheekbones, he told one of the sailors to look after the Natural still crouched in the scuppers.

Without looking at each other, the seventeen people chosen to join him silently climbed down into the yawl, one by one. Amongst them were Sub-Lieutenant de Vaudricourt, Lieutenant Lehoux, Thomas Ballu the sergeant-at-arms, the six boatmen and several slaves — including Anthonie the cook, the surly runaway, and François, the captain's personal servant. André was the last to find a place in the crowded boat. As soon as the crew took up their oars, Te Kuri's canoe, hovering a short distance away, escorted them across the bay.

It was one of those rare sun-warmed June days that broke the monotony of the continual rainstorms and grey sullen skies that had added misery to most of their daily tasks. The sun shone almost hot through the fabric of André's jacket as he sat squeezed between two boatmen on the widest thwart. Small breaking wavelets caught sparkle from the sun's rays. Ahead of the boat, he caught a glimpse of a school of herrings scatter on the surface in a thin flurry of water as they were chased by some larger fish. It was a good day for fishing. But despite his captain's reassurances, the ensign could not find the heart to appreciate the beauty all around him as the yawl danced across the lively sea and into the bush-fringed shelter of Tacoury's Cove. The words spoken by the grovelling Natural kept repeating in his head, an ominous drumbeat, and he could not rid himself of the recurring image of Te Kape's sombre face.

Determined to make the afternoon a success, as soon as they landed, Monsieur Marion chivvied the boatmen to set off again to lay out the net, folded ready in the well of the yawl. With Te Kuri standing beside him, he then seated himself on a flat-topped rock to watch as his officers split into two groups, one lining up on the net rope behind Thomas Ballu as anchor man on the shore. When the boat completed the sweep, and the rest of the officers went to join another burly sailor at the opposing anchor position further along the beach, Te Kuri sent his men to help them pull the net in. The Naturals disposed themselves along the net ropes at both ends, each alternating with a Frenchman as they had done many times before.

Te Kape took his place beside André without a word or a smile, but he squeezed his friend's hand hard where it gripped the rope before moving his own into position.

Ashore, Monsieur Marion consulted with the tall, austere chief beside him, then called the signal to start hauling the net in. 'Pull hard, mes amis!' he shouted cheerfully. 'On such a fine day we're bound to have us an excellent catch!'

Then Te Kuri also called. A harsh call, resonant and forceful.

Instinctively, André half-turned, every nerve tingling a warning. But even as he turned, a rough hand clamped itself over his mouth. Another chopped down hard on his own hands, forcing him to let go his grip on the rope. He caught a glimpse of clubs rising and falling. He saw figures struggling — dark silhouettes against the light of the late afternoon sun. He heard a choked-off scream. But before he could even try to fight off his own attackers, his skull felt as though it was exploding into myriad pieces. A wave of red-shot blackness obscured his vision. The pain swirled everything around him down into a vortex that ended in a pinprick of bright light. Then even that was mercifully extinguished.

# Chapter 12

*12–13 June 1772*
*Port Marion 35°15' S*

Somewhere nearby, low tense voices rumbled. His nose thrust into a layer of prickling, musty leaves and a suffocating weight pressing down on his back, a half-conscious André tried to turn his head sideways, looking for more air. The movement sent sharp stabs of pain through his skull, and he groaned involuntarily. The voices stopped. The weight suddenly lifted from his back, and rough hands turned him over and sat him upright. A torch flared briefly. His head throbbing in protest, André squeezed his eyes shut as the light shone full in his face, the flame close enough to sear his skin. Someone lifted his pendant on its cord, then abruptly dropped it. He felt it settle back against his chest, its cool smoothness feeling alien now, contaminated by the betrayal of trust. The torch was snuffed out and darkness descended once more. But this time he was fully conscious. He could smell the rank fish-oil and sweaty stench of savages, and hear breathing right beside him. Cautiously, he opened his eyes as the pain in his head eased to a dull throb.

Night had fallen and it was completely dark. He could barely make out the white gleam of eyes as someone leaned closer to him and spoke quietly. 'Tareka?'

He recognized Te Kape's voice. Before he could answer, a hand was placed over his mouth, gently this time. He sensed rather than saw the youth place a warning finger across his own lips. He forced himself to relax his straining muscles and Te Kape took his hand away. As his eyes slowly adjusted to the darkness, André saw the savage squatting in front of him. Two other men crouched close by, blacker bulks amongst shadows. Upright shaggy shadows that at first he thought were many other savages. His heart gave a great lurch even as he realized the shadows were clumps of dry brushwood, closely packed around them. He was wedged with these three savages into a small space deep within a dense copse of myrtle.

Somewhere, not far away, his ears picked up a multitude of other voices. Shouting, loud brays of triumphant laughter. As he peered in that direction, he saw a faint glow through the trees, too close for comfort. The young savage pointed towards the fire glow, then shook his head, placing his hand on André's shoulder to keep him still.

Images of clubs and bodies falling flashed behind André's eyes. Horror flooded back. As his muscles involuntarily tensed in the instinct to flee, Te Kape again held him down until he was still, then patted his shoulder. André could not help himself. He shrank away from his touch, the touch of a savage who had knowingly allowed the ensign's companions to be lured to their deaths. Te Kape pulled back his hand, then turned away. The ensign drew up his knees and wrapped his arms tight around his shins. He lowered his throbbing head onto his knees and closed his eyes.

Time passed in a blur of misery. What seemed like hours later, Te Kape nudged him, then pressed the cold, sweating curve of a calabash into his hand. Although he wanted nothing more to do with the savage, he could not resist the allure of quenching his thirst. He drank a long draught of water, but before he could hand the calabash back, his stomach heaved. Leaning sideways he vomited its contents, retching painfully. He sensed rather than heard the other men shuffle further away from him. So they *were* still there.

For a moment he felt nothing but despair. Then, as his emptied stomach stopped convulsing, the fuzziness in his head cleared. A single thought steadied him: he was alive. If these savages meant him harm, they would have killed him by now.

Both the fire-glow and the jubilant voices had died away. The moon had risen, its austere light casting dense black shadows under the copse where they were hidden. Slowly and without making any sound, the other two men crawled out of the hiding place, then Te Kape pushed him to follow. Although André tried to move as soundlessly as the savages, every twig he crushed crackled under him, and the dried myrtle leaves rustled loudly in his ears. He could feel Te Kape behind him, applying steady pressure against the soles of his shoes, encouraging him to keep going.

At last he emerged from the confinement of the copse and stumbled stiffly upright. He stood for a while, swaying with dizziness, before his sense of balance returned. If he kept his head still, the pain no longer stabbed so fiercely. One of the men grabbed him and drew him into the shadow extending beyond the trees, a large hand once more clapped over his mouth, warning him not to speak. The ensign nodded his head, wincing as he did so, and the hand was taken away. In silence, he followed behind the two men. Te Kape was close on his heels, sometimes steering him away from unseen hazards as they picked their way from black shadow to black shadow. Slowly, they moved further and further away from the danger that still lay behind them. Not allowing himself to think beyond the need to keep going and to be as quiet as he could, André obeyed each slight pressure from Te Kape's guiding touch.

They walked for some hours, making their way in the shadows below ridges and across valleys through concealing patches of forest and scrub. They headed steadily westwards, away from Te Kuri's village. When his silent companions at last drew him down under the screen of some bracken fern and passed him the calabash of water, the moon had long set and the eastern sky was beginning to show ominous streaks of light. He rinsed the sour taste from his parched mouth before drinking cautiously. This time the water stayed down.

After letting him rest a few brief moments, Te Kape got him back on his feet. André realized he knew where they were. He recognized the familiar silhouette of the forested hills that stretched inland behind the masting camp, hills forming a blacker mass against the lightening sky. Now, one of the men pointed through the bracken at a broad valley lying below them. At its head, faintly visible in the dim light, André could see a saddle that must be the one leading to the swampy plain traversed by the masting party each day. He looked questioningly at them, but the two men would not meet his gaze. With a brief glance at the bulge of the pendant under his shirt, they kept their faces resolutely turned away.

Only Te Kape was prepared to look directly at him. His face grave and marked with signs of weariness that made him look older than he was, the young savage pointed at all the ridges surrounding them, then tapped the club fastened at his belt in an unmistakable gesture. André swallowed. Up there, bands of armed savages must be waiting for the dawn. Now Te Kape was indicating that they did not intend going any further with him, but would leave him here. André nodded his understanding. Then, without a word or a backward glance, the three savages set off back the way they had come.

André watched until they merged into the scrub and fern like wraiths. For a long time he could not move. His legs were trembling with what he thought must be delayed shock. It only now dawned on him that the young savage had indeed acted as his loyal friend. As the realization filled his head with unwelcome thoughts, tears began running down his face. Te Kape must have taken a huge risk in spiriting him away from whatever hideous fate had befallen his captain and his companions in the cove below Te Kuri's village. Somehow Te Kape had persuaded his two reluctant allies to go along with his plans. Not only had the ensign not even acknowledged that the young savage had saved his life, he had spurned him, unable to hide his revulsion.

It was too late for amends. All he could do was make the most of the chance he had been given. Pulling himself together, André scrubbed at his wet face. Then he turned to find a way down into the valley below. He must keep going long enough to reach the masting party. He must reach them without being detected so he could warn them before they were attacked. He resolutely ignored the voice in his head saying he might already be too late.

**Extract from the Te Kape manuscript, 1841**

*It came to pass that Mariou and many of his subordinate chiefs were enticed by Te Kuri to row ashore and set their net again in that very place where they had violated tapu because of those who had drowned there. Then he and his warriors joined with those strangers, one on one, and waited until the net was being drawn into the shore. Then, each fell upon the unsuspecting stranger in front of him and clubbed him to death. The killing was quick and merciful, being ritual fulfilment of the desire expressed by that chiefly woman, Miki. All but two were so killed. One was the youth under the chiefly protection of Te Kuri himself, returned safely to the strangers at Manawa-ora. The other was the black man flogged by Mariou's men, spared his life out of sympathy for such treatment. He was allowed to swim away and went overland to Waikare, where his descendants still live today.*

*The bodies of those slain were taken by the war party, then, cooked and eaten by them as necessary retribution for the violations committed* by those strangers. The small bones of those slain were made into forks for picking up food, and their thigh-bones were made into flutes. In all these ritual ways was the mana of those slain rendered harmless. Only Te Kuri and the tohunga Tohitapu of Te Roroa had sufficient mana to eat the body of Mariou, the principal chief of those strangers. That act was carried out at Te Haumi, at the place set aside for such ritual, and the blackened stones of that cooking fire can be seen there to this day. Accordingly, that matter was brought to its necessary and inevitable conclusion.

It is often said that all the troubles visited on men stem from fights over women or land:

He wahine, he whenua, ka ngaro te tangata.
The death of men is caused by women and land.

And so it was for Mariou. A song is still sung here in Te Rawhiti about that woman, Miki, and how her craving for fish triggered his death:

Nau ra e Miki            It was you, Miki,
I tangi ki te ika         who cried for fish.
I mate ai Mariou          And as a result Marion died,
Kurikuri pau              consumed by Kurikuri [Te Kuri].

You say you have heard of the primary wife of Ruatara at Rangihoua, who also carried that name and was known to the missionaries there. Indeed, that illustrious name was further memorialized by being given to the chiefly daughter of Waraki, a woman with Ngati Rangi connections who was of high status amongst our people in that more recent time.

Stumbling with weariness, his shoulder blades tense from constantly sensing he was being watched, André slowed to a halt. From the protection of a clump of sword-grass, he scanned the slope rising ahead of him. It was fully light now, and the sun's rays were touching the rim of the saddle above. He knew he would be exposed there, as it would be hard to avoid being silhouetted against the skyline, however briefly. So far, despite that insistent prickle of premonition, he had seen no sign of savages. But he had no way of knowing who or what might lie in wait for him on the other side of the saddle — or at the masting camp beyond. Taking a deep breath, he plotted a route up a shallow gully that would provide him with the most protection. He could not linger any longer. The more he delayed, the stronger the light would become and the more likely it was he would be detected.

Then, just as he left the shelter of the sword-grass, he saw the skyline above him blur. He blinked to clear his vision, but the blurring became worse. As he watched, the slope ahead disappeared as tendrils of mist were sucked out of the damp ground by the increasing warmth of the sun. Within minutes, a wall of thicker fog rolled over the saddle and down towards him. Uttering silent prayers of thanks, he crossed himself, then plunged into the fog. He climbed as fast as he could, not knowing how long he could rely on the vapour to hide him. By some trick of terrain and air movement, the floor of the shallow gully itself was clear, the fog flowing just above his head. He was able to follow the route he had picked out.

His legs protesting with the strain, he pushed up steadily until he gained the saddle. He skirted a boggy section, then was at last moving more easily — downhill. He must be on the far side of the saddle. The fog pressed against the flank of the hill so he could not now see where he was going. At least the slope was not steep. He could hear his breathing, amplified by the fog, and pushed aside the thought that any lurking savages would surely hear him. But he sensed no other movement. He seemed to be the only thing alive in this fog-shrouded landscape.

At last the changed angle of his footing told him he had reached the floor of the valley and level ground. Pushing his way through tussock and fern, he followed around the base of the hill, heading towards the coast and the invisible sea. It would be too easy to lose his bearings in the fog if he struck out directly across the swampy plain towards the masting camp.

Almost as suddenly as the fog had descended, it began to lift. For some time he had been hearing the steady surge of waves on the beach. Now, not far ahead of him he could glimpse the sea, lit silver under the lifting layer of fog. On the far side of the plain, he could pick out the huts of the masting camp, solid shapes tucked against the slope, with moving red and blue spots of colour that must be French officers. He drew in a shuddering breath of relief.

Then, as the surrounding hills emerged through the mist, he saw what he had been anticipating ever since Te Kape left him. Armed savages massed in throngs on all the hilltops above him. By some miracle, he had made his way past them under the cover of the fog without being accosted. Instinctively, he crossed himself and muttered a prayer of thanks. As he did so, his hand brushed against the pendant still lying under his shirt. For a moment, André was tempted to wrench the alien object off and hurl it into the fern. But even as he grasped its cord intending to do just that, something gave him pause. Reluctantly, he let go. He could not ignore that the pendant had protected him somehow; and without it, those savages would not have helped Te Kape secure his escape.

With a final burst of effort, the ensign crossed the last stretch of swamp and reached the outskirts of the camp. To his dismay, he saw several savages coming from the opposite direction, intent on approaching two of the guards with baskets of fish, calling out in friendly voices. The unsuspecting guards, their muskets propped against the wall of the guard-post behind them, beckoned them closer. The sunlit scene appeared so normal that André was momentarily disorientated, the events of the past eighteen or so hours taking on the guise of hallucination. Then reality returned. But before he could find breath to shout a warning, he heard Lieutenant Le Dez's voice.

'Monsieur Tallec — you look as though you've seen a ghost!'

He turned towards the lieutenant. The senior officer was lounging against the wall of the officers' hut, a steaming mug in his hand, the picture of nonchalance. André stared, again thrown off-balance. The lieutenant looked more closely at him. Pushing himself off the wall, his voice sharpened with concern, he asked, 'Ma fois, what has befallen you? Where've you come from to be in such a state?'

André tried to tell his story, but his teeth were clattering uncontrollably. The words no sooner formed in his head than they escaped his tongue. He could only stammer, disjointed fragments of speech that sounded deluded in his own ears. He closed his mouth and stared mutely at the lieutenant. His legs were shaking again.

Lieutenant Le Dez sat him down and called for brandy. 'Take your time, sir.'

The brandy gulped and sending welcome warmth into his belly, André slowly managed to get across to the officers now clustered around him the gist of what had happened. As he spoke, the nightmare images kept flashing, a jagged visual accompaniment to his stuttered words.

Looking appalled, the lieutenant finally asked about Monsieur Marion's fate.

André shook his head. 'I did not see him, sir — I saw very little before . . .' His voice died away.

Lieutenant Le Dez touched his shoulder. His face suddenly cleared and he said comfortingly, 'Do not distress yourself. We can but hope he, too, was spared. Surely they intended no harm to him at least? Another brandy, I think.' As the glass was refilled, he gestured at the surrounding hills. 'You can see we've been having a spot of bother ourselves, but we've kept the savages at bay.'

He kept talking, at first, André thought, to give him time to recover himself. But as the senior officer talked on, he began to wonder whether Lieutenant Le Dez grasped the enormity of what he had just told him. His usual wry manner unaltered in any way, the senior officer was recounting how they had been surrounded by increasing numbers of savages since daylight. He considered their behaviour not so much threatening as merely odd. 'For some reason, they'd parcelled out the fish supplies amongst each and every one of them. They all came towards us, each holding out a single fish. We could see they were armed, so we made it clear they were to come no closer than one of their pikes we set in the ground. We did our trading from there.'

'You traded as *usual*, sir?' André found his voice to ask.

'Oui, oui — we saw no reason to forgo our breakfast fish.' Lieutenant Le Dez added, 'Never fear, we kept our weapons in full sight, so they knew we were on the alert. Don't forget we had the second lieutenant here, sent to reinforce us with another contingent of soldiers.'

The second lieutenant took up the account. 'We'd no trouble driving them off whenever they came too close to the marker — pointing a musket was enough to have them backing off. Their most serious attempt was an hour or so ago. A bunch crept up on us, squatting innocently on their heels whenever they saw us watching them. But we soon spotted what they were up to — dragging those pikes of theirs behind them out of sight in the grass, hoping to get close enough to surprise us. That's when we drove them right off the flat and up onto those hills. We've had no trouble since, just their usual shouting and stamping.'

Lieutenant Le Dez said thoughtfully, 'We did think we heard cannon being fired from the ships mid-morning — three or four shots. That gave us some pause, but nothing else has happened to give us any reason for alarm.'

Monsieur Le Corre said, 'Why, you were here yourself, Monsieur Tallec, the other day when such displays of strength proved merely that — displays. These savages do posture a lot . . .' His voice faltered as he saw André's bleak expression. He said defensively, 'There was nothing to indicate anything was other than usual. So much so that Monsieur Crozet took the masting party up to the masts first thing, seeing no reason not to keep on with our work.'

'Monsieur Crozet and how many others?' André's heart sank. He could not believe his senior officers were so foolhardy, when by their own reckoning they had been surrounded by many hundred armed savages. How could they *still* be so reluctant to acknowledge the seriousness of their situation?

Before anyone could answer him, the guard shouted that the *Mascarin*'s longboat was approaching. Leaving the soldiers and the guard on alert, the officers went down to the beach to meet it.

As soon as the boat grounded, Paul Chevillard leapt ashore, followed by fifteen men, all armed, most with muskets and fixed bayonets. André never thought he would be so pleased to see his fellow ensign. His presence surely meant the ships at least were still safe.

Greeting him with equal warmth, Chevillard said, 'You cannot believe my relief at finding you here, André. Can I assume by some good fortune Monsieur Marion is with you?'

As the young ensign slowly shook his head, Chevillard's face grew immediately grim. He turned to the other officers. 'Gentlemen, I fear I bring desperate news.'

The story he told them was desperate indeed.

At six-thirty that morning, Monsieur du Clesmeur had sent his longboat and a wooding party ashore to collect firewood. On board were twelve men, amongst them the *Castries'* coxswain, the quartermaster and the nine tops men — the *Castries'* élite and most experienced sailors. They landed at a beach below the long hill running between Pikiorei's village and that of Te Kuri. Greeted as usual by welcoming and friendly Zealanders, who had carried them ashore, the unsuspecting sailors began cutting firewood behind the beach. No sooner had they separated amongst the trees, armed only with their axes, than they were ruthlessly set upon, several savages to each Frenchman.

Only one man miraculously escaped. Even though he suffered two spear wounds to the stomach, this survivor somehow got away unnoticed after trying in vain to ward off the savages attacking his nearest companion. As he fled through the trees, he heard behind him the terrible howls of the savages and the anguished screams and moans of his companions as they were slaughtered, one by one. Even worse, he was close enough on occasion to witness bodies being hacked to pieces. At last emerging onto the cleared ground of Te Kuri's village, he ran the length of the parade ground, taunted by hordes of children, who followed him throwing stones. But he somehow succeeded in reaching the low saddle that led onto the beach off which the ships were anchored. Flinging himself into the sea, he swam out towards the ships. Luckily, one of the officers aboard the *Mascarin* heard his plaintive cries, and the longboat was despatched to pick him up. It was barely eight o'clock, only an hour and a half since the *Castries'* boat had gone ashore.

'The poor man was almost demented with grief and shock, his

words sounding like the ravings of a madman,' said Chevillard. 'But once we could make some sense of his account, we immediately feared Monsieur Marion and his party had met the same fate the night before. We'd neither seen nor heard anything of them since their departure.' He looked sombrely at André and crossed himself. 'Your face indicates that, alas, our fears were only too true. Our captain has indeed met the same fate.'

After a moment's silence, he went on to tell them that the *Mascarin's* first lieutenant, left in command of the ship, had sent him off to warn the masting camp once he had first skirted the coast to search for Monsieur Marion's yawl. Chevillard found both the yawl and the *Castries'* longboat beached at different spots along the landing place below Te Kuri's village, each still surrounded by swarms of armed savages. 'They beckoned for us to approach, gentlemen, but as there were up to two thousand of them and so few of us, I went close enough only to determine whether any of our people were amongst them.' He paused, then said heavily, 'Close enough to see that one of the chiefs I recognized was wearing Monsieur Marion's spotted velvet waistcoat. Not much further along, we saw another chief with Monsieur de Vaudricourt's sword. Others were flaunting articles of our companions' clothing.'

Enraged by the sight, their hearts filled with pity and foreboding, they fired several volleys from their muskets at these savages, but without much result. He explained: 'The water was shallow and we could not get close enough. As it was, we ran aground. By some good fortune we were able to refloat the boat and get back into it before the savages realized what was happening. Otherwise they could've easily overrun us.'

'Do you think there's any chance of survivors, sir?' Lieutenant Le Dez's demeanour was now sober.

'From the amount of our people's possessions we saw on show

amongst the savages, I fear not.' Chevillard hesitated, then said in a rush of words. 'I deeply regret we didn't go ashore, sir. I don't know for certain that no one has survived. I can't be sure we shouldn't be mounting a rescue operation at this very moment. I fear we might've abandoned someone yet alive.' He gestured at André. 'Despite what we saw, I pinned foolish hopes on finding Monsieur Marion here, and when I saw Monsieur Tallec . . .' His voice trailed away.

André realized the clerk was close to tears.

Lieutenant Le Dez said soothingly, 'None of us doubts you did your best, sir. You were clearly outnumbered. It would've been most unwise to venture any closer. If you had, you probably wouldn't be here now, bringing us such timely warning and welcome reinforcements.'

André could not help thinking the lieutenant seemed unaware of the irony of his words. The senior officers at the masting camp had faced a similar situation that very morning, without showing the same prudence. He suddenly remembered the cannon fire the lieutenant had mentioned. Concern for Jean, stranded with so little support on Marion Island, overwhelmed him.

As if he had anticipated André's thoughts, Chevillard turned to André, his emotions under better control. 'Before we left, we sent reinforcements to the hospital camp. Your cousin was indeed surrounded by savages overnight, but he'd taken the precaution of setting up barricades. With the blunderbusses clearly ready to fire, he and his men were quite safe. They had no trouble warning the savages off. Once we fired the ship's cannon a few times, we dropped off more soldiers. The savages then withdrew over the hill — presumably to that fortified village of theirs. I have full confidence in Monsieur Roux's ability to continue to look after himself and the men with him.'

Nodding his gratitude for such welcome news, André said to

Lieutenant Le Dez, 'I don't wish to presume, sir, but we should delay no longer in warning Monsieur Crozet. It may only be a matter of time before the savages work up enough courage to launch a full-scale attack.'

'D'accord,' the lieutenant had the grace not to take offence at being told what to do by such a junior officer. 'We should prepare to withdraw from this location, fall back on the ships, gentlemen. While we're still scattered so thinly, the savages may well think they can pick us off.' He told Chevillard to take his men and go on up to the masting party, fill them in on what had befallen the captain and so many of their companions. 'I'm relying on you to ensure they retreat in an orderly manner. It's important you stress that no one is to show any signs of alarm. If the savages see we're in control and not panicking, they may well continue their present stand-off.' He told the rest of the men to start loading the longboat with gear from the huts. 'Only essential equipment — we'll be hard put to get everybody on board as it is.' He looked ruefully at the *Castries'* yawl, pulled up on the beach beside the longboat, not needing to comment on its poor condition and small size.

Relieved the lieutenant had at last come to his senses, André asked, 'Permission to go with Monsieur Chevillard, sir?' He thought he would go mad stuck down here, waiting for yet more potentially bad news.

Lieutenant Le Dez hesitated. 'Is that wise after your ordeal, Monsieur Tallec?' Then he looked more closely at the ensign and nodded abruptly. 'Fort bien, occupation might be best.'

Monsieur Crozet had already been warned of the savages surrounding the shore camp by the escort who took midday dinner up to the masting party. He spotted the tightly bunched group of his countrymen approaching with bayonets fixed while they were some distance away. Leaving the haulers still at work, he came down the hill to meet them. The two ensigns brought him up to date as quickly as they could.

The second-in-command listened in silence. When they finished speaking, he said bleakly, 'This is indeed terrible news, gentlemen.' He shook his head. 'I always suspected Tacoury was a dangerous ruffian, but Monsieur Marion would have none of it.'

André thought this grossly unjust, considering Monsieur Crozet himself had consistently ignored the signs of escalating trouble, but he kept his mouth shut. It was too late for regrets, and in his opinion there was nothing to be gained by blame-laying. But he could not stop himself wishing with all his heart that they had been able to leave Port Marion even a week ago — before their association with the savages had so inexplicably turned from friendship to treachery.

Monsieur Crozet was still speaking. 'The price we've paid for his unfounded faith is high indeed — apart from the loss of our expedition leader, which is bad enough, we can ill afford to lose so many of our best men. How many, did you say?'

'If they have indeed all been slain, I make it twenty-eight, sir,' said Chevillard. 'Seventeen from the *Mascarin*, including Monsieur Marion, and eleven from the *Castries*.'

Such accounting would have been quite beyond André. For a moment he stared at Chevillard with a fierce loathing. Then he remembered the clerk's distress at the shore camp at the failure of his valiant attempt to mount a rescue operation and noticed the knots working in his clenched jaw. Perhaps it would be more charitable to see his reduction of everything to tallies or records of some sort as simply his way of coping with the unimaginable.

Monsieur Crozet now took charge. 'We must avoid letting any of the men know of this tragedy so we can withdraw in a controlled fashion,' he said. 'I've been keeping a close watch, but we've not had any savages come anywhere near us up here, so we should be able to pack up what we can without fuss and leave.'

André was observing the surrounding hills. 'I can see armed savages on all those hills around us now, sir.'

The second-in-command surveyed the hills, then harrumphed. 'They must've seen the boat arrive with reinforcements.'

André made no other comment, thinking it highly unlikely the savages had not been present — if concealed — all along. As they set off to the top of the hill where the masts had been dragged, the savages certainly made no further attempts to conceal themselves. They stood brandishing their weapons, shouting insults and jibes in unmistakably derisory tones.

With Monsieur Crozet maintaining firm discipline and the relief party mounting guard, the masting workers reluctantly began to dismantle all the equipment and pile it in heaps near the small tent they used overnight for shelter.

'Seems a crying shame to be abandoning the masts after all our hard work,' one of them grumbled as he added blocks and tackle to the pile. 'Just when we'd got within sight of the sea, pardieu.'

'D'accord — we do intend returning for them,' said Monsieur Crozet, overhearing. 'In the meantime, you'd do well not to question your orders.'

As soon as everything was dismantled, the second-in-command had the sailors loaded up with what they could carry. The rest, mostly utensils and personal bits and pieces he considered expendable, he ordered placed in a hole dug inside the tent. 'Pull the tent down over the top and set fire to it — it may be sufficient to fool the savages until we can return.'

But almost before they had left the hilltop, forming a solid phalanx with the laden sailors protected by armed men at back and front, more than twenty savages descended on the still-smoking ashes. They immediately began digging up the buried goods.

So much for them being nowhere near, André thought. That lot must have been concealed in the scrub right on the edge of the site, watching their every move. He cast a wary glance at the savages on the surrounding hills, where there now seemed to be a thousand or more of them, their numbers increasing every time he checked. On all sides, they began threading their way through the scrub and bracken fern, moving to intercept the French party. He alerted Monsieur Crozet that they were on the move.

'Keep your positions, if you please,' Monsieur Crozet passed the word through to the front. 'We know from past experience they're unlikely to attack if we remain calm and alert. These savages engage only if they have the advantage of surprise.'

Sure enough, the savages merely followed along behind and alongside, frequently jeering and calling out that Monsieur Marion had been killed. Although several marksmen in the detachment reacted, eager to seek vengeance, the savages stayed just beyond musket range. As the marksmen's frustration grew, the second-in-command ordered them to bide their time. 'You'd be playing right into their hands, gentlemen,' he said. 'Inciting an attack's exactly what they want. We can't afford an affray here, being so few. We must focus on getting all our men off the beach and back to the ships without further losses. Your chance for revenge will come — have no doubt of that.'

As they pushed on, determinedly ignoring the insults, André grudgingly gave Monsieur Crozet credit for their doing so. The savages had probably assumed they would panic on learning of Monsieur Marion's fate and they would then be able to pick off fleeing Frenchmen at their leisure. They would learn soon enough that Frenchmen were not cowards.

They reached the boats without mishap. Monsieur Crozet ordered the sailors to embark immediately without shedding their loads. Increasing numbers of savages gathered on the beach behind them, their cries growing ever more excited. André was increasingly uneasy, reminded of their experience in Van Diemen's Land. Surely it was only a matter of time before the savages worked themselves into sufficient frenzy to attack? They were outnumbered by at least ten to one.

It seemed Monsieur Crozet was thinking in a similar vein. He took a stick and drew a line in the sand, well above the tide line. He then paced up and down on the seaward side of this line, brandishing his musket, just as if he were one of the savages' own challengers. One by one, realizing what he was doing, the savages fell silent. Once he had gained their attention, the second-in-command gestured at the line, then pointed his musket at each of several chiefs in turn. His meaning was unmistakable. Satisfied, he turned to André. 'A bit of reinforcement would do no harm, Monsieur Tallec. Do you by any chance know the words that would make them sit down?'

Armed with the necessary phrase, the ensign faced the most important-looking chief, pointed at the line and said in threatening tones, 'Eh-noho!' At the same time, he deliberately raked his unfired musket along the line of watching savages.

Their response was successful beyond anything André would have expected. The chief quietly repeated the order. Without any fuss, each and every savage sat down on the sand. A thousand and more of them.

For a moment, the startled Frenchmen gaped at them, then got on with loading the boats. 'As fast as you can, gentlemen,' said Monsieur Crozet, flushed with his success. 'We don't know how long that will hold them.'

With nearly a hundred men to get on board as well as all the gear, embarking took some time. They then struggled to launch the two heavily laden boats. As they pushed and heaved to get the longboat afloat, the savages became restless. The last to embark, André and Monsieur Crozet had to wade up to their knees. As soon as they entered the water, the savages rose to their feet en masse and rushed towards the water's edge, uttering fierce war cries. Abandoning any semblance of dignity, the two officers splashed hastily towards the boat. By the time their companions helped them clamber on board, some of the savages had approached within a few yards, spears lifted to their shoulders ready to hurl.

'Peste!' The coxswain swore, then got the boat underway before André could squeeze in beside Chevillard, who was kneeling awkwardly on the pile of gear in the well of the boat. Monsieur Crozet was forced to stand straddling the tiller. With the boatmen struggling to find any rhythm in the overloaded boats, they slowly drew away from the shore as a shower of spears and stones fell harmlessly amongst them.

Behind the beach, André saw black smoke already billowing from the huts of the shore camp as the savages set fire to them. All along the edge of the tide line, hordes of savages capered and shouted, their voices full of triumph. It was too much for Monsieur Crozet. Gritting his teeth, he gave the fusiliers permission to fire a volley or two. 'We don't want the varmints thinking they forced our retreat. It's time to remind them of our superior weapons.'

But they were already too far offshore for the balls to cause much damage, and the crowded boat made targeted firing impossible. It was not long before the resigned second-in-command ordered the fusiliers to cease fire. As the boats slowly picked up what little speed they could, André watched over the stern as the cavorting savages at last began to recede in the distance.

❖❖

**Extract from the Te Kape manuscript, 1841**

*Next morning, when others from the ships came ashore to cut firewood nearby at Opunga, not knowing of the fate of Mariou, they were also taken by surprise by our warriors, as fitting retaliation for their earlier violation in cutting wood from the tapu pohutukawa tree. All but one were killed, and, that one escaped and swam off to the ships. The bodies of those slain were then cut up and shared amongst the people so that all could partake in the revenge for the major violations of tapu inflicted by those strangers.*

*Then, word was sent by Te Kuri to his allies at Manawa-ora that Mariou and many of his subordinate chiefs had been killed. Accordingly the war party gathered on the heights at Manawa-ora called out that news to the strangers there in the expectation they would take flight on hearing that their principal chief and many of their subordinate chiefs were dead. As was customary practice, they could then be picked off one by one as they fled, without the war party risking casualties of their own. Instead, an orderly retreat was achieved by one of Mariou's remaining subordinate chiefs, a man of great courage.*

*Although our warriors were frustrated at not being able to force the expected rout, they followed the well-armed strangers in a threatening manner so they would have no choice but to leave Manawa-ora. To make sure they would not return, and as retaliation for their earlier depredations in that place, all their houses and belongings were set on fire. When the boats fled and their guns inflicted no harm, the warriors at Manawa-ora considered the defeat of those strangers had been completed. As a defeated people, they would surely sail away from Tokerau and leave us in peace.*

# Chapter 13

'Monsieur Marion's only fault was to believe that savages had the same integrity and gentleness as himself,' said Jean, sighing heavily. 'We've lost the most able sailor and navigator I've ever known. None of our senior officers comes close to sharing his abilities, not even Monsieur Crozet.'

'D'accord,' agreed André. 'But it wasn't just Monsieur Marion: we all shared his belief.'

'To some extent,' Jean conceded. 'But the signs were there.'

'Easy to say in hindsight,' said André. 'Even you can't deny that if we'd been ready to leave a week ago, we'd have sailed away thinking these people the friendliest on earth.'

'And we all know why we're still here,' said Jean, bitterness darkening his voice. 'There's only one person to blame for that.'

André's thoughts returned to the collision months ago in the Southern Ocean. Surely no one could have predicted such dire consequences? Not even the most pessimistic person could have foreseen that the extra time needed to re-mast the *Castries* would land them in their present predicament.

His cousin burst out, 'I'll never understand how our captain could go along with the appointment of someone so incompetent as du Clesmeur. It's a huge price he's paid for his foolish aspirations to be accepted by the aristocracy.'

There was nothing André could say in response, and the two ensigns fell silent. They were keeping the evening watch inside the large rectangular entrenchment on Marion Island Jean had fashioned from filled water casks. With Monsieur Crozet's permission, the young ensign had come ashore to join his cousin late in the afternoon, as soon as the evacuated masting party returned to the ships. The senior officer, now in command of the *Mascarin*, did not hesitate in giving his consent. 'You'll be as safe ashore as on board, Monsieur Tallec. I can't fault Monsieur Roux's defences. Your mind will be easier if you're with your cousin.'

Although the ensign was exhausted and the eventful day seemed endless, he saw no point in trying to rest. Every muscle was quivering with pent-up nervous energy, and he startled at the slightest noise. So before the light faded completely, he took a good look at what Jean had put in place. He paced the length of the entrenchment before rejoining his cousin. Laid end-to-end, the sixty leaguers — each containing one hundred and sixty gallons of water — formed a substantial bulwark around the small guard-post tent. All six blunderbusses were now set up in a small battery on the side where any likely attack would come from, each with men delegated to fire and reload. Jean had also sent a dozen of the best men to guard the forge, about three hundred paces away.

The senior ensign told André how the night before the few able-bodied defenders left on the island had seen off several hundred savages without having to fire a shot. 'The savages marched up boldly at first, coming pretty close to the guard-post,' he explained. 'But as it was bright moonlight, they could see we were waiting for them, with the blunderbusses trained in their direction. They came no closer, but dropped down into the concealment of the fern.'

Although they were no more than a pistol-shot away, Jean resisted the temptation to fire at them. 'I had in mind Monsieur Marion's insistence that we shouldn't harm them, so I decided to wait until they attacked first.' He shook his head, then said fiercely. 'If I'd any inkling of what had just happened at Tacoury's Cove, I'd have made them pay with their lives — we could've mown them down, all of them.'

Much to his regret, the savages made no move. After half an hour or so, they stealthily withdrew, one by one, crouching low in the fern until they judged they were at a safe distance. 'We had no further bother during the night.'

'If you hadn't the foresight to mount the blunderbusses, things might've been very different,' André pointed out soberly. 'They could've overrun you with ease.'

'D'accord,' Jean agreed dryly. 'But if they'd been a bit more enterprising, they still could've finished us off, then destroyed all the ships' equipment into the bargain.'

They both fell silent again. It did not bear thinking about. Essential equipment was still on shore — rudders, rigging and all the spare yards. Worse, the savages could have capitalized on their attacks on Monsieur Marion and the wooding party, quite easily destroying each of the isolated French outliers, killing them all then capturing their ships. André assumed that was what the savages had indeed planned, but for whatever reason they had not carried such a diabolical strategy to its logical conclusion. Seeking distraction from such unwelcome thoughts, he urged Jean to go on with his account.

At first light, Jean had seen that the mountains behind the hospital camp were crowded with armed savages making threatening gestures. A mainland chief he recognized eventually approached the camp, on his own and unarmed. The senior ensign went to meet him, in the same way he had during the stand-off at the masting camp a few days previously. 'I did take the precaution of concealing a brace of pistols in my greatcoat pockets,' he said. 'But when he got closer, I saw he was weeping. He kept saying, "Tacoury maté Marion!" It took me a while to understand what he was saying, but foolishly I assumed he was warning me, as I thought Monsieur Marion was safe on board.' Fury and regret sparked in his eyes. 'If only I'd known . . .'

André shook his head. 'Our mistake was far worse.' He told him how a savage had come on board to warn them before the fatal fishing trip, how Monsieur Marion had refused to accept his translation. His voice choked. 'I should've been more insistent. I could've saved his life.'

It was Jean's turn to shake his head. 'He was so fixed in his good opinion of Tacoury, indeed of all the savages, nothing you or anyone else said would've swayed him. You mustn't blame yourself.' He placed his arm across André's shoulders. 'What you've just told me reinforces my feeling that Monsieur Marion was the unfortunate victim of his own delusions.' He paused, then said violently, 'Who knows what will happen to us now we're left with that young popinjay in command!'

André said cautiously, 'By his own account, Monsieur du Clesmeur seems to have done all right so far.'

Jean snorted. 'We've neither heard nor seen anything of him. Of course, with the loss of the *Castries*' longboat and his yawl being at the masting camp, he's been stranded on board his ship today — I assume he's been running around his quarterdeck like a chicken with its head chopped off.'

'Not what he told Monsieur Crozet,' said André, smiling despite himself. 'He claimed he took charge immediately the survivor from the wooding party was picked up. That he first sent reinforcements to you, then by firing the cannons he succeeded in dispersing the savages surrounding you this morning. Then he sent the boat off to relieve the masting camp, seeing that as a priority.'

'Monsieur du *Clesmeur*?' Jean snorted again. 'Mort-diable! It was our own first lieutenant who ordered all that — he put Paul Chevillard in charge of the *Mascarin*'s longboat to bring me reinforcements. Chevillard told me he was to report his actions to Monsieur du Clesmeur and the *Castries* on his way to the masting camp.'

'Monsieur du Clesmeur's not the only one gilding the lily,' said André. 'Even Monsieur Crozet couldn't resist. According to him, we fired several volleys of shot directly into the savages massed on the beach as we left the masting camp. Every shot counted, and we killed dozens. According to him, we could've killed the lot had he so wished.'

'And according to you?' Jean raised his eyebrows.

'We were too far offshore to have much impact, as far as I could see,' said André ruefully. 'Besides, the longboat was dangerously overloaded. Firing the guns came close to capsizing us — the fusiliers fired only one volley, and a ragged one at that.' He added thoughtfully, 'Maybe he exaggerated our success to compensate for his unpopular decision not to go back to Tacoury's Cove to retrieve our boats.'

'What other decision could he make?' Jean was puzzled. 'You were in no position to risk being attacked and overrun.'

'D'accord,' agreed André. 'But many of our people felt it was the only chance we'd have and he was being over-cautious.'

While they were talking, a bank of cloud had obscured the newly risen moon. Heavy rain now set in. The men off duty crowded into the one small tent for shelter, and Jean issued sheepskin covers to the sentries standing outside the entrenchment so they could keep the locks of their muskets dry. He and André stayed at their post behind the battery, the collars of their greatcoats turned up ineffectually against the driving rain, constantly having to dash the water from their faces so they could see.

'Prenez garde!' Jean shouted to the sentries on watch beyond the entrenchment. 'The savages may well take advantage of the dark and the drumming of the rain to sneak up on us.'

But for some hours they were undisturbed, so during the heaviest downpours the two ensigns eventually gave up their vigil to join the others under the shelter of the tent. Just on eleven o'clock, the savages attacked the forge. Alerted by the responding volley of musket shots, André and Jean hastened to the end of the entrenchment nearest the forge to check with the sentries, then sent another six men to support the defenders. After a few minutes of lively firing from that direction, the sentries reported that savages were approaching the entrenchment.

'It's as I thought,' said Jean. 'They attacked the forge as a diversion, hoping to draw us all out into the open.'

The men had already taken up their stations at each blunderbuss, and he ordered the sentries to fall back to the bulwark of the entrenchment. As soon as the savages came close enough to hurl their spears, the guns opened fire, each in turn so they were able to keep up a constant barrage of shot at the same time as they were reloading.

André shouted over the noise of the guns and the defiant screams of the savages, 'Should I signal the *Mascarin*?' When Jean nodded, he set off the flare they had agreed with Monsieur Crozet as a warning that they were being attacked. In the bright flash of light, he saw the savages were already beginning to retreat, carrying with them several of their dead and wounded. Even as the light of the flare faded, they were disappearing into the forest near the forge. Soon, the last of them had crept away. Jean ordered the men to cease firing.

Once the din of their own guns died away, they could hear the sound of continued volleys from the forge. At first perturbed that the men there were still being attacked, André soon realized the consistent and steady fire indicated they had firm control. Not long afterwards, that firing stopped, too, and the forge contingent sent a messenger to report that the savages had all retreated. At neither site had the Frenchmen suffered any casualties. Hundreds of savages had come close enough for a few darts and lances to fall within the entrenchment, but they did no harm. The elated men in the entrenchment sent up a victorious cry of 'Vive le Roi!', to be echoed by the defenders at the forge.

'That should show the savages they're no match for our trained men and superior weapons,' said Jean with considerable satisfaction. He snapped a few darts over his knee and flung them contemptuously over the bulwark. 'Paltry wooden toys, pardieu!'

At that moment a breathless group of armed sailors jogged onto the terrace, coming from the ships as reinforcements in response to their signal. At Jean's suggestion, André sent them back with the boat, taking some pleasure in saying, 'Tell Monsieur Crozet we've got everything under control.'

Although the savages made no further attack that night, the bouts of heavy rain continued. They kept a close watch. André's thoughts again turned to his earlier realization that the savages had mounted three co-ordinated attacks, first targeting the people on the ships, then the widely separated shore operations. Surely it was only a matter of time before they realized the vastly outnumbered Frenchmen were still vulnerable and pressed their advantage home? He shivered involuntarily, then concentrated on peering out into the sheets of driving rain.

At daybreak, he thought his fears were about to be fulfilled. The two ensigns could see that the number of savages gathering on the surrounding hills had swelled considerably, to at least a thousand. They could make out the dark shapes of several fully-laden canoes approaching from the mainland, bringing even more reinforcements. As soon as it was fully light, savages waving articles of French clothing began shouting down to them that they had killed Monsieur Marion, demonstrating with unholy glee exactly how they had done so. One of them was wielding the expedition leader's silver-mounted musket. The sight enraged Jean. 'If they think that will *intimidate* us, they've got a surprise coming,' he said, gritting his teeth.

André then spotted the mainland chief Te Kuri amongst the latest arrivals. He swallowed hard. What if Te Kape was with him? As he watched, the chief began swaggering down the mountain towards them, with ten of his men. His erstwhile friend was indeed amongst them; he could make out his familiar figure, recognize the way he moved. The savages were all armed with long pikes, bludgeons in their belts as usual.

'Peste soit du scélérat!' growled Jean. 'A plague on the scoundrel — and on all those ruffians with him!'

As they watched, Te Kuri came within earshot. He began shouting Jean's name and beckoning him. André could see Te Kape clearly now, in position behind his chief's shoulder. His face impassive, the youth showed no sign of recognizing him.

When Te Kuri called again, Jean said, 'Two can play this game.' In mocking tones, he called back, beckoning at the same time. 'Aré-maye, Tacoury! Aré-maye!'

To André's dismay, in the face of such provocation the chief and his followers promptly strolled within musket shot, calling again to Jean and making lewd gestures. What if his cousin ordered them to fire? He was not at all sure he could shoot at the youth who had saved his life. He waited and watched, the dilemma making his heart beat painfully.

Jean had already organized their six best marksmen. 'Fort bien! He's fallen right into my trap.' He turned to André and said quietly, 'You're to stay here, cousin. I'm aware your feelings might be compromised.' Out loud, he said to the men, 'Monsieur Tallec's to arrange covering fire here.'

Before the somewhat relieved André could protest, his cousin and the marksmen had left the entrenchment. They had not marched twenty purposeful paces when Te Kuri suddenly realized his folly. With his companions, he turned back up the mountain, no longer swaggering insolently but running as fast as he could.

He was too late. Jean ordered his party to fire, to aim only at Te Kuri himself. All seven shots were fired at him before the anxiously watching André saw the chief stumble and fall. His companions picked him up and continued running. In the mêlée he could not see whether Te Kape, always so close to his chief, had also been hit. His heart pounding, he watched as the savages now fled, with Jean and his men chasing after them, stopping only to fire another volley. Although more of them fell, the savages were the faster runners, even burdened with their wounded. Jean's party could not gain on them. Other savages were now pouring down the mountainside, coming to the assistance of Te Kuri's companions, so the senior ensign had the sense to turn back.

'That taught the villains a thing or two,' he said, his face flushed with success, when they returned to the entrenchment. 'I don't know whether we managed to kill Tacoury, but he certainly fell heavily.'

Much to André's relief, his cousin made no further reference to Te Kape. His head whirling with mixed emotions, the ensign busied himself helping reload the muskets.

They could see the rescue party still milling about on the mountain top leading to the fortified village, their obvious agitation expressed in shouting and wailing. Then, even as they watched, the savages crowded on all the surrounding hills suddenly began to withdraw. The noise died away. Within minutes, they had all disappeared.

Rain fell steadily again, and the morning light was dull. The wind was rising, its susurration in the nearby trees constantly causing André to cast anxious looks in that direction, thinking savages were amassing once more. But there was no sign of them, nothing to show they had ever been there. The rain swept down the surrounding hillsides, carried on gusts of wind that flattened the bracken fern. Only the heaviness of his saturated greatcoat, his uncontrollable shivers in the increasing cold, and repeating images of Te Kuri falling to the musket fire reassured the ensign that the whole episode had been real, not a nightmarish figment of his already strained mind.

Jean, aware his cousin was close to breaking point, sent him to organize the retrieval of all the essential equipment from the grass huts where it was stored. Grateful for the distraction of activity, André supervised his working party as they carried the equipment down to the beach. Late in the morning, as he stood with Jean watching the last load being transferred into the longboat, the senior ensign said suddenly, 'I think we should seize the advantage. I'm going to ask Monsieur Crozet for permission to attack the island's fortified village while so many of the savages are gathered there.'

**Extract from the Te Kape manuscript, 1841**

*One of Ngati Pou friendly with those strangers went to their settlement on Moturua to tell them of Mariou's death, hoping that on hearing this they would retreat to their ships and sail away without the need for further bloodshed. Those strangers instead prepared for battle. Accordingly, the war party gathered on Moturua took advantage of a dark, wet night to try to take those strangers by surprise. But Mariou's people were alert, and, they fired their many guns. Although our warriors fought bravely, they were forced to retreat to their stronghold, taking their dead and wounded with them.*

*Accordingly, when news of the failure of both the surprise attacks planned at Manawa-ora and on Moturua reached Te Kuri, he set out from Orokawa to take reinforcements to the island. Then, not wishing to lose any more warriors, he marched forth with ten picked men to challenge the strangers to send out their champions so the matter could be decided one on one. I was present when the strangers' champion and his best men accordingly marched out to meet us, and Te Kuri stepped forward to accept the first challenger. Instead of standing to fight, those strangers kept on approaching until they were within a stone's throw, at the same time raising their guns. We turned to flee, but it was too late. Despite the protection of his heavy war mat, Te Kuri fell mortally wounded, and, we bore him off to the stronghold on the island, where we lamented the loss of that principal chief.*

*Those strangers having thus avenged the death of Mariou, honour having been satisfied on both sides with the reciprocated deaths of both those principal chiefs, and appropriate retaliation already taken against Mariou's people for the major transgressions against tapu, we expected that peace would now be negotiated.*

Of the opinion that any savages remaining on Marion Island would constitute a continuing threat, Monsieur Crozet readily agreed to Jean's request. He sent a message at midday, saying that clearing the island of savages would ensure they could safely carry on accumulating the water and firewood supplies essential to their onward voyage. 'Having lost so many of our best men, we can't afford to lose any more if the ships are to be manned adequately.'

Monsieur Crozet seemed to be making most of the decisions. André doubted whether the *Mascarin*'s new commander even bothered to consult Monsieur du Clesmeur, now the nominal leader of the expedition. So much younger and far less experienced than any of the surviving senior officers, the hapless captain of the *Castries* must be in a difficult position whenever he tried to exert some authority.

'He should be grateful Monsieur Crozet has taken charge,' said Jean. 'Who cares about his pathetic sensitivities? We need to stay cool-headed here.' He pointed out that not only were many of the chiefs seen that morning those from the island who had been most friendly towards them, but they were also those who had constantly badgered the Frenchmen to take up arms on their behalf in skirmishes amongst themselves or against Te Kuri. 'Worse, these sworn enemies of Tacoury are obviously now in league with him — and all of them united against us.'

His words echoed André's earlier thoughts. Both ensigns were now only too aware of their precarious position. If the combined force of the savages decided on attack, they could be overwhelmed by sheer numbers. The ships could be seized and they could all perish. Jean added, 'We need to take the initiative before they do.'

André nodded. 'It's certainly our good fortune that once these savages lose the advantage of surprise, they don't seem willing to attack en masse.'

Marshalling the men, the fired-up senior ensign explained what he intended, then called for volunteers to join his selected twenty soldiers. Armed with muskets, belt pistols, cutlasses and forty rounds of ammunition each, the twenty-six-strong detachment set off at one o'clock. André was amongst them. Although Jean had suggested that he stay in charge of the camp and the remaining thirty men, the young ensign knew he would never forgive himself for not taking part. He could not go on putting his scruples about Te Kape before the interests of his own countrymen.

The wind was blowing strongly now, but the rain had eased. Led by the two ensigns and the officer in charge of the soldiers, they marched steadily up the mountain, bayonets fixed. The few savages gathered on the summit hastily withdrew towards the fortified village. When the village came into sight, André could see frantic activity within and without the palisades. Even as they wended their way down the hill into the bay, men were directing women, children and young people into a fleet of canoes drawn up at the landing place. The canoes were launched and speeding across the passage towards the mainland before the French detachment emerged onto the beach. The men had all withdrawn up the hill and were back inside the palisades. All they could see were the lookouts stationed on platforms above the defences.

'Excellent!' Jean stopped at the foot of the steep spur leading up to the village to reassess their options. 'At least they realize we mean business.'

Although they knew the path up to the village was narrow and treacherous — and would be greasy after all the rain — both Jean and André were familiar with the approach and the layout of the village. Leading the way, with the military officer close behind them, they marched on, the rest of the men following. André's stomach churned with nerves, but he clenched his jaw and straightened his shoulders. He had put any thoughts of Te Kape out of his mind. This was their chance to avenge the slaughter of Monsieur Marion and his companions, the chance to show these treacherous savages that Frenchmen were not to be taken so lightly.

Buffeted by gusts of wind, they negotiated the first part of the path and had almost reached the narrowest section, which traversed a steep ridge with an angry sea pounding the rocks below, when André spotted two chiefs emerging from the palisades. They were beyond musket range. 'Mort-diable!' he exclaimed. 'They're coming to parley for peace.' To his surprise, his heart lurched with disappointment at the thought they were to be denied their revenge.

But even as he spoke, the two chiefs hurled whip darts towards them. It was immediately clear these would not reach anywhere near them in the strong cross-wind, and Jean ordered his men to ignore them. 'Keep your eyes on your footing and don't look down.'

Bracing themselves against the gusts of wind that threatened their already precarious balance, they picked their way across the crumbling clay path, taking care not to look down at the foaming sea surging amongst the rocks far below. Ahead of them, the two chiefs gestured and pranced in challenge, protruding their tongues and rolling their eyes fiercely. They then held their ground, holding their war mats up against their bodies for protection as the Frenchmen approached within musket range. André could not help but admire their courage at the same time as he pitied their foolhardy and futile stance. Jean and the military officer aimed carefully, taking their time. As the smoke blew clear, one of the chiefs fell clutching a stomach wound, his thigh bone also smashed. His less severely wounded companion hastily retreated inside the gate as the French contingent marched towards the outer palisade.

Now the defenders poured calabashes of water onto the path skirting the inner palisade to the low entrance into the village. Jean cursed, 'Foutre! It's slippery enough without that.' He again cautioned his men to watch their footing, but to move as fast as they could without risking a fall into the deep fosse below, at the same time maintaining a running fire. 'Fire, then move on quickly, not stopping until you reach the entrance. Watch out for darts and spears.'

As they started along the track, André saw several savages climbing the ladder to the platform towering above the inner palisade. Without hesitating, he raised his musket, aimed carefully and fired just as they reached the platform. Beside him, Jean followed suit, then the military officer. To his satisfaction, the man he had targeted fell silently back to the ground, obviously dead. The others sprawled unmoving on the platform. They were soon replaced, but their showers of darts lost all force in the unpredictable gusts of wind. At Jean's shouted command, the French party pressed on, one by one negotiating the treacherous path below the palisade while the others maintained their running fire. When it was his turn to cross, André held on tightly to the rough poles of the palisade with one hand and pressed his feet as close to their base as he could, each slippery step threatening to send him toppling into the fosse below. The three hundred or so paces seemed to take forever, but at last he was across and took up his station beside Jean and the military officer. One by one, the others joined them in the narrow space in front of the entrance.

For a brief moment, they stared at the closed entrance, defended by two more chiefs. Crouched in fighting stance, their long pikes twirling, these fighting chiefs hurled insults and defiance at the Frenchmen, now within ten paces of them. Then Jean ordered his companions to begin a fusillade of fire into the village.

The savages inside showed great fortitude under fire, fighting without a sound. Only the chiefs' voices could be heard, calmly giving orders. Although the two chiefs defending the entrance soon fell, it quickly became clear to André that the palisade was deflecting most of the musket balls. 'We should get close enough to poke our muskets through the palisade,' he shouted to his cousin over the din of the fusillade. 'We're wasting ammunition.'

Once they had the barrels of their muskets inserted through gaps in the palisade, André saw they had gained an even greater advantage. As each wave of savages came out into the open parade ground behind the palisade to attack, the Frenchmen had plenty of time to target individuals before they could get close enough to throw their darts or in turn thrust their lances through the palisade. 'Aim at their chiefs first and foremost!' Jean shouted. 'They're the ones standing out in the open, behind that low barricade.'

As the wind whipped the smoke of their firing away, André saw an old woman standing with the chiefs, calmly handing them prepared dart-throwers. Even as he stared in amazement at her courage, she was hit and fell, her armful of weapons clattering to the ground. Neither the barricade nor their war mats gave the chiefs any protection. One by one, they too fell to musket balls. The seventh and last one rushed out, his long lance held at the ready. Before anyone could shoot him down, he launched his lance directly at the military officer, who cried out and clutched at his eye, blood streaming between his fingers. The force of the blow sent him staggering, and André just managed to catch him before he fell backwards into the fosse.

'I'm indebted to you, Monsieur Tallec,' he said breathlessly, then shrugged him off. 'I'm not hurt badly, sir. That spear missed my eye.'

The chief was killed almost before he had time to yell his delight at finding such a target. No others followed him outside the entrance and the showers of darts and spears ebbed to a trickle. The savages had resisted their attack on the entrance for more than forty minutes.

'Excellent,' said Jean, blowing the smoke away from the lock of his musket. 'He must've been the last of their chiefs. We should be able to break through into the village now.'

It took many blows with the butts of the muskets and the help of several rocks before they could breach the closed entrance. As they pushed their way inside the village, André saw that the few savages remaining had retreated to the far rampart. Without their chiefs, the rest seemed to have lost their courage. He could just make out a stream of men scrambling down the path to the landing cove where canoes were waiting. The savages left behind were already facing the French party, their lances ready for hurling.

'Foutre!' Jean exclaimed as a lance hit him in the thigh. He lurched, then brushed André away as he rushed to assist him. 'No matter — it's minor.' He turned to his men and raised his musket in the air and shook it, shouting, 'In your own time, gentlemen! Finish these varmints off!'

With a great shout of 'Vive le Roi!' the Frenchmen fired at the few savages still inside the rampart, valiantly trying to cover the retreat of the last of their people.

Before long, André was clambering down the path towards the landing cove, chasing after the remaining fugitives. Behind them in the village, none were left alive. Bodies lay sprawled, amongst them all of the chiefs. Below, two large canoes laden with men were being paddled swiftly out into a turbulent sea. The final defenders were flinging themselves into the one remaining canoe. No longer sparing any thought for their bravery, his eyes red with blood lust, the ensign joined in the last few volleys that killed most of them. Other fugitives hurled themselves directly into the sea and began swimming. The mainland was half a league away and the waves were precipitous. They were unlikely to make it.

Along with the rest of his party, André now threw aside his emptied musket to take up his cutlass. The vengeful Frenchmen attacked without mercy, cutting down any savage they came across. None of those left stranded on shore escaped with their lives. Although Monsieur Crozet had requested that they take captives, offering fifty piastres for each one, Jean's small party were in no mind to comply. Without mercy, they hacked and slashed their way along the beach, then worked their way methodically back up the hill slope towards the village, killing any wounded they came across.

It was not until they re-entered the now silent palisades that André came back to his senses. Panting with exertion, his bloodied cutlass still raised above his head, he stared around at the parade ground littered with the bodies of savages, then slowly lowered his sword to his side. It fell unheeded from his fingers.

'Search the village,' he heard Jean say from somewhere close by. 'Check all the huts and houses carefully.' Dully, André turned to see his cousin strapping his bloodied thigh with a sleeve torn from his shirt. Jean looked up as he approached, his eyes still alight with excitement. 'Pardieu, André!' he exclaimed, 'We've surely shown them that despite us being vastly outnumbered, their flimsy defences and futile weapons are no match for our firepower.'

When André shook his head mutely, overcome by reaction, his face white, Jean took him by the shoulder. 'Cousin, why so shaken? You've fought in battle before.'

André found his voice. 'Not this way,' he said slowly, trying to untangle his thoughts. 'I'd assumed we were facing great odds, but it's clear now that despite their courage, these savages never stood a chance.'

Jean nodded, his excitement ebbing. He looked searchingly at his cousin. 'You're not suggesting something dishonourable in our action?' he asked in disbelief. 'We wouldn't have succeeded if our men hadn't shown equal courage. Besides, compared to Tacoury's treachery, our intentions were nothing but obvious. As I see it we had no choice but to hit them hard, show them we're not dependent on the presence of our chiefs to be a force to be reckoned with.'

When André could not meet his gaze, he shrugged then clapped him on the back. He said briskly, 'Allons donc, we've work to do.'

Slowly, André followed his cousin as he limped through the village. Although they searched each and every hut and storehouse, they found nothing of value. Nor did they find any trace of Monsieur Marion or their massacred people. Jean could not resist saying to André, 'You see? They removed all their booty and their possessions to safety, obviously expecting us to attack.'

The bodies of about forty savages lay strewn around the parade ground and below the fighting platform. André found his heart thudding painfully as they checked each one. Te Kape was not among them. Indeed, none were youths like him, but mature men. All he could hope was that the young savage was not amongst those slain on the slopes below the village, that he had reached the mainland earlier with the evacuated villagers.

Piled around the gate were the bodies of all the chiefs who had challenged them one by one. Jean examined each body closely. His voice full of respect, he said: 'Each and every one of them has three or four musket wounds, any one of which should've proved fatal.' His voice hardened as he looked at André. 'I don't deny these chiefs are amongst the bravest of men when it comes to a direct fight, cousin. But equally, you can't deny they prefer the advantage of treachery.'

André nodded in reluctant agreement, but could not help thinking that the savages had paid a heavy price for that treachery. Of the four hundred or so men Jean estimated had defended the village, he thought maybe two hundred had escaped in the canoes. Their small party had killed the rest. They themselves had only three injured, and none seriously. Jean, wounded in the thigh, the military officer with his head wound, and a soldier with a chest wound had all been able to continue fighting.

After Jean had the village searched once more, he ordered the men to set fire to the huts on the windward side. They retreated across the approach path and watched as the wind quickly carried fragments of burning thatch to the other huts in the compound. Soon everything inside the palisades was ablaze. The black smoke billowing across the narrow peninsula was shot with flares of yellow flame. In less than an hour and a half, the buildings had all been razed to the ground. Only the fighting platform and the palisades escaped destruction.

**Extract from the Te Kape manuscript, 1841**

*We were greatly surprised when those strangers sent another party of picked men to attack the stronghold on Moturua where five hundred of our people were gathered. Alerted by the sentries of their approach, the chiefs hastened to send away the women and children and those not yet of fighting age, and, they went away safely on the canoes to the mainland.*

*In the passion of the moment, those left to defend the stronghold forgot the deadly effect of the strangers' guns. Instead, the fighting chiefs went out boldly in pairs to challenge those strangers, as was our custom, their throwing darts and spears in their hands, their war mats slung about their bodies. Their courage served no purpose, and, a wind called up by those strangers averted their darts. Even though those chiefs withstood the attack, they fell one by one to the guns, their bodies riddled with wounds. Our people fought as long as they could, and, all the chiefs fell, and, those defending from the fighting platform were plucked from the heights like pigeons from a tree. Accordingly, those remaining took flight.*

*None was spared and great was the slaughter, both within the stronghold and on the beach where the people fled in a vain effort to escape by canoe. Those victorious strangers from the sea then set fire to the stronghold.*

# Chapter 14

Shouldn't we immediately take advantage of our rout on Marion Island, gentlemen?' Jean appealed to Messieurs Crozet and du Clesmeur on board the *Mascarin* the next morning. 'We'll get no better opportunity to seize Tacoury's village. The savages will be demoralized and unlikely to put up much resistance without so many of their chiefs — especially if we indeed succeeded earlier in killing Tacoury himself.'

'Prenez garde, Monsieur Roux — you're letting a small success go to your head.' Monsieur Crozet took snuff then offered the box to the two ensigns who were reporting the events of the previous day in the great cabin. 'Those savages who escaped from the island have undoubtedly reported how lethal our weapons are. It'd be foolhardy to assume we'd take them unawares again.'

Monsieur du Clesmeur nodded his agreement. 'The island savages would hardly expect to be attacked by such a small detachment, also giving you some advantage of surprise.' He looked down his long nose, drawing his head back in that supercilious manner guaranteed to offend. 'In my opinion, sir, your actions will no doubt have roused the savages further against us. We already know that several *thousand* of them have gathered on the mainland. Besides, tackling such a large mainland village as Tacoury's would risk losing more lives we can ill afford.'

André bridled at the senior officers' downplaying of Jean's successful attack on the village. But his cousin, showing what the ensign felt was admirable restraint, ignored both the barely disguised disparagement and the proffered snuff box. He changed tack. 'Apart from anything else, we've yet to determine exactly what happened to Monsieur Marion and his unfortunate companions. There may yet be survivors. Monsieur Tallec was hardly in a position to ascertain their fate, being immediately knocked unconscious.'

'D'accord,' André hastened to support him. 'Isn't it possible others from the wooding party may also have survived and still be hiding, awaiting rescue? Barely two days have passed.'

Now Paul Chevillard looked up from his pen and paper. 'My thinking also, gentlemen. The best men from the *Castries* were amongst those attacked — some of them surely fought hard enough to escape.' It was not like him to question his senior officers. He was clearly recalling his inability to go to the rescue the morning of the attack, but, just as André's sympathy was aroused, the clerk in Chevillard could not help adding, 'If nothing else, we should try to retrieve our boats — we cannot afford to abandon such expensive items.'

Monsieur Crozet brushed all their arguments aside. 'You speak with the optimism of youth. The risks are too great. We should stick as close to the ships as we can from now on.' He then looked searchingly at Jean. 'I noticed you're limping heavily, Monsieur Roux. Is your wound troubling you?'

Jean shrugged impatiently. 'I've seen the surgeon, sir. He thinks it unlikely the savages tip their weapons with poison — in his experience we would've been dead by now if they did so.'

André realized his cousin had no intention of telling the senior officer that he had been awake before dawn, his thigh grossly swollen and throbbing, and whenever he moved he experienced sharp stabs of pain. The other two wounded men had also woken in pain, and the young ensign had insisted they all visit the surgeon as soon as they returned to the ship. Monsieur Thirion had bled them, cleansed the wounds and bound them tightly, but felt he could do no more. Only time would tell whether they faced anything more sinister. He opened his mouth to tell Monsieur Crozet the real situation, but closed it hastily when Jean glared a warning at him.

'Fort bien.' The senior officer was easily satisfied. He ordered them to return to the island to dismantle the forge, then remove all the men and equipment to the safety of the ships.

When the frustrated ensigns took their leave, Monsieur du Clesmeur fired a parting shot. 'You'd do far better to spend your time ensuring the repairs to the ships are completed as soon as possible and our provisions secured rather than seeking glory by attacking the savages.'

As soon as they were out of hearing, Jean muttered, 'The incompetent sot *would* see that as a priority, seeing his ship still has no masts.'

'And those we worked so hard for are likely lost,' André added. 'The savages probably set fire to the logs, knowing how important they are to us.' He considered their superior officers had objected over-much to their proposal, maybe realizing the successful attack on the village had shown up their own lack of initiative. It was not much comfort. His thoughts returned to the possibility of survivors, and he burst out, 'Mort-diable, Jean — I can't believe they refuse to do everything in their power to mount a rescue operation. How *could* Monsieur du Clesmeur think it's mere glory-seeking?'

'He's an aristocrat — his own skin and reputation mean more to him than the safety of his men.' Jean shrugged. 'I'm surprised at Monsieur Crozet, though. I'm beginning to think my former good opinion of him was misplaced.'

They had no choice but to return to the island, where they spent the day supervising the dismantling of the forge and the guard-post. As a precaution against being ambushed, Monsieur Crozet told them to cut down the head-high bracken fern that encroached on the shore camp on all sides. According to Jean, it was the first sensible decision he made. Although the rain had stopped, the wind still blew hard enough to prevent any savages from crossing the turbulent passage to the island, and their tasks were completed without interruption.

Earning more of the ensigns' scorn, Monsieur du Clesmeur on board the *Castries* then fired several cannon shots at canoes negotiating the inner bays, even though they were clearly well out of range. 'No doubt he'll claim a hit or two,' said Jean, snorting. 'Trying to make up for his inaction.'

When the wind died down at last a few days later, Monsieur Crozet sent André and Jean with the longboat to the burnt-out village on the island to arrange retrieval of any usable timbers, that being the only part of their report he had accepted as worth pursuing. By then Jean's thigh had begun to heal, the swelling much reduced and the puckered edges of the wound a healthy pink. Although he was still limping slightly, the pain had gone and he was back to his vigorous self. Even so, he confessed to André that the wound had given him a nasty moment or two. 'It was a long few days until we knew for certain that these savages don't use poisons.'

As they made their way up the steep path to the village from the landing cove, accompanied by a detachment of soldiers, the last gusts of wind carried the acrid stink of burnt timber tainted with the unmistakable sweetness of charred human flesh down the slope towards them. They stopped to tie handkerchiefs over their mouths. André could not help starting at every rustle in the clumps of sword-grass, his hand going to the pistol on his belt.

Jean noticed his nervousness and scoffed at him. 'You shy like a startled horse! We're not about to come across any savages — they're all holed up in their fortifications on the mainland, reduced to sounding their trumpets and lighting signal fires at our every move.' He added, looking pointedly at the bulge under André's shirt, 'Besides, aren't you protected?'

The young ensign flushed, but said nothing. Although Jean thought him perverse in continuing to wear the pendant Te Kuri had given him, André was unwilling to discard it. He knew he was being superstitious about the protection it gave him, but the gift had indeed saved his life. Despite the treachery of the savages, neither could he dismiss his friendship with Te Kape as meaningless. Deep down, and barely formulated, was the hope that continuing to wear the pendant might in some way also protect the youth who had saved him.

Now, as Jean waggled his eyebrows at him, grinning provocatively, André realized something else was troubling him. He seized the chance to change the subject. 'Haven't you noticed there are no bodies lying around? Despite our watchfulness, the savages have been back here undetected.'

He was right. When they reached the site of the burnt village, its blackened palisades still standing silent sentinel, they found no trace of the corpses they had left piled at the entrance gate. The soldiers reported recently disturbed ground in several places, and when they dug down, they discovered charred human remains.

'They must've returned under cover of darkness,' said Jean, trying to hide his consternation.

André was more disconcerted by these signs that despite their savagery, the Zealanders respected their dead in much the same way as civilized peoples. Once again, his thoughts strayed to Monsieur Marion and his unknown fate. Although he knew the wooding party survivor's reports of bodies being dismembered and shared amongst the savages did not bode well, he took some comfort from a new hope that maybe they had respected the expedition leader's status as their chief and at least given *him* proper burial.

Keeping a wary eye on the mainland, where they could now see canoes plying back and forth along the northeastern coast and amongst the islands on that side of Port Marion, the men started to dismantle the charred palisades. Others knocked down the fighting platform. As Jean had predicted, inspection soon showed that the timbers of both structures would prove ideal for firewood. It would take many trips with their one remaining longboat to transport all the usable timber back to the ships.

During the next few weeks, the ship's people were kept busy laying in necessary supplies of firewood and water. The longboat alternated trips to the burnt village to collect timber — enough to provide the seventy cords of firewood still needed — and to the watering place where they were filling seven hundred leaguers for the two ships. The blacksmith erected his forge on the deck of the *Mascarin* to assist the carpenters in fashioning a new jury rig for the *Castries*. The senior officers had quickly decided it would be futile to try to retrieve the two logs that had been hauled so tantalizingly close to the shore in the southern bay. Apart from the danger of being attacked while they hauled them the last half-league to the sea, it was highly unlikely the savages had not already destroyed them. Even Jean conceded that going to check was not worth the risk.

The carpenters accordingly set to. They converted the *Castries'* mizzenmast to serve as the main piece for a new foremast, as it could be stepped down into the hold. Its length was extended by fishing together the remaining spare yards. The new mast was made up of nine pieces of timber in all, held secure by iron hoops and hawsers tightened with wooden wedges. As the carpenters worked, they could not help constantly lamenting the superb logs they had been forced to abandon. A spare topmast then had to serve as the replacement mizzenmast. At the same time, another group put together a new bowsprit on the deck of the *Castries*, using the last spare topmast also strongly fished with lengths of timber for reinforcement. All this meant that the rigging had to be shortened accordingly and sections removed from all the sails to reduce the overall proportions of canvas to mast height. As the sailmaker commented ruefully, losing the main mast would have caused them less trouble, the foremast being crucial in maintaining the necessary balance of the sail plan. Despite his calculations and careful adjustments, he complained to anyone who had time to listen, 'She was awkward to steer before, but she'll be ten times worse now.'

The loss of their boats caused almost as much frustration — the *Mascarin*'s clerk not being the only one concerned. Every now and then, someone on board their surviving longboat, as it beat across the bay on the way from the ships towards Marion Island, would insist he had seen the other longboat or the yawl lost to the savages in Tacoury's Cove. On one such occasion, Lieutenant Le Dez succumbed to the concerted testimony of the twenty men on board that they had seen both boats close to the mainland. Against his better judgement, he set off in pursuit. The exasperated Monsieur Crozet sent the yawl with reinforcements after him when he failed to respond to signals ordering him to return immediately. When the lieutenant did return to the ships, he reported they had found no trace of their boats, but had managed to seize a length of newly worked timber he thought would serve well for the mast repairs.

The lieutenant had an extraordinary tale to tell. 'We'd barely landed when several savages came down to the beach from a nearby hamlet, bringing us fish — *fish!*' He spread his hands in disbelief.

'Ma fois, I'll never understand what drives these people. What could possess them to approach us so calmly and with such confidence, as though nothing dire had happened between us?'

'What did you do, sir?' André could not help asking, even though he feared the response.

'We soon showed them their folly in thinking we'd be willing to trade with such treacherous beings.' His party of men had promptly fired a volley of musket shots at them, wounding several. Lieutenant Le Dez shook his head. 'We tried to take those wounded captive, in the hope we'd learn what happened to Monsieur Marion and his companions, but they were still too strong for us and got away.'

Finally, the detachment took pleasure in setting fire to the hamlet behind the beach, making it the third village they had razed in the wider bay.

It was only a few days after this that the savages tried to mount a surprise attack on the party fetching timber from the village burnt on Marion Island. In charge for the day, André and Jean anticipated that the savages might seek retaliation for Lieutenant Le Dez's foray. They took care to set a sentry on the mountain above the village where he could see the country on all sides, leaving the rest of the soldiers on alert at the start of the narrow path along the ridge to the village entrance. They were precautions well taken. Almost before the wooding party had crossed the most difficult section of the path, the sentry fired off his musket and shouted a warning that he could see savages lurking in the fern. He reported later how one dressed in sailor's clothes and wearing a sailor's hat tried to stroll past him, his head down to hide his tattooed face. When the man failed to respond to his challenge, he shot him.

Realizing they were discovered and all advantage of surprise was lost, about fifty armed savages rose up out of the fern. Many of them were dressed in the clothes of the sailors killed on the mainland.

André could not help a snort of laughter. 'Quelle folie! They thought they'd take us by surprise, that we'd not notice them approaching in such a guise.'

As the savages now took to their heels, Jean shouted, 'After them!' He drew out his pistol and set off in pursuit, with his cousin and the soldiers close behind.

It seemed like déjà vu to André as they plunged down the steep fern-covered slope to a small beach on the far side of the headland from the usual landing cove, with savages fleeing before them. They cut most of them off before they could launch the canoes hidden amongst some rocks. Half a dozen fell to pistol shot or cutlass blow on the beach, and twenty or so more were killed in the water. Others drowned trying to swim away after being injured. The survivors landed their canoes at a fortified village on a small rocky islet just off Marion Island. Two canoes were left behind, and Jean immediately had them chopped up for firewood.

After this defeat, the savages made no further attempts to attack them — perhaps at last realizing that the Frenchmen were in no mood to seek peace, nor likely to be caught napping. Any canoes that foolishly ventured near the ships were fired upon. One was split in two by a lucky cannon shot from the *Castries*, which had Monsieur du Clesmeur preening as though he had blown an English warship out of the water. From then on, the savages contented themselves with keeping a close watch on the French activities from the safety of their fortified villages on the mainland, their sentries calling with loud voices that could be heard from the ships. Every night, the signal fires flared along the coast. But with no further skirmishes to distract them, the ship's people were able to complete their repairs by the end of the month.

**Extract from the Te Kape manuscript, 1841**

*Those ships continued to stay in Tokerau, but the strangers from the sea no longer ventured ashore on the mainland, remaining instead on their ships or on Moturua, which they took as conquest. The people of Tokerau made a few more attempts to surprise te iwi o Mariou, seeking blood for the blood shed, but to no avail as they suffered yet more deaths at the hands of the guns. Accordingly, some tried to sue for peace, bringing fish to a party of the strangers who came ashore at Manawa-ora. But their efforts were spurned by those strangers, who proved ignorant of the traditional way of quenching the fires of war. Instead, those peacemakers were fired upon, then, their village was burnt. Honour required that this further blood-letting should be reciprocated, and, accordingly a war party was sent to surprise those strangers at the burnt-out stronghold on Moturua. That too ended in disaster, for the vengeful appetite of the strangers from the sea knew no bounds, and, in spite of their difference from us, they were proven to be a brave fighting people.*

*Before those ships left our waters, te iwi o Mariou came ashore once more to burn both Te Kuri's and Pikiorei's strongholds on Orokawa. Despite all our efforts to ameliorate the harm done to us by the transgressions of those strangers, their atua and their weapons prevailed. Accordingly, with so many fighting men already lost in the revenge wreaked by those strangers, fighting men from Te Rawhiti, from Hokianga, and from Taiamai, we could do no more.*

It was only now, at the end of the first week in July, when the ships were almost ready to leave Port Marion that the two commanders took it into their heads to send an armed force to Tacoury's Cove in an attempt to ascertain what had befallen Monsieur Marion. It was twenty-five days since his disappearance. No one believed such an expedition could achieve anything, it being far too late to save any who might have initially survived.

Monsieur Crozet tried to justify their reasoning to his officers. 'On our return to the Île-de-France, we'll need to put in an official report to confirm the death of our leader and his unfortunate companions. I want you to search scrupulously through Tacoury's village and retrieve any of their belongings, taking careful note of any signs that might tell us what took place.'

'And if the savages object to our search, sir?' Jean kept his tone neutral.

Monsieur du Clesmeur looked sharply at him, detecting the sarcasm. 'You'll have a well-armed detachment with you, Monsieur Roux,' he said impatiently. 'We take it for granted you'll be only too willing to exterminate any savages you come across.'

Monsieur Crozet told them they were also to search for the boats. 'Once you've completed your searches, gentlemen, you're to set fire to Tacoury's village and carry off any war canoes from the landing place — or set fire to them if you can't remove them.'

Arming the longboat with blunderbusses mounted on swivels and equipping a large detachment of soldiers with muskets and cutlasses, André and Jean set off at eight o'clock the following morning to carry out orders they considered futile. Chevillard accompanied them so he could compile the official report.

Jean was not in a good mood. He grumbled to André, 'Mort-diable — this is nothing but face-saving. We won't find anything that'll tell us more than we already know.'

André shrugged. 'If we're lucky, we might retrieve our boats.'

As the boat approached the landing place, they could see savages laden with possessions streaming out of Te Kuri's village, making their way into the hills beyond. By the time they reached the beach where the ship's boats had been spotted the day of the massacres, the savages had withdrawn well beyond musket range. They gathered on the hilltops above the cove, some of them still waving items of French clothing.

'Cowards!' Jean muttered. 'Traitors and cowards, all of them — where's their vaunted courage now?'

They searched the length of the beach, but there was no sign of either boat, no sign of their seine net, and no clue to the fate of Monsieur Marion. It was the first time André had returned. His heart was heavy as he looked around the cove, the gnarled tree hanging over the rippled sand, the oyster-encrusted rocks and the quiet water lapping the shore. It was hard to believe such dreadful events had taken place here, that this peaceful spot was the setting of his continuing night-marish flash-backs. But he was secretly relieved that they would not be forced to fight their way into the village. His own instinctive urge to avenge Monsieur Marion and their slain people had diminished after the successful rout of the savages on Marion Island.

Now, so long after the event and with many more savages killed in the meantime, he was sickened by the bloodshed. It was not like killing anonymous strangers in sea battles, each ship similarly armed and victory going to the most skilled or the luckiest. Killing savages armed only with wooden weapons and wearing flimsy mats, giving them no quarter despite their undoubted courage and their defencelessness against superior weapons, had soon palled. Besides, many of those killed were savages he knew by name, whose houses he had visited, whose food he had shared. Traitors they might be, their treachery inexplicable and unforgivable, but they had already paid a heavy price for their betrayal of friendship.

Abandoning their fruitless search of the beach, the armed detachment marched with fixed bayonets up to the now-deserted village. At first they did not notice one old man, too feeble to walk, who had been left behind, sitting hunched outside his house. When he jabbed at a passing soldier with his spear, the man rounded on him and slew him before the ensigns could intervene. In the distance, where the rest of the savages had gathered on the hilltop to watch them, they could make out a savage flaunting Monsieur Marion's distinctive mantle, blue English cloth with a scarlet lining.

Jean gritted his teeth. 'Malheureux! Coquin! Infâme!' he growled. 'You villain! You rogue! You traitor!'

'Is that Tacoury?' asked Chevillard. 'Do you recognize him?'

André shook his head. 'He's too far away to be sure. That could be anybody.'

Jean agreed. 'We've not seen that double-dyed scoundrel since we shot him down on Marion Island — I'm assuming he died of his wounds, if he wasn't killed outright.'

André was thinking they had not seen Te Kape either. He could not help hoping that the young savage had escaped unhurt, but doing so felt like a betrayal of his own people. He sighed heavily and involuntarily touched the pendant hidden inside his shirt opening.

Jean looked at him sharply, but made no comment.

Reluctantly and without much expectation, they began a systematic search of the huts in the village, starting with Te Kuri's large house in the centre of the parade ground. As André stooped to enter, he happened to glance into the lean-to cooking place beside its entrance. He reared back in horror. There, mounted on a stake was a smoke-blackened human head. He pointed it out wordlessly to Jean. Covering their noses with their handkerchiefs, they forced themselves to inspect these gruesome remains. The head had been cooked, and strips of decaying flesh still hung from it. André made out unmistakable human tooth marks before his gorge rose and he was forced to turn aside and vomit.

Grim-faced, they searched all the cooking places and found other evidence of cannibalism; a human thigh-bone still attached to a spit, partially eaten, shreds of cooked and dried-out flesh clinging to the bone. In a house nearby, André found a torn and bloodied shirt he recognized as Monsieur Marion's. Its neck was saturated with dried blood, and there were several blood-smeared holes in its side. He carried the shirt outside and reported to Chevillard, busy making his inventory. His voice gruff with distress, he said bitterly, 'Here's the evidence of our captain's fate so desired by our new commanders.'

Chevillard merely nodded, then took the shirt from André's trembling fingers to add to his small pile of pathetic bits and pieces that had once been their companions' belongings. André was about to abuse him roundly for his callousness when he noticed the clerk's face was greenish-white, his Adam's apple jerking as he repeatedly swallowed his revulsion. So he touched him on the shoulder, then left to carry on the search.

By the time they finished, they had added Sub-Lieutenant de Vaudricourt's silver-mounted pistols and his bloodstained jacket to the pile, as well as a heap of torn rags that were all that remained of the sailors' clothing. In the armoury, they found the longboat's oars, darkened with blood, and part of its stem post, as well as a few carefully stacked muskets and iron axes.

Jean said sourly, 'We know now it's too late to find our boats — they must've destroyed them to get at the iron.'

At Chevillard's insistence, they carried all these proofs of the fate of their companions outside the village before they set fire to the huts. In silence, they watched as the village blazed, waiting until it was reduced to ashes. As the last hut collapsed into a smouldering heap, the clerk crossed himself, then quietly began reciting an Ave Maria. After a startled glance at him, André joined in. Slowly, other voices took up the familiar words. When the prayer was finished, they all stood for some time, doffed hats clasped to their chests, their heads bowed.

At last, Jean lifted his head and put his hat back on. 'Thank you for that, Paul,' he said brusquely.

While they were burning Te Kuri's village, some of the soldiers had noticed savages fleeing from Pikiorei's fortified village further along the peninsula. Chevillard suggested their investigation would not be complete without searching it also. 'We know Piquioré was Tacoury's henchman,' he pointed out.

Although Jean and André could see nothing more to be gained, the soldiers were keen to seek vengeance there, too. Without further ado, they marched along the ridge and entered the deserted village. There, the searchers found more evidence of the fate of their companions; torn clothing, personal belongings and articles from the boats. Human remains were scattered around Pikiorei's kitchen. After adding to Chevillard's collection, they burned this village, too. The longboat crew then towed two war canoes back to the ships, where they were dismantled for their top planks and any other wood that could be used for firewood. The hulls were burned, being too long at sixty feet to be of any use. When they returned to the ships, Chevillard drew up the formal report requested by their two commanders.

Over the next few days, disregarding the ensigns' conclusions about the fate of their boats, Monsieur du Clesmeur insisted the longboat continue its tardy search of the coastline whenever the weather allowed. Although the savages mostly kept their distance, on one such occasion a crowd of several hundred followed the *Mascarin*'s boat along the shore, yelling abuse. The officer in charge reported his chagrin at being mocked by one of these savages, who came right down to the water's edge. When they fired at him several times, he merely flung himself down on the beach, then stood up again once the shot had passed overhead. 'He pranced about opening that mat they wear as if to show us he'd not been hurt.'

Jean did not like the sound of this. 'The savages grow bold again,' he said to André. 'If we're not careful they may at last realize they have the numbers to overwhelm us regardless of our superior weapons.'

'D'accord, just what I was thinking.' André listened to the distant shouts of the savages' sentries, still keeping close watch on all their activities. 'We're almost ready to leave, though.'

'Then pray to God we do so in time,' said Jean, crossing himself. 'Despite everything that's happened, our new commanders won't perceive any threat.'

On 11 July, Monsieur du Clesmeur summonsed all the officers to his great cabin. Although he was now ostensibly the leader of the expedition, to Jean's surprise the young aristocrat had constantly deferred to Monsieur Crozet and the other more experienced officers during the month they were preparing to leave. Now, he made it clear he wished to hear their opinions before he decided what action and course they should take.

While they waited to board the longboat to cross to the *Castries*, the senior ensign commented to André, 'He's merely showing his true colours — he's no idea what we should do. He needs some options having come up with none of his own.'

'A bit harsh, cousin,' said André. 'Maybe he's learned some humility after all that's happened.'

It still seemed strange to be gathering in the other ship's great cabin, not on the *Mascarin*. Although Monsieur du Clesmeur's officers made them welcome around the handsome table, and his servants were punctilious in pouring them wine in crystal goblets, André could not help noticing that, despite his undoubted belief in his own superiority, the captain lacked the easy authority shown by Monsieur Marion. He fussed too much. Jean scarcely lowered his voice in remarking, 'Who's the toady now?'

That the captain overheard was clear from the flush that rose up his neck. He rapped his silver snuff box nervously for a moment or two, then cleared his throat. 'Gentlemen, I've called you here because as you know we've found no specific instructions amongst Monsieur Marion's papers to determine how we should proceed.' He nodded at Monsieur Le Corre. 'My second-in-command has drawn up some reckoning of our position to guide what decisions we now make.'

When the beefy senior officer finished speaking, they looked at each other bleakly. Their situation was not good. Both ships had lost their best sailors — amongst them the *Castries'* entire gang of tops men. Of those left, many were still suffering from scurvy. Their dry provisions were sufficient for only another eight or nine months, and that on the assumption they were still in reasonable condition. Not only would the *Castries* be sailing under jury rig, but she was also without the three anchors and cables lost when they first made landfall on the New Zealand coast.

Monsieur Crozet pulled no punches. 'Considering the state of your ship, sir, we've no choice but to head back to the Île-de-France by the shortest and easiest route possible.'

Monsieur du Clesmeur flushed again. 'You're suggesting we abandon any further explorations?'

'No question of continuing exploration — sir,' Monsieur Crozet added a little late. 'Manila it is, then. With that letter of recommendation from the Court of Spain you found amongst Monsieur Marion's papers, we should get assistance there to affect better repairs to the ships. We can go via Guam, pick up a pilot there and re-provision.'

'Not Chile?' Monsieur du Clesmeur tried to regain some semblance of control.

'We certainly shouldn't risk staying any longer in these storm-ridden southern waters,' Monsieur Le Corre pointed out. 'Winter's not yet over. Who knows what tempests would befall us.'

'Fort bien,' said the discomfited captain. 'I take your reasoning, gentlemen.'

'Beyond any other considerations, Manila would give us reasonable opportunities to get some return for our cargoes,' said Monsieur Crozet in conciliatory tones.

If he thought Monsieur du Clesmeur would be mollified by this observation, he was much mistaken. The aristocrat drew himself together and said haughtily, 'I've no desire to be mixed up in *trade*, sir. Naturally I've had no involvement in such matters.' He took snuff, and stared down his nose at the commander of the *Mascarin*.

'Be that as it may,' Monsieur Crozet became a little terse, 'at the very least we owe it to Monsieur Marion to reduce the burden on his estate. You've surely not forgotten that he took on the expenses of this voyage himself? We need to recoup what we can to offset them.'

'Oui, oui!' The captain waved his hand in dismissal. 'But I'm happy to leave such matters to you.'

For a few moments there was silence, an unmistakable atmosphere of dislike thickening in the room. André was left wondering whether the captain was in any way aware that his own ineptitude had triggered the long sequence of events leading to their present predicament. If he did, he was certainly showing no signs of it. Ruefully, the ensign recalled his earlier attempts to stick up for him. He would not bother again.

Paul Chevillard hastened to divert their attention onto other things. 'We've yet to formally claim these territories for the King,' he pointed out. 'What are your intentions, sir?'

'These matters I *do* have in hand,' said Monsieur du Clesmeur. 'At first light tomorrow morning I intend sending men ashore on Marion Island to bury the usual documents.' He turned to Jean. 'I thought it might be appropriate for you and the other ensigns from the *Mascarin* to do this, Monsieur Roux, in honour of your unfortunate captain.'

Jean nodded. 'That would seem fitting,' he said quietly, his tone neutral. He was not about to make any concessions to Monsieur du Clesmeur, regardless of this unexpected consideration.

So, in the grey chill of a windy dawn, the three ensigns from the *Mascarin* found themselves standing on the terrace behind the watering place on Marion Island. They waited in silence while two burly sailors dug a four-foot deep hole fifty paces from the water's edge and ten from the bank of the stream. Chevillard held the sealed bottle containing the declaration the two commanders had drawn up and which they had all signed, claiming possession of the harbour and all the coastline from here to the far north and Cape Maria. Monsieur Marion had called this tract of land France Australe — Southern France, and that was the name they gave it in the document.

As they doffed their hats and intoned the necessary words claiming possession, André's thoughts could not help returning to that earlier occasion, on the island they named Prise de Possession. Now he wondered how he could have been so excited, so full of hope for the success of their ill-fated expedition. He wondered how he could have taken it so for granted that his superior officers would make the right decisions no matter what befell them. It seemed a long time since he was such a naïve youth.

Soon after sunrise on the morning of 13 July, more than two long months since they had first anchored in Port Marion, the two ships slowly sailed out of the western passage. Once they cleared the line of islands that protected the inner harbour, they set sail to the northeast. As the range of blue mountains, the line of rocky forest-clad islands and the shimmering waters of the inner harbour receded behind them, Ensign André Tallec resolutely kept his eyes on the sea opening out ahead. He did not once look back.

### Extract from the Te Kape manuscript, 1841

*Before their departure from Tokerau, those strangers buried on Moturua a container in which they enclosed an item of power, by which action it was understood they intended us further harm. Accordingly, that container was dug up by our tohunga, and, its contents were rendered harmless by being eaten. Even today, our children still go up the stream on Moturua to search for that container out of innocent curiosity. Despite its power being so dissipated, the atua of those strangers from the sea continued to assail us long after their departure from Tokerau, and, many of our people sickened and died, their guts gnawed by ngarara, the lizards sent by those atua. Accordingly, the tides and currents flowing in Tokerau became ever more turbulent as compensation was sought for the calamities that had befallen us. First, those Ngati Pou people were driven out of Tokerau for their failure to prevent those strangers from violating the tapu at Manawa-ora. Those people fled to Whangaroa where they were given land for living. Some time later, those people were in turn pushed out of Whangaroa, and, they returned to Hokianga to their ancestral stronghold at Rangiahua, near Okaihau, many of them dying in their attempt to reach safety. Over the years, after many battles and changing alliances, the descent lines of incomers from the west have become ever more closely intermingled with those of Tokerau, so that today our children often share ancestors with their children, and, those links will persist into the future.*

*In such ways, ripples from the stone flung into the waters of Tokerau by te iwi o Mariou have spread wider and wider throughout my lifetime until they have touched many of the peoples of the north. Accordingly, when more strangers from the sea began arriving in their ships in more recent years, some of our chiefs moved away from Tokerau, having no wish to associate with treacherous people whose behaviour could result in such far-flung repercussions.*

*Ka mutu* – [this account] *is finished.*

[Editor's note: Under the command of du Clesmeur and Crozet, the French ships reached Guam on 20 September 1772. With the assistance of a pilot provided by the Governor, they continued to Manila in the Philippines, where both ships stayed for several months undergoing extensive repairs. The *Castries* sailed first, arriving back at the Île-de-France on 8 April 1773. Crozet, who sold the trade cargo in Manila, sailed a month later and arrived on 7 May. The profit was insufficient to pay the sailors or reimburse the King for the costs of the expedition. Despite Marion's distinguished service to his country, the authorities were disinclined to be generous; all his property and possessions on the Île-de-France were duly forfeited and his widow left penniless — the Marion family itself finally being declared bankrupt in Brittany in 1788. It was not until 1790 that the unpaid surviving sailors were eventually granted a naval gratuity as compensation. Jean Roux went on to become a lieutenant before disappearing from the records after 1776. Paul Chevillard held the rank of capitaine de vaisseau (retired) — equivalent to an army colonel — when he died in Rochefort in 1820. Julien Crozet rose to the rank of fireship captain (the same rank attained by Marion) in the French Navy, in which he served until he died in Paris in 1782. Crozet had met Cook at the Cape of Good Hope in 1775, where they swapped notes about their respective voyages to New Zealand, and Cook acknowledged Marion's prior discovery of the Prince Edward Islands by renaming the largest island after him. Du Clesmeur continued his career in the French Navy, achieving the rank of capitaine de vaisseau at the beginning of 1792 before he disappeared from the records, perhaps suffering the fate of many aristocrats during the French Revolution. Like Marion, both du Clesmeur and Chevillard became Chevaliers of the Order of St Louis, awarded for outstanding service.]

# Author's note and acknowledgements

With historical fiction, readers often want to know where history ends and fiction begins. *Collision* is based primarily on retrospective eye-witness accounts of the French sojourn in the Bay of Islands written by some of the surviving officers — Crozet, Roux and Chevillard from the *Mascarin*, Du Clesmeur (who also left an enlightening navigational log) and Le Dez from the *Marquis de Castries*. I have drawn heavily on Robert McNabb's translations in *Historical Records of New Zealand* (1908–1914) and Isobel Ollivier's translations in *Extracts from journals relating to the visit to New Zealand in May–July 1772 of the French ships Mascarin and Marquis de Castries under the command of M. J. Marion du Fresne* (1985). All named French officers in the novel were real people except for my narrator, the seventeen-year-old ensign André Tallec. My depiction of their personalities, attitudes and interactions reflects my interpretation of their own versions of events; any physical attributes ascribed to them are mostly fictional. Unfortunately, Marion's journals and logs have not survived, and my portrayal of him has evolved from his contemporaries' opinions of him, his actions and what he was reported as saying. Apart from the specific retrospective accounts noted, I found E. Duyker's 1994 biography *An Officer of the Blue: Marc-Joseph Marion Dufresne, South Sea explorer 1724–1772* particularly useful for gleaning aspects of Marion's personality from his earlier life and exploits.

Named Maori characters in the novel were also real people, except for the youth Te Kape, who is fictional. Different tribal accounts

attribute Marion's death to two different chiefs with similar names —
Te Kuri and Te Kauri. Both seem to have been present in the Bay of
Islands at the time, and both had Western connections. Although I use
the name Te Kuri — mainly because the French phonetic rendering
'Tacoury' seems to favour Te Kuri over Te Kauri, and a later European
visitor reported that he was told a chief named 'Cooley' or 'the dog'
(te kuri) was responsible (Peter Dillon in 1829) — I acknowledge
that claims for the name Te Kauri are equally valid. Unfortunately,
no detailed published Maori version of all the events is available; Te
Kape's manuscript, like Te Kape himself, is fictional. However, this
fictional manuscript draws on several genuine short Maori accounts
of Marion's death and its aftermath recorded in the mid-nineteenth
century, notably in John White's manuscript collections or published
in his *Ancient History of the Maori, Vol. 10*, including a version told by
Hakiro, son of Tareha (copy courtesy of Auckland Public Library).
I also borrowed material from Maori manuscripts about other early
encounters with European ships. These published sources were
supplemented by traditional information entrusted to me by Paeata
Clark, Ngati Hine and a descendant of Te Rawhiti people involved
in the events of 1772, who not only gave me access to her immense
collection of Bay of Islands cultural and historical material, but also
provided extensive and illuminating comments on the draft Te Kape
manuscript.

I have tried to reconstruct as accurate a sequence of events as
possible, using all the available sources, but readers should note that
the eye-witness accounts themselves contain some discrepancies
and obscurities. The only totally fictional episodes are those which
feature the friendship between my narrator André Tallec and Te
Kape, and André's experience at Te Kuri's village. Useful modern
analyses of the events of 1772 came primarily from Anne Salmond's
*Two Worlds* (1991) and *Between Worlds* (1997); John Dunmore's various

books on French explorers in the Pacific; Katherine Shallcross's 1966 masterate thesis, *Maoris of the Bay of Islands 1769–1840: A study in changing Maori attitudes towards Europeans*; and Fergus Clunie's draft unpublished document 'Kerikeri and Colonisation' (kindly provided by the Department of Conservation, Kerikeri). Inevitably, my interpretation of motivations and events sometimes deviates from these analyses. Events have been located geographically as accurately as possible.

I am indebted to many people who assisted with the research for this novel: first and foremost Paeata Clark for her guidance and support throughout, and to her and Neville Clark for their extended hospitality at Kohukohu; Erima Henare for persuading Paeata to take me under her wing; Wiremu Wiremu for insights on the contact period; the staff of the Macmillan Brown Library (University of Canterbury) — in particular, Jill Durney — for extended loans of research material; Peter Tremewan for an invaluable reading list on eighteenth-century French social and political history; Barry Thompson for his meticulous elucidation of nautical matters; the crew of the replica nineteenth-century schooner *R. Tucker Thompson* for a memorable five-day voyage that helped me recreate 1770s' Bay of Islands from the sea; my partner, Ron, for accompanying me on several northern research trips; and, as always, my family, John, Sally and Kate, for their continuing support. A grant from Creative New Zealand gave me the freedom to immerse myself in the fictional recreation of this fascinating episode in New Zealand's history.